**Captain Edward Dryden:** A leg wound sent him home from the fighting war—and fluency in German sent him to guard POWs at Camp McLean. Now *he* was a prisoner—and the odds were stacked against him, twenty-five to one. . . .

**Colonel Hamilton Christopher:** A drunkard, the camp commander ignored Dryden's warnings about lax security. When the captain disappeared on Christmas Eve, Colonel Christopher reported him AWOL. . . .

**Hauptfeldwebel Konrad Pavel:** A veteran of Rommel's elite Afrika Korps, the Panzer sergeant's knowledge of English made him vital to the Christmas Project. He respected Dryden—but his duty was to the Fatherland. . . .

**Oberst Heinz Kleber:** The highest ranking German at Camp McLean, he inspired fierce loyalty in his fellow Panzers—but he was forced to share command of the Christmas Project with the SS. . . .

**Standartenführer Ulrich Waldau:** Cold and uncompromising, the SS colonel would kill anyone who stood in the way of the assault. . . .

**Captain Dieter Grebling:** The handsome SS man was good at licking Waldau's boots—but in the heat of battle, his nerves would betray him. . . .

**Otto Boberach:** The short, aging scientist wasn't much of a soldier—but only he knew how to cripple Los Alamos. . . .

# STALAG TEXAS

## John Lee

POCKET BOOKS

New York   London   Toronto   Sydney   Tokyo   Singapore

An *Original* Publication of POCKET BOOKS

POCKET BOOKS, a division of Simon & Schuster Inc.
1230 Avenue of the Americas, New York, NY 10020

ISBN: 0-671-66814-5

First Pocket Books printing February 1990

10 9 8 7 6 5 4 3 2 1

POCKET and colophon are registered trademarks of
Simon & Schuster Inc.

Printed in the U.S.A.

# STALAG TEXAS

*Wednesday*
*December 20, 1944*

# ONE

Wehrmacht Sergeant Konrad Pavel blew on numb fingers and waited for the Amtsgericht officers to arrive. The midnight ritual couldn't begin without them. Pavel scanned the darkened barracks building. Men waiting with plumed breath. Candles flickering. Uneasy silence. Bunks had been pushed aside and a wooden table drawn to the wall for the judges.

Pavel edged closer to a potbellied stove, feeling uncomfortable. He wasn't sure why they had summoned him to tonight's disciplinary session. He scarcely knew the man who was to face the court. A corporal named Felix Leiser from C Compound, they had told him. Suspected of political activities against the Fatherland. Pavel had no interest in political matters. He was a soldier, not a lawyer. To cuff a noncom for sloth, or harangue a man for dereliction of duty, certainly. That was Pavel's job. He was a career soldier, a veteran of Rommel's elite Afrika Korps, and, as Hauptfeldwebel, a full sergeant-major, he was the ranking noncommissioned officer in camp. It was his obligation to remind the men constantly that they were soldiers of the German Third Reich and to make damned sure they acted like it. But to sit in judgment of a man charged with illicit political activities? A man he barely knew?

Footsteps thumped on the wooden stoop outside the barracks door. Jürgen Frischauer, a Panzer private who bunked in Pavel's building and had soldiered with Pavel in Africa, hastily put out his cigarette and nudged Pavel's arm. The door opened and the officers of the court filed in, wearing mufflers and longcoats. Oberst Heinz Kleber, the camp Standrechtkommandant and chief judge, led the way across the room. Behind him strode the other two Amtsgericht officers, a pair of majors with legal experience who would act as Kleber's supporting judges. Every man in the room snapped to attention. Kleber, dressed in desert tans under his long coat, walked silently among the rows of rigid men, eyeing each as he passed, as if taking some silent roll. When he reached Pavel he hesitated. The two majors held back, allowing Kleber a moment to speak to Pavel alone.

Kleber placed a hand on Pavel's shoulder. "Ah, Pavel," he said. "I'm glad you're here. These sessions are less distasteful with men like you surrounding me."

Pavel immediately felt more at ease. Heinz Kleber was the best Panzer officer he'd ever known. A ruddy-faced man with a wide mouth and tight, weathered skin that was permanently sun-creased, Kleber wore the scars and decorations of two world wars. But even the Knight's Cross at his throat, the highest award for valor that a German warrior could receive, would never speak as eloquently of bravery as Kleber's somber eyes. They would squint forever after the white-hot hell of the African deserts, and no loyal German could look into them without seeing the depths of pain and courage behind the drooping lids. Pavel worshiped the man. A perfect officer. Pavel would do anything for him. Fight for him. Kill for him. Even, if necessary, die for him.

Kleber's voice became serious. "You know what this is about tonight?" His breath misted in the cold.

"Yes, Herr Oberst. I was informed at mess."

"Incredible business," Kleber said. "Corporal Leiser may have put our most secret plans at risk. Pay close attention to the evidence."

"Sir, I'm not qualified to judge—"

Kleber stopped him. "Vote as your conscience dictates, Pavel. I'm not concerned with your judicial expertise. I asked specifically for you tonight because I want you to understand what is happening. I have an important assignment for you. A matter related to this unfortunate business with Corporal Leiser. And with Christmas Project. A task that I cannot trust to anyone else."

Christmas Project? Pavel had heard rumors that the officers were working on some important new operation, but he had no direct knowledge of it. He said, "I am at your orders, Herr Oberst."

Kleber nodded, satisfied. "A Wehrmacht private will arrive on the train tomorrow," he said. "Part of the new consignment from Camp Butner. He will be traveling under the name Karl Zolling. You will meet him. I want you to place him under your personal protection for the next few days. At least until we determine how much damage Leiser may have done."

"Sir? A private?"

"Yes, but don't be deceived by his rank or name. Both are false. He's the man for whom the Christmas Project officers have been waiting. We'll talk about it after this proceeding is concluded."

Kleber beckoned to the two associate judges and led them behind the table. They took their places, Kleber in the center. Two candles, thick cylinders of red wax, shimmered on the table. Tacked to the wall above the judges, cloaked in shifting shadow, hung the Hakenkreuz, with its black swastika standing out starkly against a field of red and white cloth.

A tall, acid-faced SS officer approached the judge's table. He removed his cap, exposing a thatch of curly red hair, and leaned over to murmur in Kleber's ear. Pavel regarded the officer warily. This was SS Standartenführer Ulrich Waldau, chief of inner-camp security. Fully three quarters of the men in camp were Afrika Korps Panzer veterans like Pavel and Oberst Kleber. The rest were a hodgepodge of quartermaster corps, Wehrmacht infantry, Waffen-SS, and a compact cadre of hard-core Nazis like Waldau. Waldau was an aloof man, cold and uncompromising. He had no friends that Pavel was aware of. Certainly not among the enlisted men. He was said to be a good officer, daring and resourceful on the battlefield, but he was also a full-fledged member of the NSDAP, a political animal whose allegiance to the Nazi cause superseded all else. The frequency of these disciplinary hearings had trebled in the four months since Waldau arrived in camp. So had the frequency of convictions.

The SS colonel finished with Kleber and turned to regard the men in the room. Cold eyes swept from face to face, seeing nothing, registering everything. He took a seat on the edge of a bunk.

Kleber said, "This court is now in session. Summon the prisoner." One of the enlisted men opened the front door and spoke to the sergeant on watch. Pavel and the others stayed at hushed attention. The sergeant flashed a hand signal to the barracks building next door. Pavel heard hurried footsteps approaching through the darkness. Heavy boots clambered up on the stoop.

The prosecution advocate, a handsome young SS captain named Dieter Grebling, entered first, followed by two muscular guards and a trembling prisoner. The prisoner stumbled as the guards manhandled him over the sill. He would have fallen if they hadn't supported him. His mouth was muffled by a gag, and his wrists were bound securely at the back. He didn't resist as the two guards dragged him across the room to the judges' table.

Dieter Grebling faced the judges and the flickering candles and extended his right arm in stiff Nazi salute. "Heil Hitler," he said. He had a thin, high voice. "In the cause of our Führer, we deliver before you the traitor Felix Leiser and declare him ready to face the judgment of this court."

Kleber asked, "Were you seen?"

Grebling said, "No, Herr Oberst. Attention has been diverted to the edge of camp. A mattress burning in the A Compound courtyard. I am assured by Colonel Waldau that another diversion will commence as soon as the court has reached its verdict and the punishment committee takes the prisoner to meet the consequences of his sentence."

Pavel's eyebrows went up. The SS captain seemed to be presuming a great deal, speaking of sentences and consequences when the trial hadn't even begun. But no one objected. Not with SS Colonel Waldau looking on. It was said that Waldau could have a man arrested and dragged before the secret court with a simple nod of the chin. Nacht und Nebel. Night and fog, into which a man could disappear without a whisper. With sycophants like Grebling and the

4

other hard-core SS officers backing him, Waldau usually got his way. Only Oberst Kleber outranked him.

"Let the prisoner approach," Kleber said.

The two guards shoved the prisoner to the tribunal table and left him there, swaying on wobbly legs, eyes wide and fearful. The guards backed away and took positions beside a cheap wireless radio set. Pavel glanced at the radio, then at the guards. One was a grenadier, a private named Erwin Maschmann, whom Pavel had seen once or twice lumbering among the soccer players on the camp recreation field. A big man, but clumsy. The other guard was Albert Voight.

Voight. Of course. Pavel should have known Voight would be among the regular participants in these midnight Amtsgericht rituals. Voight was a pig. A great potato-headed Panzer corporal with broad muscles and a wide streak of sadism, Voight no doubt delighted in these disciplinary sessions. They would make him feel superior. A chance to kick a man when he was in the dust, to suck up to the officers and wheedle praise for his tireless devotion and attention to detail.

"Present the charges," Kleber ordered.

Dieter Grebling produced a charge slip and began to read in a high, fastidious voice. Felix Leiser, assigned to Barracks 12C in the east compound, was accused of policital adventurism, treachery, and conduct unbecoming a loyal German soldier. He had been overheard on two occasions to speak disrespectfully of the Führer and had recently expressed the opinion that Allied landings in France might well have rendered the German cause hopeless. Further, Corporal Leiser had displayed a stubborn disregard for inner-camp discipline and had refused to punish two men in his barracks who had been caught reading unacceptable literature from the camp library.

The list went on. A litany of petty and imagined crimes. Pavel tried to listen closely, but his mind kept wandering. He thought again of the brief exchange with Oberst Kleber. A man arriving on the train tomorrow? A private soldier, traveling under a false name? Was that really the reason Pavel had been summoned to this secret session of the Amtsgericht? He hoped so. He didn't want to take on the added duties of midnight juror. Certainly not on a permanent basis. From the sound of it, this poor lout Leiser was guilty of nothing more than faulty judgment. That he had spoken disrespectfully of the Führer was reprehensible, but not unusual. Pavel and Frischauer and every other man in this room had groused quietly from time to time when there were no officers about. As for Leiser's occasional defeatist comments, what difference did it make? Words, nothing more. Words wouldn't change anything. Like Pavel, everyone in camp knew that Germany would eventually win the war. The German Army was, without doubt, the finest military machine in the world. Outnumbered, perhaps, but never outfought. In the end, Germany would prevail.

Pavel sneaked a look at the regular Amtsgericht jurors, to see how they were taking it. Several were his friends, from better days in Africa. Veterans of Libya and Tunisia. Good soldiers, all. Franz Eggers, wounded at Maknassy and still unable to straighten his left arm, following Grebling's evidence with hooded eyes. Willi Roh, a mouse-sized rifleman with the face of an unshaven angel, standing rigid and attentive in the second row, breathing through his mouth and listening with cocked head. Jürgen Frischauer, Pavel's oldest friend among the Afrika Korps veterans at this camp, shifting from foot to foot, looking uncomfortable and bored by it all. But Pavel knew better. Frischauer, a one-time farmer from Pegnitz, had complained privately to Pavel that he didn't have the stomach for the legal duties of the midnight Amtsgericht, that the frightened victims and the nasty punishments depressed and distressed him. He had asked the officers numerous times to be relieved. Without success.

Pavel sighed solemnly. Perhaps this tiresome session would end soon, if Captain Grebling would get on with it. The usual punishment for defeatist talk and disobedience was the "holy ghost" treatment, a lesson in barracks comradeship that called for the guilty party to be placed under a blanket or a sheet, then beaten severely with fists and clubs by everyone on the punishment committee. Pavel hoped it wouldn't go that far tonight. Leiser looked too frail to take much of a beating, and a soldier crippled by his comrades wasn't much use to anyone.

But the charges took a serious turn as Grebling squeaked on in his tiresome, high-pitched voice, adding statements and depositions from witnesses. He piled them up like strokes of a hammer on coffin nails. Leiser had been observed standing outside the window of a room in which certain officers had met secretly this afternoon. The building had been declared off-limits, but Leiser had approached it anyway, close enough to eavesdrop. He was confronted by one of Waldau's security men, a former Hitler Youth named Erich Huber, and told to move on. The prisoner Leiser had obeyed, but he had done so in what was described as a guilty manner. Furthermore, when Erich Huber marched off to continue his rounds, several men saw Leiser return furtively to the window. He remained there, listening, until Corporal Huber was again notified of his deliberate disobedience. When Huber came back with a squad of three security guards to remove Leiser forcibly, Leiser saw them coming and ran away. Huber and his men followed Leiser to the camp gate, where they observed him speaking to a sentry. They heard him ask for an immediate audience with one Edward Dryden.

Kleber looked up sharply at the name. "Are Corporal Huber and his men certain the prisoner asked for Dryden?"

Grebling said, "Yes, Herr Oberst. That was verified."

Kleber frowned. "Could the prisoner be aware of the role Dryden is to play in Christmas Project?"

"Possibly, sir," Grebling said. "Witnesses said Leiser lingered at the window for some time before the security men returned."

"Did he manage to speak to Dryden?"

"No, sir. Corporal Huber and the security detail arrested him just after he spoke to the sentry. He was taken before SS Standartenführer Waldau for questioning."

"And the sentry? He made no protest?"

"The sentry was inside the gatehouse, Herr Oberst. Presumably on the telephone. He did not see Leiser taken away."

Kleber's jaw tightened. "This is damned annoying. How much did the prisoner hear? The details of the debate? The train tomorrow? The discussion of Werner Heisenberg?"

"We can't be sure," Grebling said. "He has refused to answer questions. But he may have heard enough to create difficulties for Christmas Project. There was argument among the officers during the meeting. Voices were raised."

"Ludicrous," Kleber snapped. "Someone should have been stationed at the window during the entire meeting to

prevent such an outrage. Colonel Waldau, your people knew
the importance of today's discussion. Why did they not take
adequate steps?''

Waldau rose from the bunk, lips compressed in a thin line.
The SS colonel was reputed to have a savage temper, but it
was normally under tight control. He said, ''Security ar-
rangements were more than adequate. The proof stands
before you. The traitor is here, facing the judgment of this
court.'' He folded his arms and stared at Kleber. ''We have
done our job,'' he said. ''Now it is time for you to do yours.
Evidence shows the prisoner to be guilty. He was observed
lurking in a forbidden area, eavesdropping on a highly secret
discussion. He ran away when confronted by security men.
And he was caught attempting to betray his comrades to the
authorities. He must be punished. I call for an end to these
fruitless deliberations and an immediate vote of the Amtsgericht. Now.''

Dieter Grebling spoke quickly. ''Herr Oberst, as prosecution advocate, I agree with Standartenführer Waldau. The
prisoner's guilt has been suitably demonstrated. Such trea-
sonous intent merits only one verdict: *Sonderbehandlung*.''

Kleber rubbed his face with stubby fingers. After a lengthy
silence he said, ''Very well. All who agree with the prosecution advocate please signify by a show of hands.''

Several men raised their hands at once. Albert Voight.
The two supporting judges flanking Kleber. Erwin Maschmann. Some of the jurors lifted their hands more reluctantly.
Willi Roh. Franz Eggers. Jürgen Frischauer. One by one the
hands came up. Soon every man but Pavel had joined the
vote. Pavel's hand stayed at his side. *Sonderbehandlung* was
a bureaucratic term. ''Special treatment.'' It meant death.
To vote now and condemn a man who had yet to speak in
his own defense seemed less than fair. But to withhold his
vote was to challenge the authority of the court and risk the
wrath of SS Colonel Ulrich Waldau and Captain Dieter
Grebling.

A few heads turned toward Pavel, waiting for him to
decide. Voight watched with undisguised disdain. The two
SS officers eyed him impatiently. Oberst Kleber squinted
across the room at him, imploring him wordlessly to make
his choice without further delay. Pavel wondered if he should
insist on the prisoner's right to speak for himself. He almost

put it into words. But then he lost his nerve. With shame in his throat, he took the coward's way and thrust his hand into the air with the others.

"It is decided," Oberst Kleber said. "The accused stands convicted of crimes against the Führer and the Fatherland. It is the unanimous decision of this court that he be hanged by the neck until dead. Private Maschmann, the radio, please."

Erwin Maschmann flicked a radio knob and the dial began to glow. Felix Leiser moaned behind his gag. He cut his eyes wildly from side to side, seeking help. None came.

Kleber said, "For reasons of security, the sentence will be carried out immediately. The prisoner's death must appear as suicide. The guards will render the prisoner unconscious and take him to the tree."

As the radio warmed, music filled the room. Albert Voight turned the volume all the way up and took a folded pillowcase from his tunic. Solemnly, he advanced on the prisoner. Leiser trembled uncontrollably, still moaning. Roughly, Voight pulled the pillowcase over Leiser's head. The other guard, Erwin Maschmann, seized Leiser by his bound wrists and forced him forward at the waist, muffled head parallel to the floor. Moans continued to pour from beneath the cotton pillowcase, but the loud music covered the sound. Voight pulled a two-by-four from beneath one of the bunks and raised it above Leiser's extended head. He paused to gather his strength, then brought the two-by-four across Leiser's neck with both hands. The moans stopped abruptly and Leiser went limp.

Pavel swallowed hard. He watched as Voight and the big soccer player dragged Leiser to the door, legs trailing. A thin line of moisture followed, urine seeping down Leiser's trouser leg. A couple of jurors turned away.

The music swelled and ended, and a twangy Texas voice blasted through the radio static. "Yes, sir, that was 'Slow Boat to China,' a request from Darlene Henry right here in Amarillo, Texas, and dedicated to her guy, Private First Class Hershel Remington, over at Camp Barkeley in Taylor County. And now, from the senior girls at Pampa High School, we have a musical plea for the boys of the 343d Military Police Escort Guard Company down the road in McLean, Texas, at the McLean Prisoner of War Detention

Camp. It's Cole Porter's new hit, 'Don't Fence Me In.' Take it away, fellas.''

Kleber caught Pavel's eye and nodded toward the blaring radio in disgust. Pavel hurried over and turned it off.

"Soldiers of the Reich," Kleber said, addressing them all. "I need not remind you that you are prisoners of war in an enemy camp. You will disregard all mention of Christmas Project and related topics that may have arisen during prosecution of this case. You will say nothing to anyone about what you have seen or heard here this night. There must be no further erosion of inner-camp security. You will now return to your separate barracks before the tower guards notice something is amiss. Pavel, you stay here for a moment. There are vital matters Colonel Waldau and I must discuss with you.''

# TWO

The sun rose like an iceberg above the sprawling West Texas horizon. Raw orange light cast morning shadows and scattered frosty shards on rows of silent barracks windows. A rooster crowed in the distance. Tower guards stamped their feet in the December chill, thinking of coffee. Giant loudspeakers located around three cheek-by-jowl barbed-wire enclosures hummed uncertainly, then sputtered to life. Needle clicked into groove, and a recorded bugler blasted an amplified reveille across the crisp morning. Groans and Teutonic curses rose from the sleeping compounds. The McLean Detention Camp, with its complement of 3,021 German prisoners of war, stretched and yawned and woke up to its 592nd day of World War II duty.

As prisoners staggered from their cots behind the barbed wire an American officer parked an olive-drab army-issue Dodge near the camp headquarters and climbed out. In spite of the keen knifeblade of cold wind that greeted him, Captain Edward Dryden felt warm and happy. He'd spent another night away from his bachelor quarters, trading army blankets and rough sheets for the languorous comfort of Beverly's bed. Mischievous Beverly. Sweet and sexy. Waking with her

11

full, warm body beside him in the big rented house on Barton Street was the only thing that made this temporary duty at a Texas prison camp bearable. It beat the hell out of waking in a foxhole, knee-deep in Italian mud. Or in a military hospital with pins in his hip and a cast on his leg.

Dryden strapped on his service holster and walked into the main office of the administration building. Kenneth Jenkins, a corporal who filled out the duty rosters and supervised an office staff of enlisted men augmented by German volunteers, looked up from his desk and said, "Morning, Captain. You're early today."

Dryden murmured a greeting in return and headed for the coffee pot, still basking in Beverly's afterglow. Even her raucous alarm clock, set for an ungodly hour so he could shower and shave and get back to camp before he was missed, hadn't dampened his spirits. Sneaking back to camp at daybreak was her idea, of course. McLean, like any small town, harbored a gaggle of wagging tongues, both civilian and military. While Dryden didn't really care what people might say or think about him, Beverly's reputation was another matter. She was the offspring of a very staid Cleveland family, and she wasn't quite modern enough to admit she had a live-in lover.

He poured coffee into a crockery cup and glanced at the corporal. "You're pretty early yourself, Kenneth. What's up?"

Jenkins said, "Oh, the usual screw-ups, sir. I'm having a tough time setting up the duty schedules for next week. Colonel Christopher has authorized Christmas leave for half the guard force. I can't make the numbers come out."

"Yeah, I saw the memo," Dryden said. He sipped coffee and glanced at a copy of a confiscated German leaflet on his desk. It was poorly printed, obviously cranked out by a prisoner on one of the camp mimeograph machines. He picked it up and read it. Dryden's German was fair, thanks to his maternal grandmother. He'd tried to improve his use of the language over the years—a couple of prep-school classes at Mr. Connell's private ranch school up on the mesa above Santa Fe, another two years of college-level German at the University of New Mexico, a refresher course at OTS. He still stumbled over some of the complex word combinations, but there was nothing complex about this particular

12

leaflet. It was hasty and vitriolic and called for deliberate disobedience of all camp commands. Dryden grunted. Nothing new. The camp's hard-core Nazis produced such diatribes by the dozens. He crumpled the leaflet and tossed it in a trash can. "Anything for me?"

"Yes, sir," Jenkins said. "A call from the base hospital, reminding you of your appointment with Dr. Brody today."

"Oh?" Dryden said. He sipped coffee and smiled to himself, thinking of Beverly on Barton Street, sliding into her crisp nurse's uniform. "Who called? Lieutenant Bennington?"

"No, sir. One of the orderlies. I put a tickler on your calendar. Oh, and there was another suicide last night. In the center compound. One of the prisoners hanged himself."

Dryden lowered his cup. "Who this time?"

"Corporal Felix Leiser. One of the noncoms from C Compound. Alva Franks found him at six o'clock this morning when the watch changed."

The front door creaked open and two tousled Germans appeared, adjusting their tunics. One bowed stiffly from the waist. The other slid quietly behind a desk. Clerk/typists from the inner compound. The camp commandant had authorized the use of German prisoners to relieve the camp's chronic manpower shortage. Mail sorters, laundry, office duties. Most of the Germans were eager to volunteer. Clerical duty took them off the winter work lists for the area's farms and ranches.

"Where did it happen?" Dryden asked.

"That cottonwood tree inside B Compound. You know, where we found that German sergeant last month. Private Franks said there was a chair under the man's legs, tipped over. The body was pretty stiff. Must have hanged himself around midnight." The two Germans, listening, bent over their desks and tried to look busy.

"Where is Franks now?"

"Down in the duty room with Sergeant Kieran, making out a report. Colonel Christopher likes these suicides cleared up as fast as possible."

"Yes, I know," Dryden said. He drained his coffee.

"We've had too damned many suicides lately. I'd better take a look."

The sun was a few degrees higher when Dryden stepped outside, but it gave no warmth. Cold wind whipped his cotton field jacket, and he drew the collar closer. He headed down the road toward the stockade entrance, trying hard not to limp. Blue northers, the Texans called them, these chill winds that gusted down across the barren plains of the Texas Panhandle. The cutting cold brought fresh misery to his hip as he walked. He frowned and catalogued the aches. Hip, socket, thigh. Lousy luck. All the way through North Africa and Sicily without a scratch. Then splintered bones and puckered flesh left by a brace of hidden gunners on an Italian ridge. Mementos of the disastrous charge across the Rapido River. Dryden's last stand.

That was months ago. Almost a year. Would the aches and twinges never go away? This was his first prolonged taste of winter weather since the military doctors nodded over his wounds and pronounced him sufficiently recovered for reassignment. Texas winters were considered mild by the military mind when compared to the snows of the northern United States, so the doctors had sent him here. But the unending wind of the Texas Panhandle drove the cold deep to the bone, bringing bitter lament to slow-mending flesh. If this was an example of how his mangled hip would react to winter in years to come, it might mean an end to his pleasant pre-war existence. The Dryden ranch was on high ground, at the foot of the Sangre de Cristo range in New Mexico. When the snows came and the winds blew, only hardy men and hardy animals dared go out. Cripples need not apply. No more blustery afternoons in the saddle, riding fence. No more midnight sessions with a brood mare about to foal. No more two-year-olds to be trained the way his father had once trained them, and no more strong, square quarter horses to cheer on at the track. An end to the intense, happy life in the stables his father had founded. Dryden's older brother, Sam, would have to take over. Dryden didn't much care for the idea. Sam was more interested in real estate than horses.

Dryden studied the sweeping stretch of barbed wire. He could see activity beyond the guardhouses and the gun towers, prisoners drifting out of the three fenced sleeping

14

compounds and converging on the POW mess hall. The McLean camp was only one of 155 main base camps and 511 branch camps for prisoners of war scattered across the United States. Most of the POW camps were situated in the South and Southwest to take advantage of the more temperate climate and to save money on heating bills. Texas had thirty-three base camps just like this one. Twice as many as any other state. But in December, here on the high plains where the wind blew ceaselessly and the mercury plummeted, it was hard to understand why.

And they were big camps. This one had almost three hundred buildings inside and outside the stockade fence. Most of the buildings were cheaply constructed barracks for the German prisoners, long rectangular huts covered with black tar paper and lined in tidy rows inside three contiguous barbed-wire sleeping compounds. A larger compound fronted the three sleeping enclosures, a fenced field that served as a parade ground where morning roll call was taken. The Germans had their own medical clinic inside the wire. They also had their own laundry, kitchens, barber shop, cafeteria, library, and recreation hall. And there was a well-stocked post exchange where prisoners could trade canteen coupons for cigarettes and candy bars, hair oil, American newspapers and magazines, peanuts and soft drinks. They could even use their coupons for a regular ration of beer, up to two bottles a day per man. All the comforts of home.

Here on the outside of the fence, where Dryden and the rest of the American personnel lived and worked, the architecture was the same. Early temporary. A gravel road ran from the narrow highway to the stockade entrance, separating the officers from the enlisted men. On the south side of the road, peon territory, stood a ramshackle canteen, a game room with Ping-Pong and pool tables, and more of the black tar-paper barracks, called "black beauties" by the American enlisted men who slept in them. Further south rested a big motor pool where army mechanics tinkered tirelessly on the battered trucks that were used to transport POW work parties to outlying farms and ranches. On the north side of the gravel road, where the officers congregated, were the administration buildings, a fully equipped camp hospital, and the officers' club. A few of the married officers rented quarters in town, but there were several small frame build-

15

ings behind the hospital for bachelor officers like Dryden, and a slightly bigger house tucked near the officers' club for the camp commandant. The current inhabitant was Lieutenant Colonel Hamilton Christopher.

Dryden stopped at the guard post beside the stockade gate. A slouching corporal sat just inside the front door with his feet up on a desk, reading a newspaper. He didn't see Dryden. As the corporal turned pages a prim, pretty-faced SS captain came out of the duty room behind him. The German officer murmured to the corporal, who waved him on toward the gate. The German brushed past Dryden on his way out.

"Where's Sergeant Kieran?" Dryden asked.

The corporal raised indifferent eyes, then closed the newspaper rapidly and stood up. "He's in the duty room, sir, talking to Private Franks. We had a suicide last night. One of the prisoners hanged himself. Seventh hanging since July."

"I heard about it," Dryden said. He glanced over his shoulder at the SS captain. The German was letting himself through the gate and into the compound. "What was that officer doing in the duty room?" Dryden asked. "Was he here to talk about the suicide?"

"No, sir. That was Captain Dieter Grebling, sir. He came to offer one of the noncoms as translator. A Sergeant Pavel. There's a train coming in at noon."

"A POW train? Today?"

The corporal said, "Yes, sir. From North Carolina. We're expecting fifty new prisoners from Camp Butner. Sergeant Kieran says they're troublemakers. He says the Camp Butner people are shipping them here to the boonies so they can't make waves."

Dryden nodded. "We often get the bad apples. Why didn't the captain sign his man on the roster out here?"

"He couldn't, sir," the corporal said. "It hasn't been posted. I sent him in to talk to Sergeant Kieran."

Dryden looked at the corporal sharply. "The train roster hasn't been posted yet?"

"No, sir. Sergeant Kieran just started working on it."

"How did the German know about the train? Did you tell him?"

The corporal shook his head. "No, sir. Information about

16

POW movements is classified. None of us even knew it was coming until Sergeant Kieran opened the priority dispatches this morning."

Dryden nodded thoughtfully. "That's very intersting. And puzzling. How do you suppose the Germans learn these things before we do? The train comes at noon, you say?"

"Yes, sir. About half past."

"Curious. I may take a noon run to the depot myself." Dryden glanced toward the duty room. "Ask Sergeant Kieran to meet me at the gate. Tell him I want to talk to Franks."

The corporal picked up a telephone. Dryden stepped outside and strolled over to peer through the strands of barbed wire. The SS captain had reached the POW mess hall, where he stopped briefly to speak to a tall, blond sergeant in Afrika Korps tans. Masses of German enlisted men were already lined up in front of the mess hall, waiting for the second breakfast shift to begin. They would eat in rotation until time for the trucks to appear and cart them off to their work assignments.

Most of the enlisted men in front of the mess hall were wearing regulation uniforms, a mixture of Wehrmacht gray-green and desert tan, depending on where they had been captured. Some of the uniforms were shabby, but the only alternative was to wear the American-issue POW fatigues, blue-denim work clothes with "PW" stenciled in yellow on the fronts and backs of shirts, and on the knees and seats of trousers, mute testimony to each wearer's individual defeat. The average prisoner was too proud to use the fatigues except when working in the fields, to save wear and tear on his uniform. On cold winter days like this, when the cotton stubble had been turned and the winter wheat long since planted, there weren't as many work details to go around, and most of the off-duty Germans wouldn't be caught dead in the denims. They would rather wear their old uniforms until the seams fell apart. Even then they would take their gray-greens and desert tans to German POWs who could sew and try to get them patched.

As Dryden watched, the mess hall doors swung open for the second breakfast shift. The lines of enlisted men began to inch forward. A group of German officers strolled past lazily, boots shining in the morning sunlight, heading for the smaller officers' mess. Dieter Grebling joined them. All the

17

German officers wore uniforms, of course, complete with Nazi medals and campaign ribbons. One rarely saw officers in denims, even when they worked on small personal gardens outside their stockade quarters. According to the Geneva Convention, officers could not be forced to join organized work parties, and since they continued to get their German military pay in canteen coupons, twenty to forty dollars a month depending on rank, most of them elected not to work at all. No one was paid in real money, of course, not even the enlisted men, who earned up to eighty cents a day from their American jailers for toiling on the work gangs. Money could be used in escape attempts. Canteen coupons, clearly marked, could not.

Escape attempts were rare, fortunately. It had nothing to do with camp security. The guard system was chronically sloppy. Many of the American enlisted men assigned to POW camps were rejects from other units. Some were older, considered unfit for active duty. Others, like Dryden, had been trapped in the deadly routine of guard detail for the simple reason that they could speak a smattering of German. A few, also like Dryden, were assigned to the camp while recovering from wounds. Then there were the dregs from the bottom of the military barrel—the slackers, the unlucky, the careless, the recalcitrant, the punctured eardrums and fallen arches—men shunted to one side, doomed to share an imprisonment with the Germans that seemed severe no matter which side of the wire they were on.

And because camp routine was dull, the guards had grown lax. Dryden could see one of the tower guards now, leaning on the rail of his elevated platform, reading a comic book. At the beginning, when the camp was freshly opened and the trucks went out to dehorn cattle or pick West Texas cotton fields, there was a guard for every ten Germans on a work detail. Now it wasn't unusual to see as many as seventy or eighty prisoners in an unfenced field with only one or two guards assigned to watch them. It was surprising that more of the POWs didn't try to escape. At most, eight or nine a year might wander away from the work gangs, or cut through the wire here at the stockade, but they were usually rounded up in a day or two. More could have escaped, easily. But most of the Germans admitted that there seemed no point to it. Texas was too big. Too desolate. Too far from Europe and civilization. There was just no place to go.

Max Kieran and Alva Franks came through the corporal's cubicle and out to the wire. Kieran, a rotund sergeant with ballooning hips and a pugnacious face, pulled to a stop in front of Dryden and tossed him a halfhearted salute. "You want to see us, Cap'n?" His voice was impatient, his tone insolent.

Dryden returned the salute more crisply and said, "Yes, thank you, Sergeant. I want to talk to Private Franks."

Alva Franks, a long-necked farm youth from Georgia, looked pale, as though still in shock from his early-morning discovery in the prison compound. Sergeant Kieran hooked his thumbs in his belt and said, "This gonna take long, Cap'n? Franks and me was filling out a report on that dead Kraut."

"The report can wait a few minutes," Dryden said.

Kieran was aware that Dryden, a front-line officer, was contemptuous of some of the sloppier camp procedures, many of which the sergeant himself had set up. He seemed to hate Dryden for it. He grinned, showing small teeth with slight gaps between, like seeds set too far apart in gum-pink soil, and said, "Colonel Christopher ain't gonna like it if we don't get the paperwork done in time for the morning mail. He likes his suicides nice and tidy."

Dryden ignored Kieran's studied insolence. "Are you so certain it was suicide?" he said.

Kieran said, "It was suicide all right. Jerk hanged himself. Colonel Christopher said mark it down and forget it."

"Did you see the body?" Dryden asked.

"I didn't have to," Kieran said. "Lots of these Krauts get depressed. They do themselves in all the time. Couple of months before the doctors shipped you down here, a guy walked away from a highway work crew and stepped in front of a steam roller. Just stood there, waiting for it to get him. Mashed him flatter than a tin can in a scrap-metal drive."

Dryden glanced at the young private. "You found the body?"

Franks swallowed and said, "Yes, sir. When we changed the guard. He was hanging . . . hanging from the tree just inside the B Compound fence. There was a chair under him."

Dryden said, "Show me."

Kieran puffed up. "I need Private Franks in the duty room for that report, Cap'n. The colonel wants it in the mail by eight o'clock this morning. He gets real ticked off if I don't do things on time."

"You can tell the colonel it was my fault," Dryden said.

Kieran nodded. "Yes, sir. You can be sure I'll do that."

Dryden unbuckled his holster and handed it to the corporal at the gatehouse. No weapons were allowed inside the barbed wire. The corporal stuck the gun and holster inside his cubicle, then opened the gate for Dryden and the private.

The early breakfast shift, now out of the POW mess hall, had broken into surly groups on the parade ground. Dryden scanned faces as he and Franks walked through them. Most of the Germans stared back openly, but some averted their eyes. There was an air of restlessness in the way they huddled together in the raw morning chill. Many of them exchanged whispers when they saw where Dryden and the young private were headed. Word of Leiser's death had spread quickly.

The gate to B Compound was open. Once the bugle sounded reveille, the gates to the sleeping compounds swung wide, allowing free access to the recreational facilities and service buildings of the outer compound. The three inner gates would stay open until the work crews returned from the countryside and the evening chow lines had cleared.

Franks and Dryden entered the dusty central sleeping compound. In spite of the cold, a number of German prisoners waited in line outside the B Compound community shower room. A few of them, braver than the others, stood bare-chested under the chill December sun, towels draped around their necks. A timpani of shower sprays drummed inside the shower hut. German voices rose above the cascading water in a mixture of laughter and rude horseplay. No broken spirits here.

One of the bare-chested men outside the shower hut, a lanky blond, saw Dryden and murmured quickly to his companions. Heads turned to stare. The lanky German watched Dryden to see where he was headed, then stepped out of line and hurried toward the outer compound.

"Looks like we're going to have company," Dryden said.

Franks blinked. "Company, sir? What do you mean?"

Dryden nodded toward the shower hut. "One of the Germans just took off. Probably looking for an officer or a noncom. They don't like us poking around in the sleeping compounds."

Franks glanced nervously over his shoulder. "Should I go back to the main gate and get a few guards?"

"Don't worry about it," Dryden said. "We'll be okay."

The tree loomed in front of them. It was a big cottonwood, the only tree in the whole stockade, a solitary windblown shape with crooked branches. The sparse brush that had once covered this bleak square of land had all been bulldozed by the Army construction crew, but trees were so rare on the Texas Panhandle that even the army engineers had felt compelled to spare this single tree that huddled forlornly on the camp site. It wasn't close to any of the fences. It posed no escape threat. So the engineers had left it standing in a red-dirt clearing midway between the B Compound gate and a community latrine. In spite of its proximity to the latrine and its misshapen look, it was a popular favorite among the prisoners. A few could always be found beneath its branches in the late afternoons, sharing a smoke before dinner. There would be no one under it for the next few days, though. Leiser's death would keep them away.

"This is B Compound," Dryden said. "Wasn't Leiser quartered in C Compound?"

"Yes, sir. That's what Sergeant Kieran said." Some of the prisoners drifted closer. Franks watched them anxiously.

Dryden stared up at the cottonwood. It would be a pity to cut it down, but he knew the subject would come up at the next staff meeting. Too many men had died dangling from its pale, twisted arms. "Doesn't it seem odd to you that a man would come to a different compound to kill himself?"

Franks said, "Well, it's the only tree they've got, sir. Maybe the guy sneaked over after hours to do it." He started to say something more, but movement caught his eye. The ring of German spectators parted to let someone through. Franks said, "Uh-oh, Captain. You were right. Here comes one of the noncoms now."

Dryden swung his head. He saw a tall, rawboned sergeant

21

bearing down on them, a muscular soldier in desert tans. The same blond soldier he had seen talking to Dieter Grübling outside the mess hall. And ready for combat, from the look of him. His brow was furrowed and his Nordic blue eyes were locked on Dryden. The German stalked up and planted his feet wide, almost a boxer's stance. In passable English he said, "You wish something?"

Dryden looked him over. The German had a leathery, sandblasted face etched with deep lines, burnished by the sun to a dusky bronze. Yellow tufty eyebrows, as golden as the sun-bleached hair on his head, stood out against his dark skin. His eyes were old and tired, but he couldn't have been much over thirty. Dryden said, "Relax, Sergeant. We're just having a look around. You're Pavel, aren't you? One of Kleber's people?"

The German looked surprised. "You know me?"

Dryden switched to German. "Yes, I know you, Sergeant. I always check the terrain when it's in enemy hands. It's a simple matter of tactics."

The sergeant's eyes narrowed. He glanced at Franks, then lowered his voice and spoke in German himself. "You speak our language well, Captain. Are you one of us?"

"No. I'm not one of you."

The man's jaw hardened. "Then what do you want? Why have you come to our sleeping compound?"

"I'm looking for information," Dryden said. "Perhaps you can provide it. They tell me you're Kleber's right hand. You must know what's happening to your men out here."

The German sergeant said, "Our men are our business, Captain, not yours. I have nothing to say to you."

Franks seemed puzzled by the rapid exchange of German. He watched them both nervously.

"I'm sorry you feel that way," Dryden said. "I had hoped someone among you would give a damn."

The German drew himself up. "Pfui Teufel! We care greatly for our men, Captain. More than you, apparently. Be good enough to show respect. A German soldier died at this tree last night."

"Yes, I know," Dryden said. "One of many to die these past few months. That's what bothers me. Who is helping them on their way, Sergeant? Oberst Kleber? The Amtsge-richt? Are your secret courts operating again?''

The German hesitated. Uncertainty flickered across his face, then quickly dissipated. He said, "I know nothing of any Amtsgericht.''

"What do you know about meeting trains?" Dryden asked.

The German sergeant scowled. He said, "Finish your business here at the tree quickly, Captain. My men do not appreciate your attention. I cannot guarantee their actions.'' He spun on his heel and stalked away. As he approached the ring of German spectators a man stepped forward and asked a question. Pavel walked past the man without answering.

"What was that all about?'' Franks asked.

"He told us to finish up and get lost,'' Dryden said. "He suggested there might be trouble if we don't.''

Franks flicked an uneasy look at the Germans. "Maybe he's right. Maybe we should get out of here.''

"When we're ready,'' Dryden said. He looked back at the tree. "Where was Leiser hanging?''

Franks pointed. "That limb up there. The one with the raw rub spot. That's where the rope was tied. The chair was flopped on its side underneath, like maybe he kicked it.''

"And you took him down?''

"I tried, sir. But I couldn't reach the rope. I had to call for help.''

"Why didn't you use the chair?''

"I did, Captain, I put it right under him. I could get my hands on the noose, but I couldn't lift him and work it off at the same time. I got some of the guys from the 620th to come and help me.''

Dryden sighed. "Why did you have to lift him?''

"To get slack,'' Franks said. "He was heavy, sir, and he was just hanging there, dead weight, and . . . Oh, crap. I see what you're driving at. His feet weren't touching the chair. He was a good six or eight inches above it.''

"Which would make it difficult for him to slip a noose around his own neck and kick the chair away. Right?''

Franks swallowed. "Yes, sir. Damned near impossible.'' He looked at Dryden. "You don't think it was suicide, do you?''

"Do you?''

23

"Well, no, I guess I don't. Not any more. Damn. Sergeant Kieran is going to be pissed when I change my story."

Dryden shrugged. "Tell Kieran whatever you want. He'll write it up the way Colonel Christopher wants it anyway."

Franks cleared his throat. "You mean that, Captain? You wouldn't mind if I just let the report ride?"

"It doesn't seem to matter what I think," Dryden said. "This camp runs on its own momentum." He took a last look at the cottonwood. "I've seen enough," he said. "Let's go."

Four hours later, with the wind whistling and the cold noon sun glaring on the flat steel railroad tracks, the Camp Butner train chuffed into sight. Konrad Pavel waited silently on the platform in front of the McLean railroad depot. Three American guards huddled nearby, smoking.

Pavel was accustomed to meeting trains. He was one of a handful of top noncommissioned German POWs who had been proposed by Oberst Kleber as translator/overseers back when the Americans first realized they needed someone to smooth the long march from depot to the isolated prison stockade. Without a German topkick to translate, the new prisoners frequently made things difficult, pretending not to understand the most basic of commands. It was a mild form of rebellion, but it irritated the Americans, and they had hit upon what they considered an agreeable solution, requiring German officers to designate a pool of authoritative noncoms to form up the prisoners and get them on the road without delay.

Pavel's English was good enough to understand what the guards wanted and turn it into crisp German commands. In the process of translation Pavel found he could usually sneak in a few tidbits about Camp McLean for the new prisoners, what it was like, which guards to avoid, which works details to shun, how to hide their personal possessions—especially money—during the long march to camp, to avoid confiscation.

But there would be no translation tricks played on the American guards today. Today was special. Today he was to seek out a special prisoner, a man named Otto Boberach, carrying the paybook of a Schütze named Karl Zolling. And

24

he was to do it quietly. Without drawing notice from the guards.

Kleber hadn't said much the night before about the man Pavel was to meet at the depot. Only that he was a specialist who had been captured near Paris and shipped to the American mainland without the Allies realizing who he really was. Once the man had surfaced at Camp Butner, German officers at both camps had gone to a great deal of trouble to get him transferred to Texas. It had taken almost two months to set it up, using the clandestine POW mail system and volunteer clerks in the American military offices, and it had culminated only this week when Boberach switched clothing and identity papers with a German private at Camp Butner, a man named Zolling who had broken enough rules to earn the punishment of exile to Camp McLean. Oberst Kleber said it was vital that no one discover Boberach/Zolling's true identity. Pavel was puzzled by it all but prepared to do his duty.

The train chuffed closer. One of the American guards field-stripped his cigarette, then unslung his carbine. Pavel tried to remain calm. He studied the wooden depot building, brown and yellow, with soot smudges on all the wood-framed windows and the overhanging wooden roof. Wood everywhere. So many American homes and public structures appeared to be made of wood. A temporary country, this America, with only a few of the good, solid stone structures one found in Germany. Almost as if the Americans realized the impermanence of their mongrelized culture and expected everything to crumble about them and blow away.

The train hissed and rumbled to a stop. Metal panels clanged and steps dropped from the passenger cars. Two military escort guards jumped to the platform and checked the area perfunctorily, then gestured for the prisoners to detrain. Out they came, fifty of them, spilling awkwardly and slowly from the passenger cars, accompanied by more guards. They looked sallow, most of them, and tired after the long train ride from North Carolina. Uniforms sagged. Buttons were undone. They shuffled sloppily to the depot platform and milled in confusion. Not one held his head high. These were the flower of German manhood? Pavel glared. He'd soon set these bastards straight. There would be no slovenly men in his charge.

25

Pavel could see a number of local residents gathered near the tracks to watch. Their presence irritated him. Most of the McLean townspeople were accustomed to the comings and goings of German prisoners, seeing them often enough on the streets when the work details motored through town on their way to outlying farms. But these local Texas swine apparently took some perverse pleasure in watching subdued new German arrivals climb off the train. People always gathered. Today, with county schools closed for the Christmas holidays, there were even a number of children and teenagers standing around. Pavel noted a scattering of young boys, eager to trade red-hots and packets of Bull Durham and cigarette papers for German military patches and ersatz metal insignia, and farther away, too shy to come close, a few teenage girls put their heads together, giggling among themselves over some of the younger, better-looking German prisoners.

One of the Camp Butner guards produced a roll sheet. "Fall in for roll call," he barked. He waited for the prisoners to assemble, but they shuffled indecisively, as though failing to comprehend.

The McLean guard grinned and said, "Okay, Pavel, take over. Show these visiting dogfaces how we do it in Texas."

Pavel strode forward and called the prisoners together. He told them gruffly to line up and be quick about it. Some of the prisoners gave him startled looks, uncertain why one of their own, a German topkick, should interfere in their mild demonstration of passive resistance. But Pavel's voice carried authority, and they complied.

The Camp Butner guard scowled and raised his roll sheet. He started calling names in a broad midwestern American accent, but the POW rebellion wasn't finished. The prisoners responded slowly, hesitantly, as if having difficulty understanding the mangled pronunciation of their names. This time Pavel didn't interfere. Finally, with the roll barely into the D names, the Camp Butner guard gave up. He thrust the roll sheet into Pavel's hands and said, "Here, you smart-aleck Kraut. Let's see you do it."

Pavel rapped out names, "Deichmann . . . Dietl . . ." He paused only long enough for replies and a chance to look the men over at close range. Most wore the cuffbands of Sepp Dietrich's Fifth Panzer Army, which meant they had been

26

captured in France, probably in the late summer battles along the Oise. Some of them looked well fed, which indicated that they had been in American hands at least three or four months, long enough to fatten up on the excellent American POW diets. The Geneva terms required the capturing force to feed its prisoners the same food and rations that it fed its own army. But the average American soldier ate considerably more than his German counterpart. And a much better diet. German POW's were astonished by the quantity and quality of meats, vegetables, and fruits that passed through the barbed wire to their tables.

". . . Kaufmann . . . Krause . . ." Pavel studied the faces, wondering which would be the bigshot specialist Boberach. The sharp-nosed man in the second row with a hard mouth and granite chin? No, that one wore the shoulder strap of a Gefreiter, a corporal. Boberach was supposed to be masquerading as a private. What about the beetle-browed man in the rear? Was that Boberach? Or the soldier on the end, the one with scowl lines an inch deep?

". . . Schirmer . . . Stumme . . ." A guttural response from the back row. There went the beetle-browed man. Two names later, the soldier with the deep scowl lines spoke up. Not him, either. Then who? There weren't many left. A couple of square-jawed tankers. A gangly scarecrow with bad teeth. A little old man who looked like a janitor. A kid with peach fuzz.

". . . Ziegler . . . Zolling . . ." Good God, it was the janitor. A short, dumpy little man with a face like a mistreated hound. Big, sad eyes. Cheeks sagging around a downturned mouth. An air of complete hopelessness. Not at all what Pavel was expecting. The man's lower lip trembled when he answered the roll call, as if he expected a rap on the ear for his audacity.

Pavel called the last names and handed the sheet to the guard. He stepped back and glanced again at Boberach/Zolling, wondering why the man seemed so timorous. There was nothing remotely military or authoritative about him. Soft body and stooped shoulders. Gear bag hanging across his arm. This was Oberst Kleber's anonymous Nazi specialist? How could such a mild, frightened little man be so important?

Pavel was deep in thought, pondering how best to approach Boberach/Zolling, when a hand touched his shoulder and a voice said in accented German, "Well, Pavel, did you get what you wanted from the train?"

The touch startled Pavel, and the words chilled him. He looked around into the intense gray eyes of Edward Dryden, the American officer who had disrupted inner-camp routine this morning at the tree.

Pavel forced himself to stand motionless, with an expression of polite incomprehension, as if he hadn't understood the question. Dryden was a relatively recent addition to the Camp McLean hierarchy, but he had already tangled with several of Pavel's fellow noncoms over lax security procedures. Dryden was a problem. He had the look and manner of a man who had ridden the tiger too long. A war lover, but one who had been badly burned. Pavel could understand that. He had seen such men in Africa, men who fought too zealously, with too much abandon, and left their souls on the scorched desert floor. Some became pathetic cowards who quaked at shadows. Others turned into killing machines, monsters without conscience. Dryden could go either way. The American was as dangerous as a starving animal, impractical, unpredictable. Someday would come the explosion, a triggering event that would push him over the brink. Which way would he go? Would he become rabbit or raving maniac? Pavel didn't want to be on hand to find out.

"Well?" Dryden prompted. "Has the day worked out as planned? Did you find what you expected on the train?"

Pavel controlled his face. "I have no idea what you mean, Captain."

"Oh?" Dryden said. "I checked, Pavel. One of your officers came to the gatehouse to volunteer you for train duty only minutes after the wake-up bugle. Something about this train must have caught his attention."

"Camp routine is dull for those of us behind the wire, Captain. Perhaps he wished only to vary my day."

"Perhaps. But he was there before the notice was posted. How did he manage that, Pavel? How did your officer know there was to be a train today? How does word get behind the wire so fast?"

Pavel said, "Excuse me, Captain. I am on duty. It is time to start the men toward camp."

Dryden smiled at him coldly. "Duty. Yes, of course. The ultimate German refuge."

"You don't believe in duty?" Pavel asked.

"Not when it's used as a shield. What about it, Pavel? Was it duty last night when Felix Leiser was tried and executed by the Amtsgericht?"

Pavel felt the skin go tight at his temples. How could Dryden know of such things? Or was he guessing? Pavel said, "I told you earlier, Captain, I have no knowledge of any Amtsgericht. Now, if you will permit me, I must continue with my assigned duties."

Dryden's intense eyes probed deep. Finally he said, "As you wish, Sergeant. Carry on. It's your conscience. You must live with it."

Pavel turned away, his ears burning. The German prisoners stood at ease, murmuring among themselves. Pavel shouted them to attention. They formed up slowly and sloppily. More of their passive resistance. Pavel decided he wouldn't allow it. He stalked closer to the formation and came to a stop near the sad-faced little man who was Boberach/Zolling. He shouted, "Listen to me, you lazy bastards. Dress up those lines. Remember, you are soldiers of the German Reich. By God, let's see you act like it."

The prisoners jolted to attention. Pavel sneaked an uneasy look over his shoulder. Dryden had drifted to the train and was talking to Camp Butner guards. Satisfied that Dryden wouldn't notice, Pavel turned back to the prisoners and said quietly, just loud enough for the sad-faced man in the private's uniform to hear, "You, Schütze Zolling. Say nothing. Listen to me."

The man looked up at Pavel with liquid blue eyes.

Pavel gazed down the line, checking the crispness of the ranks, and continued quietly. "You have friends here," he said. "But we are being watched. Say nothing. Do nothing. We will talk more at camp."

Boberach/Zolling's face came briefly to life. For a moment Pavel feared the man might give himself away through some foolish demonstration of gratitude. To forestall it, Pavel stepped back quickly and addressed the full complement of prisoners.

He said, "German soldiers. You are now consigned to an American hell called Texas. And I am the devil who will

29

command your fate. These American puppies would like to see you slog to camp like defeated men with heads hung low. I won't have it. Any man among you who gratifies the Americans will have to deal with me personally. When I give the command you will move out smartly, with a spring in your step and your chins held high. Is that clearly understood?"

Some of the prisoners muttered, but there was a tilt to the shoulders and fresh steel in the backbones when they grew quiet. A McLean guard signed the transfer papers and gave Pavel a nod.

"Prepare yourselves," Pavel roared. "Show these American rearguard warriors how real soldiers move on parade. I want to hear those feet slap in unison. Ready? For the Führer and the Fatherland, march!"

The ragtag group of prisoners moved out crisply, a solid phalanx of marching men. Even little Boberach/Zolling stepped off with his chest and chin jutting. Pavel marched beside them, feeling proud. But he didn't permit his face to show it until they had marched past the American, Edward Dryden, and turned onto the road to begin the trek to the stockade. Then Pavel smiled and said, "Well done, troopers."

From the depot platform behind them, Dryden watched thoughtfully.

"Lieutenant Bennington?"

"Yes?"

"This is Edward Dryden."

"Yes, Captain Dryden. How may I help you?" Her voice was soft but businesslike, very professional over the telephone.

He reached for the pile of Camp Butner file folders and pulled one across his desk. "I'm afraid I'll have to postpone my therapy session this afternoon. A load of new prisoners just arrived, and I need to go through the transfer papers. It's apt to take the rest of the day."

"I see. Perhaps we can fit you in tomorrow."

"Yes, that would help. Thank you."

A slight hesitation, then her voice changed timbre and she said, "Ned? Is everything all right?"

He grinned. She was beginning to read his mind as easily

30

as his words. He'd heard that old married folks sometimes did that, after years of living in each other's hip pockets. He'd known Lieutenant Beverly Bennington less than two months, only since coming to Texas. But they'd been a very intense two months.

He said, "Yes, everything is fine. Just a problem with some new prisoners that I have to work out."

"Will I see you tonight?"

"Damn straight. About six?"

"Don't be late. I'm selling my body to the local butcher for a pair of steaks."

He rang off, grinning. Then, with a sigh, he opened the first folder from Camp Butner. He didn't really expect to find anything useful in the transfer information. POW records were embarrassingly skimpy. With almost 400,000 Axis prisoners bulging the POW rolls in the continental United States, most files contained only sketchy entries regarding point of capture, unit, rank, and general behavior behind the wire. No one had time for careful evaluation and precise notation. There were too many prisoners, and the detention camps were understaffed.

Still, he had to start somewhere. The Germans had known the train was coming. How? And why was the SS officer so eager to sign Pavel up for train duty? Was there something on the train that the Germans wanted? Contraband from Camp Butner, hidden somewhere in the chair car? Unlikely. Dryden had questioned the escort guards from North Carolina, and they swore none of the prisoners had removed anything from the chair car that wasn't already in their travel kits. Was it a someone, then? Could the camp POW hierarchy have been expecting some particular prisoner? Perhaps some important officer or a nameless Nazi party official who had slipped through the identity net during the clamor of capture and was masquerading as a common soldier? It happened often enough. A man needed only to switch paybooks with a corpse when capture seemed inevitable. But the Camp Butner guards said no. They had noticed nothing out of the ordinary. If anyone of importance had been in their charge, even traveling incognito, surely his own arrogance would have betrayed him.

Dryden frowned. Maybe there was nothing to it. POW trains came to McLean all the time. Still, word of this particular train had obviously reached the Germans behind the wire early. How? And the SS captain had been eager to sign up a particular man to meet the train. Why? What did they expect Pavel to find? Could Dryden afford to ignore the danger signals?

He stared at the pile of folders. Fifty files for fifty prisoners. Somewhere among them, possibly, just possibly, a ringer. Perhaps if he sifted through them carefully, he would find a background or face that didn't fit. Something out of the ordinary. Age. Rank. Enlistment date. Maybe he could select ten or twelve of the most likely candidates and sneak them onto the farm and ranch work lists for tomorrow. Get them out of the compound before the German officers and inner-camp sleight-of-hand experts could close ranks around them. If Dryden could isolate the suspicious ones on dusty farms, he could drive around and look them over more closely at his leisure. And if that didn't work, he could do it again, pick a different ten or twelve the next day. And keep it up until he found the man he was looking for. If such a man existed.

Oberst Kleber looked up from his book when the door to the recreation room opened. Pavel came in, ushering a small man before him. They came to Kleber's table. Pavel snapped his heels together and said, "Herr Oberst, I have the honor to present . . . Schütze Karl Zolling."

Kleber laid his book aside and smiled warmly at the little man. "No need for subterfuge, Pavel. We're all friends here. Herr Boberach, how delighted I am to welcome you. Here, come and sit. Tell me about your trip. Any difficulty with your papers?"

"None that I could discern," the man said wearily. He shuffled to a chair and perched on the edge.

Pavel cleared his throat and said, "Sir, the American, Edward Dryden. He was at the train station, asking questions."

Kleber became alert. "Did he show any special interest in Herr Boberach?"

"No, sir. But he spoke of my motives for meeting the train." Pavel fidgeted, embarrassed at having to point a finger of blame at an officer. "Sir, Captain Grebling may

32

have gone too early to the guardhouse to volunteer my services. The train announcement hadn't been posted yet."

"You told Dryden nothing?"

"No, Herr Oberst. Nothing."

Kleber hesitated, then smiled. "No matter. Let Dryden ask his questions. Now that Herr Boberach is here, nothing can stop us. If we move quickly enough, Captain Dryden's suspicions will no longer be a factor."

Pavel didn't understand, but he said, "Yes, sir."

Kleber turned back to the little man and said, "So, Herr Boberach. You know, of course, why we worked so hard to have you transferred here?"

"Yes, I know."

Kleber studied his face. "We must have confirmation. Tell me, you are sure of the location?"

The man nodded. "There are three facilities, but we have isolated the primary target. Shipment of special equipment has made it a certainty. The American army tried to disguise the intent, but a few of the larger pieces were too massive to move without notice."

"We will have only the one opportunity," Kleber said. "You are absolutely certain?"

The man looked hurt. "I'm a scientist," he said. "I know what I'm talking about. Our intelligence people tracked two electrostatic generators from Wisconsin, a Cockcroft-Walton high-voltage device from Illinois, a particle accelerator from Harvard, and three carloads of apparatus from Princeton. They were all transported to the same location more than a year ago. There can be no doubt."

"Will we reach them in time?"

"We have no choice," the man said. His face drooped. "If Germany is to survive, we must stop them instantly. Before they solve their problems and test the apparatus. They've already had a year. Perhaps two. Time is short."

"We can be ready to move on the instant," Kleber said. "Much has been arranged already. Clothing. Team leaders. We have access to a man who knows the terrain intimately. An American officer. We are waiting only for a letter from an outside contact. A day or two. No more. Have no fear. We will reach the site in time."

33

The man blinked watery eyes. "I pray that you are right."

Dryden saw a spill of light coming from the front window as he drove past the large frame house. He pulled the Dodge to the curb and climbed out. Bright yellow light flooded through half-closed drapes, touching darkened shrubbery. He stalked toward the house, favoring his hip. A dog barked in lonely warning from a nearby fenced yard.

Dryden glared at the spill of light playing through the window, then rapped at the front door. Movement sounded in the house, bare feet coming from a back room. The door opened, and a young woman appeared. "Yes?" she said.

Dryden put his hands on his hips. "Lady, do you realize your curtains are open?"

"So?" she said. She was hard to see with the light behind her and a screen door between them, but she seemed to be wearing a robe and toweling her hair.

"So don't you know there's a war on?" he said. "Your window is lighting up the whole goddamn block."

She was momentarily flustered. "I . . . I'm sorry. I forgot."

"Sure," he said. "It's careless people like you who keep soldiers like me on the streets. What if a wave of German bombers came over about now? They could home in on your light and head straight for downtown McLean."

"Oh, my God," she said. "The city clerk's office in flames. McPherson's hardware a shambles. I'm so ashamed."

His jaw tightened. "You're taking this pretty lightly. Do you know the penalty for aiding and abetting the enemy?"

"I hope it's something physical," she said.

He glowered. "That does it. Unlatch the screen, lady. You're under arrest."

She released the latch. "You ass," she said. "Get yourself in here."

He stepped into the hallway and gathered her in his arms. She smelled of soap, and her body was still damp beneath the robe. She printed quick kisses all over his chin, then drew back and smiled up at him. "Well, Captain Dryden," she said.

"Well, Lieutenant Bennington."

34

"You're late. You said you'd be here by six."

"I had to manipulate the work lists for tomorrow. A private project."

"It serves you right if dinner is spoiled," she said. "The salad has been ready for an hour. The potatoes are limp. The steak is in the refrigerator, getting tired of waiting."

"You managed steaks?"

"Only one. I didn't have enough red points for two. But it's a big one. A nice porterhouse. Mr. Lattimore was saving it under the meat counter. I think he has the hots for me."

"Who doesn't?" Dryden said.

She took him by the hand and led him into the living room. The furniture was overstuffed and covered with a red-rose pattern. Not at all what she was accustomed to. Beverly had grown up in a big Shaker Heights house filled with antiques, many of them American Empire mahogany handed down through her mother's side of the family, others bought by her father, an M.D. with a solid practice. But even here in the rented house on Barton Street, near the edge of McLean, amid shabby secondhand furniture and faded drapes, she looked perfectly at ease. It was a trait Dryden admired.

There were times when he wondered if their backgrounds were too dissimilar. Both came from moneyed families, but Dryden's was dirty-fingernail money, earned through hard work and good luck by a loud, good-natured ranching father who took his supper in shirt sleeves, eating beef and beans at the kitchen table. Hers was aspiring manicured-pinkie wealth, earned by a father who devoted the same conscientious thought to his investment portfolio as he did to his patients, and spent by a mother preoccupied with whether an English Regency mirror would look good over a Queen Anne lowboy. Would Beverly be comfortable in a ranch house in New Mexico? They had talked about it on long evenings in front of the Barton Street fireplace, daydreaming about the end of the war and what they would do with the rest of their lives. Beverly had assured him she could be at home anywhere, so long as he was there. Dreams. Honeyed talk.

Beverly left him to close the drapes over the front windows, not to evade marauding German bombers, but to shut out prying eyes. She turned wantonly, taking from the pocket of her robe the ring and gold chain he had given her

35

that one glorious weekend in Dallas, the only time they had so far been able to steal away together from Camp McLean. An exchange of gifts to mark their commitment. The ring caught light, glowing. It was a square-cut emerald with a blue flame in its depths, exactly the color of her eyes. She wore the ring not on her hand but on the gold chain around her neck, and she fastened the chain now as she faced him. She had bought him a watch on that same trip. An expensive watch with a radium dial that glowed in the dark. She often made him wear it when they were making love. She said she liked to see the green shimmer as his hand moved on her body.

His heart pulled. She was so damned beautiful, standing there in front of the closed drapes. She had the look of a classic Grecian statue. Flawless white skin, as white as the finest marble, and black hair. Her body, fresh from the shower, looked full and smooth and solid beneath the robe. He suddenly felt misshapen. Knobby. Clumsy in comparison. But, again like a statue, there was a mysterious calm about her that put him at ease, a great stillness that drew one closer to study the mystery.

"I missed you," he said.

"I missed you, too." She linked her arm in his and guided him toward the kitchen. "I ran into Colonel Christopher at the officers' club this afternoon."

"That bastard. He didn't show up at the office today. He sent word that he was sick. What was he doing at the officers' club?"

"He only dropped in for a few minutes. The decorating committee met to talk about the Christmas Eve dance Sunday. Colonel Christopher wants mistletoe and holly wreaths."

"That figures. Mistletoe, huh? The old goat. He'll probably use it as an excuse to slobber on every woman in sight. You in particular. Come to think of it, I might take minor advantage of the mistletoe myself."

"Now, now, remember the rules," she said. "No displays in public. What we have is just for us." She took a package from the refrigerator and unwrapped the steak. She held it out to show him, a handsome slab of meat on a platter of crinkled butcher paper. "Isn't it lovely?"

"Stunning," he said. He leaned close and kissed her.

"Flatterer. I mean the steak." She set it on the kitchen counter and picked up a butcher knife to cut away the fat. "Awfully expensive, though. Can you believe Mr. Lattimore charged me forty-nine cents a pound?"

"War is hell," Dryden said.

It was apparently the wrong thing to say, even in jest. Her face clouded and she turned her back on him, busying herself with the butcher knife. As she trimmed the porterhouse she said, "Dr. Brody is on the decorating committee. We talked about you after the meeting broke up."

Dryden cocked his head. "Oh?"

"Yes." She glanced over her shoulder at him. "Dr. Brody tells me you've come through therapy splendidly. He's thinking about changing your medical status. He wants to honor your request for a return to active duty."

Dryden's breath caught. "He said that?"

She nodded. "He's very impressed with your progress. He asked me if I thought you were ready."

"And what did you tell him?"

She set the knife on the counter and turned to face him, brows knit. "I didn't mention the blackouts or the terrible dreams, if that's what worries you. How could I? I've painted myself into a corner. I can't admit to intimate knowledge without explaining how I got it."

"Hey, don't fret," Dryden said. "I'm okay, babe. Honest."

"You are *not* okay," she said forcefully. "You've lied to your doctor, Ned. You didn't tell him about the pain in your hip, or the nights when you wake up in a cold sweat, yelling at shadows. You've convinced him everything is satisfactory, when you know it isn't."

"Hey, an achy hip," he said. "It's no big deal." He put his hands on her shoulders. "Come on, Bev, try to understand. I'm wasted here in Texas. I'm a combat soldier. I belong back at the front. Besides, the hip doesn't bother me that much."

She looked exasperated. "Since when?" she said. "There are days when you can't even walk without hurting. If you let them ship you back to the war with your leg and hip still banged up, you'll probably get yourself killed. Is that what you want?"

"No, of course not." He pulled her closer, nestling her cheek to his chest, stroking her, soothing her.

She sighed against him. "Why didn't you tell me?" she murmured. "How could you ask Dr. Brody to send you back to the fighting without even mentioning it to me?"

"I would have said something eventually." He ran a hand gently over her hair, but his unblinking gaze fell across the top of her head, taking in the kitchen with its pots and pans and red, raw steak lying limp on the butcher paper. Like the red, raw wounds beside the Rapido River. He had friends there. Men who had pulled him away from the ridge and risked their lives to carry him to safety. Men who still faced death every day. How could he explain his debt to her? His sense of guilt? How could he make her understand?

He said, "Don't worry, Bev. I won't go off half-cocked. I'll talk to Brody tomorrow. I'll even tell him about the occasional twinges, if you insist. And I won't do anything without talking it over with you first. I promise."

It seemed to satisfy her. She lifted her face and kissed him. Quietly at first, and then with urgency. He found himself responding, mouth merging with hers, bodies mingling, loins touching. His hands drifted to her waist, undoing the terry-cloth belt. The robe fell open and he slid his hands inside, seeking the warmth of her flesh, still damp from the shower. He cupped her breast, round and ready for his touch. Her nipple quivered insistently. He allowed his hand to roam lower, tracing a pattern across her belly, down to the thatch between her legs.

A moan rose from her throat and she whispered huskily, "Let's forget dinner and go to bed."

"No, here," he said. "In the kitchen."

Her eyes flickered and she said, "You're crazy. Totally insane." But she acquiesced without protest, sinking with him to the linoleum, fumbling with his uniform belt and trouser buttons.

It was not a comfortable coupling, but it was memorable. They joined in a frenzy, like eager animals, laughing at the lack of dignity, the absurdity, twining together on the cold floor, filling each other with pleasure and tingling release. It seemed to last forever. Days. Years. An eternity.

When it was done she rested her head on his arm, exhausted, and said, "Stay with me, Ned. Don't go back to the war. Stay with me always."

"Sure," he said. He held her close and nuzzled her, loving her, wanting to please her. But his eyes rose to the kitchen counter, to a ragged edge of the butcher paper, barely visible above the rim. A raw, red image filled his mind. He said, "Sure, babe. There's no place I'd rather be."

*Friday*
*December 22, 1944*

# THREE

The pig laid its ears flat and squealed in terror when Jürgen Frischauer and baby-faced Willi Roh dragged it from the pen. Smart pig, Pavel thought. It knew something was terribly wrong. Pigs, like soldiers, were selected and nurtured with one purpose in mind—to die for the good of others. You could shove a pig in a muddy sty and let it eat scraps like the German soldier, or you could stuff it full of food and watch it snooze through a short lifetime of luxury like the American soldier, but in the end it came down to the same thing. A whack between the eyes and a knife in the jugular, all for some rashers of bacon. Or a few kilometers of devastated ground.

Pavel watched sourly as Albert Voight shed his denim work shirt with the yellow POW letters. Voight waved the men and the pig closer to the butchering table. Voight had splendid arms and a wide, sturdy chest, but Pavel could see that easy living in the sties of the American POW camp had softened his belly and changed his color. Voight's skin, except for the ruddy hue of his face, neck, and arms, had the pallor of a sick fish.

"Get it over with," Pavel said. "They need us out in the field, to help prepare the bonfires."

Voight grinned. "The trouble with you, Pavel, is that you never know how to enjoy the good times. Relax. We can stretch this out all morning, killing, cleaning, butchering. The guards will never miss us."

"Killing a pig is good times?" Pavel said.

"It's better than wrestling with a pitchfork and those damned Texas weeds."

The pig smelled death now. Jürgen Frischauer murmured a warning. Just in time. The pig wrenched, then dug in with stubby legs, squealing continuously, and tried to escape the pressure of the ropes.

"Is the water ready?" Voight called.

Franz Eggers, using his crooked left arm to feed a fire beneath a black cauldron, said, "It's coming to a boil."

Frischauer and Roh dragged the straining pig to the table and stood apart, keeping their ropes taut. Voight whistled tunelessly between his teeth. He leaned over the table to study an assortment of knives, a saw, a cleaver, and several scrubbing brushes. He selected a wicked-looking knife with a steel blade about ten inches long. With a quick glance for guards he hefted it and said, "These are damned good cutters, Pavel. We could use a couple of them when the Christmas Project gets underway. You're in charge of the crew today. Why don't you hide a few among the lunch boxes when we head back to camp?"

"Find your own hiding places," Pavel said. "I'm under orders from Kleber to play nursemaid. I can't afford trouble."

"That soft little man from Camp Butner?" Voight said. "Let him look out for himself."

The pig planted all four legs, peering up at the men in work denims, dreading what would happen next. Pavel could see that it was quivering.

"Here goes," Voight said. He looped a slipnoose over the pig's snout and pulled. The pig squealed again.

Frischauer said, "Come, man. Aren't you going to knock him in the head first?"

"That's the woman's way," Voight said. "Watch. I'll show you how my father did it. He was a tough old bastard."

Voight straddled the squirming pig and stroked it, crooning

41

softly in German. As the pig calmed, lulled by the quiet words, Voight slid the knife below the pig's chin. He stroked a few seconds longer, then shouted a string of curses and raked the blade across the pig's neck. The pig screamed, and Voight drove the blade deep in its throat, severing the carotid artery. Blood gushed to the ground and the pig's legs crumpled. Voight stood over the kicking body, grinning.

Sickened but not wishing to show it, Pavel said, "Why did you curse at the last moment?"

"That's the way my father taught me," Voight said. "He said you should always work up a good, righteous anger before you strike. Me, I don't much care. I only curse for effect."

*"Schweinerei,"* Pavel muttered. "Pick up your brother and get him in the water."

Voight flashed a look at Pavel, then laughed it off. He said, "Boys, give me a hand."

Frischauer and Willi Roh helped him wrestle the pig into the black cauldron. A cloud of steam hissed into the air. Voight scraped bristles from the body with quick, hard strokes of the knife. Roh took a brush from the table and joined him. The hot water began to turn red.

Frischauer asked Voight hesitantly as they worked, "What did you mean about the knives, Albert? You said they would be useful when Christmas Project begins. Do you know what the officers are planning?"

"I've heard rumors," Voight said. "A man in C Compound told me there might be an escape. He said the officers plan to break through the wire and raise hell. You know, burn a few ammunition dumps and wreck some trains. Things like that."

Pavel scoffed. "Escape? That's nonsense. I talk to the officers every day, and I never heard anything like that."

Willi Roh said, "I hear the officers are planning a demonstration in the stockade. A corporal I know says we're going to pile up cots and mattresses and burn them, then refuse to leave the sleeping compounds until they improve our conditions."

Voight said importantly, "You're both wrong. It has to be an escape. Why else would men on work details be instructed to steal civilian clothing from farms and ranches? Why would old uniforms be gathered and soaked in lye to bleach the color out? Why would the camp tailors cut and sew late into the night?''

"Who says such things are happening?"

Voight shrugged. "My friend from C Compound. He saw a tailor using lye on a tunic and a greatcoat. All the insignia had been removed, but he said the coat belonged to an officer."

"Rumors," Pavel said. "Nothing ever comes of rumors."

Frischauer stopped scrubbing. "What if it's true?" he said. "Suppose the officers are planning an escape, like Albert says. Do you think they might take some of us with them?"

Voight sneered. "A few of us, maybe. People like Pavel and me. We're good soldiers. They'll need us to create chaos. But not you, farmer. They'll never pick you. They need fighting men, not perverts who pant after little girls."

Frischauer stiffened. "What do you mean by that?"

"You know what I mean," Voight said. "Do you think the rest of us don't notice, the way you hang around little girls who live on these farms? Talking baby talk to them. Always making trinkets for them. I'm surprised you haven't tried to drag some little darling into a barn by now."

Frischauer rose from the cauldron, his face red and the cords on his neck bulging. He reached for Voight, but Pavel stepped in quickly to pull him away. "Easy," Pavel said. "You'll get the guards on us."

Voight rose, knife in hand, and grinned. "Let him come, Pavel. I'll carve his pecker down to little-girl size."

"Shut up," Pavel snapped. "Both of you. Voight, finish cleaning your damned pig. And you, Jürgen, get a grip on your temper. It's time we joined the others in the field."

Frischauer glared, then allowed Pavel to pull him away from the cauldron and push him toward the fields where the other prisoners were working. Voight cackled as they walked away.

"Filthy bastard," Frischauer muttered. "He has no business saying such things. You should have let me fight him, Pavel."

Pavel shook his head. "I probably saved you from the worst beating of your life. Be grateful."

"I can handle myself," Frischauer said. "I'm almost as big as he is. And I'm stronger than I look."

Pavel smiled. "Maybe. But Voight is easily the strongest man in camp. He would have beaten you to mush. Or worse. He might have sliced you open the way he did the pig."

Frischauer kicked a clod of dirt. "Good God. I'm not interested in little girls."

"Voight was just blowing air," Pavel said. "No one paid attention."

"Surely, I find pleasure in the children we see on the farms," Frischauer said. "I'm a family man myself. And the little girls, well, they remind me of my own daughter. My little Gerda. Gerda had six red hens of her very own when she . . . before . . . hell, you know."

Pavel did know. Frischauer grieved about it often enough. Back at the start of the war, when the army had summoned Frischauer from his farm near Pegnitz, he had sent his wife and daughter to Hamburg to stay with relatives for the duration. It had seemed a sensible move at the time. Then in July of 1943, two months after Pavel and Frischauer were captured in North Africa, Allied bombers had dumped more than 7,000 tons of bombs on Hamburg, causing 80,000 civilian casualites and turning the stately old city to rubble. Frischauer hadn't heard from his wife or child in all the months since. Almost a year and a half. Perhaps it was only the usual complexities of transferring mail between belligerents. Or perhaps they were dead. The agony was not knowing.

Frischauer said, "Do you think Voight might be right about Christmas Project? Do you suppose the officers are really going to try to break out of here?"

"Voight talks too much," Pavel said. "It's not our business to speculate on what the officers intend."

"It must be something important," Frischauer said. "You saw what they did to poor old Felix Leiser."

"Leiser was asking for it."

"Yes, but why? What do you suppose he heard?"

Pavel scowled. "I don't know what the officers have in mind. But you're probably right about it being important. Oberst Kleber talks as if it could affect history. Maybe even secure the German victory."

"Is he serious? How could any of us do that?"

"I'm damned if I know," Pavel said. "But I trust Oberst Kleber. If he says it's possible, then I'll accept it."

Frischauer said, "Leiser must have known what it was about. Why do you think he was trying to get to the Americans, Pavel? That was crazy, you know. With everyone watching. Why would Leiser do a thing like that?"

"Who can say? Maybe he thought the Americans would reward him."

Frischauer plunged his hands in his pockets. "I don't know. Maybe Leiser just wanted to make sure he would survive. Be alive when this is all over."

"He certainly picked the wrong way to go about it."

Frischauer walked in silence for a moment, then said, "They mentioned odd things that night at the Amtsgericht. Not only Christmas Project. The American captain, Dryden. Someone named Heisenberg. Did the Oberst tell you what that was about?"

"He doesn't confide in enlisted men like me," Pavel said impatiently. "Everything I know, I've gathered on my own from observation. Come, Jürgen, get off the subject. We're not supposed to be discussing any of this."

"I don't know anyone named Heisenberg," Frischauer insisted. "Not in this camp, anyway. Do you?"

"No. And I don't care to."

Out beyond a hog-wire fence Pavel could see the rest of the work crew busily gathering tumbleweed and stacking it into vast piles. It was a rare windless morning, and the German work gang would soon set the piles on fire. A scourge on these flat Panhandle plains, tumbleweed rolled and cartwheeled after the first frost to the nearest fence, then clung together in deep scraggly drifts. If the Texas farmers didn't clear them periodically, sand would blow up and cover the drifts, creating sand mounds. Pavel watched as German backs bent to scoop up the prickly weeds. Was Boberach among them? Probably. Pavel had told him to take it easy, just go through the motions unless one of the American guards was close at hand and watching. But no American guards were in sight. Not out here in the chill air. They were no doubt hanging around the farmhouse. They never did much guarding.

What fury when Oberst Kleber found Boberach's Camp Butner alias on today's work lists. Dryden's doing, most likely. Several of the Camp Butner names had appeared on the various lists. Kleber had considered making a formal protest but had decided against it. Best not to draw attention to Boberach or the others. Not with the time so near. Instead, he had asked Pavel to volunteer for the same work crew and to act as Boberach's bodyguard. Just as well. Boberach looked as if he'd never done a day's labor in his life. Soft hands. A white-collar man. Some kind of technician, from the way he talked yeasterday. What was that all about? What were the officers planning?

Apparently Frischauer was still wondering about the same thing. Hesitantly he said, "If there's really going to be an escape, Pavel, maybe we could go along. With a little luck I'll bet we could make it all the way home."

Pavel laid a hand on Frischauer's shoulder. "Forget it, my friend. The only way either of us will see home again is for this damned war to end."

Colonel Christopher's eyebrows came together in a stern gray line, and he sniffed into a handkerchief. He refused to look directly at Dryden. He said, "I received your memo this morning, Edward. I must admit it disturbed me."

Morning sunlight streamed through a big window in the colonel's living room, dappling an assortment of pill bottles and cough medicines at Christopher's elbow. Equally prominent was a fresh bottle of bourbon, uncapped and on its way to an early death. A glass tumbler showed traces of whiskey and sugar. A spoon lay on a saucer beside the tumbler. The Lone Star cure, Christopher called it. A toddy for his apparently permanent Texas cold.

"Are you prepared to act on it?" Dryden asked.

Christopher adjusted his hips uneasily on the rubber doughnut that had been prescribed by camp doctors for a newer ailment, hemorrhoids. He said, "I don't know, Edward. You're suggesting we tighten our security?"

"Yes, double the guard," Dryden said. "And run some search-and-explore operations behind the wire."

Christopher, a spare man in his fifties, wore a graying mustache over a sensitive mouth. The mustache twitched, and he said, "We don't have the manpower, Edward. Not with half our men going on leave."

"Cancel the leaves," Dryden said.

Christopher looked shocked. "We can't do that. Not with Christmas coming up. Most of the men are packed and

46

ready. Changing signals now would be disastrous for morale."

"That's the whole point," Dryden said. "The Germans know about the leaves as well. They know we're going to be shorthanded."

"We have no reason to expect trouble from the Germans." Christopher objected. "As a matter of fact, they've been quite cooperative lately. General Kleber asked permission just last week for a Christmas celebration in the prison stockade. He promised his men would congregate only in small groups and confine the festivities to their barracks. Does that sound like a man planning mischief?"

Dryden shook his head. "I don't think a Christmas party is what Kleber and his officers have in mind. Something is happening out there. Something important enough to cause the death of Felix Leiser."

"Now, now," Christopher said. He stirred a fresh toddy for himself, a spoon of sugar and a dollop of bourbon. "I wish you could control your zeal, Edward. Sergeant Kieran told me you might make a fuss over that poor man's death. Why don't you just accept it for what it was? A suicide, nothing more."

Dryden stared at the toddy. Colonel Hamilton Christopher, like Dryden, was a war invalid, but without a damaged body or visible scar tissue. He had absorbed his wounds at the Kasserine Pass. When Rommel's Afrika Korps made its sweeping breakthrough in February 1943, Christopher's battalion was trapped in Sidi Bou Zid. A lot of good men died. It wasn't Christopher's fault, but rear-echelon quarterbacks looked for sacrificial lambs to lay on the altar of blame, and Christopher was one of the lambs they selected. He was summarily relieved of his combat command and yanked back home to finish out the war in an unimportant POW post. In Roman times a disgraced officer would have fallen on his sword. Christopher had fallen on a bourbon bottle. It cut just as deeply.

Dryden said, "No, sir. Leiser didn't kill himself. The facts won't support it."

"Yes, yes, I know." Christopher said. "You explained all that in your memorandum." His eyebrows dipped as if he were seeking a solution, but his mind was obviously already made up. "Very well," he said. "We'll do it your way,

Edward. As soon as the men are back from holiday leave we'll strengthen the perimeter guard and run a few shake-up crews into the compounds. Is that acceptable?"

"That might be too late," Dryden said.

"I understand," Christopher said. He sipped his toddy. A tower of compromise, the younger officers called him. Old Blood and Gutless. "But I can't disappoint the men. We'll just have to get along with what we have. Resign yourself to being shorthanded the next few days, Edward. Then, when everyone is back, we'll start the new year right and do what we can about beefing up camp security." He tossed off the toddy and nodded vaguely in dismissal.

Dryden suppressed a sigh. Once Christopher's mind was set, further discussion was useless. He thanked the commandant for his time and headed for the door. He heard the spoon stirring a fresh toddy as he let himself out.

Dryden slipped into the Dodge and switched on the engine. No point in dwelling on matters he couldn't change. What next? He checked his watch. Still early. Time to check out a couple of the farms before lunch. At least he could take a closer look at some of the Camp Butner prisoners he had dragooned for the day's work lists.

Sergeant Konrad Pavel looked up from his lunch carton to see the olive-drab army Dodge curling up the dirt road toward the small farmhouse. Most of the prisoners were squatting around the Camp McLean truck, finishing their sandwiches and oranges. Two American guards, loafing on the porch and paying scant attention to the prisoners, caught sight of the approaching Dodge and quickly grabbed their weapons. They bustled into the sunlight and barked orders, trying to look busy. Schnell, schnell, they shouted. Clean up that debris. Stop dawdling. Get back to work.

Pavel watched as the army sedan eased in behind the truck. The American officer, Edward Dryden, climbed out. Pavel muttered under his breath. He should have known the man would show up. Albert Voight, sitting near Boberach, also saw Dryden emerge from the car. Voight stiffened and turned away. Pavel thought he saw the big man reach beneath his denim shirt. His hand shifted to his discarded lunch carton before he rose to his feet and ambled off. Pavel crumpled his sandwich wrappings, wondering what Voight was up to.

"Hurry up, burrheads," the oldest guard yelled. "Let's get those cartons stacked and in the truck."

Boberach seemed confused by the guard's shouted English. Jürgen Frischauer leaned over and told him what was expected of him. Boberach nodded and stuffed his sandwich wrappers and orange peels into his lunch carton, then gathered several empty cartons, including Voight's, and piled them precariously atop his own. Dryden came around the rear of the truck.

The guard kept ranting, trying to impress Dryden. "Come on, *mach schnell*," he rasped. "Upanzee pick. Let's go, let's go."

Boberach's load was unwieldy. The guard gave him a push and the top cartons teetered and toppled. Wrappers and rinds spilled across the dirt. A long, shiny pig knife rolled out among them, glinting in the sunlight.

The guard goggled. "Hey, you," he yelled. "Whoa. What the hell are you trying to pull?"

Boberach blinked at him, not understanding.

The guard grabbed Boberach by the tunic. "Where did you get that knife?" he demanded. "Do you know the penalty for stealing? This will mean the sweatbox for you, you Kraut bastard."

"Nein, nein," Boberach protested. He blinked in confusion.

Pavel groaned. He shouldn't interfere. It would be foolish to speak on Boberach's behalf while Dryden was nearby. But he had to do something. If he didn't, Boberach was apt to be slapped into solitary confinement. Kleber would be furious.

Pavel edged forward. Quietly and in his most careful English, he said, "Excuse me, Corporal. The knife was not stolen. We made use of it during lunch to peel the fruit."

The guard glared. "Are you saying you took it?"

Pavel kept his voice low. "No. I am saying no one took it. It is a knife used to butcher the pigs. We kept it briefly to cut the oranges. It was to be replaced, but you called us to order before we could do so. This man picked it up by accident."

"Trouble, Corporal?"

Pavel grimaced. It was Dryden.

"Yes, sir," the guard said. "I caught one of the prisoners swiping a knife. Now Pavel says he and the others only borrowed the knife and were using it to peel oranges. I didn't see nobody peeling oranges with no knife. They're lying."

Dryden raised an eyebrow. "Good to see you again, Sergeant Pavel. And this is one of your new Camp Butner comrades, isn't it?"

"Yes, sir," Pavel said reluctantly. "Schütze Karl Zolling." He sought Voight, standing a few feet away, and blistered him with a look. Voight shrugged.

Dryden switched to German, speaking directly to Boberach. He said, "Tell me, Zolling. Did you take the knife?"

Boberach blinked again, surprised to hear German from an American officer. He said, "Knife? No, sir. I saw no knife. I picked up some boxes. It must have been among them."

Dryden told the guard, "It's all right, Corporal. This man says he was unaware of the knife. I believe him. I think we can overlook the incident. Just have someone return the knife to its proper place."

The guard nodded sullenly, not pleased that Dryden was taking up for a prisoner. He scowled at the surrounding faces, looking for someone to take the knife. Voight hesitated, then stepped forward. "I will replace it," he said.

The guard handed the long knife to him. Voight flicked a smirk of triumph at Pavel and hurried away, holding the blade close to his chest. Boberach started to leave, too, but Dryden wasn't through with him.

In German, Dryden said, "One moment, Zolling. I'd like to talk to you a moment, if you don't mind."

Boberach turned. He took a fragile pair of spectacles from his tunic pocket and slipped them onto his nose so he could see Dryden more clearly. One earpiece was broken and had been mended with adhesive tape. He peered at Dryden and said, "Yes, Herr Hauptmann?"

Dryden studied Boberach's Wehrmacht tunic, checking the insignia and cuff bands. His gaze settled on a small chest decoration, a diagonal strip of colored ribbon running from the second buttonhole to the flap where it turned under. It was a common ribbon, black stripe on white, bordered in red.

"I see you've won the Iron Cross," Dryden said. "Will you tell me where?"

Boberach said, "In . . . in France, Herr Hauptmann."

Pavel winced. A mistake. If this went further, he'd have to step in again. He looked for help. Jürgen Frischauer was watching from the rear of the army truck. Pavel gestured unobtrusively. Frischauer seemed to understand. Franz Eggers and Willi Roh moved closer as well.

"Where in France?" Dryden asked.

"Er . . . in Caen, Herr Hauptmann. For action against the British."

Pavel tried to catch Boberach's eye.

"Is it first class or second class?" Dryden asked.

"Second class, Herr Hauptmann."

Pavel expelled breath. The fool had gone too far. What to do? How could he distract Dryden? Frischauer may have sensed Pavel's dilemma. The big farmer reached suddenly to the side of the truck for a heavy grinding stone on which the Germans were allowed to hone their tools. For an instant Pavel thought his friend was about to use the stone to attack the American. He almost called to him to stop. But Frischauer deliberately wavered and seemed to stumble under the stone's weight. It fell from his hands and bounced off his foot. Frischauer shrieked in pain.

"Jesus, what now?" the guard growled.

Pavel, surprised to silence, waited and watched. Frischauer played his part well, making enough noise to keep Dryden's attention, hobbling beside the truck with just the right mixture of pain and embarrassment. The guard hurried to check him. Frischauer cursed and tried to keep his weight off the injured foot. He cursed even louder when, at the guard's insistence, he was forced to sit and remove his boot and sock. He flinched in agony when the guard probed the damaged arch. The guard came back to Dryden with a worried look.

"Sorry, sir," the guard said. "That dumb bastard may have busted his foot. Someone ought to take him back to the camp infirmary for an examination. I'd take him myself, but we only got two people here to watch the prisoners."

Dryden glanced at Frischauer impatiently, then at Pavel and Boberach. He seemed unwilling to break off the interrogation. To Pavel's relief, Dryden said, "Very well, Corporal. Put the man in my car."

The two guards helped Frischauer hobble to the Dodge. They lingered until Dryden backed away from the truck and drove down the dirt road toward the highway. Then they grinned at each other and headed back to the porch to resume their loafing.

Pavel turned on Boberach angrily. "You fool," he hissed. "You let the American trick you."

Boberach was startled. "He tricked me? How?"

"The ribbon on your tunic," Pavel said. "It isn't the Iron Cross. It's the Kriegsverdienstkreuz. The War Merit Cross. The Iron Cross ribbonette is a red band bordered by black. Yours is the opposite, a black band bordered by red. Any real German soldier would have known that."

Boberach dropped his eyes to the ribbon. "I . . . I'm sorry. Nobody told me."

Willi Roh and Franz Eggers, crowding closely, overheard. Willi said, "It's a little thing, Pavel. Colors reversed. Maybe the American captain doesn't know the difference either."

"He knows," Pavel said. He gazed across the distance at the highway, watching Dryden's car. "Dryden knows too many things."


Erwin Maschmann, one of the German enlisted men assigned to postal duty in the camp mail center, was sorting incoming letters when he came to an envelope bearing one of the five names set aside for the use of the officers. His throat tightened. He caught the eye of one of his fellow mail workers, a Waffen-SS corporal, and tapped the letter surreptitiously.

The Waffen-SS man worked on, sneaking glances across the room, then nodded, a sign that the nearest guard was looking elsewhere. Maschmann stuffed the envelope into the front of his shirt. The paper slid across his chest like an ice cube. It was cold in the camp postal center. There was a gas space heater at the other end of the building, where the American guards congregated, but its warmth never reached the Germans.

The special letters with the special names were to be delivered to Oberst Kleber immediately. Maschmann backed away from the counter and headed for the front of the building, holding a hand to his stomach. He didn't have to say a word. The guard took one look at the queasy expression on his face and said, "A little grippe, Maschmann? Go on over to the clinic. I'll put you on the Krankenliste and check you out."

Maschmann nodded gratefully and went out into the fresh air. It was warmer in the sunshine. The wind had calmed today, and the temperature was in the mid-fifties. Even so, Maschmann felt a chill. Why couldn't he be stalwart like the others? For most of the Germans on mail-sorting duty, slipping letters past the American censor was a grand game. They played it with roguish glee, tampering with postmarks and labels under the very gaze of the guards. Not so for Maschmann. Each letter clutched at him like a cold vise. Maschmann was a direct man, uncomfortable with trickery and subterfuge. It wasn't so much that he dreaded punishment in case he was caught. It was worse than that. What turned him into six feet of quivering jelly was the fear that he might, through some clumsy act of carelessness, cause the complex mail system so carefully wrought by the German officers to come crashing down in ruins.

And it was a fine, intricate system. German prisoners could receive unlimited mail, thanks to the Geneva accords. And, subject to American censorship, they could send two letters a week per man, either to friends and family in Europe, or to blood relatives in the United States. The German officers had worked things out so a letter could be sent almost anywhere. Easiest was shuffling letters back and forth among the 150 base camps in the American POW chain. In theory, only relatives could write each other from one prison camp to another. A POW father could send a letter to a POW son. A nephew could write an uncle or a cousin. Once a legitimate family letter, twenty-four lines of writing, had passed the camp censor, Maschmann and the other mail sorters could easily add several additional messages to the same envelope before sending it. The family member at the other end always passed the extra notes along.

Other postal schemes were more complex. In POW camps across this barren America, German officers had issued standing orders that when a German soldier was transferred from one stockade to another he was to leave his old enve-

53

lopes behind, already marked with the official censor's stamp. Here at Camp McLean, for example, Kleber con trolled the envelopes. He kept a list of the camps where transferred men had been sent. If something urgent needed to be forwarded from one camp to another, Kleber selected the proper envelope, stuffed a new message into it, and sealed it. He could then pass it to the postal volunteers, who would stamp it "No Longer at Camp McLean." Since it already bore the censor's stamp, it was automatically forwarded to the new camp. The man at the other end would receive it, then carry the message to the person for whom it was actually intended.

Maschmann thought of himself as uneducated and unsophisticated, but even he could see the value of this marvelous subterfuge. Message after message could be sneaked past the camp authorities, either directly to the proper camp or through a series of envelope changes until it reached its goal. Oberst Kleber had used the system most recently, Maschmann knew, to arrange some form of complicated prisoner exchange with a POW camp in North Carolina. At least that's what everyone at the postal center said. But a train had come in from Camp Butner yesterday, and as far as Maschmann could tell there were no important people on it. Only common soldiers like himself.

There were other intricacies in the mail system that Maschmann didn't fully understand. This letter today, for example. When letters of extreme importance came from the outside they had to be slipped out of the mail building and delivered before they ended up on the censor's table. Maschmann had no idea who wrote the letters, or how they learned of the special list of names. Such complexities were better left to officers. And to answer such special letters without censorship, the officers relied on a false censor's stamp carved by one of the best POW artisans. It looked as good as the real thing, Maschmann thought, but the officers preferred to save it for emergencies.

Maschmann shielded his eyes and gauged the sun. It was getting on toward the end of the lunch hour. Oberst Kleber would probably be in the officers' mess. The officers always lingered at table longer than the enlisted men. And why shouldn't they? They had the best cuts of meat, and the best German POW cooks to prepare their meals. They had real linen and crystal. They even had fresh flowers on their table every day, provided by the American army. The first German officers to be interned at Camp McLean had objected to the spartan quality of the mess and had refused to eat in it until the Americans purchased fresh fittings. The American commandant, a Colonel Christopher, was a mild man with no wish to offend. He had arranged for proper china and linen and had even budgeted five dollars a day in military funds so a McLean florist would provide roses and white carnations for the tables.

As Maschmann entered the officers' mess he took the envelope from his shirt. A young artillery lieutenant, Bernd Strikfeldt, saw the envelope in Maschmann's hand and nodded toward the rear of the room. Maschmann was gratified. Like most of the German enlisted men, Maschmann liked Lieutenant Strikfeldt. He was a decent officer who never took advantage of his rank. An explosives expert and cocky as hell, but willing to mix with common soldiers. Strikfeldt even joined the enlisted men occasionally on the soccer field. A good outside forward. Fast, aggressive, and willing to share the glory when someone as big and lumbering as Maschmann chanced to get open.

Maschmann followed the direction of Strikfeldt's nod and saw Oberst Kleber back at the biggest table, sharing ice cream and cigars with SS Colonel Ulrich Waldau and SS Captain Dieter Grebling. Maschmann hesitated. Kleber wasn't so bad, but he hated to brace Waldau and Grebling. Both SS officers thought highly of themselves and didn't appreciate being interrupted by lowly enlisted men.

But Kleber had seen him. The Oberst glanced at the envelope, then beckoned. Maschmann inhaled deeply and hurried.

"Is that for us?" Kleber asked.

"Yes, Herr Oberst. It just arrived."

Kleber took the envelope eagerly and checked the name on the front. He seemed pleased by what he saw. He laid the letter reverently on the tablecloth and told the two SS officers, "Gentlemen, this is the one we have been waiting for."

Officers at nearby tables stopped talking. Waldau and Grebling leaned forward intently. Maschmann felt conspicuous, standing at attention. He wished the Oberst would remember to dismiss him.

Kleber's voice rose. "Leutnant Spielberger, will you do the honors?"

A junior officer at Bernd Strikfeldt's table, a slim, owlish Wehrmacht lieutenant with a university degree and an understanding of cryptanalysis, pushed quietly from his chair and came to Kleber's table. He studied the envelope carefully, turning it first one way, then the other.

"It's the stamp," the young lieutenant murmured. He produced a leather cigarette case from which he extracted a tiny tool, a sliver of sharp steel about two inches long. With tender slowness he inserted the sharp edge of the tool under each corner of the postage stamp, peeling and lifting. When the corners were loose he put the steel tool back in his case and brought out a pair of tweezers. Carefully, gently, he lifted the stamp free. It didn't take much effort. Only the corners had been moistened.

Maschmann rocked back on his heels, his mind racing. God in heaven. The stamp. And he had placed the verdammt thing under his shirt. What if it had been hot today instead of cold? What if he had sweated through to the envelope and gotten the stamp stuck? They would have killed him.

The young lieutenant laid the stamp on a napkin, face down, and put the tweezers away. He took a small magnifying lens from his breast pocket and leaned over the stamp, studying it. "It's in code," he said. "I'll have to make some transpositions."

Kleber gestured, and a notepad and pencil materialized from the tunic of Dieter Grebling. Using the magnifying glass, the lieutenant studied and scribbled, transferring symbols from the back of the stamp to the notepad. He worked in silence, doing it all in his head without a codebook or any memory guides. When he was done he handed the pad to Kleber.

Kleber read it slowly, then smiled and said, "Auf Draht! This is the final link, gentlemen. Transport and weapons will be in place by Sunday and will remain on standby for five days."

Waldau, the SS colonel, brushed a lock of red hair from his forehead and allowed his thin mouth to quirk up at the corner. Grebling, more demonstrative, laughed out loud.

Some of the nearby officers drummed fingers on tablecloths in quiet applause. The young lieutenant collected his tools and returned to his seat.

Kleber tore the sheet from the notepad. He took his cigar lighter from his pocket and touched a flame to the paper. As the sheet curled and burned, Kleber laid it in the ashtray and added the stamp to it. "Officers of the Christmas Committee will meet in my quarters tonight," he told the men around him. "We will select the names of men who are to accompany us and inform them tomorrow morning. If everything is ready, we will go on Monday."

Dryden handed a fresh roll of tape to Beverly. "It looked like a phony accident to me. The timing was too pat."

She applied an anchor strip three inches above the German soldier's ankle and said, "No matter how it looked, the injury is real. He'll have trouble walking for a day or two. Does he speak English?"

Dryden shook his head. "I tried him in the car. He knows a few words. They all do. But not enough to follow a conversation."

She tore pieces of adhesive tape and looped stirrup strips from the anchor below the heel and back up. "You're convinced there's a problem?"

"I think so. We've got a suicide that smells to high heaven. A prisoner who isn't what he seems to be. Now we're crippled by holiday leaves and a depleted guard roster. If ever the Germans wanted to hurt us, the time is ripe."

"So what will you do?"

"I'm not sure. Talk to the little guy again, I suppose. A soldier who doesn't know his medals isn't much of a soldier."

She taped a gauze pad to the instep. "Perhaps you should tell Colonel Christopher about him."

"No point. Christopher won't listen. Not without solid evidence. I don't know, Bev. It's frustrating, working in a vacuum. I feel like a car stuck in the mud, spinning its wheels. My engine is running, but I'm not getting anywhere. Maybe I should go ahead and ask Dr. Brody to process my reassignment papers."

"We've talked about that," she said. She started laying cross strips.

"Yes, and nothing has changed."

She said, "Do whatever you have to, Ned, but don't expect my blessing." She applied the last cross strip and finished taping with a heel lock, then stood. "I have other patients waiting," she said. "Tell him to stay off the foot. At least until tomorrow."

He reached out and touched her, a finger to the curls at her neck. "You still don't understand, do you?"

She resisted his caress for a moment, then softened. "You haven't made it easy," she said. "You keep talking about your debt to others, but I have the feeling there's more. What is it really, Ned?"

He remembered his discussion with Pavel at the train depot. "Duty is a part of it," he said. "A man has to believe in duty."

"But there's something else, isn't there? Is it the wound? Is that what bothers you? You don't have to rush back to war just to prove you're still a hell of a man, you know. Not for me, you don't."

"I know." He looked inward, weighing his motives. A secret truth glistened among the darker cobwebs of his psyche. Duty was part of it, sure. Proof of manhood? Perhaps. But even stronger was a shimmering nugget of personal, selfish greed. He felt useless here. Crippled, pushed aside, forgotten. A zero. A cipher. He wanted to count for something again. How did one explain that?

She regarded him quizzically for a moment, then patted his hand and left the room.

Dryden sighed and faced the German. Frischauer already had his sock on and was trying to slide into his shoe.

"How do you feel?" Dryden asked him in German.

The big German raised gloomy eyes. He said, "The foot hurts. But I will survive."

"You're more fortunate than many," Dryden said. "The war will end soon, and you can go home. Some of your comrades aren't so lucky. Corporal Leiser, for example."

Frischauer looked away. "I know nothing of that," he said. He hesitated, then glanced again at Dryden. "Do you really think the war will end soon?"

Dryden nodded. "A couple of months. Maybe earlier."

"Your American newspapers speak of a new German

58

offensive in the Ardennes," Frischauer said. "They say our Panzer armies are closing in on a place called Bastogne."

"It won't last," Dryden said. "You've got no air cover."

Frischauer slipped off the examination table, testing his foot. "I hope you are right. I know I should not say such a thing. I am a German soldier, and loyal to my comrades. But I have a family."

"We all have families," Dryden said.

"Your American families are not being bombed day and night," the man murmured. He leaned against the table, eyes downcast. "Captain, do you think it possible that the war could be prolonged by desperate men? If they . . . if they were willing to do anything? Make any sacrifice?"

Dryden was puzzled. "I suppose so," he said. "It would depend on the caliber of men. On their commitment. And what they had in mind."

Frischauer grimaced. "What if you knew something about it? Not precisely what they were planning, perhaps. Only that an event of importance was about to take place, and that a few people think it might conceivably change the course of the war. What if the men were your friends, but you knew that they were determined to make the war go on and on, exposing more women and children to death?"

"I'd try to stop them," Dryden said.

Frischauer stared at Dryden, then said, "Thank you for bringing me to the infirmary, Captain. I'll return to my quarters. I have many things to consider."

*Saturday*
*December 23, 1944*

# FOUR

A German lookout stepped smartly in front of Pavel at the library door, blocking his way, and said, "You can't go in."

Pavel took his time and studied the young man in his path. Huber, his name was. Erich Huber, barely in his twenties, one of Dieter Grebling's security clowns. He was a handsome young man, blond hair and wide hazel eyes above smooth cheeks and a straight nose. His mouth, full and sensuous and cherry-lipped, was set in a thrusting jaw and suggested insolence. Pavel knew the type well. This was another of those arrogant young bastards from the Hitlerjugend, weaned on patriotic songs and Nazi idealism, who had grown into strapping manhood and the firm belief that everything they did, every sentence they uttered, every thought and sinew and fiber of their bodies, was dedicated to the greater glory of the thousand-year Reich.

The most irritating thing about these Hitler Youth puppies was that they considered devotion and loyalty to be their own exclusive province. They never gave a thought to the loyalty of the common foot soldier. Pavel gave passing consideration to grabbing the young prick and hurling him bodily into the dust in front of the library door, to teach him some manners. Instead, he said quietly, "I have been summoned. Oberst Kleber sent for me."

"Your name?"

"You know my name," Pavel said. "Hauptfeldwebel Konrad Pavel. Move aside."

"Rank means nothing today," the little prick said. "This is a restricted zone." He pulled a crinkled sheet of paper from his tunic and checked a list of names. He seemed disappointed to find Pavel's name among them. He said, "You may enter. Speak no word to anyone about what you see inside."

"Thank you for telling me my duty," Pavel said. He couldn't resist jostling Huber aside with his elbow before entering the library.

It was a long, narrow hut like the others, wood frame with black tar paper on the outside and exposed studs on the inside, but with long shelves lining the walls and several reading tables scattered along the narrow length of the building. It contained more than four thousand books, about two thirds of which were in English, and the balance in German. Most of the English-language books, provided by Texas schools and public libraries, were educational—textbooks on agriculture and accounting, on mathematics and music, on American history and government and gardening. The rest of the books, a mixture of aging entertainments and moldy volumes of nonfiction in the German language, had been culled from home libraries and donated by German-American families scattered across the polyglot state of Texas.

There were at least twenty men crowded around the tables. Most of them were reading. Pavel saw several faces he recognized. Willi Roh and Franz Eggers, flipping magazine pages and making notes. The resident explosives ace, artillery lieutenant Bernd Strikfeldt, studying a big atlas of the United States. Erwin Maschmann, the hulking grenadier who worked in the mail-sorting room. Albert Voight, his piggy face creased in concentration, sharing a newspaper with Horst Baumhof and a Panzer corporal named Lampe who had been wounded and captured in the last retreat toward Bizerte.

A friendly voice hailed Pavel. "Good soldier Pavel. Thank you for coming so quickly."

It was Oberst Kleber, standing beside one of the tables. Pavel drew himself to attention. "You wished to see me, sir?"

"Yes, indeed." Kleber took Pavel's arm and drew him to a window, away from the crowded tables. Quietly, he said, "Once again I need the help of a good man, Sergeant Pavel. Would you be willing to take on a complex and dangerous obligation?"

"Of course, Herr Oberst."

"Excellent. Within the next forty-eight hours there will be an organized escape attempt from this camp. A special force, operating under orders. Four officers and twenty enlisted men. I want you to come with us."

Pavel's heart missed a beat. "Come with you, sir?"

Kleber gestured at the crowded tables. "These are the men selected for the adventure. The best the camp has to offer. Even now they are studying survival materials. What Americans wear. Food. Drink. Railroad timetables. Prices. Will you come?"

Pavel tried to conceal his glee. "With pleasure, sir."

"I feel I should warn you," Kleber said. "The odds are against us. Before we can separate to flee the country we must answer a serious challenge. In a few days you and I and the rest of the men in this room will be fighting for our lives. And the lives of our families. Many of us will die. Perhaps all of us. Here. In America."

"A battle, sir? With the Americans?"

Kleber's eyes flashed. "Yes, a battle. Every step has been planned. Transportation. Route. Weapons. You're the best combat sergeant in camp, Pavel. When the time comes, I want you to lead the assault force."

"Thank you, sir. I would be honored."

"There's more," Kleber said. "Otto Boberach. He will accompany us. I want you to protect him with your life. Until we reach the assault area, he must be shielded from all danger. He is essential to the success of our mission. Colonel Waldau will share the command with me. Grebling and Strikfeldt will act as junior officers. Waldau is an excellent leader, but he is SS, trained to meet problems with harsh expedience. No matter how precisely we make our plans, there are always imponderables. If anything happens to me, and the Americans close in on us before we reach our objective, Colonel Waldau might be tempted to abandon Herr Boberach. That must not happen. Do you understand what I am saying?''

"Yes, sir. I think so.''

"Good,'' Kleber said. "The men trust you. Most of them will stand with you, if circumstances compel a confrontation. I'm not asking you to disobey direct orders, Pavel. Only to use your best judgment and do everything in your power to see that Herr Boberach reaches our final destination. Even if it calls for your own life's blood.''

"I promise, Herr Oberst.''

Kleber grasped Pavel's shoulder. "I knew I could count on you.'' He led Pavel away toward the door. "Take heart, my friend. It won't be all hardship and danger. After we have completed our mission the survivors still have a good chance for escape. The Fatherland has provided a U-boat.''

"A U-boat, sir?''

Kleber touched a finger to his lips, cautioning silence. "It lies now off the coast of Mexico, waiting. Starting from the moment we break free, we will have five days to reach the target area, and another five days to fight our way to the submarine. Those of us who are still alive to reach it will see Germany again. Family. Friends. Home. Where is your home, Pavel?''

"Westphalia, Herr Oberst. Near Cologne.''

"Ah, the Rhine Valley. Beautiful country. I used to go to Cologne every January with my wife for the masked balls. Karneval. Before the war, of course. I'm a Bavarian myself. Munich. I think of it often, especially at this time of the year. Christmas was wonderful in Munich. Shopping for presents at the Christkindl Markt. Crepes Barbara at the Spatenhaus. Children caroling in the snow on street corners. God, I miss Germany.''

"We'll see it again together, sir.''

"Yes, perhaps,'' Kleber said without conviction. He paused with Pavel at the door. "I have a more immediate task for you, Pavel. Please find Herr Boberach and bring him to my quarters. It's time to assemble the officers who will lead this expedition and explain the true nature of our mission."

"At once, Herr Oberst."

"Ah, and the man who assisted you at the farm yesterday. What was his name? Frischauer?"

"Yes, sir. Private Jürgen Frischauer. Had it not been for his quick action, we might all have ended up in solitary confinement."

"You say Dryden took him to the camp clinic, and the nurse, Lieutenant Bennington, tended his foot? He saw the two of them together?"

"Yes, sir. I asked him about it myself."

"Excellent," Kleber said. "We need confirmation of one last piece of information about Captain Dryden. Perhaps Private Frischauer can provide it. Ask him to come to my quarters right away."

"Yes, sir." Pavel hesitated. "Sir, about Private Frischauer. Is he to accompany the expedition as well?"

"No, I'm afraid not," Kleber said. "Why do you ask?"

"He's a good soldier, sir. I served with him in Africa. And he proved his value yesterday, at the farm."

Kleber's eyes mellowed. "I see. You'd like your friend to come with us?"

"We've been through many battles together," Pavel said. "And he has special reasons for wanting to see home."

"Very well," Kleber said. "I think it can be arranged. I'll speak to Colonel Waldau. You may so inform Private Frischauer."

"Thank you, Herr Oberst."

Kleber grew more businesslike. "Keep these matters to yourself, Pavel. Tell no one. Not even the men in this room who are to take part in it. For reasons of security, the special nature of this escape must remain a closely guarded secret until we are clear of the camp and on our way. Do you understand?"

"Yes, sir," Pavel said. He saluted smartly and left.

Pavel's spirits soared as he stepped out into the sunlight. Escape. How glorious the concept. And more. A battle. He hummed a few bars from the Afrika Korps anthem. Erich Huber, the snotty Hitlerjugend lookout, gave him a haughty look. Pavel was inexplicably pleased. He fixed his eyes on the arrogant youngster and broke into a roaring refrain:

> *Es rasseln die Ketten . . .*
> *Es dröhnt der Motor!*
> *Panzer rollen in Afrika vor!*

The Hitlerjugend youngster blinked, startled, and Pavel shoved past him, savoring the words. He sang them again to himself. *The tank treads clatter . . . The engines roar! Panzers roll forward in Africa!* Yes, roll on. But roll through America this time. Across Texas to some unknown battlefield. Pavel's brain teemed. To fight again. Right in the enemy's backyard. Prodigious undertaking! And freedom. *Auskneifen!* Unfenced horizons. An end to the debased existence of a conquered soldier. No more *hundsmiserabel* barbed wire and elevated gun towers. No more demeaning work details and domineering guards. Deliverance. Revenge.

Across the parade ground, loitering near the small medical clinic, Jürgen Frischauer waited for Dryden to appear. The clinic, a tar-paper hut like the others inside the wire, offered partitioned cubicles where German prisoners could bring their ingrown toenails and gastrointestinal upsets and minor cuts and bruises to be treated by the American nurses and orderlies who took turns on day duty. More serious cases went to the fully equipped camp hospital outside the stockade fence, where American doctors were on perpetual call.

Frischauer was fairly certain now. It was to be an escape attempt of some sort. Vague rumors had been spreading since daybreak. A few lucky enlisted men had apparently been selected to participate and had only just been notified. They had been warned not to say anything, but their stunned expressions and growing excitement spoke for them. It had to be an escape. Nothing else could bring such unbridled glee to somber faces.

Frischauer rubbed a hand across his face. Did he really have the nerve to talk to Dryden about it? He shouldn't. There was no guarantee that the Americans could stop the Christmas adventure, whatever it was. It had to be more than just an escape. The officers would never have been so guarded about Weinachten Entwurf, the Christmas Project, if escape were the only goal. And even if the Americans could stop this undenned project, the war might go on and on. What if he betrayed his comrades for nothing? What if his betrayal was even counterproductive? For all he knew, the Christmas plan might itself lead to the shortening of the war.

Frischauer glanced at the stockade gate. Dryden's woman was standing there as promised, a handsome brunette woman in a white nurse's uniform, wearing the silver bars of an American lieutenant. Frischauer had taken the note to her after breakfast. Just three words. *Christmas Project,* and the name he had heard at the midnight trial of Felix Leiser, *Heisenberg.* The woman spoke no German, but Frischauer managed to convey to her that he wanted to meet with Dryden. And she had made signs and gestures to indicate that she understood. She would summon Dryden to the gate and bring him to the clinic. Frischauer could then speak with him under guise of having his foot rebandaged. But Dryden hadn't yet appeared. Had Frischauer understood the woman correctly? If so, where was Captain Dryden?

He took a deep breath. God, was he doing the right thing? And if he actually did it, would he be able to face his friends? Perhaps the Americans would send him immediately to another camp, one of the prison stockades in Arizona or California. He had heard they were warm camps, filled with Germans who were proven anti-Nazis.

Ah, there. Dryden. Coming down from the headquarters building, walking with a slight limp toward his woman. Frischauer breathed more easily. Good. Now Dryden was at the gate with her, chin lifted as if checking the guard towers. They were speaking. There was tension in the set of the woman's shoulders. They talked quietly, the American officer and the woman, scarcely looking at each other as they came through the stockade gate.

Frischauer edged into the sunlight, steeling himself for the walk across the parade ground. If he hurried, he could reach the clinic ahead of them. But before he could gather his nerve a hand gripped his biceps and a voice said, "Ho, Jürgen. I've been looking for you."

He swiveled his head. It was Pavel, standing right behind

him. Frischauer threw a panicky look at the medical clinic, then ducked his chin.

"So," Pavel said. "How is the foot today?"

"A . . . a trifle sore," Frischauer stammered. God in heaven. The foot. Why was Pavel asking about his foot? Did he know? Had he somehow guessed what Frischauer was up to?

"Is it sound enough to march across Texas?" Pavel asked.

Frischauer hesitated, confused. "Why do you ask?"

Pavel shook him by the shoulders, a soldier's playful roughness toward a comrade. "We're going to break out of this sinkhole, Jürgen. You and me. Oberst Kleber just added us to the Christmas Project list."

"Us? He picked us?" Frischauer's eyes narrowed. Was this a trick of some kind? Was Pavel serious?

Pavel shrugged. "Actually he picked me. Then he said he wanted to talk to you about something, and told me to come find you. So I put in a good word for you. I told him you were a damned fine soldier and we could use a man like you once we make it to the outside, and he agreed. What do you think of that?"

Frischauer tried to control his voice. "He . . . he asked to see me? Why? Did he say what he wants?"

"It has to do with your visit to the clinic yesterday. Something about Dryden and the nurse, I think. The Oberst said it was important."

Frischauer's chest squeezed. The clinic? Dryden and the woman? They must have guessed everything. He said, "Does the Oberst want to see me now? This very moment?"

"Yes, you're to go to his quarters," Pavel said. "I'll follow you later." He swung his head, gazing across the field and the milling prisoners. "Have you seen Zolling? The little private from Camp Butner?"

Frischauer shook his head, trying to think.

"The Oberst wants to see him, too," Pavel said. "I told Zolling to wait out here on the parade ground for me." His eyes swept from side to side. "I'm supposed to be keeping a watch on him, but the Oberst summoned me to the library, and I . . . Oh, there he is, over by the horseshoe pit."

Frischauer followed Pavel's gaze numbly. Across the parade ground, near the entrance to the south sleeping compound, German enlisted men took turns aiming and looping horseshoes in graceful arcs toward a metal pin. Watching listlessly among a small crowd of spectators, the sad-faced little private from Camp Butner stood with shoulders bent, looking like a lost dog. Frischauer stared at him. Poor Zolling. So he was in trouble, too. The hanging tree would be busy tonight.

Frischauer sneaked another quick look at the clinic, then said, "Pavel, I have things to do. Do you suppose the Oberst would mind if I came a few minutes later?"

Pavel's friendly face became stern. "Enlisted men do not keep officers waiting," he said. "What's the matter with you, Jürgen? Damn all, man, you should be joyful at the news. This is what we've all been waiting for. A chance to get out of this place. Now you're acting like a witling. For God's sake, go see the Oberst and tell him what he wants to know. I'll follow along in a few moments, as soon as I collect Zolling."

Frischauer gazed longingly at the clinic, then at Dryden and the woman, moving toward it. He swallowed hard and turned away, sloping across the field toward the inner compounds. To the Oberst's quarters. To confront his fate, whatever it might be.

"He's going away," Beverly said. "I told him to meet us at the clinic."

Dryden watched Frischauer walk slowly across the parade ground, leaving Pavel behind. "Are you sure he understood?"

"I don't know. I thought he did. He kept nodding at all my gestures. It was like a game of charades."

Dryden glanced at the piece of paper with the three scrawled words on it. *Weinachten Entwurf. Heisenberg.* "Did he explain this note? Did he give you any idea why he wanted to talk to me?"

"Not in words I could understand. The orderly was in another examining room, so we didn't have anyone to translate for us. We just stood there, talking baby talk like Tarzan and Jane and making hand signs at one another. He seemed very nervous."

Pavel started toward the horseshoe pit. Dryden watched

him for a moment, then said, "Yeah, I got the idea he was nervous yesterday after you bandaged his foot, too. He acted like he wanted to talk about something but couldn't work up the nerve."

"You could send a guard after him."

Dryden shook his head. "No, he'll have to come to me. I can't force him to talk. And if a guard went in now and pulled him out, his buddies in the compound might get suspicious. He could end up like Leiser."

He watched as Pavel paused beside the elderly private from Camp Butner. They spoke briefly, then walked away from the horseshoe pit together. Dryden frowned. What was Pavel up to? First Frischauer, now the little soldier from the POW train. Where were they going?

"Perhaps he'll come back," she said. "If it's important, I'm sure he'll try again."

Pavel and the private walked along the inner fence line, heading toward the same gate that had swallowed Frischauer. Dryden's curiosity got the best of him. He said, "You might be right. If he does, give me a call. I'll be back in my office as soon as I finish here. There's something I want to check."

She clutched his arm. "You're not going out in the compound alone, are you?"

"Sure. I just want to talk to a couple of people."

"Is that wise? They know you've been asking questions. What if they decided to stop you? How could you defend yourself, with three thousand German prisoners surrounding you?"

"Don't worry," he told her. He waved up at the wooden gun towers. "I'll be in full view the whole time. Nothing is going to happen."

Pavel and the aging private were approaching the sleeping-compound gate. Dryden hustled across the field on an interception course, hurrying through groups of gray-green and desert-tan uniforms. There were no POW work crews this holiday Saturday, since half the guard force was gone, and the parade ground was packed. With Christmas coming on Monday the Germans were assured of a full three-day weekend, and most of them were already taking advantage of it, loafing and strolling in the sun. A few were busily decorating

69

the POW mess hall, using the foil from countless commissary cigarette packages to spell out noel messages.

Dryden reached the inner gate first and turned to wait. He watched the squat private roll along beside Pavel, short legs churning to keep up. This was supposed to be Karl Zolling, the Schütze from Camp Butner. What was his real name? Not Zolling, surely. Zolling was a ten-year veteran, according to his papers. He would know the difference between an Iron Cross and a War Merit Cross. Who, then? Could this be the man named in Frischauer's note? Heisenberg?

Pavel's stride faltered when he saw Dryden blocking the path. He came to a complete stop. Dryden said, "Well, Pavel. Out for a morning stroll?"

In icy German, Pavel said, "It is Saturday morning, Captain. My time is my own."

"So I see," Dryden said. "And you seem to be spending a lot of it with Private Zolling. Yesterday, and now today."

"I try to know all of my men," Pavel said.

"Commendable," Dryden said. "And very democratic." He nodded pleasantly at the squat little private. "How are you getting on, Zolling? Beginning to feel at home in your new surroundings?"

The man dropped his eyes. "No one can be comfortable in a prison compound."

"Perhaps not," Dryden said. "And yet it must be comforting to make new friends so quickly. You should be flattered. Sergeant Pavel is the top noncom in camp. And a close associate of Oberst Kleber. That's heady company for a private soldier."

Pavel stirred uneasily. "Private Zolling was in a training camp near my home in Germany. We were sharing memories."

"Oh?" Dryden said. "Where did you train, Zolling?"

Pavel spoke first. "Westphalia. He trained in Westphalia. Isn't that right, Private Zolling?"

The little man shrugged. "Yes. It was Westphalia."

"I see," Dryden said. "And where is your family home, Zolling? Let him answer for himself this time, Pavel."

The little man's unhappy gaze lingered in the vicinity of Dryden's knees. "Berlin. I lived in Berlin."

"You have a family there?" Dryden asked.

"A sister," the man mumbled. "My sister lives in Berlin. With her daughter and granddaughter."

"Have you pictures of your family?"

Pavel scowled impatiently. "What is the purpose of this inquisition, Captain? You have no right to badger this man about his family."

"I mean no harm," Dryden said. "I'm only trying to be friendly. Most men are proud to show family pictures. If they have them."

"I . . . I have pictures," the private murmured. He reached for a cracked wallet and opened it. Extending it, he said, "See? Here is my sister. She exists. I am not lying."

Dryden took the wallet and looked. He saw two small tinted photographs facing each other in isinglass sleeves. One was of a gray-haired matron, short and aging like the private himself. The other picture showed a young woman in a flowered dress holding a chubby-cheeked little girl.

"Very pretty," Dryden said. "Your sister resembles you."

Pavel said, "So they resemble each other. May we go now?"

Dryden had one more question. As the private reclaimed his wallet Dryden said innocently, "What's your sister's married name? Heisenberg?"

He was hoping for a reaction, but not the stunned response he got. The man's fingers twitched spastically and he dropped the wallet, spilling pictures and identification papers across the ground. His face turned parchment white. He stared at Dryden in horrified silence, then sank to his knees to retrieve his belongings.

"I seem to have touched a nerve," Dryden said.

Pavel was confused. He knew something had gone wrong in the conversation, but he obviously had no idea what it was. He said, "You have intruded on our privacy long enough, Captain. Go away and leave us alone."

"Was it the name?" Dryden said. "My German is faulty. Did I pronounce it incorrectly?"

"Baumer," the private blurted from his knees. "My sister married a man named Baumer. Ernst Baumer. He died before the war."

"Enough," Pavel snapped. He helped the chubby private

71

to his feet and brushed him off. Then he looked sullenly at Dryden and said, "Are you finished with us, Captain? May we go now?"

Dryden nodded. "Yes, I think I have what I need. Carry on, Sergeant-Major Pavel."

Pavel nudged the private through the gate into the center sleeping compound. They walked away quickly and stiffly.

Dryden watched them disappear among the clustered barracks. He shook his head, bewildered. Yes, he had what he needed. There was obviously a link between the aging private and the name scrawled on Frischauer's note. But what link? Who the hell was Heisenberg? Why had the name startled the man so? What the devil was going on?

"He knew the name," Boberach wailed. "He spoke it out loud. He knows everything."

"Calm yourself," Kleber said. "He can't know anything of substance. Certainly nothing about the Heisenberg project. Otherwise he would not have used the name so casually."

Pavel regarded the other men gathered in Oberst Kleber's private quarters. Dieter Grebling, the SS captain, sitting by a writing table. Lieutenant Bernd Strikfeldt, lazing against the single window. The red-haired SS Colonel, Ulrich Waldau, perched like a vulture on the edge of the bunk, watching solemnly.

Grebling grunted. "Even so, the American captain knows too much. Pavel should have killed him on the instant."

Pavel firmed his chin, prepared to argue in his own defense if necessary. How could he have known the danger? No one had told him anything about anyone named Heisenberg.

Kleber defused the tension with laughter. He said, "Now, now, Dieter. Pavel was right to walk away. Would you kill the golden goose before he hatches our golden egg?"

Grebling said stubbornly, "I fail to understand your gentle treatment of this American officer. How can you consider him important to this undertaking?"

"It's all in his file," Kleber said. He removed a slim folder from a magazine on the writing table and passed it to Grebling. "Our volunteer clerks in the American headquarters building liberated a few of the more pertinent facts.

72

Read through them when you have time. My reasons are all there. His childhood in New Mexico. His schooling. His ranch at the edge of the mountains. In particular, his intimate knowledge of the terrain surrounding the target site. All will be necessary before we're done. In fact, had it not been for the presence of Captain Dryden, this entire project might well have fallen to some other prison camp. You will understand everything when we reach his home territory."

Waldau said, "Nevertheless, Captain Grebling has a point. If Dryden has learned the name, there must be a traitor in camp. That could be dangerous. Once Dryden learns the truth about Herr Heisenberg he could easily guess the rest. He could destroy our plans in a moment."

"Then he must not be given time to learn the truth," Kleber said. "We will move the project forward. A full twenty-four hours. Tomorrow. We will go tomorrow night."

Grebling's head jerked. "Tomorrow? We can't possibly. What about the diversion? The escape plan depends entirely on the confusion of the Christmas celebration in the outer compound Monday night. We dare not change it."

"We will move the celebration forward," Kleber said. "The men must work harder to prepare. Don't worry. We'll be ready. In truth, Christmas Eve may be a better time. A Sunday, with the townspeople on holiday and surrounding farms gathered about their Christmas trees. The American officers engaged in their own festivities at the officers' club. Enlisted men shorthanded at their posts. Better yet, the next day is Christmas. There will be no roll call inside the wire. With Dryden to show us the way, we can be a hundred miles away before they even know we're gone."

Bernd Strikfeldt said, "How can we be sure this Dryden will cooperate? He seems a contentious officer, full of himself."

Kleber smiled thinly. "He will cooperate. Give me a few moments and I think I can guarantee it." He glanced at Pavel. "Sergeant, ask Private Frischauer to come inside."

Jürgen Frischauer was waiting nervously at the far end of the narrow corridor. He came quickly. Inside the Oberst's room he snapped to attention, with his spine as straight as a rifle barrel and his chin tucked into his tunic collar.

"At ease," Kleber told him.

Frischauer relaxed, but only minimally. His eyes darted

73

around the room. Pavel watched him and thought he knew what Frischauer was thinking. The officers' quarters were spacious and private compared to the crowded barracks for enlisted men where each iron cot shared the available floor space with twenty other cots. Officers were billeted only six to a building, each with a walled private room. Oberst Kleber's narrow bunk looked no more accommodating than the one on which Pavel slept, but the Oberst also had a writing table and a chair and a real lamp, with a fabric lamp shade. There was a shelf above the writing desk with books on it. And on the wall, framed photographs, mostly of a pleasant woman in a variety of fine clothes. The Oberst's wife? The enlisted men had pictures of women on their walls, too, but they were usually magazine clippings of American movie stars. Pavel's favorites were Dorothy Lamour and Esther Williams.

But no, perhaps it wasn't the spacious room that had captured Frischauer's attention. He was staring at the walls, true, but he seemed more intent on avoiding eye contact with the officers than in checking out the comparative luxury of the Oberst's living quarters. Pavel frowned quietly to himself, wondering why his friend should be so nervous. Frischauer had never shown any particular fear of officers before.

Kleber said, "Answer carefully, soldier. You saw Dryden and the woman together at the clinic?"

Frischauer swallowed. "Yes, sir."

"Did they seem to be fond of each other?"

Frischauer blinked. "Sir?"

Waldau grumbled impatiently. "Come, man. Answer the question. We have made certain observations that we wish to have verified. Do Dryden and the woman appear to have more than a casual relationship with each other?"

Frischauer seemed confused. He said, "Yes, sir. They seemed quite friendly. At one point they . . . they touched."

Kleber looked pleased. "You see?" he said to Waldau. "It's as I told you. They have been seen in each other's company frequently, and often with some special hint of affection. One of our people, returning late on a work truck, saw Dryden enter a house in town with her. The guards made obscene remarks and laughed. Apparently the whole camp knows."

Waldau said, "The question is not whether he is fond of the woman, but rather how fond. A good soldier would put duty first."

"You don't understand Americans," Kleber said. "They regard their women in a different light. I'm correct about this. You'll see." He addressed Frischauer again. "Private, you will hold yourself in readiness. Tomorrow night, when the time is right, Hauptsturmführer Grebling will send for you. You will accompany him to the camp clinic and identify the woman. You will make no mistakes. Is that understood?"

"Yes, Herr Oberst."

"Thank you, soldier. You may go."

Frischauer's eyes widened. "That . . . that's all?" His shoulders sagged with relief. He glanced at Pavel and stepped quickly outside.

The Oberst turned to Grebling. "I want the strongest, most obedient man in our ranks to accompany you when you go to the clinic. I will instruct him myself."

"Yes, sir," Grebling said. "Sergeant Pavel?"

Kleber shook his head. "No, Pavel is an excellent man, but not for this. I want a man not hampered by conscience. A man who will obey on the instant, without reflection, no matter how distasteful his orders. Albert Voight. Take Voight with you."

"Yes, Herr Oberst."

Kleber smiled broadly and rubbed his hands together. "And now, gentlemen, to business. Security is paramount. Certain facets of this operation are to be revealed to the men only as they become important. However, since we in this room are to act as leaders of this expedition, I am now prepared to tell you the full and true purpose of the Christmas Project. And about the secret research findings of Herr Heisenberg and his associates that have prompted this expedition."

Bernd Strikfeldt, never a man for strict military niceties, nodded vigorously. "It's about time someone told us what's going on. Who the devil is this Heisenberg? Why does his name keep cropping up?"

"He's a scientist," Kleber said. "His full name is Werner Karl Heisenberg, and he's head of a special weapons project

75

in the Fatherland. A weapon so secret that it is known only by a code reference number. Am I correct, Herr Boberach?"

"Yes," Boberach murmured. "We call it 811-RΓR-111. Until four months ago I was part of the Heisenberg research team myself. I was in Paris, confirming Abwehr reports from America, when I was captured." He looked desperately sad about it.

"I don't understand," Strikfeldt said. "A German weapon? What has that to do with our mission here, in this country?"

Kleber made a face. "A great deal, I fear. That's what Herr Boberach learned in Paris. Unfortunately, the Americans appear to be working on a similar weapon. Our intelligence sources report that the American army has gathered a team of scientists from the American and British scientific communities to work around the clock on the project. They have sequestered them in an isolated mountainous region not far from here."

Waldau said stiffly, "Yes, a rat's nest of self-appointed scientific geniuses. Aided by renegade German scientists and a pack of Jewish scoundrels who fled Europe to help them."

"It is a weapon of enormous destructive power," Kleber said. "Herr Boberach tells me that our own device, unless the course of the war improves and we are given breathing space, cannot possibly be ready in time to make a difference. It appears that the American weapon will. *Das ist zum kotzen*. If they complete it on schedule, they intend to use it to break the will of the German fighting man by destroying civilian populations. A barbaric notion. Our job is to delay the American weapon by fighting our way to their hidden research installation and smashing vital equipment."

"And executing the renegade scientists," Waldau put in. "We have a list of the refugee scum and key American personnel. Herr Boberach will identify not only the equipment we are to destroy, but the men who must die as well."

"Yes," Kleber said reluctantly. "That was one of the many specifications delivered to us. If necessary, we are to eliminate some of the key people."

Grebling said, "Who will lead?"

Pavel's mouth turned down disapprovingly. It was an impertinent question. Grebling would no doubt prefer Waldau, an SS man like himself, as leader. But Kleber was the ranking officer. And a damned good soldier. Pavel knew that firsthand.

Kleber may have been irritated as well. He said grimly, "I will lead. I am aware of Colonel Waldau's special SS training in assault tactics. For that reason, he will be my second in command. You and Lieutenant Strikfeldt will handle the explosives. Pavel will lead the actual strike."

Strikfeldt spoke again. "Is it permitted to ask exactly where we are going?"

Kleber nodded and took a Texaco road map from his writing table, one of the common variety of maps handed out free by American petrol stations and carried in the glove compartments of every American car and truck on the road. Pavel wondered which of his fellow prisoners had stolen it.

"Attend closely, gentlemen." Kleber unfolded the map and spread it on the bunk. "The Americans have endeavored to keep their intentions secret, even from their own population. But Herr Boberach and other members of the Heisenberg team alerted Abwehr intelligence officials more than a year ago as to the types of special machinery and equipment necessary for the development of this terrible weapon. Our agents have been monitoring equipment movements ever since. The information has been slow in coming, but several large pieces of such vital equipment have finally been traced here, to a remote area in the mountains of northern New Mexico."

Strikfeldt leaned over to study the map. "That's more than three hundred miles away," he said. "How do we get there? What do we use for arms?"

"Already arranged," Kleber said. "A German intelligence specialist in Mexico City was instructed to forage vehicles for us. Arms and explosive materials were delivered to him by submarine a few days ago. Both vehicles and ordnance are now in place. We will rendezvous with the vehicles tomorrow night and travel to a secluded staging point in New Mexico, here in the foothills. This is where Captain Dryden assumes his most important role. After we have rested and acquired adequate food and supplies we will continue the journey on horseback, trekking overland through mountainous terrain, avoiding all contact until we are in position to swoop down from the trees and attack."

77

"And what is our final destination?" Grebling asked.

Kleber pointed to a small area northwest of Santa Fe. "Here," he said. "On a plateau surrounded by forest. You won't find it on the map. It's an obscure settlement, hidden deep in the mountains. Surprise will be vital. They are cut off from the rest of the world, but extremely well guarded. They call the place Los Alamos."

# FIVE

Sunday was a day of frenzied preparation behind the wire. German cooks started baking long before dawn. Waldau's security people took up posts, and several barracks buildings were suddenly declared off limits. German officers hurried from billet to billet throughout the day. Tailors tailored. Carpenters hammered. Foragers rummaged. Most of the prisoners had no idea what was behind the activity. There were whispers of a special Yule celebration being prepared by the officers, with extra food rations and Red Cross parcels from Germany. A feeling of euphoria began to spread. And because Sunday was Heiliger Abend, Christmas Eve, and most of the prisoners had no duties, they spent the day trading trinkets and good wishes, waiting to see what Christmas Monday would bring.

But they didn't have to wait that long. That same evening, as the Texas sun sagged below the horizon and American officers assembled at the officers' club near the highway for their own Christmas Eve celebration, a radio monitor reported to Oberst Kleber with a summary of the American evening news. For the past week or so American newspapers and radio announcers had given guarded reports of a massive

79

German offensive in the Ardennes, a surprise attack which the American press had peculiarly dubbed "The Battle of the Bulge," designed to drive the Americans and British back into the sea. Kleber selected one news item, a wire-service bulletin from an American SHAEF correspondent, and dressed it in the most optimistic German terms, then sent runners swarming through the compounds to notify officers and ranking noncoms that General Heinrich von Luttwitz and his XLVII Panzer Korps had smashed through the American defenses and completed the encirclement of Bastogne. The American garrison was surrounded, Kleber's dispatch announced, and would soon surrender. A great German victory was within easy grasp. There would be gaiety and libation in the outer compound. Now. Tonight.

Word of the imminent German triumph, carefully orchestrated by Kleber's officers, rippled through the camp. Jubilation brought excited soldiers streaming from their tarpaper barracks. A victory celebration *and* a Christmas Eve party? Their spirits soared as they poured through the sleeping-compound gates and came together on the parade ground, jostling for position, waiting to see what the officers had planned.

At first the Americans were uneasy. Twilight deepened the parade-ground shadows, and holiday leaves had thinned the guards' ranks. The milling masses of prisoners narrowed their courage. A searchlight clicked on atop the northwest tower and was joined by beams from other towers, dancing across the figures below. Even above the din of expectant German voices one could hear rifle bolts being slammed home outside the wire and the ratchet of actuator knobs priming tower machine guns.

Then, to the astonishment of the American guards, the German mess hall and kitchen doors swung open and POW kitchen details lugged newly built tables out and set them up at the edge of the parade ground. Cooks and cooks' helpers trundled back and forth, carrying heaping platters of sausages and potato turnovers, sweetmeats and small cakes. The POW orchestra, a twelve-prisoner group that practiced nightly with tired musical instruments donated from the local high school, filed out of the mess hall and put violin to cheek, clarinet and sousaphone to mouth, and began to serenade the cheering crowd with Christmas carols. Miraculously, Yule trees appeared. Small, scrawny trees with paper and popcorn decorations rose to the tops of tables as if by magic. Then, from the depths of C Compound, twenty men, heavy jugs dangling from their hands, ran in single file like ammunition carriers across the open ground toward two special tables on which no food had been set. Illicit schnapps from the camp's hidden stills, a fiery brew concocted of potato peelings and raw courage in equal doses. A fresh cheer went up, louder than before.

The guards didn't know what to do. The Germans had been granted permission to hold Christmas celebrations, but Christmas wasn't until tomorrow, and the permission covered only smaller parties in barracks. The jugs of schnapps were illegal, the extra rations were unwarranted, and the mass gathering was unauthorized. The proper response would have been to drive the prisoners back to their sleeping compounds and lock the three inner gates. But prisoners outnumbered the skeleton crew of guards by more than twenty to one, and it was, after all, Christmas Eve, and the few guards on duty felt miserable anyway, having missed out on holiday home visits. So they did nothing. The POW party picked up steam.

For a time the guards continued to finger their weapons, wondering if they should notify the duty officer. But the gathering seemed innocent enough. Hordes of Germans linked arms around the musicians and lustily sang a string of German carols. Others swarmed around the dining tables, gorging on treats. Prisoners descended on the schnapps supply, where, even with forty jugs constantly tipping and sloshing, the lines grew long and cheerfully rowdy. As the mood behind the wire turned mellow the guards relaxed. Cocked hammers were lowered. Rifle bolts opened. The searchlights stayed on, but machine guns were allowed to tip back in their sockets, threatening only the darkening sky. Tower guards slouched in their lofty perches and listened wistfully to the joyful Christmas music. Perimeter guards drifted slowly in twos and threes to the stockade fence, eyeing the schnapps tables and feeling sorry for themselves.

Later, when it was time to fill out reports and explain how the evening went to hell, no one could remember which prisoner first brought a jug of schnapps to the wire and offered it to the guards, nor could anyone remember which guard was the first to accept it. But there was plenty of blame to go around.

Pavel waited until the revelry was well under way, then slipped through the darkness to the staging area, one of the off-limits barracks buildings at the back of Compound B. No light showed from the windows, and he thought perhaps he had misunderstood Kleber's directions, but when he cracked the door to slide inside he saw blackout curtains pinned along the walls. He found himself in a pool of flickering candlelight, facing a roomful of silent men, most of whom had frozen like statues at the opening of the door.

"It's only Pavel," someone murmured.

The human statues melted with relief and bent back to their tasks. Jürgen Frischauer grinned and came to join Pavel at the door. He said, "You scared the hell out of us, Pavel."

Pavel found that understandable. A man could cut the tension in the room with a bayonet. He checked faces. Lieutenant Strikfeldt, wearing a windbreaker, was checking a large sketch pad. Erwin Maschmann and Franz Eggers, dressed in baggy civilian clothing, huddled in a corner, packing knapsacks. Willi Roh, on a bunk near them, sorted tins of food. Others—Herbert Schönbeck, Wolf Lampe, a man named Detthard—were in their underwear, just now in the process of changing. Of the twenty or so men in the room only Frischauer, Albert Voight, and Erich Huber were still in full uniform.

Frischauer leaned close. "Listen, Pavel. We've talked of this before. If the officers let us scatter and go our separate ways once we get clear of camp, let's travel together. I have a plan. I'm pretty sure I can get us to Mexico."

Pavel felt an ache of guilt. None of the others, including Frischauer, had been told about the dangerous mission that lay ahead of them. Nor could they be told until Kleber gave the word. Pavel said vaguely, "I imagine the officers will instruct us."

"I wish they'd hurry," Frischauer said. "Some of the men are ready to jump out of their skins. To tell the truth, I'm a little nervous myself."

"Of course," Pavel said. "We're all a bit . . ." A rustle of gray at the edge of his vision distracted him. He looked around and saw Erich Huber, the Hitler Youth fanatic, drifting closer to listen. Pavel glared at him. "What the hell do you want?"

Huber scowled back. "Nothing from you."

"Then go away," Pavel said. "We're talking."

The young man retreated sullenly.

Frischauer giggled, an uneasy sound in the silence of the room. "Take it easy," he told Pavel. "Speaking of nerves, what's wrong with you? Why so touchy?"

"I don't like him hanging around."

Frischauer shrugged. "Huber? He's not so bad. Captain Grebling told him to stay close. It has something to do with Dryden's woman. The captain and I are going over to the clinic later. Huber and Voight are going with us."

"I don't trust Huber," Pavel said. "I don't think much of Voight either, for that matter."

"Oh, they're both pretty good soldiers," Frischauer said. He moistened his lips and said, "Pavel, I . . . I may have done a couple of things I shouldn't have. But everything will turn out well. You'll see. Escape makes all the difference."

"What things?" Pavel asked.

Frischauer shook his head. "It doesn't matter now. The situation has changed. Ah, here comes Haupsturmführer Grebling. Good. The sooner we finish this episode at the clinic, the sooner I can get out of this uniform and into my escape clothing. Remember, Pavel, once we are through the wire it's you and me. We'll go the rest of the way together. Agreed?"

Pavel hesitated. "Listen," he said. "Don't let your hopes soar too high."

"What do you mean?"

Pavel looked over his shoulder to make sure no one was listening. "Delays sometimes occur," he said vaguely. "Important obstacles have to be overcome. So keep yourself calm. Be flexible."

Frischauer paled. "What? What's happening? Do they know?"

Pavel raised an eyebrow, startled by the note of panic in his friend's voice. "Calmly, Jürgen. Everything is fine. It's just that there are unseen wheels turning. Now I must go. Oberst Kleber expects me in the outer compound. We'll talk more when everyone has gathered. I'll explain as much as I can then."

He headed for the door, forehead creased in thought. Explain? Yes, he could say a few things about the escape without breaking his word to Kleber. Just enough to put Frischauer at ease. But how could he explain his friend's abrupt shift from good humor to white-knuckled fear? What the devil was wrong with Frischauer? Why was he behaving so strangely?

Beverly hung up her white nurse's uniform and slipped into her khaki blouse and skirt, then looked at herself in the clinic mirror. Ghastly, she decided. Dark smudges under the eyes, hair lifeless, breasts flattened by the stiff lines of her starched uniform blouse. "Snow White lives," she murmured.

She brushed her hair and put on her service cap, angling it to one side. What a pity she couldn't abandon regulation attire on this one special night. She had an evening gown in sea-green chiffon, something her mother had sent her, that would knock Ned's eyes out. Lots of skin. With time to apply a fresh layer of makeup she might transform this mirrored wreck into some semblance of a woman. Oh, well, if love was truly blind, and Edward Dryden truly loved her, perhaps he wouldn't notice how awful she looked. She checked her reflection more closely. Still horrible. It had been a long Sunday in the clinic, filling in for nurses on leave, and every hour was etched on her face, visible in the tiny lines around her mouth and the flesh below her eyes. If only there was some way to divert Ned's attention.

She felt for the gold chain she wore under her uniform, drawing it out. She fondled the emerald ring, considering, then reached behind her neck for the clasp. She would wear the ring openly tonight, on her ring finger where it belonged. She would leave the prison compound and stroll up to the officers' club and walk in with Ned's beautiful ring in plain sight, for everyone to see. Wearing the ring openly would be a signal. A sign that she was ready to end the subterfuge. Tonight she would dance every dance with him. And later, in the solitude of her bedroom, she would give herself to him with athletic abandon, fulfill his wildest fantasies.

The face in the mirror startled her. She whirled to look at the door. It was one of the German officers, a man with pretty features and oddly shiny eyes.

"How did you get in here?" she demanded. "What do you want? Where is the orderly?" Then she saw another German soldier standing behind him, the elusive private with the bruised foot. She said, "Oh, it's you."

The officer advanced a few paces and bowed politely. "The orderly is . . . how to say? beschäftigen? . . . occupying himself with the Yule festivities in the parading ground. Please, you come. An accident. In the compound."

"You know the rules," she said. "I can't enter the compound without an orderly. We'll have to wait for him to come back."

Like a tourist in a foreign country, the German officer seemed to be able to string together a few phrases in English yet understand little of what was said back to him. He looked blankly at Beverly and said, "A man has broken the leg."

"Then bring the man here."

The officer shook his head. "It is a badful accident. The leg is broken so." He chopped a hand at his own leg, just below the knee. "He cannot be move. You come. Now."

She slipped the ring and gold chain into her blouse pocket. "I'm sorry," she said, her tone softening. "I know it's a silly rule, but we'll really have to wait while I call for another orderly."

"The man is American," the officer said. "He is in much pain. For you he is asking. Much agony. Morphine, I think he is needing."

"An American?" she said. "Calling for me?"

"A captain," the German officer said. He turned and spoke briefly to Frischauer, then said, "Yes, a captain. *Der Name ist* Dryden. Edward Dryden." He pronounced it Edvard.

"Ned?" she said. Her heart automatically sped up. "What happened? What was he doing in the compound?" Then, to Frischauer, "You, damn it. He went looking for you, didn't he?"

The officer said, "A floor plank in *die Kaserne,* the barracks, is breaking. Through the hole he fell. The leg, like a stick, is snapping."

"Oh, my God. Which leg? His bad one?"

The officer looked puzzled for a moment, then forged on. "The bone shows. Much pain and agony. Morphine we are needing. You come now. Someone we will leave to bring the orderly and a stretcher."

"Yes, of course," she said. She grabbed a medical bag half-filled with a jumble of first-aid supplies. She hurriedly threw in more gauze and bandages, then rummaged in a cabinet for morphine ampules and a syringe. In growing panic she found herself scooping up surgical scrub and sterile pads. Oh, God, which would be hardest on him, she wondered. To have rebroken his damaged leg or to break the sound one? He was already so depressed about being hurt. How would this affect him?

The sounds of celebration were louder as they hurried from the clinic to the parade ground. Beverly was startled to see another pair of Germans waiting for them outside the clinic doors, a huge man with a bull neck and an intense blond youth. Both of them fell in behind the officer and Frischauer. "Wait," Beverly said. "Who's going to bring the orderly?"

The officer waved vaguely. "Do not worry," he said. "Another man will make the telephone call in the clinic office. He is knowing where to bring help. Come. The center compound. We must hurry. The American officer there is waiting for you."

She felt a wash of uncertainty, striding along in the night with four Germans toward one of the inner sleeping compounds. She craned her neck toward the stockade entrance and saw three American guards slip through the gate. She experienced a brief moment of relief, thinking they might be the stretcher detail already on their way to help. But the three guards sidled self-consciously across the parade ground, hands in pockets, toward a table bearing several large crockery containers. Other Americans were already at the table, standing in line with canteen cups.

The gate loomed ahead of her. Beverly felt an inner alarm bell ring, not in her brain but in the vicinity of her intestines. She stopped and said, "Just a moment. I see some guards at that table over there. They can help carry him out."

"No time," the officer said. He spoke sharply to the German with the bull neck. The big man put a hand in Beverly's back and shoved. "We will continue," the officer said.

"You can't do this," Beverly objected. The big man's

86

hand clamped over her mouth. She struggled, but the big man propelled her through the gate. Her eyes darted wildly. No one was watching. No one had seen. She turned helpless eyes on Frischauer, but he refused to look at her. And then they were in the darkness of the inner compound, between the rows of huts.

Up on the highway, far from Beverly and her four-man German escort, the Camp McLean officers' club was ablaze with lights. A ragged ring of parked cars, both military and civilian, circled the building, nosed in like suckling piglets. Loud music and laughter echoed inside. Unaware of the mushrooming festivities in the prison stockade, Camp McLean officers and their ladies busily entertained the town's leading citizens in a noisy celebration of their own.

Edward Dryden pulled impatiently on his second Scotch, glaring at the holiday decorations. Loops of red and green tinsel dangled from walls. Glittering white Christmas bells hung from rafters. Angel hair shimmered. A big Christmas tree, loaded with colored globes and blinking lights, crowded the bandstand. And in every corner and doorway, strategically placed, Colonel Christopher's sprigs of mistletoe invited Christmas smooches. It all looked so damned cheerful. Too damned cheerful.

Beverly was late. Her shift at the POW clinic should have ended at least fifteen minutes ago. How long could it take to walk from the stockade to the officers' club? He had talked to her earlier in the day at the officers' mess. She had looked gorgeous as usual. Velvety face a perfect oval. Soft black hair framing invitation. She said she would join him at the officers' club as soon as she finished her shift and changed. So what was keeping her?

"Enjoying the music, Edward?"

Dryden looked into the flushed face of Colonel Hamilton Christopher, the camp commandant. The usual Texas cold had abated, but not the cure. There was a sheen of perspiration filming his face and a lightly glazed look in his eyes. From the look of him, the commandant had been busily keeping the toddies coming from the bar.

"I'll enjoy it more when Lieutenant Bennington gets here," Dryden said.

"Frankly, so will I," Christopher said. Camp social functions were about the only activities that could tempt him from his self-imposed exile in the big house. He'd already spent much of the earlier evening dancing with the wives of his junior officers. Willowy young wraiths, glowing with health, towering over the frail commandant. Milkmaids and faery princesses, paying homage to the frog king. "She's an excellent dancer, our Beverly."

"Our Beverly?" Dryden said. He put his nose in his glass, experiencing a mild surge of jealousy.

Christopher chuckled, a low, raspy sound. He gestured to the enlisted man behind the bar, signaling for a drink. "Come now, Edward. We used to see a lot more of Beverly here at the club before you joined us. Tell me, my boy, is there something serious between you two?"

"I like to think so."

The bartender brought a drink. Christopher said, "Pity you aren't interested enough to stay around and let it develop."

"Who says I'm not interested?"

"I understand you've been talking to Dr. Brody about returning to active duty."

"Oh, that," Dryden said. "Maybe a word or two."

"I'm not surprised," Christopher said. "You young people are always so energetic, always looking for a way to get ahead. Not much chance for promotion, buried in a hole like this."

"I'm not looking for promotion," Dryden said.

Christopher shrugged. "Motive doesn't matter. A camp doesn't run well unless its people are happy. I want you to know, Edward, I'm behind you on this. If you want a transfer, I'll do everything I can to see that you get it. I can even arrange a bit of vacation for you while you make up your mind."

Dryden cocked his head. "What brought this on?"

"I've noticed how busy you've been these past few days. Talking to Germans. Changing work schedules. Questioning suicide reports. A man who indulges in fantasy sometimes does irrational things."

"It isn't fantasy, it's fact," Dryden said. Across the dance floor one of the younger second lieutenants came from the front of the building, picking his way through couples. "We have a tense situation building out in the stockade."

"I'm aware of your conspiracy notions," Christopher said. "I discount them. You're tired, Edward. You need to relax for a few days. Why don't you go visit your family? Or go to Dallas and hit the night spots. But get away from here and give your imagination a rest. We can talk about the possibility of a transfer when you get back."

"Is that an order, sir?"

Christopher winced. "No, of course not, my boy. I'd rather you decide on your own. There's no need for a hostile relationship between us, Edward. I like you. I really do. And I'd be delighted to have you come back to serve on my staff, rested and ready for duty, if that's what you want."

The young lieutenant reached them and leaned to whisper in Christopher's ear. Christopher nodded slowly, then said, "Yes, all right. Tell him to watch them and call me if things get out of hand." The lieutenant saluted and made his way back across the dance floor.

"Problems?" Dryden asked.

"Hmmm?" Christopher said. "Oh, no. A phone call from the stockade. One of the corporals says the Germans have embarked on some form of Christmas celebration."

"I thought you approved a celebration."

"Yes. But it was scheduled for tomorrow, and only in small groups. The corporal says they've gathered in the outer compound. He wanted to know if he should find Sergeant Kieran and put a stop to it."

"What did you tell him?"

"Oh, I don't think it will do any harm. The Germans are only singing a few carols and munching a few Christmas treats. Let them have their fun. It it gets unruly, we can always call in fire hoses."

Dryden raised an eyebrow. The timing was troublesome. If the Germans were in the mood for mischief, this would be a perfect moment for it, with most of the officers away from their posts. And Beverly was still down there. He said, "I think I'll take a look."

Christopher smiled sadly. "More conspiracy notions?"

"I was thinking of Lieutenant Bennington," Dryden said. "She's overdue from the clinic. I'm going to walk down to the stockade and have a quick look. If things are running smoothly, I'll pick her up and bring her back."

\* \* \*

But things were not running smoothly. Dryden had scarcely left the club when he saw three guards away from their posts, lurking in night shadow between the road and the guard barracks, trading pulls at a crockery jug. They jerked to attention, trying to hide the jug behind them. Dryden walked faster.

The noise level rose as he neared the stockade. At least the clinic was dark. He could see the unlit windows through the barbed wire. Maybe Beverly had decided to go home and change before coming to the party at the officers' club. Odd that she hadn't bothered to warn him.

He turned his attention to the guards along the perimeter. Some were still in position, and many were in pretty good shape. But all of them seemed to have joined the party. Dryden saw cups pass back and forth through the wire. Half the tower guards had come down from their perches to accept food and drink. Sergeant Max Kieran was there, the strong odor of alcohol on his breath. Even so, Kieran seemed sober.

"Hey, Cap'n," Kieran said. "Come down to join the party?" Kieran sounded unexpectedly friendly, and Dryden reassessed his evaluation of the man's sobriety.

"What's going on?" Dryden asked.

Kieran waved his hand at the crowded compound. "The Krauts have brewed up the damnedest punch I ever tasted. Here, have a taste." He waved a coffee mug at Dryden. A colorless liquid sloshed from rim to rim.

"Get your men in order," Dryden said. "Some of them have left their posts."

"Aw, don't be a spoilsport," Kieran muttered. "The colonel said it was okay."

"I'm sure Colonel Christopher didn't know about the booze," Dryden said. "Where are the gate guards?"

"Out in the compound," Kieran said. "Lots of our guys are out there. These Krauts can be okay, once in a while."

A clutch of male voices switched from carols to Nazi marching songs, and a Teutonic roar of approval went up.

"Open the gate," Dryden said. "We're going in."

"What for?" Kieran said. "The Germans will bring you anything you want out here. Just waggle a cup at them."

"The drinking is finished," Dryden said. "Open the gate,

Sergeant. I want you and two of your men to accompany me. We're going to round up all American personnel and get them out of the stockade."

Kieran reached for the gate latch, muttering under his breath.

"Did you say something, Sergeant?"

Kieran pushed the gate open. "Only that it ain't fair, Cap'n. You officers are up at the club swilling martinis, and we can't even have a little holiday nip."

"You've gone beyond the nip stage," Dryden said. German voices soared militantly from the parade ground, singing "Die Fahne Hoch."

Kieran cupped a hand to his mouth and bellowed, "Private Stone, Corporal Morrison, get your asses over here. On the double. The cap'n wants to vacuum out the compound." He staggered and fell against the gatehouse. "Whups," he said.

Dryden sighed. "Maybe you'd better stay here, Sergeant. Call the mess and order several pots of coffee. I want everyone sober before word spreads to the officers' club."

"Yes'r, Cap'n," Kieran said. "Coffee it is, Cap'n. Shit."

Two men came quickly toward the open gate, looking sheepish but relatively clearheaded. Dryden led them into the prison compound. Most of the Germans were pleasantly smashed, arms linked, faces red with drink and excitement, cords standing out on their necks as they sang. But Dryden also noticed a number of sober Germans on the edges of the crowd who seemed to have as their sole responsibility the entertainment of American personnel. Several crews at the fences replenished canteens and tin cups as quickly as they emptied. Kitchen helpers stood below the gun towers with trays of tidbits, trying to tempt the remaining tower guards down. Runners attached themselves like tour guides to guards bold enough to enter the compound, leading them from table to table.

Massed German voices moved smoothly from "Die Fahne Hoch" to a somber rendition of "Deutschland über Alles." Extraneous noise died down. Ruddy faces sobered. Heels clicked as German POWs snapped to attention to honor the slow, stately anthem. Voices across the parade ground rose in solemn song.

As Dryden watched, three tipsy Americans, mellowed by home-brewed schnapps, put their heads together and bellowed a bawdy Americanized version of the German anthem, words calculated to drive German listeners into a state of frenzy. In drunken three-part harmony, keepng time with the voice and music in the background, they sang:

> Life presents a dis-mal pi-ic-ture,
> Dark and dreary as a-a tomb.
> Marshal Rommel's had a stri-ic-ture,
> His wife's in bed with a fa-all-en womb.
>
> Himmler's mother has been abor-or-ted
> For the forty-second time.
> Her-mann Goering has been depor-or-ted
> For a-a ho-oh-mo-sex-u-al crime.
>
> Joseph Goebbels has been cas-tra-a-ted
> And he very seldom smiles.
> He has the di-is-mal oc-cu-pa-a-tion,
> Crushing ice fo-or Hit-ler-er's piles.

It was a klutzy, insulting set of lyrics, well known to most of the American guards, and it usually infuriated the German prisoners when they heard the words wafting down from one of the towers, but now three inebriated American guards were singing the damned song in their midst. Instead of outrage, the Germans greeted the words with strained smiles. A few of the Germans even egged the guards on, calling for an encore. That was when Dryden knew for sure that something was badly wrong. He had to clear the compound. Fast.

"Fetch those three first," he said. "Get them out of here."

Pavel found Oberst Heinz Kleber with a group of officers. He tugged the Oberst's sleeve and said urgently, "Sir, Dryden is here. In the compound."

Kleber's face showed surprise, then concern. *"Zum Kotzen!"* He checked his watch. "Where? At the clinic?"

"No, sir. In the midst of the singers. With two men. Clearing out the American guards."

Kleber said nothing for a moment, then nodded his chin decisively. "Good. We'll do it now. This will save our having to summon him by telephone. Captain Grebling, take Herr Boberach and retire to Compound B."

"It's early," Grebling said. "The men may not be ready."

"It can't be helped," Kleber said. "Once the American guards are driven back to their posts, natural resentment will eventually persuade them to break up the merriment. We must be clear before that happens."

One of the officers, the major who was to take over as Standrechtkommandant once Kleber was gone, said, "Herr Oberst, if you wish more time, we can prolong the demonstration. If necessary, we will stand our ground and fight until they force us back to our quarters."

"No, no, be cooperative," Kleber said. "I wish nothing to alert or alarm them." He smiled at the circle of officers and said farewell to each in turn. Then he gestured to Pavel and said, "Come with me, Sergeant-Major."

The compound was almost clear. Dryden's two helpers had worked quickly and efficiently. When they paused again for instructions, one of them asked, "Sir? Are you going to put these guys on report?"

Dryden shook his head. "No, I just want everyone out of here before this thing blows up in our faces. Do a last circuit. See if we've overlooked anyone. Make it fast."

As the two men hurried toward the schnapps table, checking for khaki uniforms among the carolers, Dryden saw Oberst Kleber and Konrad Pavel bearing down on him. He waited grimly, wondering what the Oberst wanted.

Kleber smiled cheerfully as he drew up. "Good evening, Captain Dryden. I'm pleased you could join our jubilee. We had planned to extend you a special invitation. Now you have saved us the trouble."

Dryden stared. "Whatever you're planning, forget it. As soon as my people are clear, I'm shutting you down."

"This?" Kleber said, regarding the happy throng. "I assure you, Captain, you have nothing to fear from them. There will be no confrontations. They will be more than willing to collaborate with anyone in authority. When told to retire, they will retire."

"Then call them off now," Dryden said.

"Ah, but I specified collaboration with someone in authority. You, Captain Dryden, no longer fit that description."

"What the hell does that mean?"

Kleber reached slowly into the flap of his desert-tan tunic and produced a golden chain on which hung an emerald ring. He let it dangle in front of Dryden, twisting to catch the light. "Do you recognize this jewel, Captain?"

Beverly's ring. All sound vanished for Dryden, the murmur of voices, the music, the clink of cups. His eyes darted involuntarily to the darkened windows of the clinic. In the shocked silence of his mind, his question sounded like a scream. "Where is she?"

"Patience," Kleber said. "You will see her shortly. But first you must dismiss your two escorts and send them back through the gate. Tell them you will return at your leisure to the gala at your own officers' club. I would not want them to worry about you."

"Why should I tell them anything?" Dryden asked.

Kleber's voice turned hard. "Be convinced, Captain. This is no bluff. The life of your lady depends on your words and actions in the next few moments." He returned the ring and chain to his tunic. "Your men are coming. Be careful what you say. We are desperate men."

The two enlisted men approached from the schnapps tables. One of them looked at Kleber suspiciously, then said, "That seems to be the lot, Captain."

Dryden hesitated. Kleber gave him a steely smile and touched his tunic unobtrusively, resting his hand over the square-cut emerald. Dryden said, "Okay, make a last sweep over by the kitchens to be sure. Then get out. Lock the gates after you."

"What about you, sir?"

Dryden cleared his throat. "You don't need me anymore," he said. "I'll be going back to the officers' club."

He could read the disgust in the man's face. Sure, the look said, drag us away from our harmless fun, then hurry back to your cushy club and have another drink. The man saluted and murmured, "Yes, sir. As you say, sir." He nudged his friend and the two of them set off toward the kitchens for a final check.

Kleber waited until the two guards were swallowed by

massed Germans, then said, "Well done, Captain. Now come with us."

"Where?"

"Save your questions," Kleber said. "Your lady is waiting."

With Pavel on one side and Kleber on the other, Dryden allowed himself to be guided toward the B Compound gate, away from the music and voices and into the shadows. As they hurried into the sleeping compound a German soldier materialized from the darkness and closed the gate behind them. They walked on through silent rows of tar-paper barracks. Music and laughter continued in the outer compound, covering their footsteps.

They walked deeper and deeper among the huts. As they neared the back fence Dryden gazed upward at the guard towers. The nearest tower was empty. He heard voices. Through the buildings he caught a glimpse of guards and Germans hovering happily on opposite sides of the fence at the foot of the empty tower, sharing a jug through the strands of barbed wire. He cursed silently to himself.

At the next-to-last sleeping hut Pavel gestured toward the wooden stoop. Dryden followed. The building was dark, not a glimmer of light from its windows. Kleber gave Dryden an enigmatic smile and opened the door.

Dryden gaped. The hut was filled with men. Twenty or more, sitting in candlelight, wearing civilian clothing, holding knapsacks and cardboard suitcases. And Beverly. Seated on a bunk near the door. Above her stood a handsome young German soldier with intense, hostile eyes. Beverly looked small and intimidated, but she said in a steady voice, "I'm all right, Ned." She started to rise. The young German pushed her roughly back to the bunk.

Dryden felt a hot, salty taste flare at the back of his throat. Instinct took over. Without a sound, without pausing for breath, he launched himself at the young soldier standing over Beverly. He grabbed the man by the throat with both hands, his fingers digging into flesh. The young soldier fell backward over the cot, Dryden on top of him. Someone shouted, and another German moved in quickly to separate them. A big man. Muscular arms snaked out to catch Dryden by the shoulders. Like an irritated animal Dryden flicked out at him, jamming his elbow back, driving it into the big man's stomach. Breath whooshed and the man doubled over. With single-minded purpose Dryden returned his hands to the young man's throat, choking, choking.

More Germans rushed in to pry him loose, but Dryden held on. He heard a high-pitched protest of pain. He thought for a moment it was the young soldier, and he dug his fingers tighter to cut the sound off. Hands clawed from behind at his head and arms, but they couldn't move him. He was determined to kill the young man, could have killed him, would have, but he suddenly realized that the sound of pain wasn't coming from the young soldier at all. It was Beverly. He looked around wildly, blindly, trying to locate her. She was on her toes by the bunk, barely touching the floor, suspended firmly against the chest of a massive German with a bull neck. The point of a long butcher knife was nestled beneath her chin, glinting in the candlelight.

Dryden took his hands from the young soldier's throat. As soon as he stopped resisting, the Germans dragged him away and yanked him to his feet. Pavel pinned his right arm, and two more Germans seized his left. Another soldier, angered by Dryden's earlier struggles, grabbed him by the hair and punched him in the face. Still another hit him in the stomach.

"Enough," Kleber barked. He marched around to face Dryden and said, "Use your intelligence, Captain. Corporal Voight will kill the woman if you persist."

The big German pressed the knife point against Beverly's chin, breaking skin. She winced, and a bright droplet of blood trickled down her throat. Dryden stared at the big German and the thin trail of red on Beverly's soft white neck. He looked at the hostile faces of the officers and enlisted men surrounding him. He caught sight of Jürgen Frischauer in the background, head down, looking guilty. Confusion filled his mind.

"Okay, okay," Dryden wheezed. "You win." It was hard to breathe with arms locked around his neck. A roaring rush of sound filled his ears. "What the hell do you want, Kleber? What's this all about?"

Kleber shrugged. "I should think it obvious, Captain. You and Miss Bennington have become, for want of a better term, prisoners of war. *Our* prisoners of war."

\* \* \*

Pavel pulled Dryden to a bunk, away from the woman. Erwin Maschmann fetched cord from one of the knapsacks and tied Dryden's hands behind his back. Pavel stood above the American and regarded him with some surprise. He'd seldom seen so fast an attack. There had been no warning. No hesitation. Dryden had leapt on the instant, like a fighting dog that strikes without wasting growl or bark. The Hitler Youth, Erich Huber, was only now untangling himself and rising from the floor beside the cot. Maschmann, who had caught Dryden's elbow to the stomach, looked sullen. But Huber, gasping and nursing his bruised throat, glared at Dryden with flaming cheeks and savage hatred in his eyes. Pavel smiled to himself, enjoying the young man's humiliation.

When the room grew quiet Kleber and Waldau faced Pavel and the other soldiers. Kleber said, "Men, I have an instruction for you of the first importance. Do not discard your uniforms. Pack them in your kits and prepare to bring them along. You will need them in a few days. This unit will function again as a viable fighting force. We will shortly do battle for the Fatherland."

A stir rustled through the room. This was the first word the men had received that this was not to be a normal escape. Some of them looked intrigued. Others looked stricken. Jürgen Frischauer raised a bewildered eyebrow at Pavel. Pavel nodded curtly, then watched with pride as the majority of the soldiers, without complaint or question, bent over knapsack or suitcase to make room for the discarded uniforms. Others followed. Even Frischauer, Pavel noted with satisfaction, packed his uniform without further comment.

"You will be given further details as circumstance requires," Kleber said. "In the meantime, we will now split apart and slip through the wire in three separate groups. The first contingent will leave in five minutes under the direction of Captain Grebling. The second group will follow shortly with Lieutenant Strikfeldt. Colonel Waldau will lead the final group. Stay close to your team leaders. When you are clear of the camp they will direct you to a special staging area where we will reassemble. Good luck to you all."

Strikfeldt stuffed his sketch pad in a cloth bag. While Grebling and Strikfeldt assembled the first groups, Waldau and Kleber came to inspect Dryden's bonds. Kleber nodded, satisfied, and summoned Albert Voight and Erich Huber. They came, holding the woman between them. Pavel pulled Dryden to his feet.

"Are you all right?" Dryden asked.

She nodded.

Kleber gestured for Voight to release the woman. "Young Huber will attend her from now on," he told Voight. "I would rather you assist Sergeant Pavel in controlling Captain Dryden. Keep him quiet. I wish no difficulties between here and the rendezvous point."

"Yes, Herr Oberst," Voight said. He stepped in beside Dryden. Erich Huber, now in sole charge of the woman, dug his fingers into her arm and twisted it with unnecessary force.

Dryden's eyes blazed. But he spoke to the Oberst, not Erich Huber. He said, "You haven't got a chance, Kleber. Not a man in this room will get more than five miles. By dawn there'll be patrols everywhere."

"Let them come," Kleber said. "We'll be a hundred miles away by the time the alarm is given. Traveling in comfort. And you, Captain, will be guiding us to our destination."

"You'll get no help from me," Dryden said.

"Ah, but we will," Kleber said. "If you value the woman, you will do exactly as you are told. In a few moments Private Huber will take her away with the first group. After the second and third groups depart, you will accompany us. If anything unexpected occurs to keep us from joining the others at the staging point, young Huber will kill her. Once we reach our transport and begin our journey you will continue to cooperate. If you do not, Private Huber will kill her. If anything goes wrong at any time from now until the end of our mission, the same end awaits her. Huber will kill her. She is hostage to your good behavior."

The woman looked searchingly at Dryden and said, "Don't listen to them, Ned. You mustn't help them. They're going to kill us anyway."

Kleber smiled thinly. "Perhaps. Perhaps not. But the captain will listen. Count on it. The captain will do everything we tell him to do, because it's the only certain way to keep you alive, Miss Bennington. He will submit because it is the nature of the human animal to survive. And every hour of sweet life he provides will give him another hour to hope. To wait for a miracle. A chance to escape. The miracle won't come. But he won't stop hoping. No one ever does.''

Dryden let his breath out slowly. "Okay," he said. "I'll do as I'm told. But leave her here. You don't need her. I'll do whatever you ask. You have my word.''

Kebler nodded, smiling. "And we trust your word, Captain. But we prefer the absolute advantage provided by the presence of Miss Bennington. We may also need her medical abilities." He looked at Erich Huber. "Soldier, guard this woman will all care. If Captain Dryden keeps his head and behaves in a proper manner, they will be permitted to see each other again at the rendezvous point. Is that clear?''

"Yes, Herr Oberst.''

"Very good. Take the medical bag. It may prove useful before this is done. Now go. Captain Grebling is ready to leave with the first group.''

Huber picked up the woman's black bag and raised his arm in stiff Nazi salute. The gesture looked peculiar on a man dressed as a farm laborer. He yanked the woman toward the door, joining the others. Grebling's men began to edge through into the darkness. Pavel saw the woman look over her shoulder at Dryden, a long, steady look, then disappear into the night.

Bernd Strikfeldt, wearing brown trousers and a dark wind-breaker, reported to the Oberst that the second group was gathered and ready. The Oberst grunted and told him to get underway as soon as Grebling's detachment was clear. Then the Oberst put his hand on Pavel's shoulder and said, "Come, let us change. Our time is almost here.''

Pavel left Dryden in Voight's charge and retired to strip out of his uniform. As he unbuttoned his tunic he watched Dryden. The American stood quietly in Voight's grasp, seemingly resigned, but Pavel saw banked fire behind the stony expression. There was a profound stillness about the man. As if he were marking time. Waiting. A mistake, Pavel decided. Taking Dryden along was a dangerous mistake. The man was too unpredictable.

As soon as the second team had departed, Ulrich Waldau moved into place with the final group. The men began to disappear through the door. Pavel folded his uniform and packed it, then hurried back to Voight and Dryden. Kleber came moments later. The Oberst had replaced his Afrika

Korps tans with a tailored suit that might have come off the rack at some American department store. His eyes briefly inspected Pavel's new clothing. "Good," he said. "We will leave immediately after Colonel Waldau's men. Herr Boberach and I will go first. You and Voight will follow with Captain Dryden. We will wait for you beyond the fence."

Pavel stiffened. In the crush of happenings he had forgotten completely about the little technician from Camp Butner. And Boberach had been assigned to him as part of his duties. He was supposed to be watching out for the man, not neglecting him. He looked around the room quickly, hoping the Oberst wouldn't notice, seeking Boberach. He found him near the door, bundled in a bulky overcoat, looking anxious. Thank God. Pavel let a sigh flutter up from deep in his chest.

Pavel picked up Voight's knapsack and his own and waited. Time ticked slowly. Waldau's men darted into the night one after another. Waldau clasped Kleber's hand and disappeared after them. Soon only Kleber and the overcoated Boberach were left. Kleber nodded to Pavel and took Boberach's arm. Then they, too, were gone.

"It's time," Pavel told Voight. He slung the knapsacks over his shoulder and clamped a fist around Dryden's elbow. He hurried to the door, hesitated long enough to draw a deep breath, then dragged Dryden down the stoop and across the darkened space between buildings. A man, one of the spotters, waved from the shadows. Pavel ran to him, pulling Dryden along.

The wind was rising again. The spotter waited until Voight joined them, then pointed. Pavel saw two figures, black lumps in the night, dart to the wire fence. Kleber and Boberach. A series of cuts below one of the guard towers made a small opening just large enough for one man at a time. Kleber scrambled through to the clearing outside the wire, then waited to help Boberach to his feet. They took off at a crouch, running across the clearing, coattails flapping, and were quickly swallowed by the black, moonless night.

Sounds of laughter and music still echoed from the parade ground, but the din was dying down. The spotter put a finger to his lips and whispered, "The guards are below the tower. Drugged. As soon as everyone is clear, the wire will be repaired and the guards revived. They will think they have

100

drunk too much. They will say nothing. With luck, none of you will be missed until roll call two days from now."

"Did all make it through?" Pavel whispered hoarsely.

"Everyone," the spotter murmured. "But be careful. The guards in the next tower refused to drink. They are alert, and using their searchlight." He glanced at the wire. "Your friends are clear. Remember, the wind carries sound. Go. Now."

Pavel tugged Dryden to his feet. They ran to the cut in the wire. Voight ducked through first, and Pavel shoved the two knapsacks after him. As Voight snatched at them the searchlight at the neighboring tower made a cursory swing across the inner compound rooftops. The beam of light came nowhere near Pavel or Voight or Dryden, but all three froze until it finished probing. Even Dryden. Pavel nodded in satisfaction. Good. Dryden understood his tenuous situation and was prepared to behave properly.

Pavel nudged Dryden, who scrambled through the wire after Voight. Pavel crawled through the opening to join them. They rose quickly and scuttled at a crouch across a bull-dozed clearing. The knapsacks, dangling from Voight's arm, swayed erratically as he stumbled through furrows. Pavel kept a firm grip on Dryden's bound wrists.

"Here," someone whispered from the darkness ahead of them. Kleber's head appeared at ground level. Pavel pushed Dryden forward, into a depression beside Kleber and Boberach. Voight piled in after them. Dryden looked around at Pavel with eyes that were flat with loathing and peculiarly contemplative.

A dog barked in the distance. Baying at shadows? Or barking at one of the earlier groups, now scattered through the surrounding countryside? Pavel rubbed his eyes, thinking of his comrades darting across uncertain ground, alone in the night in a hostile environment, not knowing what the next hours might bring.

And then, unaccountably, someone in the shallow depression beside Pavel began to make a peculiar sound. Pavel looked around anxiously, wondering what was wrong. It was Oberst Kleber. The Oberst held a fist to his own mouth, trying to muffle the sound. Good God, he was laughing. Pavel gaped. Oberst Kleber couldn't seem to stop. The soft sound shook his belly and his chest. He ducked his head, biting his knuckles, quaking with quiet laughter.

The sound was infectious. Albert Voight snickered. Boberach stifled a snort, then began to giggle. In spite of his concern, Pavel found himself joining in. Quiet laughter, whispering from anxiety-tightened throats. Dryden stared at them as though they were insane. Four grown men, Dryden excluded, laughing softly in the darkness.

It was madness, and Pavel couldn't imagine what perverse catalyst had triggered it. But moments later, as he rose to his feet, laughter still bubbling in his chest, realization came to him. He suddenly knew, with intense clarity, why the laughter had come. He felt an unexpected thrill as the chill Texas wind whipped darkly around his legs. A peculiar new smell was in the air, a ripe smell, mixed with an odor of cold earth. A pleasant smell. A smell that Pavel had forgotten. It was the smell of freedom.

Freedom. Yes, freedom. By God. At long last, they were once again free men.

*Panzer rollen in Amerika vor!*

*Monday*
*December 25, 1944*

# SIX

Dark gray clouds boiled across the midnight sky, blotting
the stars. Wind moaned from the north, blowing December's
breath on Pavel's neck. He peered at the dark shape through
the fence rails, trying to make it out. Was that the vehicle
Kleber was expecting? It looked like a big truck, but very
old, very dilapidated. Pavel saw deep furrows in the fenders
and gaps in the grillwork, the scabs and scars of numerous
lost road wars. The windscreen was cracked in at least three
places. Two sagging headlights, nestled like crossed eyes
between fenders and hood, stared sightlessly. A faded canvas cover arched over the cargo bed. The truck looked sick.
Defeated. Pavel heard a rustling sound like a death rattle,
but it was only wind flapping the canvas.

The wind gusted and died. Pavel cocked an ear, listening.
A murmur of voices drifted from beyond the truck, like
furtive whispers in a vacuum. The wind huffed again, blowing the sound away. Pavel hooked his arm, summoning the
others, then waited, shivering in the darkness. His eyes
sought the distant glow of lights from Camp McLean, some
six miles to the south. Had the American guards missed
anyone yet? He heard a crunch of gravel as Kleber and

Boberach hurried to join him, followed by Voight and Dryden.

"Is that it?" Kleber asked, staring at the truck. "Only the one?"

"It's all I've seen," Pavel said.

Kleber's jaw hardened in the darkness. "Where are the men?"

"Beyond the truck," Pavel said. "I heard someone talking."

Kleber nodded and crawled over the fence. Boberach clambered after him. They moved openly toward the truck, Kleber walking erect, Boberach hurrying to keep up. Pavel and Voight boosted Dryden over the fence rail by his bound arms and followed. A blast of wind swirled dark red dust around them.

The muted murmurs choked off at Kleber's approach. Pavel saw a shadow drop to a crouch and scuttle behind the rear of the truck. A rustle of clothing. Soft impact of bodies hitting the dirt. Nothing else stirred until Kleber was close enough to be recognized. Then a figure rose tentatively. Pavel saw the pinched, nervous features of SS Captain Grebling waiting to greet Kleber. Horst Baumhof and Erwin Maschmann climbed to their feet and brushed dirt from their knees. Erich Huber and the nurse appeared briefly at the rear of the truck, then Huber dragged the woman back beneath the canvas canopy. Dryden might have seen her, too, but nothing in his demeanor betrayed him.

"Where are the other two teams?" Kleber asked. "Strikfeldt? Colonel Waldau?"

Grebling, face bloodless and tense with strain, said, "Not yet here, Herr Oberst. We've only just arrived ourselves."

Kleber frowned. "Have you forgotten how to be a soldier? Get busy, man. Post some sentries to guard the perimeter. We came near enough to hear you. No one should be permitted that close."

Grebling looked embarrassed. "Yes, Herr Oberst. I should have thought of it sooner." He quickly designated three men and sent them on the run.

Kleber stared at the truck, then kicked one of the tires. A retread. *"Das ist zum kotzen,"* he said. "Who is responsible for this?"

"I am," a voice said. A tall German, straight as an upright

steel girder, eased his way through the remainder of Grebling's men. His hair was white, or perhaps gray. Pavel couldn't tell in the darkness. He had a jaw like a bulldozer blade, and he towered over most of the soldiers, a giant with heavy-boned shoulders and elbows and knees.

"I am Oberst Heinz Kleber," Kleber said. "Who are you?"

"They call me Linares," the man said. "My real name is unimportant."

"You are the agent sent to help us?"

The man nodded. "That is correct."

Pavel, a six-footer himself, was awed by this awkward-looking giant. How could a man be a spy, someone expected to blend into the background, when he stood head and shoulders above normal men?

Kleber gestured at the truck. "Is this the best you could do?"

"It isn't much," the man admitted. "I had to buy what was available. There are no fine new trucks for sale in Mexico. Not with the war."

"Will it get us to our destination?"

"With luck and careful driving," the man said. "The tires are old, and the motor is rough. But it has brought me six hundred miles from the Mexican coast and another five hundred from the border. It should hold together the final three hundred miles. I make no guarantees."

Kleber stared at him suspiciously. "How do you know the distance? You know where we are going? What this is all about?"

"I know only as much as I need to know," the man said. "The U-boat captain said you would need transport for some three hundred miles, and then the truck was to be abandoned."

Kleber studied the man with continued skepticism. "Your accent is strange. You are from Germany?"

The man shook his head. "No longer. My home is in Guadalajara. I've lived there for years. With my brother. But I still hold German citizenship, if that's what you mean."

Kleber regarded the truck and said, "Our friends from the U-boat delivered the materials we requested?"

The man nodded. "Yes, everything was put ashore a week

105

ago. I met the U-boat myself, with two Mexican helpers. You'll find your equipment in back. Guns. Explosives. Concealed in the cotton."

"Cotton?"

The man's chin split in a gritty grin. "Two large bales of Mexican cotton. You can be thankful for war shortages. American customs officials allow Mexican trucks to bring cotton and other agricultural produce across the border without question. I crossed the border with seven bales of long-staple cotton four days ago. I sold five of them to a compress company in Del Rio. For a good price, as it happens. Then I switched license plates and drove north. The remaining two bales are still in the truck. Your materials are hidden inside them. You'll need band cutters to break them open."

"Show me," Kleber said.

The man fetched a pair of band cutters from the cab and walked Kleber to the back of the truck. He rustled the canvas aside and lowered the tailgate. Erich Huber and the woman were standing in the bed of the truck, blocking the view. Huber pushed the woman roughly to one side. Pavel, gripping Dryden's arm, felt the American's muscles tighten. He whispered, "Please keep your wits about you, Captain Dryden. This is not the time for heroics." Dryden said nothing. But his muscles stayed taut.

Kleber peered into the dark hollow of the truck bed. Beyond Huber and the woman two bulky bales of cotton lay on their sides. Behind the cotton, lashed to the front wall behind the cab, stood a brace of dark fifty-gallon drums. "What is in the barrels?" Kleber asked.

"Mexican gasoline," the man said. "It stinks to high heaven, and it knocks like devils hammering on the gates of hell, but I would prefer not to make gasoline stops at American petrol stations, even if I possessed the proper ration cards."

"Yes, of course," Kleber said. "How much gasoline is there?"

The man smiled slyly. "Enough to get us back to Mexico for the rendezvous with the U-boat, if the truck is still available to us. You might keep that in mind. There was a suggestion that anything left over when you are done—the truck, for example—would revert to me. We could sell it in

Guadalajara for a good price. Even a relic like this. Trucks are in short supply. I would be willing to share with you."

More figures approached through the night. Dieter Grebling heard them and started to duck, but one of the sentries hailed the truck from the perimeter. Everything was all right, the man called. It was only one of the two missing teams coming in. Grebling, recovering from brief panic, darted an embarrassed look at Kleber. Pavel held Dryden tightly and scowled to himself. He was accustomed to better officers than Grebling. The SS captain had bad nerves. Too jumpy. He wondered if the Oberst had noticed.

Waldau, the SS colonel, came at a crouch with six men, hurrying across dark ground. They grinned happily as they closed on the truck and the waiting soldiers. Jürgen Frischauer was among them. A couple of Waldau's men rushed up to the truck and hugged it. Frischauer made a fist of triumph. Even Waldau looked excited. "We're here," Waldau said. "We're ready. Let's go."

"Where's Lieutenant Strikfeldt?" Kleber asked. "He left the stockade before you, didn't he?"

"We saw no sign of him," Waldau said. His eyes probed the darkness, momentarily sober. "Perhaps our escape path was shorter." The cheerful look returned. "Yes, of course. That's it. He and his men were assigned the longer route around the motor pool. They will no doubt be along shortly. This is the truck? Everything is delivered? Arms? Explosives?"

"I was just on the verge of sending someone in to unpack them," Kleber said. He glanced at Pavel. "Sergeant, transfer the American to Corporal Voight. You will do the honors for us. You and Private Frischauer."

"Yes, sir," Pavel said happily. He pushed Dryden into Voight's hands and gestured Frischauer to the truck. The giant from Mexico handed Pavel the long-handled band cutters. The truck bobbed slightly as Pavel and Frischauer heaved into the bed and advanced on the cotton bales. Pavel slipped the long band cutters in place and sliced the metal bands from the first bale. Snick. Snick. Snick. They unwound with hissing fury. Swish, clatter. Swish, clatter. Metallic snakes striking at the sides of the truck. The cotton bale bulged more after each cut, like a woman removing a girdle.

When the bale was free Frischauer peeled away the burlap and tore out hunks of cotton, plowing deep until his hand encountered the first of several tightly wrapped canvas sheaths. He handed it to Pavel, then dug for more. Pavel untied the draws and unrolled the canvas, exposing a sleek Schmeisser MP-40 machine pistol with a folding stock and a corrugated thirty-two round magazine taped to its side, still smelling of cosmoline. "Maschinenpistole," Pavel announced gleefully. He wiped it clean with a hunk of loose cotton and passed it down to Kleber.

Frischauer kept digging. Pavel had expected ordinary infantry rifles, the ubiquitous Gewehr 98s, with at most a couple of Schmeissers thrown in for rapid covering fire. But his excitement mounted as he unwrapped each canvas bundle. One MP-40 after another. No rifles at all. The Abwehr or the navy, whoever had provided the weapons, had shown great generosity. The first bale was crammed with MP-40 machine pistols. Twenty of them. One for each man. Enough firepower to take on an army. Pavel passed the dark, oily submachine guns across the tailgate to the outstretched hands of eager troopers.

By the time Frischauer emptied the first bale, loose cotton lay in fluffs along the length of the truck bed, and the wind was already whipping bits of it into the night air. Grinning faces, some with cotton lint clinging to whisker stubble, waited to see what the next bale would offer. Pavel gestured Frischauer aside and unlimbered the band cutter. Snick. Snick. Snick. The bands parted. Swish, clatter. Swish, clatter. More sharp-edged snakes uncoiling against the wooden sides. More spreading cotton, freed from corseted confinement. Again Frischauer dived. Cotton flew as he ripped it away. A smaller package wrapped in oilskin. Pavel peeled it. Five leather holsters containing Walther 9mm P-38 pistols with eight-round clips. "For the officers," he called. He handed them down to Kleber.

The next package contained high-powered binoculars, two pairs of powerful navy glasses with Carl Zeiss lenses. Then came two heavy cases of ammunition, 9mm Parabellum cartridges for both the submachine guns and the pistols. After that a smaller box, some kind of scientific contraption that Pavel didn't recognize, but which drew a squeal of joy from Boberach. Deeper in the bale were three massive cases of explosives wrapped in tight bricks and surrounded by excelsior. Torpex, Composition B and Baronal. Huge rolls of special waterproofed fuse cord. One of the cases contained a sleek metal hand unit for igniting the fuses, something like an electric cigarette lighter. Frischauer helped Pavel slide the cases over against the sideboards.

While Pavel and Frischauer worked, the last contingent from the POW camp, Strikfeldt and his men, came scooting in. The enlisted men were breathless with excitement, and they claimed their own MP-40s at the tailgate like children accepting Christmas presents. Strikfeldt shoved a Walther pistol and holster into his belt and reported to Kleber, murmuring apologetically. He gave a nervous laugh and described a dark field and an encounter with a stupid, stubbornly territorial bull and a full headlong retreat, his men fleeing in disorder. He said they'd been forced to circle widely around the field to avoid disaster. Kleber told him about the explosives, and he clambered up to the bed of the truck and knelt beside Pavel and the cases. "What did they send us?" he asked.

"Three cases," Pavel said. "Torpex, Composition B, and Baronal. Enough to flatten a few city blocks."

Strikfeldt considered the cases a moment, then nodded. "I haven't used much Torpex. It's a naval explosive. Great blast effect, but mainly for hunting submarines. W-Bomben. Depth charges. It doesn't matter. I can fashion acceptable explosions. What about timers?"

"No timers," Pavel said. "They sent some rolls of fuse cord."

Strikfeldt looked distressed. "Fuse cord? You mean the kind that burns? How can I be expected to create simultaneous explosions without timers?"

"It's good fusing," Pavel said. "The label says it will burn even under water. Three rolls. Different speeds. An electric igniter. We'll make it work."

The agent from Mexico leaned in at the tailgate and checked his watch. "If you're satisfied, you'd better call in the perimeter guards. We should drive as far from here as possible before daylight."

Strikfeldt dropped to the ground to warn Kleber. The agent watched while Pavel and Frischauer gathered the loose metallic bands and strips of sacking and larger chunks of stray cotton in successive trips and dumped them to the ground. Then he said, "You might want to look behind the gas drums. There's a present from the crew of the U-boat."

Pavel leaned over the drums. Wedged tightly between them was a squat wooden keg. The markings had been burned away with a soldering iron. "What's this? A wine cask?" Pavel called. Several faces appeared at the canvas flaps, alerted by Pavel's question. Pavel reached over and rapped the keg with his knuckles. It answered with a ripe, rich sound. "By God, it is. And full. Is it German?"

"A little taste of home," the tall spy said. "A Bernkasteler from the Moselle. The U-boat captain thought you might all wish to toast Christmas and the success of your mission."

"Break it open," someone said eagerly from the tailgate. Other chins nodded in anticipation. They'd had nothing stronger than 3.2 American beer for months.

Oberst Kleber appeared among them. "Not now, boys," he said. "Let's not lose our heads. There'll be time enough for wine and celebration tomorrow." A ripple of moans. Kleber smiled indulgently. "Pavel, you will drive. I will guide you. Captain Dryden will ride in the cab with us, in case we encounter roadblocks or other hindrances. You may untie his hands now. The rest of you load up in the cargo bed. Keep the woman quiet but comfortable."

Pavel dropped to the ground and fumbled with the knots at Dryden's back, freeing his hands. Dryden rubbed the circulation back into his wrists. Boberach and the officers climbed into the back of the truck. Then came the contingent of enlisted men. The truck sagged as the weight increased. By the time the last of them had climbed in, the bed was jammed from wall to wall with twenty-four close-packed bodies. Only the massive agent from Mexico remained on the ground with Kleber, Pavel, and Dryden.

Kleber told the man, "You will ride in back with the others."

"Yes, if you wish," the tall agent said. "But first you'll need my help getting the engine started. It can be stubborn when it's cold."

Kleber's jaw stiffened at the reminder, but he offered no further complaint about the sorry state of the aging truck. He motioned Dryden into the cab, then climbed in after him

110

and slammed the door. The agent followed Pavel around to the driver's side.

"You have to pump the accelerator a few times before you hit the starter," the man told Pavel. "It may take a few tries. Then nurse it carefully. It coughs and wheezes, but it should be running smoothly by the time we hit the highway."

Pavel eased under the wheel and closed the door. The seats were badly sprung, and the cracks in the window spidered down from the top toward the passenger's side, but Kleber seemed not to notice. He sat quietly by the far door, staring straight ahead. Dryden sprawled glumly between them, legs straddling the gearshift.

"Remember, pump the gas a couple of times," the man said.

Pavel did as he was told, then switched on the ignition and hit the starter. The engine whined fitfully. Pavel tried again. Kleber's face became stonier. On the third try the engine turned over, coughed, and caught. Pavel fed gas evenly, trying to keep it going. It ran ragged, like a Panzer tank.

The man nodded. "That's good. It will settle down in a few moments." He patted the window frame affectionately, then said, "Yes, well. I will return to the back with the others. The sun will rise in about five hours. Get off the road as soon as you can. It's dangerous to drive in daylight."

"We should be at our first destination by then," Kleber said.

The man circled to the rear of the truck and climbed aboard. Pavel nursed the engine, feeding it gas, toying with the choke. He gripped the steering wheel tightly and grinned to himself. It felt good to be behind the wheel of a vehicle again, even a ramshackle old truck like this.

Kleber removed the Texaco road map from his jacket and unfurled it, trying to read it in the dim light from the dashboard. He traced a line with his finger, then said, "Go south to the highway and turn west. Stay on Highway 66. We come first to a city, a place named Amarillo, about seventy miles from here, then another seventy miles to the New Mexico border. After that we go on about a hundred miles to a little town"—he checked the map again—"called Cuervo. There we turn north. We should be there by daylight."

Dryden looked up sharply. Pavel sensed sudden movement more than actually seeing it. He put a hand against

Dryden's chest, half expecting some foolish heroic notion, but the American was only staring at Oberst Kleber.

"Don't worry, Pavel," Kleber told him calmly. "The captain is only a trifle startled. He is just now beginning to understand why he is with us. Isn't that right, Captain Dryden?" Dryden said nothing. Kleber smiled smugly to himself. "Let's go, Pavel."

Pavel had no idea what Oberst Kleber was hinting at. He shoved the truck in gear and released the clutch. The truck lurched forward, jouncing across the rough field. Bodies shifted in the rear, and someone cursed Pavel's driving talents soundly. Pavel muttered under his breath and shifted to second. The truck jerked and bobbled, swaying toward a break in the fence and a dirt road beyond. Behind them, skittering across the dark ground like shreds of newspaper, cotton tufts swirled silently on the wind. Pavel turned south toward the highway.

"Excellent," Kleber said. "If everything has gone well, there should be no alarm before tomorrow. We'll be safely hidden on Captain Dryden's ranch by then."

Dryden huddled in the cab, scheming. There must be some way to attract attention to the escaped prisoners without placing Beverly in unnecessary jeopardy. He'd thought Amarillo might be the place. A smallish city huddled in lonely isolation on the flat wastes of the Texas Panhandle, with a wartime population of about 50,000 people. Surely there would be traffic lights, cops, pedestrians, maybe even roadblocks if the breakout at the POW camp had been discovered. But Amarillo had presented no opportunities whatever. It was a sleeping town—almost two in the morning, tinsel decorations dangling above empty streets. Dryden knew that children were dozing fitfully in some of these dark houses, waiting for dawn and presents under family Christmas trees, but no adults seemed to be awake, either. The truck crept through without challenge.

They chugged on, heading westward toward the New Mexico border, swaying down the two-lane highway, the only headlights visible for miles. This was barren country, as flat as cardboard, with scarcely a tree to break the horizon. They weren't making very good time. Pavel was fighting a headwind, and the truck waddled along at forty miles per hour, clattering over worn pavement. They passed through a few sparse settlements—Bushland, Wildorado, Vega, Adrian. In the long gaps between towns an occasional farmhouse cropped up in the night. Most of the houses were dark, like abandoned shacks in a desert. But as the pre-dawn hours slipped away, one in five showed a glimmer of light, someone making breakfast perhaps, or getting ready for early chores. Kleber seemed to be growing more apprehensive by the moment.

They passed out of Texas almost without notice. The road abruptly became worse, and a sign skimmed by on the roadside welcoming them to "New Mexico—the Land of Enchantment," but nothing else changed. The land was still flat. The road still straight and deadly boring. Dryden sneaked a look at the radium dial of his watch. Half past four. And a hundred miles to go. If Kleber hoped to reach safety before daylight, they were in deep trouble. Was there a way he could slow them further? Anything to eat away more minutes of time. If he could keep them on the road past sunrise, their chances of being spotted would increase significantly. Someone might finally give the alarm. But what could he do? Suggest a wrong turn? Sabotage the truck? Overpower Pavel?

Dryden awaited his chance, but the truck did it for him. Twenty miles into New Mexico, tooling down the road toward Tucumcari, one of the Mexican retreads blew. One moment they were zipping along at forty miles an hour, then Dryden heard a bang like a howitzer shell and the truck slewed wildly, cavorting from side to side on the narrow ribbon of road. Kleber grabbed the dashboard. Curses swelled from the rear as closely packed bodies lost their balance under the canvas canopy and lurched against each other. Pavel wrestled the wheel frantically, turning against each skid, stamping hard on the brake pedal, fighting the truck to a standstill. The truck spun around broadside, teetered one last time, then settled on three haunches, leaning lamely in the direction of the blown tire. The engine wheezed and died. Silence swooped in.

Pavel's hands, locked on the wheel, were shaking. He sat still for a moment, muttering under his breath, then flicked off the lights and the ignition. He shoved his door open violently and jumped down from the cab. Kleber got out on the other side and gestured for Dryden to follow. Canvas rustled at the rear, and more Germans dropped from the truck bed. Rubber fragments littered the road behind them.

"*Schlammasel,*" called Bernd Strikfeldt. "What rotten luck. What happened?"

"Blew a tire," Pavel said glumly. He glared at the agent from Mexico.

Kleber was all business. "Fetch the spare, Herr Linares. Let us get it changed. Quickly."

The back of the truck continued to empty its human cargo to the pavement, men stretching cramped muscles. Dryden saw Beverly lean over the open tailgate and drop, helped by Frischauer and a man with a crooked arm. Her eyes sought him. She nodded quietly.

Waldau approached Kleber and asked, "How much farther? It's quite crowded in the back of the truck."

"Too far," Kleber said. "Almost eighty miles to the turnoff. And another thirty miles on dirt roads."

"We must make alternate plans," Waldau said.

"Yes, I suppose so."

Linares wheeled a spare to the side of the truck and produced a jack. Strikfeldt posted guards east and west of the truck and sent the others, Beverly among them, to seek cover in a plowed field north of the highway. Voight and a couple of German enlisted men shoved the jack under the truck and tackled the blown tire.

Kleber scanned the horizon. To Dryden he said, "I thought there were mountains in this New Mexico of yours."

"There are," Dryden said. "Further west."

Kleber said, "High mountains? The map indicates some are fairly high."

Dryden had long since made up his mind to keep his mouth shut, to offer nothing voluntarily, but there was a note of worry in Kleber's question, and he couldn't resist worrying the German further. "The highest is a little over thirteen thousand feet," he said. "That's high enough for most people."

Strikfeldt came to them, looking frustrated. "The jack doesn't work," he said. "Corporal Voight says the threads are stripped."

Kleber swore. "Where is Herr Linares?"

"Still trying with the jack," Strikfeldt said. "He's not feeling too confident at the moment. Shall I fetch him?"

"Never mind," Kleber said. "Send some men to find a large stone for a fulcrum and a fence post for a lever. We must get the tire changed quickly."

Strikfeldt summoned men from the field and gave them quick instructions. A few scattered to scout up the stone. Some swarmed to the fence and stripped barbed wire away, then began to rock a post back and forth to loosen it. Others came to the truck to wheel out the gasoline drums and cases of ammunition to lighten the load.

Thin cloud cover parted, exposing a fat moon. Yellow moonglow washed the road. The SS colonel fidgeted impatiently. "What is the next town?" he asked Kleber. "How far is it?"

Kleber pulled out his road map and thumbed a lighter, searching for names and distances in the flickering glow. "About fifteen miles," he said. "A place called Tucumcari."

"Perhaps we can hide there."

"Perhaps," Kleber said. "We dare not expose ourselves."

Two men wrestled a good-sized rock out of a ditch and lugged it to the truck. The post came loose a few moments later. A band of men came charging to the truck, carrying the pole like a battering ram. Voight guided them in, showing where he wanted the pole on the rock and where to place the prying end. They slid the pole beneath the truck quickly and efficiently, then grunted and put their weight to it.

The post was about seven feet long, and several of the biggest men had to lean in before the truck shuddered and moved. The bed heaved slowly, rising above the pavement. A murmur of triumph went up. Voight removed the nuts with a lug wrench, then pulled the shredded tire from the wheel shaft and reached for the spare.

The man from Mexico moved to them from the shadows, apparently more at ease now that the tire change was underway. Dryden watched the giant shuffle toward Kleber, hands in pockets. Kleber turned stony eyes on him. The man said defensively, "This isn't my fault. If you wanted flawless transportation, you should have asked the submarine to bring it."

"You had better be a good intelligence agent," Kleber said. "You have much to account for."

115

"I don't perform miracles," the man muttered.

Waldau swung around, still impatient. "Do you know this country well?" he asked. "We may need a place to—"

There was a sudden splintering sound, a loud *crack*, followed by shouts and curses. The truck smashed to the ground. Someone shrieked in pain. Dryden jerked his head to see men toppling to the pavement like tenpins, falling away from the truck. All but two. One man was frozen on the pavement, his mouth open in silent scream, his leg caught under the bare wheel. Another stood wide-eyed and stunned above the splintered end of the fence post, clutching a tear in his rib cage.

Kleber rushed to the man under the wheel, calling for help. A few of the fallen figures bounced to their feet and hurried back to the truck, applying shoulders to the cargo bed in an attempt to lift it. It didn't budge. Dryden had no conscious thought of helping, but he found himself adding his shoulder to the others. "Get another post!" Kleber shouted. A few men broke away. The man under the wheel was keening, "Ah, ah, ah, ah." The man with the rip in his lower chest walked whimpering from soldier to soldier, trying to catch their attention, but they were too busy straining at the truck. Dryden turned the man gently away.

Other Germans poured in from the field to help. The truck groaned and lifted slightly. The wheel rose inches above the man's leg. Dryden and the agent reached down quickly and helped Kleber pull him loose. The leg was smashed above the knee, the trousers soaked. The man's eyes rolled, showing the whites. His keening was constant now, with scarcely a stop for breath.

Dryden said, "Call Beverly. She'll know what to do."

Kleber nodded. "Summon the woman," he shouted.

The man with the torn ribs came to stand over them. He pressed his hands against his bloody shirt and looked down at his fallen comrade. "Is Schönbeck going to be all right?" he asked.

Kleber finally noticed him. "What happened to you, soldier?"

"The post caught me," the man said. He gestured vaguely with one hand. "When it broke, I fell forward. On the jagged end. I'm all right. It's just a small puncture wound."

Beverly hurried in, propelled by Erich Huber. She took a

quick look at the first man's leg and said, "I'll need my bag." Dryden translated, and Kleber told Huber to fetch it. Huber headed for the truck bed. He was back in moments.

While Beverly rummaged in the bag Germans hurried from the field with a new fence post. One of the men pushed the rock back in place, and they hefted the truck properly. Voight wheeled the spare over and lifted it onto the wheel shaft. Another man spun the nuts and tightened them.

Beverly tied a tourniquet above the man's knee, then inserted a syringe into a vial and drew off several cc's. She held it to the moon and tapped air out of the needle. "Tell them this is morphine," she said. "I'll need better light to clean the leg. And I'll have to stanch the other man's bleeding. We should find a place to stop soon. They're both badly hurt."

"Are you all right?" Dryden asked her.

"Just pissed off," she said. "And you?"

He flashed her a quick smile. "Yeah, me, too. I should have seen this coming."

Waldau, the SS colonel, glowered. "If you have something to say to the woman, say it in German," he hissed.

"She doesn't speak German," Dryden objected.

"Then keep your comments to yourself."

"Our comments were about your two injured soldiers," Dryden snapped. He hesitated, then decided to give it a try. "She's giving morphine to the man with the smashed leg. She says there's nothing else she can do for him. She says he requires immediate hospital care, or he'll lose the leg."

The spy from Mexico cleared his throat. "Excuse me, sir. That isn't what she said. She said she needs better light to clean the leg, and we should stop soon."

Dryden sighed. "You speak English, do you?"

"Fluently," the man said. "Also Spanish, French, and Portuguese." He glanced at Kleber. "Some miracles I perform with regularity."

Waldau was still impatient. "We're wasting time," he said. "If the woman needs light to minister to them, we should accommodate her. We must find a place to hide." He called to the back of the truck, "Quickly. Return the ammunition cases and the gasoline barrels to the truck. We must depart."

The morphine took effect quickly, and the man with the

117

damaged leg grew quiet. Pavel paused with one of the ammunition cases to look at the man, apparently noticed his head lying in the dust, and stripped off his jacket. He offered it to Beverly. She rolled the jacket into a bundle and put it under the man's head, making him as comfortable as possible, then turned her attention to the man with the bleeding rib cage. The gasoline barrels clanged noisily as Germans wheeled them to the tailgate and hoisted them to the truck bed.

Their luck stayed bad. A pair of headlights appeared in the distance, coming toward the truck. Waldau barked a low command, sending the Germans at the tailgate streaming into the darkness with their weapons. He hurried forward to join Kleber and Dryden. "The vehicle is slowing down," he warned.

"*Zum Kotzen,*" Kleber muttered. "What can go wrong next?" To Pavel and Voight he said, "Quickly. Get these injured men into the truck. Take the woman with them."

Pavel picked up the man with the smashed knee. He tried to be gentle, but he must have jostled the leg. In spite of the morphine the man cried out. Voight seized Beverly and the man with the bleeding rib cage by the arms and hurried them to the rear. The lights drew nearer. It was a sedan with a single driver, and it was slowing down even more.

The towering agent said to Kleber, "Let him see the American officer in uniform. Perhaps he will drive on past."

"Yes, a good idea," Kleber said. He nudged Dryden to the front of the truck. "Colonel Waldau and I will be behind you," Kleber told him. "If the car stops, you will speak. Get rid of him. For your safety, be convincing."

Dryden waved as the car coasted toward them and motioned the driver on, but the car came to a complete stop anyway. There was a chromed red light on the roof. It was a black-and-white patrol coupe with a New Mexico highway patrol emblem on the side. The driver's door swung open, and a florid-faced man climbed out, wearing a battered gray Stetson over quizzical brows. He jingled his car keys and stuffed them in his pocket. He had a protruding belly that spoke eloquently of the good life. A low-slung leather holster hugged his hip. "Kin I he'p you folks?" he asked.

"It's all right, officer," Dryden told him. "We had a tire problem. It's fixed now."

118

The man eyed Dryden's uniform and broke into a grin. "Serviceman, eh? My oldest boy's in the army. France. What outfit you with?"

Dryden glanced at the holstered gun and wondered if he could pass word to this man, alert him to the Germans. But Linares, the man from Mexico, was standing only a few feet away, listening to every word, and Beverly was in the back of the truck, probably pinned between Pavel and Voight. Not to mention all the Germans hiding in the dark field with those big guns from the bale of cotton. He said, "Corps of Engineers. I'm taking a civilian work crew down to Fort Sumner. They've got drainage problems."

The highway patrolman glanced at the battered truck. "Don't look like one of them army machines to me. You folks scrapin' the bottom of the barrel?"

"It belongs to the construction company," Dryden said. "If I'd known their tires were in such lousy shape, I'd have requisitioned one of our own trucks."

"Well, you need any he'p, you just tell me. I'm 'bout to start my mornin' shift. I can radio for a wrecker if you need one."

"Thanks anyway," Dryden said. "We can make it now."

The patrolman touched his Stetson and started to turn toward the patrol car. As he did a moan rose from the back of the truck. Dryden winced. The man with the shattered leg, most likely. The moan cut off quickly, as though some-one had clamped a hand over his mouth.

"What was that?" the patrolman asked.

Dryden said, "One of the boys got hurt when we skidded. Banged up his knee a bit. He'll be all right."

"I've got a first-aid kit in the car," the man said. "Better let me take a look." He turned again, this time toward the bed of the truck. Kleber and Waldau moved aside.

Dryden said quickly, "Sorry, officer, but we really don't have time. We're running pretty late. We're supposed to be in Fort Sumner by daybreak. I've got to get these people on the road again."

The patrolman hesitated, scarcely a foot in front of Wal-dau. "Wouldn't take but a second," the man said. "You never know. Sometimes these little hurts go nasty and turn into big ones. Won't cost you nothin' for me to look. Part of the service."

119

"It isn't necessary," Dryden said.

The man shrugged. "Well, you're the boss. I'd have him looked at pretty soon, though. It sounds to me like he's hurtin' pretty bad."

Waldau pulled his Walther P-38 from his jacket and without ceremony put it to the back of the patrolman's head and fired. Blood and bone sprayed in a fine mist, and the man plunged forward in a half run. He was brain dead already, but he took two steps before he crumpled. Heads popped from the canvas canopy.

"God in heaven!" Kleber exploded. "Why did you do that?"

"He was reaching for his gun," Waldau said.

Dryden said, "The hell he was. I had him convinced, you bloodthirsty bastard. He was about to drive away and leave us alone."

"He might have mentioned us to others," Waldau said. "Even the most innocent word could expose us to danger and complicate our movements. We dare not take such chances." He glanced at Kleber. "The mission comes first. Agreed?"

Kleber said reluctantly, "Yes. Yes, I suppose you are right. But blast it, man, you need not have acted so precipitously. We could have disarmed the man and decided his fate later. Now we must dispose of the body and find a place to hide his car."

Linares scratched his jaw. "We haven't much time," he rumbled. "Perhaps we can bury him in the field. I have a tarpaulin in the truck."

"I suppose that is our only option," Kleber said. "Very well, fetch the tarpaulin and ask Corporal Voight to select a burial detail." He turned to the truck and called. "Sergeant Pavel?"

Pavel jumped down and ran toward them. He dropped his eyes briefly to the body, then said, "Yes, Herr Oberst?"

"Herr Linares will replace you as driver of the truck," Kleber said. "The keys to the police car are in the pocket of this . . . body. Take them. I want you to drive the car ahead of us. Find a thicket of brush, or perhaps a canyon, and hide it. Go at least a few miles before you stop. I do not wish the car found near the body. If you cannot find a place to conceal the car, drive it into a field and leave it. Then wait for us beside the road. We will pick you up when we pass."

Pavel snapped his heels. "Yes, Herr Oberst." Dryden watched as Pavel bent over the body. Pavel was a soldier, accustomed to death, but he seemed reluctant to rifle the man's pockets. He hesitated before he dug the keys out.

Linares and Voight brought the burial detail to the front of the truck. As the men wrapped the body in a tarpaulin and dragged it off the pavement, Waldau said stonily, "We have wasted enough time here. Let us get underway quickly. We must find a resting place."

"For once, I quite agree," Kleber said. "Gentlemen, finish loading the truck. We have less than an hour until sunrise."

# SEVEN

The schoolroom smelled of spilled paste, stale disinfectant, and construction-paper Santa Clauses. Dryden sat on one of the writing desks and watched the Germans peer into closets and bookcases. Pavel, a Schmeisser tucked under one arm, pulled open drawers in the teacher's desk, scanning papers, gradebooks, and primers.

There were four Germans in the room with Dryden—Pavel and Frischauer and a couple of enlisted men. The others were off prowling the school. "What are you looking for?" he asked Pavel.

"Us? Anything useful," Pavel grunted. "The others are checking for food. We brought limited rations. We expected to be at our first staging point by this morning, and now it looks like we'll be stuck in this verdammt schoolhouse until dark."

"Try the cafeteria," Dryden said. "Maybe they left something there."

"Cafeteria?" Pavel said. "You feed your schoolchildren in this country? When I was a child we had to take our own lunches to school. Nobody fed us."

"It's traditional," Dryden said. "A rural area like this,

most of the kids ride to school in those big yellow school buses out back. They can't go home for lunch. School boards figure a cafeteria is the only way the kids can get a meal and a glass of milk. I used to pay a quarter for a plate of spaghetti, or franks and beans. Maybe some bread pudding. As I recall, the pudding tasted like sawdust."

"Even sawdust would help. Where do we find this cafeteria of yours?"

"Look for a big room with steam tables," Dryden said. "It's probably out back, away from the classrooms. I wouldn't expect too much. School has been closed for two weeks. And at least another week of Christmas vacation to go. They probably emptied the refrigerators before they turned the kids loose. but there might be staples."

"Do you think so?" Pavel said. He spoke to Frischauer and the other soldiers, telling them about the cafeteria. All three slung their weapons and hurried eagerly into the hallway.

Dryden was mildly surprised that Pavel let them all go. This was the first time since the break that the Germans had left him alone with only one man to guard him. What advantage could he take of it? He decided to keep Pavel talking and look for an opening. "What have they done with my friend?" he asked. "The nurse, Lieutenant Bennington. Where did they put her?"

"In the classroom down the hall," Pavel said. He peered at the blackboard, trying to make out the chalk scrawls.

"I'd like to talk to her."

Pavel shook his head. "She's tending our injured comrades. The Oberst would not want her to be bothered." He wandered to the wall and stared at crayoned sketches pinned up for the holidays. There were Santas in all shapes and sizes, and inexpertly drawn reindeer and green-paper Christmas trees. "This is a strange way to spend our first day of freedom," he said. "I haven't been in a schoolhouse for years."

"You should have stayed at the POW camp," Dryden said. "Things will go hard when they catch you."

Pavel gave him a stern look. "They won't catch us," he said. "And if they do, we'll make them sorry. None of us will go back willingly."

Dryden shrugged. "You can't win, Pavel. A handful of

men surrounded by a nation full of enemies. A big nation at that.''

''We are more than men,'' Pavel said. He left the children's sketches and walked back to Dryden, patting the machine pistol affectionately. ''We are German soldiers. The best fighters in the world. Much can be accomplished with a trained, tightly knit cadre of dedicated soldiers. And we are fearless. There's not a man among us who isn't willing to die. With Oberst Kleber to lead us we can do anything. Let no man stand in our way. Including you.''

''Bravo,'' Dryden said dryly. ''And just where does Oberst Kleber plan to lead you? What's this all about, Pavel?''

Pavel's eyes narrowed. ''You'll find out soon enough,'' he said.

''If I live that long,'' Dryden said. Pavel wasn't close enough. He needed the German just a little bit closer. ''What will happen to Beverly and me? A shot in the head like that highway patrolman last night?''

''That's up to the officers,'' Pavel said. ''If you do as you are told, I'm sure an accommodation will be made. Oberst Kleber is a fair man.''

''Yes, we saw an example of his fairness when the patrol car stopped us on the road. That poor cop never had a chance.''

''That was Colonel Waldau's doing,'' Pavel said. ''The colonel acted hastily, without orders. If it hadn't happened so quickly, I'm certain Oberst Kleber would have found alternative means.''

''Sure,'' Dryden said. Be friendly. Make eye contact. Don't look at the gun. ''I can see why you would follow a man like Kleber. He's a solid officer. A bit brusque maybe, but good instincts. That SS colonel is something else. I'm surprised Kleber brought him along. What's his name?''

''Waldau,'' Pavel said. ''SS Standartenführer Ulrich Waldau.''

''Yeah, Waldau. I get the idea you don't much like him.''

''A soldier doesn't have to like his officers,'' Pavel said.

''Maybe not,'' Dryden said. His eyes drifted toward the door. He tensed and lowered his voice conspiratorially, hoping Pavel would lean closer. ''But in a tight spot, I'd rather—''

Pavel cocked the bolt and put the MP40 under Dryden's chin. "I'm not a fool, Captain," he said. "What would you do if you could take it from me? Rescue the woman? Shoot your way out of here?"

Dryden's chin rose with the lift of the MP-40 barrel. He held very still for a moment, then smiled sheepishly. "Was I so obvious?"

"Not necessarily," Pavel said. "It's what I would have done. We're alike in many ways, Captain." He lowered the machine pistol but kept it pointed at Dryden's midsection. "One thing. If you had managed to seize the gun, who would have died first? Me?"

Heels clicked in the hallway, coming toward their door. Pavel stepped away from Dryden and planted himself by the blackboard. He removed the magazine and eased the bolt home, then cradled the machine pistol in his arms. Dryden sighed.

Kleber strode into the room accompanied by Lieutenant Strikfeldt and Otto Boberach, the man Dryden had known until last night as Karl Zolling. Kleber was all smiles. He said, "This place is marvelous. Drinking water. Toilet facilities. All the space we need. Not a soul in sight. We could hide here for days."

Boberach raised sad eyes and said, "We don't have days." He looked tired and sat down at one of the smaller desks. He was holding the strange device from the cotton bale, nestling it protectively to his chest. It looked like a big flare gun, or a signal light without a lens. A kind of box on a handle, with a protruding tube. The open end of the tube was covered by a thin mesh.

Kleber gave Boberach an encouraging smile and clapped him on the shoulder. "Don't worry," Kleber said. "We'll be safe here. We can rest through the day, then drive on as soon as it gets dark. Pavel, where is the truck? Is it well hidden?"

"Yes, Herr Oberst. We parked it far in back, among the buses. It can't be seen from the road."

Kleber turned serious. "The engine runs like a threshing machine. And it was heating badly during the last hour on the road. Pavel, you know the men. Tell me, do we have any good mechanics among us?"

Pavel thought for a moment. "Willi Roh and Franz Eggers

do good work," he said. "They used to work on our tanks in Africa, after the parts stopped coming."

"Good. Later, when they have stretched their legs, I want you to take them out and have them put that miserable truck in order. Ask them to check the radiator hoses. Perhaps replacements can be taken from the buses. Check the water pump, too. Do the best you can. I don't want another breakdown once we start the last leg of our drive."

"Yes, Herr Oberst."

Kleber turned to Dryden. "Well, Captain. You are back in your home state at last. How does it feel?"

"I've kept better company."

Kleber laughed. "I dare say. Miss Bennington is a handsome woman."

Whoops sounded in the hallway. Frischauer charged into the room, arms loaded with booty. He skidded to a halt when he saw Kleber and Strikfeldt and snapped to awkward attention, clutching sacks and cans to his chest. Two small brightly colored boxes toppled from his grasp and fell to the floor. He cast a look in Pavel's direction.

Kleber cocked his head at the pile in Frischauer's arms. "What are you carrying, soldier?"

"Food, Herr Oberst. Canned beans, crackers, peanut butter."

"And the boxes?"

"Little individual servings of dry cereal, sir. They apparently package them for the children."

"Is there enough for everyone?"

"Yes, sir. In the dining hall. My two comrades are there now, sorting through it." He hesitated. "There were big sacks of potatoes, sir. I'm not much of a cook, but I can boil potatoes. And flour and baking powder. Maybe I could make some dumplings. There's no milk, but I can try using water. With your permission, I can put a meal together. It won't be a Christmas feast, but perhaps breakfast for all of us."

Kleber seemed tempted, but he shook his head. "No, no fires, no cooking odors. Just tell the men where you found the food. Tell them they may eat anything they wish, so long as it requires no cooking."

"Yes, sir," Frischauer said. He dumped his load on the teacher's desk and hurried back into the hall.

Kleber and Strikfeldt prodded the packages, checking

126

Frischauer's booty. Pavel picked up one of the cereal boxes and broke it open, shoveling flakes into his mouth.

"How is it?" Kleber asked.

"Like cardboard," Pavel said. "But perhaps nourishing."

Dryden cut his eyes to Boberach. The little man was sitting at one of the children's desks, hips bulging over the sides. He was working busily on the odd contraption from the cotton bale. He had a small screwdriver, and he adjusted a screw, testing a dial. The machine clicked, and Boberach looked up, startled. He glanced around the room, then pointed the machine at Dryden. It clicked again.

"What is that thing?" Dryden asked.

Boberach adjusted his glasses. "A scientific device," he said. "It was invented by one of my German colleagues, Hans Geiger. It's called a Geiger counter. It's used to measure radioactive emissions."

"Radio what?"

Boberach smiled shyly. "A term we use in atomic science. Some atoms are less stable than others and shed parts of themselves. It's called *Radioaktivität*. The Geiger device counts emissions and measures them for us. It can be used to seek radioactive elements, or it can warn you when levels of radioactivity are dangerously high."

"How does it work?"

Boberach warmed to the question. "It's relatively simple," he said eagerly. "The device contains an electrically charged wire inside a gas-filled tube. When a charged particle enters the window it ionizes gas atoms, stripping away electrons. The electrons are then drawn to the positively charged wire, which automatically changes the level of current in the wire. That's what we measure. The change of current runs through a small amplifier, like an electrical pulse, and you hear a click. The more clicks you hear, the more emissions there are."

"I heard it click a moment ago," Dryden said. "Are there radioactive elements in this school?"

"That was you," Boberach said.

Dryden was startled. "Me?"

Boberach grinned. "Your watch. It has a radium dial?"

Dryden glanced at his wrist, at the watch Beverly had given him. "I guess so," he said. "It glows in the dark."

"I thought as much. Notice what happens when I point

the device at you." He turned the counter's mesh window in Dryden's direction. A slow stutter of clicks sounded.

"Now see what happens when I bring it closer," the little man said. He wiggled out of the cramped desk and carried the counter toward Dryden. The clicks came faster. Boberach lowered the barrel of the device slowly to Dryden's wrist. The machine chattered. It sounded like radio static in a bad thunderstorm. Kleber glanced in their direction, his curiosity aroused.

"That's all coming from my watch?" Dryden asked.

Boberach nodded. "As long as you're wearing that watch, you shouldn't sit with your hands in your lap. Not if you hope to marry some day and have sons."

"I beg your pardon?"

Boberach chuckled slyly. "A jest," he said. "A small joke we use in our atomic physics laboratory. Radioactivity does strange things. Especially to reproductive organs."

Dryden stared at his watch. "Are you serious?"

"Not at all," Boberach said. "The danger is slight."

Dryden looked at the radium watch, then took it off and started to put it in his pocket. His hand stopped when he realized his pocket was potentially more dangerous than his wrist. He hesitated. He couldn't just discard it. It was a special gift from Beverly. She might not understand. Besides, the little man had just assured him there was no real danger. He slipped the watch back on his wrist where it belonged. Even so, he draped his arm casually along the back of the desk, extended well to one side.

Kleber strolled over to them and said, "Perhaps you should put the mechanism back in its box, Herr Boberach. We wouldn't want to clutter Captain Dryden's mind with unnecessary details."

"Yes, of course. I'm sorry, Herr Oberst. I meant no harm."

"And none has been done, I'm sure," Kleber said. "There's no way the captain can pass any knowledge along. It would appear no one knows anything about us. I doubt the alarm has even been given back at the POW camp. There have been no roadblocks. No sign of patrols. No aerial surveillance. The road is clear. Once darkness falls we may do as we wish."

*     *     *

128

Colonel Hamilton Christopher cast a worried glance at the clock on the wall, then drummed his fingers on the desk. Almost noon. The final roll call should be done by now. Why hadn't that young lieutenant reported back with the results? And why couldn't anyone find Oberst Kleber? Or Captain Dryden? He stared at Max Kieran, standing at hangdog attention in front of the desk. Should he inform the sergeant about the breach in the wire? Blame Kieran for everything? No, not yet. Wait until the roll call of prisoners was finished. Christopher allowed himself a frown for emphasis and said, "You shouldn't have let the Christmas celebration get out of hand, Sergeant."

A bead of sweat ran down Kieran's temple. His hands shook. His face was deathly white, and his eyes were frantic. Christopher decided the man's discomfort was not so much from the dressing down he was receiving as from the weight of demons clawing at his temples. Kieran obviously had a roaring hangover. The sergeant said, "Sir, you okayed the party."

"Yes, but I didn't approve alcoholic beverages," Christopher snapped. "Not for the Germans. Certainly not for our own men. You were supposed to be on duty." The frown turned inward. Had he approved the use of alcoholic beverages? He couldn't remember. All instructions had been oral, hadn't they? Nothing on paper? Then, for the record, it would be better to stick to his story.

"It was just a little friendly nip, sir. In the spirit of Christmas."

Christopher slapped his palm on the desk. "Damn it, man. This is an army post. No one is allowed to drink on duty. You're lucky I don't have you up on charges."

The sergeant shrugged. "Begging your pardon, sir, but the officers were all drinking. Up at the officers' club."

Christopher was irritated by the sergeant's apparent lack of regret, his unwillingness to accept responsibility. Perhaps it was time to show the man just how serious the situation had become. He said heavily, "The officers weren't on duty, Sergeant. You were. Your conduct last night caused a dangerous disruption of camp discipline. Our guard force was already depleted, and now most of the remainder are on sick call. There's debris scattered all over the parade ground.

The Germans refuse to come out of their barracks. I sent four men to the stockade an hour ago to find Oberst Kleber and escort him to my office for an explanation. They couldn't locate him. He's missing. Do you hear me, Sergeant? The highest-ranking German officer in camp, and he's missing."

"Yes, sir," Kieran said. At least he had the decency to wince. Or was it the hangover again?

Angered, Christopher decided to lay the full horror before him. "That's not all," he said. "While you were snoring in your bed, the early patrol found a breach in the wire. Five strands cut at ground level, then mended. It appears Kleber may have slipped through and escaped last night while you were guzzling contraband liquor. How do you explain that, Sergeant?"

That seemed to catch Kieran's attention. He sucked in a bushel of air and started scrambling for high ground. "It isn't my fault, sir. I'm only an enlisted man. There should have been an officer on duty."

Christopher looked up at him sharply. "Are you trying to push the responsibility off on me, Sergeant?"

"No, sir. I was thinking of Captain Dryden, sir. He came to the stockade last night. He stormed in like a Baptist preacher and stopped the party. The party you approved, sir. And he was damned rude about it. He got the Germans all pissed off. If anything went wrong, I'd say it was his fault."

"Don't try to lay the blame on a superior officer," Christopher said. "As it happens, I ordered Captain Dryden down to the stockade myself. With instructions to see that discipline was maintained." As soon as he said it, he was sorry. He hadn't actually given any orders to Dryden. Dryden had gone of his own volition. He tugged at his lip, exploring the ramifications. If only he could remember everything that had happened at the officers' club last night. Too many toddies. He had argued with Dryden mildly. Had he sent Dryden away? Told him to take a few days off to visit his brother? What would happen when Dryden finally returned? Would Dryden back him up?

The sergeant might have noticed Christopher's indecision. He pressed on. "Maybe so, sir. But I'm sure Captain Dryden exceeded your orders. I'll bet you didn't tell him to send our guards off to drink coffee when they should have been patrolling the fences. They can't watch prisoners if they aren't at their posts. If someone cut the wire and Oberst Kleber is missing. I'll bet that's when it happened.''

"Yes, well, of course," Christopher said. "I certainly didn't tell him to pull any guards off the fences. Did he do that?''

Someone rapped on the door. Christopher blinked, fearing it might be Dryden reporting for duty after all. He picked up a handful of papers and shuffled them. "Enter," he called.

A young second lieutenant came in, looking stern. "We've got problems, sir. Bad tally on the roll call.''

Christopher took a deep breath. "How bad? Is Oberst Kleber missing?''

"More than just Kleber, sir. And the Germans refuse to cooperate. I had to send teams into all three compounds to count them in their barracks. The tally is way off. We're short twenty men and four officers.''

Christopher gasped. The papers fluttered in his hands. "So many? Are you sure?''

"We checked every building, sir. And we did roll call three times. Each time it came out the same. Twenty-four men. They're gone.''

Christopher shot a look at Kieran. The sergeant looked wary. Perhaps Kieran was right after all. Perhaps Dryden was responsible for this fiasco. Christopher cleared his throat and asked the lieutenant, "Did you, ah, find Captain Dryden?''

"No, sir. He's not in his quarters.''

Christopher sighed. Thank heavens for that, at least. It might leave room to maneuver. He said, "Did you check with Lieutenant Bennington? He sometimes visits her.''

"No, sir. Not yet.''

"Well, call her. Do it now. Use one of the phones in the outer office. If Captain Dryden is with her, let me know immediately.'' The young lieutenant saluted and backed out of the office.

As soon as the door closed, Kieran said, "There, you see. Dryden's gone AWOL. That proves my point. He knows he's at fault.''

Christopher passed a hand over his eyes. "Not necessarily," he said. "I may have suggested he go. It was to see his

131

brother, I think. If I could just remember where he was going. Was it Dallas? Oklahoma City?"

"You sent Dryden away?"

"Yes. As least I think I did. I was . . . busy . . . last night. Damn it, man, I was hosting a party. I can't remember every little thing I said. But I think I told him to take a couple of weeks off. He must have cut his own papers."

"Did he leave a copy for you?"

"No, none that I've seen."

Kieran grinned. "Then we've got him. Technically, he has to file his leave papers with his superior officer. If he didn't notify you, it doesn't matter whether he cut his own papers or not. He's absent without leave."

A glimmer of hope attended Kieran's words. Christopher gazed at him eagerly. "Do you really think so?"

"Yes, sir," Kieran said. "Twenty-four men missing? We'll have investigators all over this place when word gets out. Heads are going to roll. Wouldn't you like to have Dryden's head ready to serve up on a platter? It might keep them busy for a while."

"I can't entertain a notion like that," Christopher said. "I'm commandant of the camp. The responsibility is mine." He hesitated. "Still, I suppose we must be honest with any potential investigators. It wouldn't hurt to make sure everyone understands Captain Dryden's culpability in this reprehensible situation."

Kieran beamed like a proud father. "That's the ticket, sir."

The lieutenant poked his head back in the door. "Sir, I tried Lieutenant Bennington's house. No answer."

Christopher drew himself up and looked businesslike. "That's too bad. Captain Dryden has been depressed lately. I tried to talk him out of leaving camp. Well, we'll just have to put him on report as absent without leave. See to it, will you, Lieutenant?"

"Yes, sir," the young lieutenant said. Then, "Sir, about the break. Shall we notify the authorities? Call in the FBI?"

Christopher glanced quickly at Kieran. Kieran nodded.

"Yes, I suppose we must," Christopher said. "In the meantime, see if you can scrape up a few men to patrol the roads and search some of the farms. They can't have gotten very far. It will look better if we appear to be doing as much as we can."

Pavel wiped the grease from his hands and grinned at Willi Roh. "You're lying," he said.

Willi plunged his hands under the truck hood and wrestled with a wrench. "No, it's true. I swear it. I was born in Ankershagen, so I know. The ghost appears every year. Not the whole ghost. Just the leg."

A slow-witted Panzer turret master named Basil nodded eagerly. "I believe you, Willi. There are things in this world that we're not supposed to understand." Willi ignored him.

They were working on the truck in the late afternoon sun, nestled between dormant school buses at the back of the building. Willi and Franz Eggers, with Basil's help, had torn the engine down. The radiator, drained and flushed with buckets of water from the school, lay propped in the sunlight. Willi was now deep under the hood, removing the water pump. Parts were scattered in mild disarray around the front of the truck. They'd been at it for a couple of hours.

"Honest," Willi said. "There's this old medieval castle by the lake in Ankershagen." He grunted, struggling with the wrench. "Back in ancient times the castle belonged to a man called Henning von Holstein. He was a terrible man who stole and robbed from everyone. But the Duke of Mecklenburg was ruler of the district, and he started giving people safe-conducts, and von Holstein couldn't steal from them without getting into trouble."

"Sure," Pavel said.

"So von Holstein invited the duke to come to his castle for a visit," Willi said. "He intended to grab the duke, see, and kill him as soon as he was inside the walls. And the duke came. He would have gone in the castle, but a local cow herder warned him and told him what von Holstein was going to do. I know that's what happened, because my Aunt Mathilde told me the cow herder was one of my old-time relatives, a great-great-great-great uncle or something."

Franz Eggers leaned his crooked arm on the fender. "A medieval relative who was a cow herder? I'm surprised. I figured you would claim he was a prince, or a wealthy merchant."

133

"I'm only telling it like it happened," Willi said, hurt. "Besides, no one knows if my great-great uncle could ever have amounted to anything, because he didn't live long enough to find out. After the Duke of Mecklenburg stormed off, von Holstein came roaring out of the castle and grabbed the poor guy and kicked him in the nuts, then roasted him alive."

"And that's when your uncle became a ghost?" Eggers asked.

"No, not my uncle," Willi said heatedly. He waved the wrench. "It's von Holstein who became a ghost. Aren't you listening? See, the Duke of Mecklenburg went home and got his army, and when they came marching back von Holstein could see that there was no way to escape. So he dug a hole under the tower and hid his plunder in it, and then he killed himself. They buried him in the churchyard cemetery. That's when it started. They say von Holstein's leg grows out of the grave one night every year, like a black flower. The same leg he used to kick my uncle in the nuts. The sexton at the church said he once saw the leg sticking up out of the dirt. It was in a long black stocking. Silk, he said. I never actually saw it myself."

"Is the treasure still under the tower?" Basil asked.

Willi looked up in disgust. A long smear of oil trailed from his brow to his cheek. "What difference does it make?" he said. "We're talking about a ghost, not treasure."

"Basil's right," Pavel said. "We'd rather talk about the treasure. There's no profit in ghosts."

Willi thought that over for a moment, then nodded. "As far as I know, the treasure is still there. I never heard of anyone getting rich in our town. Unless it's old man Heidiger, who makes sausages for our district. I guess people have always been afraid von Holstein's ghost will rise up and haunt them."

"It wouldn't be much of a haunt." Pavel scoffed. "Pfui Teufel. One leg? I'd be willing to risk it." He grinned at Franz Eggers. "We're not afraid of a leg in a silk stocking, are we? When this is over, and we get back to Germany, let's go to Willi's town and dig for treasure. The four of us."

Eggers bunched his shoulders. "I'm not sure any of us will ever get back to Germany," he said.

"Oh, I don't know," Pavel said. "Once the mission is over, maybe Oberst Kleber has a surprise in store for us."

Willi's head came up from the engine pit. "A surprise?" he said. "What kind of surprise? Has Oberst Kleber talked to you about the mission?"

"He may have told me a few things. In confidence."

"Well, give, man. Where the hell are we going? Why did he tell us to keep our uniforms? And why the guns? Are we going to fight someone?"

"Yes, there may be a battle," Pavel said. "Perhaps a difficult one. With Schönbeck and Baumhof down it will take full effort from the rest of us to pull it off."

Eggers shifted his crooked arm. "How are they? Nobody has seen them since we got here. Someone told me they were in a special room with that American nurse to tend them. Are they badly hurt?"

Pavel nodded. "Bad enough. Schönbeck's leg is terribly mangled. Baumhof isn't much better. Lieutenant Strikfeldt says he's conscious, but he's having trouble. Neither one of them is likely to be on his feet in time to help us launch the attack."

"I always liked Baumhof," Willi said. "The attack is to happen soon, then?"

"Sooner than you think," Pavel said. "And there may be good news for after. Oberst Kleber says—"

From the front of the nearest bus a youthful voice said, "Who are you guys? What are you doing to the truck?"

Pavel jerked around. Willi's head rose so fast from the engine that he bumped it on the hood. Eggers and Basil froze. Two small boys stood by the bumper of the bus staring up at them. One had an oversized leather mitt dangling from his hand. The other carried a wooden bat and a small white ball.

Pavel switched quickly to English. "Where did you come from?"

One of the boys, the smaller one, pointed east. "Down the road. Jody and me live there. Why are you working on Christmas Day?"

Pavel glanced at Willi Roh, then at Basil and Eggers. None of them spoke any English. All three looked horrified. He made a calming gesture and said to the boys, "Some people are not allowed to rest. Work must be done."

135

"What was that language you were speaking?" the older boy asked.

"You heard us?" Pavel said. He forced a smile. "I see. Well, we were just talking a little nonsense. Practicing. That was French."

"It didn't sound like anything I ever heard," the youth said.

"It was Moroccan French," Pavel said gruffly. "We're from Morocco. Workers from across the sea. We're here to help the American war effort."

"Why are you working in the schoolyard?" piped the littler one. "School's closed."

"We were told to wait at the school," Pavel said. "For truck parts from the next town. More important, why are you here? Little boys are not allowed to come to the school when it is closed."

"Daddy told us to," said the older one. "He doesn't like it when we make noise. Weed and me come here all the time to play."

The smaller boy held up the big leather mitt. "See what I got for Christmas?" he said. "A catcher's mitt. Just like Moe Berg. Jody got a bat. Show him your bat, Jody."

"Yes, both are nice," Pavel said. "I am sorry, little boys. You will have to leave. You cannot play at the school today."

"Why not?" asked the older suspiciously.

"Because that is the rule," Pavel said. "You will have to go home."

The older boy firmed his mouth and took the younger by the hand. "Come on, Weed. Let's go home. Maybe Daddy's feeling better now."

Pavel watched them trudge away from the parking area. "They're going home to their father," he said. "They may tell him about us. We'll have to leave immediately. Put the truck together. I'll warn Oberst Kleber."

Willi looked at Pavel in disbelief. "Immediately?" he said. "Look around you, man. Even if I put the water pump back in without checking it, with such poor tools it'll take at least an hour to put the rest back together."

"We may not have an hour," Pavel said. "Do the best you can. As soon as I've spoken to Kleber I'll come back and help."

He rushed into the building. Several of the soldiers were

136

sprawled in the hallway, grabbing naps. He threaded his way through them, murmuring, "Get up. Get up. Gather your things." A couple of the soldiers snarled back at him, irritated at being awakened, but most of them quietly roused themselves and reached for their knapsacks and weapons.

Pavel stuck his head in the room where the two wounded men were resting on a pallet. Albert Voight was standing guard. The nurse was curled up in a corner near the two injured men, her head cradled in her arm. She looked tired. "Make yourself ready," Pavel told Voight. "We may have to leave soon. Where's Kleber?"

"In the schoolmaster's office with Colonel Waldau and the other officers," Voight said. "What is it? What's wrong?"

"Just get ready," Pavel said.

He bobbed across the hall to a big office and let himself in. Kleber stood over a desk, making marks with a red pencil on his road map. The towering spy from Mexico, Herr Linares, had a ruler and appeared to be measuring distances. Waldau, Grebling, and Strikfeldt watched carefully.

Kleber looked up. "Yes, Pavel? What is it?"

Pavel said, "Sir, two boys. They may be on their way for help. They saw us in back, working on the truck."

"Boys?" Waldau said. "Why didn't you stop them?"

"They were just children," Pavel said.

"How long do we have?" Kleber asked, gathering his map.

"A few minutes, perhaps. They said they live along the road. There's a house about a mile away."

"You were close enough to speak to them?" Waldau snapped. "Good God, man. You should have killed them."

Pavel stiffened. "They were children, sir," he repeated.

"Leave it," Kleber said. "Alert the men. We'll leave at once."

Pavel swallowed. "Sir, we . . . the truck isn't ready. Private Roh says it will take an hour to put it back together."

Kleber folded the map and put it away. "We can't wait," he said. "We'll take one of the buses."

The man from Mexico looked startled. "Wait. You can't do that. A school bus? They're marked with the name of the town. Tucumcari School District. What if someone stops us?"

"We have no choice," Kleber said. "With luck, the risk will be minimal. In less than two hours we leave the highway and turn north. From that point we can resort to dirt roads."

"But you can't abandon the truck," the man insisted. "It isn't fair. The truck is mine. It was part of my agreement."

"Would you rather wait here and be captured?" Kleber asked sourly. "For us it would mean a return to the prison camp. We will have failed in our mission, nothing more. For you, Herr Linares, it would be quite different. They execute spies in America. I'm told they hang them."

The man's hands turned into fists the size of hams and braced against the desk. He didn't look at all pleased with Kleber's decision.

Kleber grunted. "Captain Grebling, ask the mechanics to pick out the most appropriate bus. Make sure the tanks are full. Transfer gasoline from the barrels in the truck, if necessary. If there are no keys, tell them to bypass the ignition wires. We'll leave immediately."

Grebling saluted and hurried away.

"And you, Herr Linares, notify Captain Dryden and his guards and make certain all the men are alerted. Colonel Waldau and Lieutenant Strikfeldt will see to the wounded. Pavel, you and I will go with them for the moment. They'll need your English to talk to the nurse."

They crossed the hall to the makeshift first-aid room. Pavel held the door for the three officers. Albert Voight snapped to attention. The nurse raised a tired but defiant chin from her corner. Kleber glanced at them both, then walked across the room to kneel by the two injured men. Schönbeck didn't move a muscle, but Baumhof, lower chest swathed in gauze, rolled his eyes in apprehension and struggled to lift himself to his elbows. Kleber gestured him back.

Pavel was shocked by the appearance of his two comrades. Baumhof, though conscious, was unnaturally pale. Pavel couldn't understand. The man had suffered only a small puncture wound. But he had apparently lost more blood than anyone had realized last night in the darkness of the road. Schönbeck, lying beside him, looked even worse. He was apparently deep in the protective embrace of opiates. His eyes were closed, and a dribble of saliva trailed down his cheek. His leg looked terrible. The nurse had done her best to clean the wound. A wastebasket beneath the blackboard

138

was mounded with blood-soaked wadding. Even so, the torn flesh around the knee and shin was puckered and festering. A distinct smell rose from the pallet. Fetid, like tainted meat.

Kleber regarded Schönbeck's leg, then smiled down at Baumhof. "How are you, soldier?"

Baumhof gritted his teeth. "I'm ready to go, sir. Please don't leave me. I can make it."

Kleber nodded. "Don't worry, son. We'll do what's best for you." He backed away from the pallet and lowered his voice. "Ask the nurse to come," he said to Voight. "I must talk with her."

Voight grabbed the woman by the arm and jerked her to her feet. She came quietly, too tired to resist.

"Are these men fit to travel?" Kleber asked.

Pavel translated the question, then listened to her weary answer. He looked at Kleber and shook his head. "She says not, Herr Oberst. She claims they both need hospital care. She says the infection in Schönbeck's leg is too advanced. She says it must be controlled with proper treatment or he will lose the leg. And she says Baumhof needs plasma."

Kleber waved his hand in irritation. "Nonsense. Tell her Captain Dryden has already tried that subterfuge."

Pavel repeated the Oberst's objection. The woman said, "Tell him to smell the leg himself. I've been working on it all day. There's nothing more I can do."

Kleber listened to Pavel's hasty translation, then nodded. "Very well," he told Pavel. "Perhaps she is right. Perhaps it would be best to leave them. We'll find a telephone when we reach safety, and either Captain Dryden or the nurse will make an anonymous call and inform hospital authorities of their presence." He swung his chin to the SS Colonel Waldau. "See that these two men are stripped of all identifying materials. Instruct them they are to say nothing to anyone beyond answering basic medical questions. Under no circumstances will they admit that they are escaped prisoners of war, nor are they to divulge any information about the rest of us."

"As you wish," Waldau said.

Kleber's face softened, and he touched Pavel on the arm. "Please thank the woman for all she has done on behalf of our two injured comrades. I know it's been a trying day for her. Tell her we appreciate her efforts. Tell her Lieutenant Strikfeldt will now escort her to the bus."

Pavel translated Kleber's words of gratitude, and the woman nodded, accepting them without emotion or apparent concern. She allowed Strikfeldt to take her elbow and escort her from the room. Pavel and Kleber followed, leaving Waldau and Albert Voight with the two wounded men. As Pavel stepped into the busy corridor he saw Jürgen Frischauer threading his way through milling soldiers with the American captain, Edward Dryden. There was a brief moment in which Dryden's eyes met the woman's across the crowded hallway. Her spine grew straighter and her spirit seemed to return, then Strikfeldt ushered her into a departing stream of men toward the rear of the building.

"I wish to check the bus," Kleber told Pavel. "You keep the men moving."

"Yes, Herr Oberst."

Frischauer waited until Kleber was gone, then pulled Dryden across the hallway. Several men were still gathering their knapsacks and weapons. "What's happening?" Frischauer asked. "Why are we leaving so suddenly? It's still daylight."

"A precaution," Pavel murmured. "We were seen working on the truck. By two children."

"God in heaven," Frischauer said. "Who was dumb enough to work outside without setting up a watchpost?"

"The Oberst felt it best not to post guards," Pavel said. He flushed. "The school is supposed to be empty at this time of year." As he spoke SS Colonel Waldau came out of the first-aid room. He shot a scathing look at Pavel, then marched across the corridor to the principal's office.

Frischauer shivered. "That man has the coldest eyes I've ever seen. What's he mad at now?"

"He's angry with me," Pavel said. "I was there. I had a chance to stop the children and didn't."

Frischauer's rubbery face split in a grin. "You? It was you? Konrad Pavel, the toughest sergeant-major in Africa, let two children sneak up on him? I don't believe it. You've gone rusty."

The hallway was clearing. Pavel shifted uncomfortably. "We were out of sight between two wings of the building. There was no reason to think—"

140

A sharp cry sounded from the first-aid room. It lingered, a note of sheer terror, echoing loudly down the empty corridor.

"Holy Christ!" Frischauer gasped. "What was that?"

"The sick room," Pavel said. "It came from there."

He yanked the door open and plunged into the classroom. Frischauer, dragging Dryden, tumbled after him. Schönbeck lay dead on the pallet in a spreading pool of blood, his throat cut. Albert Voight stood above Baumhof, knife poised at his throat. Baumhof's eyes, wide with horror, swiveled beseechingly toward the three men at the door.

Pavel shrieked, "Good God, man! Have you gone mad?"

Voight glowered at them, then plunged the knife, raking it across Baumhof's throat. Blood gushed from the cut like water from a broken balloon. With a bellow of rage Pavel flew across the room. Frischauer clattered after him. The knife came up quickly, but Pavel kicked it aside. He grabbed Voight and threw him away from the pallet. Voight fell to the floor and scrambled for the knife, but Frischauer rushed in and locked an arm around his throat. He yanked Voight to his feet, then seized him in a bear hug and slammed him against the wall.

Pavel dropped to the pallet beside Baumhof. Death came in seconds. Pavel actually saw the light leave the man's eyes. One moment they were human, questing, filled with pain and confusion. Then they were dull and empty, two staring stones.

Pavel rose, seething. Faces appeared at the doorway, lured by the shouts and sounds of struggle. Voight still squirmed in Frischauer's grasp, but the farmer held him firmly. "Turn him loose," Pavel said. Frischauer looked doubtful but relaxed his grip and stepped back. Voight stumbled to his knees, choking, clawing at his collar. Pavel unslung the machine pistol and primed it. In a voice he scarcely recognized as his own, Pavel snarled, "Explain yourself, man. Have you lost your sanity?"

"Go fuck yourself," Voight muttered.

Pavel pressed the barrel of the machine pistol to Voight's head. "Then meet your maker, you stupid son of a pig."

There was a stir at the doorway as someone elbowed through the stunned clutch of bodies. A deep voice, Oberst Kleber's, roared, "Pavel, stop!"

Pavel's finger was on the trigger. He heard Kleber's voice, but he didn't want to listen. His hand twitched with indecision. Fueled by shock and outrage, he wanted to fire, to send a stream of bullets into Voight's broad face. To blow him to hell.

"That's an order!" Kleber bellowed.

Pavel hesitated. His brain shrieked for justice. He stared at Voight, finger lingering on the trigger. He wanted desperately to tighten his grip and feel the buck of the Schmeisser in his hands. But in the end he was too good a soldier to disobey a direct order. The gun stayed at Voight's cheek a moment longer, then dropped reluctantly to Pavel's side.

"He killed them," Pavel said. "Killed two of our own men."

Kleber pushed Dryden out of the way and stared at the two bodies. He advanced on Voight, white-faced, and said, "Is this true?"

There were more murmurs at the door. Waldau barged through the tangle of horrified gawkers. His quick gaze darted from Kleber to Voight, then to the bodies, taking in everything. "Leave the corporal alone," he said. "He was acting on my orders."

Kleber's body tensed. He swung to face Waldau. His eyes were embers, hot with hatred, burning across the room. His voice, however, was even and measured. He said, "Would you care to tell me why?"

"It was necessary." Waldau said calmly. "You left me no recourse when you decided to leave them behind. The mission comes first. Our ultimate goal is far too important to risk on the semiconscious ramblings of wounded men. One wrong word could finish us."

Kleber's temples throbbed. He was obviously angry, but he held it in. "Someone clean this up," he said. "Private Frischauer, you do it. Use a bucket. Douse this room with water." He studied faces, then jabbed a finger at Erwin Maschmann and Erich Huber. "You two. Find a place to rest our comrades. Use the steam room. Hide them well. We don't want them found before the school reopens." He regarded the cluster of remaining spectators at the door. "The rest of you will continue to the bus. We will leave as soon as all signs of this debacle are cleared away."

The room began to empty. Frischauer hurried off to find a

bucket. Maschmann and Huber made the pallet into a litter and carted one of the bodies from the room. Kleber waited until they were gone, then fixed a look of pure granite on Waldau and said, "From this point on, Standartenführer, you will remember that I am in command. I will make all decisions. Is that clear?"

Waldau gazed at him indifferently. "As you wish."

"As I command," Kleber corrected. He glanced toward the corridor and saw Dryden standing silently in the doorway, watching. Kleber seemed surprised by the American's presence. Even chagrined. He said curtly, "Pavel, take charge of the prisoner. Escort him to the bus."

"Yes, sir," Pavel said. He chucked his chin at Albert Voight. "What about him?" Voight, on his knees by the wall, nursed his throat and flicked a look of intense loathing at Pavel.

Kleber regarded Voight briefly, then said, "The corporal acted under orders. He can't be held accountable. Let him be." Voight's mouth quirked in triumph.

Pavel sighed and slung his weapon. "Yes, sir," he said. He gestured Dryden into the hallway. Dryden didn't move, just kept watching. Pavel stopped a foot in front of him, feet planted. "You have something to say?" he demanded.

Dryden muttered under his breath, "You have some great friends, Pavel. Nazi to the core. You must be very proud."

Pavel's jaw bulged. "You heard the Oberst," he snarled. "Get moving."

Dryden shrugged. "Anything you say, Pavel. We mustn't disobey orders. Follow the leader. Let's be good little robots and do as we're told. Orders are everything."

Pavel shoved him into the hallway and prodded him viciously toward the bus. But it didn't make him feel any better.

143

# EIGHT

The shaggy black dog running in the headlights of the bus had Dryden's full attention, so he missed the question. The dog's delighted barking continued to beat against his eardrums, but Kleber repeated himself, and this time it came through clearly: "You realize, of course, that we had full access to your personnel files."

Dryden nodded. The totality of German knowledge about his private life had been clear to him since Kleber's remark in the truck the night before. He would have known it anyway once the bus turned off the highway west of Cuervo, heading north. Where else could they be going in the middle of a New Mexico nowhere? But stolen personnel files couldn't pinpoint which anonymous private road turned off to the ranch. There was no sign. Out here you already knew the way if you were a friend, and if you were a stranger, you weren't always welcome. Dryden nudged the driver beside whom he was standing, supposedly watching for the turnoff to the ranch gate. Maschmann, that was the man's name. A big burly private. In German, Dryden said sharply, "Stop the bus. That's my dog."

There was no gate in sight, just long stretches of post-and-rail fence lining both sides of the dusty road. Maschmann glanced at Kleber, looking confused. "We are here? But there's no place to turn."

"Stop the bus!" Dryden snapped. "You're going to hit her!"

The dog darted in as if to bite at the right front tire of the school bus. She darted back just as agilely, but Maschmann hit the brakes in a panic, and the bus lumbered to a stop. The dog stopped, too, and regarded the bus uncertainly. She was big, weighing close to eighty pounds, and from the shape of her head and the texture of her coat the Dryden family had always figured she had a fair share of Irish wolfhound in her mongrel mix. She was nowhere near as big as a purebred wolfhound, but she looked formidable.

"Is the dog dangerous?" Kleber asked.

"Her name is Pots," Dryden said impatiently. "She's almost ten years old, and she has bad arthritis. She isn't going to chew up your mighty German soldiers."

"Where is the turnoff to your ranch?" Kleber demanded.

"We already passed it," Dryden admitted. "A quarter mile ago. Open the door and let Pots in. She can ride back with us."

Dryden was in no mood for further bargaining. He hadn't been at all sure he was going to tell Kleber which two-rut track led to the rolling foothill ranch Big Sam Dryden had pieced together in pursuit of a dream. Let the Germans wander through the sprawling Pecos River valley until they ran out of gas, ran out of time, ran out of hope. This country was big enough to swallow them. As the bus bumped past the ranch road only moments before, Dryden had kept his head firmly turned away from Beverly, sitting pale and expressionless two seats behind him. Now, somehow, seeing the old ranch dog appear from the early darkness made Dryden change his mind. Getting Kleber lost was at best only a play for time, and a diversion the German could easily counter through threats to Beverly. Dryden turned to stare at Kleber in the dim dashboard lights, waiting to see if the man would curse him for letting the bus overshoot the turn. Kleber stared measuringly back at Dryden for several heartbeats, then told Maschmann to open the bus door.

Pots retreated two steps and barked. Dryden grinned. Pots never chased cars, but she specialized in chasing any truck that came to the ranch, and here was a marvelous lost bus for her to chase. He knew it was one thing for Pots to happen upon such a wonderful surprise, but it was quite another thing for her quarry to stop and confront her.

"Potsie, girl," Dryden called. "It's me. Been out hunting, girl? Come here, Pots. How's my good old Potsie?"

He could have coaxed the big black dog into the bus sooner had not one of the Germans, a little man called Willi Roh, joined him on the steps of the bus and started crooning to the dog. Pots hung back, even after she recognized Dryden, and started whimpering and wriggling, but she was too exuberant to hold back for long. She bounded past Willi Roh onto the bus, favoring her arthritic left hip, and greeted Dryden with a series of wet kisses that sloshed from his chin to his eyes. Little Willi was the first German to pat her shaggy head. Other hands reached out. Pots shied from the strangers at first, then unpatriotically gave herself over to the enemy, delighted by the attention. As the bus jockeyed and turned and rumbled back to the Dryden ranch turnoff the dog bounded back and forth along the aisle, greeting everyone who spoke to her. The German enlisted men, morose and tense since whispered word had spread among them about the death of the two wounded men at the schoolhouse, finally began to smile.

After the big gate led them off the main dirt road it was another bumpy mile to the ranch house. The main house was dark, of course. So was the bunkhouse, between the main house and the stables. Only the foreman's house was lighted, and before the bus could stop and Kleber could motion for Dryden to precede him to the steps a tall figure with a flashlight had appeared on the front porch. It was Clarence Creighton, Big Sam's longtime foreman, looking puzzled.

Pots dashed out of the bus first. She ran to Creighton, then ran back to Dryden, pausing only to stare at two younger dogs that rushed out of the darkness, telling them to stay back, this bus and its contents were her special prize. Two Germans fell in smoothly behind Kleber and Dryden, and behind them came Erich Huber with Beverly.

"Mr. Dryden!" the foreman called out. "Holy Jesus, is that really you, Mr. Dryden?" His eyes went from the bus to Beverly to the Germans. He looked uneasy at the sight of so many strange men, but the woman, the bouncing dog, and the innocent yellow-and-black school bus seemed to reassure him. A big smile came, and he sang out, "Christmas gift!"

Dryden didn't wait for Kleber to object. He strode forward and embraced the older man. "You got me, pal," he said to Creighton. "I owe you a present."

"Look like you already brought one," Creighton said. He nodded politely toward Beverly. "Is that the pretty lady you wrote me about? I sure hope so. It's time you settled down." Then he lowered his voice. "But all these men. Who in the world are all these men, Mr. Dryden?"

Kleber and all the other Germans stared wide-eyed at the ranch foreman. Clarence Creighton looked every inch the typical rancher. Tall. Lean. Slightly bowed legs encased in faded jeans. Sheepskin jacket. A Stetson tilted back on his graying hair. And he was black. There was a long tradition of black cowboys in the West, but Dryden had counted on the Europeans' initial surprise to give him a chance for a few private words with his father's foreman. He said swiftly, "They're trouble, Mr. Creighton. Germans. We're their prisoners. Be damned careful what you say and do. We'll get our chance."

Kleber recovered before the others. He demanded in German, "Is this man alone? Who else is here?"

Dryden wanted to know, too. He translated Kleber's questions.

"The boys are all off for Christmas," Creighton said. "Shorty and Martinez should be back in the morning, but you can bet Shorty will ride in drunk. We're down now to just them and Old Man Newsom and his grandson. The Newsoms caught a ride to Albuquerque. Family. They're not due back until day after tomorrow." Creighton watched the Germans as he spoke. Quietly, he added, "Reckon I ought to lock up the dogs? These fellows look spooked enough to shoot one of them."

Kleber approved. In rapid order he organized a search of the foreman's house and the other outbuildings to be led by Grebling, then he assigned Bernd Strikfeldt to accompany the foreman to the stables to put away the dogs. He directed Dryden and Beverly to the main ranch house.

Beverly was shivering as they stepped into the front hall

of the big house and Dryden turned on the lights. Kleber apparently noticed Beverly shivering. He said to Dryden, "There is no heat?"

"Sure there is," Dryden said. "A coal furnace. Mr. Creighton just doesn't heat the main house when there's no one in it. The furnace is in the basement. I'll go down and fire it up."

"No," Kleber said. "You will precede us to all rooms and turn on the lights, but one of my men will light the furnace. You will stay within sight at all times. You will touch nothing except the light switches. Do you understand?"

"All too well," Dryden said. He had to admire the German's caution. Like any ranch, Big Sam Dryden's rambling rock house had guns all over it. Dryden remembered a sawed-off .410 shotgun that always leaned in a corner by the back door, loaded, ready for any passing rattlesnake. A twelve-gauge was similarly placed, left over from the days when his mother had raised chickens and frowned upon the eating habits of the local hawks. There was his dad's Colt .45 automatic that lived in a bedside drawer in the master bedroom, ready for burglars. There was Dryden's own Ruger .44 with a 7½-inch barrel, a present on his twelfth birthday, used mainly for target shooting and plinking tin cans. And Little Sam's Smith & Wesson .38, similarly a birthday present and similarly used for target shooting, until the day Sam casually dropped it along with a load of library books in this same hallway and accidentally blew a hole in the front door. Dryden's mother confiscated the pistol, left it in her sewing basket for young Sam to peek at sadly, and left the front door unrepaired until the next cold season to teach Sam a lasting lesson in gun safety.

In closets all over the house were boyhood .22s and deerhunting .30-.30s and other miscellaneous rifles and pistols, not to mention the finer contents of Big Sam's gun case, which was filled with antiques and collector's items like his Winchester lever-action and his Henry .44 and an old Peabody breech-loading rifle and a few modern custom-built sporters, among them a Mauser-action that his dad loved and a custom single-shot modeled on a British Farquharson. There was even a Bowie knife that Big Sam always swore had belonged to Jim Bowie, but no one else in the family ever believed that.

Big Sam's guns were in the living room. The glass case was locked, and judging from the blue fire that leapt into the SS colonel's eyes, the panes of the case wouldn't have lasted ten seconds, so Dryden lost no time fishing the key from a San Ildefonso pot atop the piano. The Germans crowded around, exulting over the guns. The man from Mexico, Herr Linares, saw something he liked even better: an old walnut Philco radio sitting on a sideboard. Linares turned it on and began searching through the static, probably wondering if word of the escape had made any of the evening news programs.

Beverly's guard, Erich Huber, stayed close. She still shivered. The house, unoccupied since Dryden's last home leave, was nearly as cold as the chilly outdoors. Dryden knelt by a copper tub on the hearth and efficiently laid old newspaper, kindling, and piñon logs on the firedogs. Before the Germans finished inspecting the guncase he had a good blaze going. Kleber gestured Beverly to it, then the Germans fanned through the ranch house to look it over.

Dryden stretched out his hands to the fire, using the warmth as an excuse to stand close to Beverly. He gave her a wry look and murmured, "Sorry. This isn't exactly the way I wanted to introduce you to the old family homestead. I had in mind a more private showing."

"Maybe we can come again some day," she whispered back.

Neither Beverly nor Dryden got to enjoy the silence or the fire for long. As Kleber poked through the drawers and papers in Big Sam's desk Willi Roh bounded in from the back of the house and smartly clicked his heels before saluting. "Herr Oberst, there is food!" Willi said excitedly. "Not normal rations like the POW camp. A great cooler off the kitchen! Like a butcher shop. Beef. Venison. Real food!"

Kleber didn't reprimand the little rifleman for interrupting his search of the big rolltop desk. He said, "Excellent, Private Roh. We shall have a proper Christmas yet. Tell Sergeant Pavel to take the nurse and the black man into the kitchen to start cooking. Something that doesn't take long, but something good. Then take two men to the bus and see that the cask of wine from the U-boat is brought into the house. We will feast this night."

Dryden objected. "Miss Bennington and Mr. Creighton

149

aren't servants," he said. "Take food, if you need it, but have your own men cook it."

Waldau came down the stairs from Big Sam's bedroom carrying a confiscated gun, Big Sam's .45 automatic, in his hands. "Loaded," he said. "Every gun in this house has been left loaded. These are violent people." To Dryden he added, "As for you, Captain, you should allow your friends to make themselves useful. It might provide a reason to keep them alive."

In the end it was Dryden who offered to be chief cook. For some odd reason, Clarence Creighton was still at the stables with Strikfeldt, and Dryden was damned if he would have Beverly struggling alone to cook for two dozen hungry Germans in a strange kitchen. Pavel was summoned to act as kitchen guardian, since Waldau and Kleber seemed to think so many knives and sharp utensils might give Dryden ideas. The mouse-sized man, Willi, was assigned to act as helper as soon as he got back with the wine cask, and, to Dryden's surprise, Willi's fellow mouse, Otto Boberach, volunteered to help. Maybe it was Christmas feeling or maybe it was just a means of staying out of everyone else's way. Boberach scarcely seemed to know how to open a can efficiently, but he was a willing worker.

With Willi and Boberach fetching and carrying they assembled potatoes, steaks, canned peas, biscuit makings, canned pears, and fresh apples grown on the ranch. Maliciously, Dryden chose the freshest side of beef in the cooler for the unwelcome dinner guests. The steaks would be tough. Too damned bad for the Germans.

His mother's dining table was temporarily commandeered by Waldau for the growing number of guns the search parties were still turning up. Waldau's underling, the SS Captain Grebling, officiously gave instructions. There would be two menus. One hasty menu for six German enlisted men who would eat early at one end of the table and turn in for a few hours of sleep before taking the first shift of overnight guard duty. Only then was Dryden to prepare a full feast for the remaining Germans. For the early eaters Grebling decreed fried potatoes. The rest, Grebling decided, could wait long enough for baked.

"I'll make the biscuits," Dryden told Beverly. He flashed her a smile. To be able to speak to her, even about potatoes or biscuits, was a welcome change. But the SS captain objected.

"What are you saying?" Grebling asked suspiciously.

"I told her I would prepare the biscuits for your dinner," Dryden said. "On a ranch, all men know how to cook, and we're accustomed to cooking for large numbers of people."

"Ah, at your harvest times," Grebling said.

"Roundups," Dryden corrected in English. He reached to open the flour bin. Grebling beat him to it. He jerked open the bin to inspect it, then moved back fastidiously as a puff of flour floated out. Worth noting, thought Dryden. This particular German had little English and little desire to get dirty. Grebling also seemed to have a fixation about knives. He made Pavel go through the kitchen drawers and count knives and arrange them carefully on a kitchen counter away from the cooking action. When Beverly or one of the German helpers needed a knife the SS captain issued them one, then insisted it be washed and handed back to Pavel as soon as the chopping job was finished.

The fool. Dryden put the first pan of biscuits in the hot oven and gathered heavy iron skillets for the steaks. He set the skillets by the stove, then laid a sharp-tined kitchen fork beside them. Let Grebling keep the knives. One swat in the face with a red-hot skillet and he would be out of commission. The kitchen fork couldn't stab to the heart, but it would be damaging. Dryden worked on, entertaining himself with thoughts of Grebling writhing on the floor, the fork quivering in his chest. It was a pleasant fantasy, but nothing could come of it. Pavel, less careless, watched his every move. And there were too many Germans still ranging through the house.

As Dryden labored to break down the rib and loin sections of the beef side to get at the steaks a cheer went up: Someone had discovered Big Sam's liquor supply in the basement. A half-dozen bottles came through the kitchen. The Germans, unaccustomed to American whiskey, left the good bourbon and chose the indifferent domestic brandy, Dryden noted with pleasure. Other Germans came through carrying stacks of blankets and warm clothing—jackets, hats, boots, woolen socks. Another gathered tins of food, candles, utensils. They seemed to be rifling the bunkhouse as well as the main house. Once there was a sound of breakage from the living room, followed by Kleber's stern rebuke, "Be soldiers! No looting. We are not here to break and pillage. Only to gather supplies for our mission."

Dryden put the skillets on to heat, wondering silently. What mission? What the hell were the Germans after? And why his ranch? When Clarence Creighton, his gray-haired black foreman, finally came back to the ranch house and was pressed into service in the kitchen to help them, Dryden was presented with one of the first pieces of the puzzle, and a new worry.

"Mr. Dryden," Creighton said softly as he measured coffee into the huge percolator, "that damned German officer sure is interested in our horses. He acts like he maybe knows something about horseflesh. He spotted Southern Starr in a loose box, and he all but sang him a song."

"Strikfeldt? What did he say?"

"I'm damned if I know. He wasn't talking English or Spanish, and that's as far as I stretch. But I like to never got him out of Starr's box. I thought he was going to spend the night in there. He didn't pay too much attention to Starrs and Bars, and Shorty rode out on old Quantrill, but Shorty and Martinez are due back by chore time tomorrow, and drunk or sober, Shorty always turns up. What'll that German fellow say when he sees Quantrill?"

"You think they're after our horses?"

"Sure looks that way to me," the foreman said.

Dryden made a soft shushing sound. Grebling approached the stove. Dryden flipped a drop of water onto a skillet to test its heat, half hoping it would splatter on the SS captain.

"When will the food be ready?" Grebling asked.

Dryden said, "The first shift can eat in about fifteen minutes, the rest in about forty-five. There's nothing left here but to wait for the potatoes. I should go to the dining room now to set the table."

"What about the meat?" Grebling objected. "You haven't even started to cook it yet." Though the Germans had eaten well in the prison camp, Dryden could see that the big steaks, home-grown like so much on the ranch, were a strange and beautiful sight to the captain.

"The steaks will only take five minutes. They should be served the moment they come off the skillets."

"Very well, but you stay," Grebling said. "The woman must set the table."

"She doesn't know where the plates and silver are," Dryden said stuffily. "You should have Sergeant Pavel tell the first shift of men to be ready to dine. In addition, Lieutenant Bennington should change her clothing. As Oberst Kleber observed, her uniform is not heavy enough for this freezing weather. Clothing of my mother's will fit her. Now is the best time. She will be occupied once the men begin to eat. I will tell her where to look. One of your men, of course, may accompany her."

Dryden won. The hypnotic spell of the steaks surely helped. Grebling told Pavel to go out and alert the early shift that they would soon be called to the table. The bumbling little man, Boberach, had no chores at the moment, so Grebling assigned him to go with Beverly. As soon as Pavel left the room, taking his better command of English with him, Dryden seized the seconds he figured he had to speak to Beverly.

"Upstairs, third door on the right, there's a sewing room off a bedroom," he said quickly. "My mother's things are there. Change into something warm. Be sure to forget something vital. A sweater, maybe. Something you'll have to go back for. I want you to look in a big blue sewing basket. There should be a revolver there. Loaded. Don't take it. Just check the basket. Later we'll go back for it."

Beverly may have straightened too alertly. Grebling, listening to the murmured English from across the room, looked alert, too. Beverly chose to laugh. "Why don't I forget something really interesting?" she gurgled. "How about my panties?"

"What is this? What are you saying?" Grebling puffed.

"Lieutenant Bennington asks if there is warm underclothing she may wear," Dryden said. "I don't know the precise word in German, but what she requests specifically in English is 'hot panties.' *Unterwäsche?*"

Grebling's face reddened. He may have known the English words, Dryden decided. Odd, the words one picks up first in a foreign language. Grebling sent Beverly and Boberach on their way, then accompanied Dryden to the dining area to see to the table.

Dryden pondered. Where was the good silver? Better yet,

153

where was the regular silver? This was Christmas night, but there was no need to pull out the plugs for a house full of enemies. The regular silver was tarnished, but Dryden didn't let that bother him. As he laid plates his eyes counted the weapons heaped on the other end of the table. He saw his own Ruger .44 and Big Sam's Colt .45 automatic among the welter of rifles and shotguns. Then his heart sank. There, two rifles to the left of his Ruger, was the Smith & Wesson .38 he had last seen in his mother's blue sewing basket. Little Sam's confiscated target pistol. He had sent Beverly on a futile errand. One more half-baked plan down the drain.

Could he work his way closer to the guns? He walked along the table, dealing plates, but Grebling had no intention of letting him near the guns. The SS man looked contemptuous as Dryden folded napkins and rattled silver, but what he clearly regarded as sissy behavior didn't lull him into sufficient carelessness. Then Pavel, with his watchful eye and his cradled MP-40 machine pistol, came back from his errand to join Grebling.

Another chance lost. Dryden found bowls for the canned pears and regarded his arrangement of plates and silver. To his eyes, the array of guns at the far end looked a hell of a lot better. Through the open double doors from the living room, raised voices greeted the opening of the wine cask from the U-boat. Even the sounds of gaiety didn't draw Pavel or Grebling away from their posts. That was left for the SS colonel, Waldau, who a moment later hurried through the doors.

"Cognac glasses. At once," he snapped to Dryden. To Grebling he breathed, "My God, the Moselle is Bernkasteler Doktor. Would you believe it? Some of the men with lesser palates prefer the California cognac. I shall be the last person to dissuade them. Come, Grebling, and join the toast."

Grebling gestured toward the guns. He said, "Sir, I dare not."

"Have Captain Dryden come with you to bring the glasses. You come too, Pavel. Join us. Quickly, please. Bernkasteler Doktor. The elegance. The delicacy. An astonishing wine."

Brandy glasses were in short supply. Dryden supplemented them with tequila glasses. Who would care about the difference? He carried the glasses into the living room

154

on a tray and passed them out to the score of eagerly waiting Germans, then backed to the door, standing out of the way. He wanted no part of the German celebration. But Kleber kept it simple. The commanding officer raised his glass, and, when all other glasses lifted, he said quietly, "To our loved ones."

Waldau frowned slightly, perhaps preferring a toast to his Führer, but a dreamy smile came over his face as he sipped the wine. He sat down at the piano. Two voices called out simultaneously, one for a patriotic song and one for a Christmas carol. The SS colonel shook his head. He fingered the keys, then lightly, smoothly played a few bars of a waltz from *Der Rosenkavalier,* as gay and elegant as his wine. The Germans roared approval.

The wine and brandy tipped back and forth, not enough to get anybody sloshed but certainly enough to make them all mellow, and Waldau drifted into a medley of cabaret tunes that drew more than a few of them to the piano to join in lusty song. They seemed to have forgotten, at least for the moment, the fate of their two companions at the schoolhouse. Grebling downed his wine nervously and hooked a chin at Pavel, indicating it was time to corral Dryden and return to kitchen chores.

Dryden was still shaking his head as he followed Pavel into the kitchen. A pitiless SS killer who was devoted to delicate wines and Strauss waltzes? Men who could overlook the needless death of comrades and melt into maudlin reveries over a few tinkly beer-hall tunes? Big Sam would have turned red in the face and roared them all out of his house. So why didn't Big Sam's youngest and favorite son do something about it?

The reason was waiting in the kitchen. Beverly was back, dressed in dark blue woolen slacks and a bright red sweater. A warm-looking jacket that Dryden didn't recognize hung over the back of a kitchen chair, sending a strong odor of mothballs to mix with the aroma of two broiled ribeyes that the kitchen helpers, Willi Roh and Otto Boberach, were wolfing down at the kitchen table.

"Asses!" Grebling exploded. "Dryden and the woman are to taste everything first. Do you not care that the food may be poisoned?"

Willi's fork halted on the way to his mouth. He looked

apprehensive. Boberach didn't. Whether he had been at the cooking sherry or found courage elsewhere, he said, "Nonsense, Captain. We have watched and helped in all preparations. The food is wholesome."

"That may be," Grebling said. "Even so, it is not your place to eat now. The early guard unit was to have been served first."

"As assistant chefs, we may sample all foods. That is the way an American ranch kitchen works. Herr Creighton told us so."

Grebling shot an angry look at the black foreman, leaning quietly against the kitchen counter, Stetson tipped forward over his eyebrows. "How?" Grebling demanded. "He speaks no German."

"Cuisine is a language of and by itself," Boberach said grandly.

The argument was going so well that Dryden risked a whispered moment with Beverly. "So what did you forget?" he asked. He stared longingly at her full breasts. "Not your bra, I see."

"I forgot the matching cardigan for this sweater, you lecher," she whispered back. "They're a set. I couldn't find the gun. I found two pairs of scissors and about a half-dozen hatpins. I hid them in the towel drawer by the sink. But damn it, no gun."

"I know," he said. "Dad must have moved it. Anyway, the Germans found it first. It's out on the dining table."

Grebling told Willi Roh and Boberach to finish their meals quickly. Dryden forked six more steaks onto the hot skillets. The party continued in the living room while the six men assigned to early guard duty eagerly trooped to the dining table for their meal.

When the first shift finished eating Dryden went to clear the table and found that the guns had all been moved to some unknown site. He shrugged to himself, put in the table's extra leaves, and set more plates. Grebling bustled officiously, like a maitre d' in a grand hotel. A word in his colonel's ear. A word in the ear of Oberst Kleber. Through the open doors Dryden heard the party grind to a halt, heard Kleber call for attention, then say, "Finish your wine and cognac, gentlemen. Captain Grebling has overseen the prep-

156

aration of excellent food. We shall feast, then everyone will go early to well-earned rest. Tomorrow will be a busy day.''

For Dryden the next two hours were busy. None of the rest of the Germans were shy or slow about eating. After that there was kitchen cleanup and time to grill the best steaks for Beverly and Creighton, then Kleber came with crisp requests: Make more biscuits for the next morning, bring more apples from the barrels in the basement, put big beef roasts in the oven to cook slowly all night. Pavel brought two new Germans to help.

Soon all the work was done. Most of the enlisted men, gorged on food and wine, had already been sent happily to the bunkhouse to sleep. Pavel dismissed the rest, then escorted Dryden, Beverly, and Creighton to the living room, where two guards, Jürgen Frischauer and Erwin Maschmann, awaited them. Outside Dryden could see another guard pacing the front porch as if it were a crenellated watchtower.

"Here are blankets, pillows, and the divan for Lieutenant Bennington," Pavel said. His little speech sounded rehearsed. "The officers have taken the bedrooms. There are only the big chairs for you and the cowboy, but Oberst Kleber hopes you will be comfortable. You will sleep now."

Dryden said, "How about five minutes for a cigarette in front of the fire, Pavel? We've been working our asses off all evening while you and your Nazi playmates have been enjoying Christmas cheer."

Pavel looked apologetic. He glanced at the brandy bottles on the piano. Four were left. "You wish a glass of cognac before you sleep?"

"We wish," Dryden assured him.

"I will so instruct the guards. Then you will sleep," Pavel said.

The big German sergeant even went back to the butler's pantry for cognac glasses before going upstairs, presumably to seek his own bed among the officers. Dryden raised his glass to Beverly and Creighton. "At last," he said. "I can introduce the two of you properly. Miss Beverly Bennington, Mr. Clarence Creighton. I'm sorry as hell I got both of you into this mess. But here's to a better Christmas next year."

Beverly looked as if she would like to snuggle closer, but the German guards were staring at them. She inched out her hand to Dryden instead. "Point me to a machine gun, and I'll end this Christmas real fast," she whispered. "I'm so goddamned mad, I could kill them all. Pardon my language, Mr. Creighton."

"The language sounds fine to me," Creighton said. "I like the part about machine guns, too."

Frischauer rattled his Schmeisser and stalked over to them. "The orders were to drink and smoke, not talk," he said.

Dryden raised hostile eyes. "Excuse me, private. I don't think you really want to interrupt us just now."

Frischauer bunched his eyebrows, perplexed. "What do you mean? Why should I not interrupt you?"

"It wouldn't be prudent," Dryden said. "As it happens, the three of us were just discussing the note you left with Miss Bennington two days ago, when you asked for a meeting with me. If we argue now, officers might come. I'd have to tell them what we're talking about."

Frischauer glanced over his shoulder at the other guard. His voice was lower and tinged with panic when he answered. "The note told you nothing!" he hissed. "Nothing at all. I'm a good soldier."

"Nothing?" Dryden said. "I seem to recall a mention of something called the Christmas Project. And a Herr Heisenberg. I'm sure Colonel Waldau would be interested in how I came to know of such names."

Frischauer's leathery face creased, and he squared his shoulders. "I admit nothing," he said. "I told you nothing. Nevertheless, in the spirit of Christmas, you may have a brief conversation. Five minutes, no more." He withdrew and stood by the other guard, looking edgy.

Puzzled by the rapid exchange of German, Beverly said, "What was that all about?"

"I just bought us a few moments of privacy," Dryden said. "And maybe some help later, when we make our move."

Creighton's eyes flashed. "Now you're talking my language. What about it, Mr. Dryden? We gonna do anything soon?"

"Not yet, Mr. Creighton," Dryden said. "We're too damned outnumbered at the moment. Give it time. We're playing on home court. They're not. We'll get our chance."

Beverly closed her eyes with a tired sigh. "Why do you two keep calling each other 'Mr.'?" she said. "Don't you like each other?"

Dryden grinned. "You'd have to ask Mr. Creighton that," he said. "All I know is, I used to be 'Eddie' to him, and he was always 'Clarence' to me. I grew up riding a pony three feet behind him, like a calf following momma. Then on the day my dad died, I suddenly became 'Mr. Dryden.' "

"That's the day you stopped being a snot-nosed kid and had to start being boss," Creighton said. "It seemed the right thing to do."

"Yeah, well, things have changed," Dryden said. "Under the circumstances, maybe we could go back to being 'Clarence' and 'Eddie.' "

Creighton mulled it over, then shook his head. "It just wouldn't seem right," he said.

Dryden sighed. "I'm never going to be the man my daddy was, Mr. Creighton. Maybe you should quit trying."

"The score's not ready to add up yet," Creighton said. "I got a feeling you're about to be tested." He looked at the two guards. "What's this all about, anyway? What do these Germans want?"

"That's the problem," Dryden said. "We don't have the faintest idea."

In the quiet hours of morning, while it was still dark, Dryden jerked upright in his chair, ears straining. Outside Pots howled from the stable. As if in reply, from the front road a human voice howled, *"Siete Leguas, el caballo, que Villa mas estima-a-ba-a-a-a-a-a-a."*

"Oh, Christ," Dryden said. "It's Martinez."

"No, that's Shorty," Creighton said.

Dryden checked his watch. It was barely past five in the morning. The German guards must have been dozing. Frischauer stumbled sleepily to his feet and yelped, "What is it? What is happening?"

Outside the howling voice disagreed with Dryden's watch: *"Como a las seis de la tarde silvan la locomoto-o-ra-a-a-a-a,"* it sang. Pots howled louder, frustrated at not being able to rush out in greeting. The other two dogs were barking. Feet hit the stairs. Konrad Pavel, dressed only in a long woolen shirt and socks, rushed into the living room carrying his pants and boots. Within seconds, trousered if not fully dressed, Kleber and Linares came charging in.

Kleber fumbled his gun from a loose holster. "The other men?" he asked Dryden swiftly. "They are returning at this hour?"

"Right on time for chores," Dryden said. He hastily laced his own shoes. Home-court advantage gave him the right words. "Listen to me, Kleber, and listen fast. I'm going out there, and I'm going to send those men away. Mr. Creighton is coming with me. They're drunk, but they're accustomed to taking orders from him."

"They are armed?" Kleber said.

"It wouldn't surprise me," Dryden said. "Plenty of animals around here are night hunters."

Kleber nodded to himself. "You will disarm them and bring them inside."

"No," Dryden said.

There wasn't much light in the room. One lamp, and a red glow from the embers in the fireplace. Kleber stared somewhat uncertainly at Dryden, then gestured at Beverly and said firmly, "You will do precisely as I say. Your mind is misted by sleep, Captain Dryden. Kindly remember I have hostages. Not only Miss Bennington, but also the *schwarze Neger* cowboy."

"Then kill them," Dryden said. "Kill us all." He was glad Beverly didn't speak German. "Kill them, kill me, then try to kill the two men outside. Even drunk they'll give you a run for your money. Do it now."

"You . . . you have lost your senses," Kleber said.

"No. Those two men leave, and they live. They're extra baggage. If I bring them in here, they'll die anyway. Your shithead SS colonel will see to that. Just as he's already killed two of your own people. Just as he's no doubt planning to kill the three of us. So be a man, Kleber. Kill us yourself."

"I have no wish to harm innocent people," Kleber said.

"Then make damned sure nothing happens to those two men. Let me give them some good excuse and send them away. And promise me no harm will come to Lieutenant Bennington and Mr. Creighton. Or everything stops. Right now."

The embers in the fireplace popped and settled. Kleber

160

glanced toward the sound. His head still turned, he said to Dryden, "They will leave if you speak to them?"

"Why not? It's the Christmas season, remember? Eat, drink and be merry. They'll be glad to have some extra time off."

"I must be certain you say nothing of our presence," Kleber warned. "I will have to send one of my men with you."

"Send Pavel," Dryden said. "He speaks English. Or send your spy from Mexico."

There was a sound from above, Waldau and Grebling coming toward the staircase. Kleber said quickly, "I will send both. Go!"

Dryden grabbed one of the brandy bottles and Clarence Creighton's arm. Pavel and Linares hastened after them. Dryden was out the front door and explaining the agreement hastily to Creighton before Shorty, having started a second rendering of the ballad of Pancho Villa's favorite horse, could get the Bracamontes Brigade into formal battle again at the Irapuato train station. Creighton hollered loudly, "Okay, Shorty, shut up that damned caterwauling."

All was darkness. Then, dimly, plodding up the two-rut road, Dryden could see two horses and riders. One rider slumped silently in the saddle. That would be Martinez. Liquor always made him morose. The other rider was all but reclining on the back of William Clarke Quantrill, sire of both Southern Starr and Starrs and Bars, out of Belle Starr; Quantrill, the big bay quarter horse found by Dryden's father in a calf lot in Colorado when he was already eight; Quantrill, the most prolific sire of the Dryden line, now a beloved nineteen-year-old still going out on toots with his best friend, an Hispanic cowboy named Shorty.

Dryden called, "Get your butts up here, you mangy sons of bitches. Come have a drink to congratulate me. I've brought my bride home! I'm married!"

"Boss?" The little figure lolling on the big horse made an effort at straightening up. "That you, boss? Well, fry my fanny! Hurry up, Martinez, that's the boss! El patrón is home!"

In the bilingual confusion that followed it took Creighton to explain the presence of the two strangers standing behind them. "These are Mr. Dryden's best men," he lied blandly.

"He couldn't wait for no one from the ranch, since he's got to get back to the army soon, so he had to choose two friends to stand in for us. And his bride chose two maids of honor, too. They're all here. The whole bridal party, taking up every bedroom in the big house. They've got me chaperoning, 'cause young Mrs. Dryden is too busy just now. What with being newly married and all." He smiled, only his white teeth showing in the darkness.

Dryden was busy blinking away fat tears that had welled in his eyes. Quantrill remembered him. The big bay dropped his muzzle to Dryden's hand and snorted, then delicately bit him on the shoulder.

Creighton passed the bottle around. Shorty and Martinez drank gratefully. Dryden wiped his nose on his sleeve like the awkward kid he'd been when Quantrill first came to the ranch, and took a pull, then remembered to pass the bottle back to his "friends," Pavel and Linares.

Martinez had perked up after his moment with the full brandy bottle. He said to Creighton, "The bride—a beauty?"

Creighton nodded. "Hair like midnight, skin like a lily, voice like a song."

"A dove," Shorty crooned. "A dove to share the lonely nest. Let us meet this dove."

"Not today, boys," Dryden said. "You're going to take the rest of this bottle, and you're going to ride back to whatever party or honky-tonk you've been to, and you're not going to come back for a full week. A week off, boys! Our other friends are going on today, and then Mrs. Dryden and I want to be alone."

Shorty would have objected. He was determined to meet Dryden's lovely bride. But Creighton said, "It's honeymoon time, Shorty. Don't nobody even want me around, but someone's got to stay to look after the stock. Reckon Mr. Dryden won't have much time for that himself."

The bottle went around once more to accompany the inevitable lewd remarks about newlyweds, then Martinez took the brandy bottle firmly in hand and turned his horse around. He wasn't much better mounted than Shorty. Dryden saw that Martinez was riding Toothache, a Quantrill grandson his father had bought back after the young horse was lamed on the rodeo circuit. Dryden worried about both

162

horses, one gimpy and one too old, as the two hands rode away. But he knew they'd be well cared for. Shorty felt about Quantrill the way Pancho Villa must have felt about Siete Leguas.

A duet floated back as Shorty and Martinez left. *Cucuru-cucu-u-u-u-u, paloma. Cucurucucu-u-u-u-u-u, no llores*. The white dove comes. Don't cry now, lonely dove.

# NINE

Waldau's startled face screwed up in puzzlement. " 'Nuts'? What means this 'Nuts'?"

The whole household was up early, thanks to Shorty's pre-dawn serenade. While Dryden made coffee Linares had turned on the radio and found an Amarillo station, and its early news brought every German in the big house to a state of alarm. The Battle of the Bulge had turned against the German Panzer divisions. The radio announcer was crowing about some brief exchange between Brigadier General Anthony McAuliffe, the acting commander of Bastogne, and Fifth Panzer emissaries demanding surrender of the town. McAuliffe had become an immediate media hero by replying to the surrender terms with one word of American slang, "Nuts!" Now the stranglehold around Bastogne was broken. As of Christmas Day, the day before, Patton's Third Army tanks had broken through and relieved the beleaguered garrison. The entire German advance had been halted after only eighty kilometers. German troops were retiring in confusion.

It was bad news for the Germans, and word spread quickly as guards on the porch called to their friends. By the time the announcer moved to local news the full complement of enlisted men had streamed in from the bunkhouse, buttoning shirts and whispering about the collapse of the offensive. The local news also made them uneasy: A Texas POW camp had released an announcement about a "small" breakout; three men were reported to have wandered away from a prisoner-of-war camp in McLean but were expected to be caught momentarily. In the meantime, citizens were asked to be on the lookout and report any suspicious parties to local authorities. The whispers broke out anew. Only three men? Could the Americans be unaware of the full-scale size of the escape? Or was this a trick to lull them into a false sense of security?

Dryden knew it was more likely that the number had been pared drastically for public consumption in order to avoid panic, but he didn't say so to anyone. He assessed the murmuring troops silently. Yesterday's brief Christmas cheerfulness had evaporated. Waldau wore an expression of grim disapproval, perhaps because the two ranch hands had been allowed to depart unscathed, and his disapproval was matched by uneasy looks from the men toward him and Voight. They were clearly thinking about the deaths of their comrades the day before, and wondering if the war news meant the two men had died for nothing. After all, if von Rundstedt's last-ditch Ardennes offensive had failed, then total collapse of German troops and defenses was sure to follow. It was only a matter of time. The Allies commanded the air. German troops were exhausted and demoralized. And if the end was in sight, was there any reason for them to go on?

Kleber seemed to make up his mind about something. He nodded, apparently to himself, and stepped in front of the fireplace. Dryden expected him to call on the kitchen crew for breakfast to cheer up the men, but Kleber called for attention instead.

"Men, I have told you this would be for you a busy and interesting day. It is also an important day. Now more than ever. Our homeland is in jeopardy. Our comrades need us. Today you will learn the true purpose of the Christmas Project."

Dryden's ears came to a point. He gestured silently for Beverly and Creighton to sit still. He wanted to listen, and he had no intention of moving unless someone insisted.

165

Fortunately, no one did. Kleber looked at him full in the face and apparently decided he had a right to hear. Or the need.

"Our mission is vital to the survival of the Fatherland," Kleber said ponderously. "If we are not successful, our homes and our families may well vanish in a rain of fire and destruction. So that you will fully understand the complexity of our mission and the peril that awaits our loved ones, I call upon Herr Boberach to address you. Please be seated. Everyone. Herr Boberach?"

The little man looked less comfortable in the spotlight than he had in the kitchen the night before. A few of the Germans drew dining-room chairs close to the double doors. Others squatted or sat on the floor. Boberach touched a trembling finger to his lips. "I . . . I should have a blackboard," he said.

"You do not need one," Kleber told him. "These are soldiers, not university students. Kindly begin."

Boberach said hesitantly, "Well, ah. Yes, ah. Yes, well, I should start with something that occurred in Germany. In 1938, the year before the war began, a remarkable thing happened. One of my German colleagues, Otto Hahn, working at the Kaiser Wilhelm Institute in Berlin, split a uranium atom with a bombardment of neutrons. It was the first atomic fission ever to take place under observable laboratory conditions."

The atom? The men looked puzzled. Dryden translated quietly for Beverly and Creighton, but he was just as puzzled himself.

Boberach's voice gained strength as he charged on. "Consider the implications," he said. "As each atom splits it throws off fragments, fragments that can then collide with other atoms, causing more separations. It might be possible, through a kind of instantaneous chain reaction, to shatter billions of atoms, to split them apart in a microsecond. The release of energy would be enormous."

Boberach happily droned on . . . actonide elements . . . radium, thorium, and uranium . . . new atoms of barium. By now the German enlisted men were looking at one another. Boberach was losing them. The little scientist sounded excited, but his excitement hadn't translated to their understanding. Boberach must have seen it. He stopped, thought, then started again.

"Word of Hahn's remarkable accomplishment stunned scientists around the world. Within two weeks speculation had begun—in Germany, in England, in America, Russia, Japan, everywhere—that a bomb might be possible, harnessing the energy of atomic fission. An incredible bomb. Unlike anything the world has ever known."

Mention of the bomb did it. An excited buzz began among the soldiers. Bombs were something they understood. Or thought they did.

"By September of 1939, Kurt Diebner's new War Department took over German fission research. The War Office moved a team of scientists into the Kaiser Wilhelm Institute of Physics, and the German atomic bomb project was well begun. The project was placed in the hands of one of our more exceptional young physicists, Werner Heisenberg. He assembled . . ."

Dryden looked up sharply. There was the other shoe. First "Christmas Project." Now "Heisenberg." He glanced at Jürgen Frischauer and saw recognition and relief dawning slowly. The big farmer took a deep breath and returned Dryden's gaze. So much for blackmail threats, his calm face seemed to say. How would Dryden convince anyone now that he had heard the two names before this meeting?

"We were well ahead of the rest of the world," Boberach continued with a trace of bitterness. "Unfortunately, some of Germany's finest atomic physicists were no longer available to us. Brilliant men and women. People like Albert Einstein, Hans Bethe, Otto Frisch, Lise Meitner, Rudolf Peierls, Victor Weisskopf. They were respected companions in our small community of atomic scientists, people who had once worked side by side with us at German universities. But they were cursed by an accident of birth."

"They were Jews," a loud voice interrupted contemptuously. Waldau. Of course.

"Yes, Jews," Boberach said. "And they were hounded from our country by intolerance. Men and women who could have helped the Fatherland, forced to migrate to England and America. Even Nobel laureates. Our universities lost more than a hundred trained physicists when the Reichstag passed the anti-Jewish Civil Service Law in 1933. German science, once the envy of the world, was radically altered by the stroke of an anti-Semitic pen.''

Albert Voight, taking his lead from Waldau, said, ''Germany is better off without them. Jews are subhuman. Everyone knows it.''

The Germans near Voight hissed and catcalled. They didn't dare hiss Waldau, and Dryden knew the propaganda-fed German mind well enough to know that the soldiers wouldn't ordinarily have defended Jews, but they seemed to welcome a chance to curse Voight and, by implication, Waldau.

Boberach gazed around the crowded room. ''We worked hard in Germany, trying to solve the riddle of atomic fission. But the Führer has not seen fit to give us the financial and physical resources we need. He appears to be more interested in miracle weapons like the V-1 and V-2 rockets. As a result, our project is still far from bearing fruit.''

''Faugh!'' Waldau said. ''Are we to listen to this? Get on with it. Explain why we are here.''

''Yes, continue,'' Kleber said sternly to Boberach. But he leveled at Waldau a look so antagonistic that it may have salved the antagonism of the restive audience. The men grew hushed.

Boberach nodded solemnly. ''We knew the British and the Americans might also be probing the military potential of atomic fission. By 1940 we were certain. The names of prominent physicists began to disappear from the pages of international journals. Within months we noticed an absence of research findings from metallurgists, chemists, and mathematicians as well. Where British and American scientists had once written and published with great frequency, suddenly no papers appeared. It was inconceivable that all Allied atomic research had ended. The only answer was that a mutual conspiracy of silence had choked off all findings. And there was only one possible reason for such silence. We scientists, if nothing else, know how to draw inferences. Peculiarly, the British and Americans had given themselves away through their very insistence of secrecy.''

Boberach was speaking so fervently now that Dryden no longer bothered to translate. He was too engrossed in what the man was saying.

''The realization that our enemies were working on an

168

atomic device caused great concern," Boberach said. "At the time Germany's forces were consistently victorious, winning battle after battle, but we knew all would be lost if the Allies were allowed to complete their device before our own. So, with the Führer's permission, we enlisted the aid of our intelligence organizations. We provided them with key information—the scientists most likely to be involved, the various types of large equipment needed for experimentation, the universities and institutions where such equipment might be found, the massive stores of chemicals and radioactive elements necessary."

Boberach had everyone's attention now. Even Linares looked keenly attentive. Boberach continued, "The Americans were working under a heavy curtain of secrecy and covered their movements well. It took almost two years, but our people finally managed to trace portions of the combined British and American atomic effort to three locations in this country. Two of these—a huge installation in a place called Oak Ridge in Tennessee and another in Hanford, Washington—we determined to be specialized plants for isotope separation. The crippling of either might well delay progress on the atomic device. But it was the third location that interested us the most. The Americans also purchased a small boys' school hidden on a plateau in the mountains, most difficult of access, a place called Los Alamos, near Santa Fe, and moved the teachers and the boys away."

Dryden's eyebrows shot up. He almost called out, *"What? Say that again?"* But he realized he had no formal place in this classroom. Had he missed a line? No, Boberach was still talking.

"This place, called Site Y by the Americans, is the area where most of the scientists on our lists—American, British, refugees from occupied countries, our own disenfranchised Germans—have vanished. We know very little about it, except that it has grown enormously in the past two years. Our agents estimate that there are as many as two thousand technicians and scientists living on the Los Alamos plateau, concentrating their efforts on the successful development of the atomic device."

Beverly, concerned by the look on Dryden's face, whispered "What is it? What is he saying?" Dryden gestured abruptly, begging for silence. He didn't want to miss a beat.

169

Boberach didn't raise his voice, but a note of despair captured the full attention of the German listeners. He was nearing the end of his story, and it was obvious that what he had to say frightened him. "The Americans are thought to be very close," he murmured. "Unless someone stops them, they may soon be able to ferry an atomic device by boat or by airplane to Germany and crash it into our cities. It would be an explosion such as no man has ever seen. Consider this: A flight of two hundred American B-17s can carry and drop two thousand tons of high explosive in a single day. They can lay waste large portions of a city. We've seen it happen in Allied bombing raids. But if the atomic device is perfected, one plane, one alone, carrying only one bomb filled with a few hundred pounds of purified uranium, could completely devastate a city, causing as much destruction as twenty thousand tons of regular high-explosive bombs. It would take ten flights of two hundred planes each, as many as two thousand American bombers, a constant stream, to drop an equivalent amount of ordinary bombs. A city could disappear. Vanish in an instant."

A stunned hush fell. Soldiers looked at each other. One, little Willi Roh, raised a hand shyly and said, "Not Frankfurt."

Boberach nodded firmly. "Every building, every stone."

"But not Berlin," Franz Eggers said.

Boberach said, "Possibly. If the bomb were big enough, Berlin could become a desert. Every man, woman, and child would vanish. Every tree. Every dog and cat. Every canary. Boiled to vapor in miniseconds."

"But that isn't warfare," said another. "That's slaughter."

Kleber rose to stand beside Boberach. "Yes, it is," he said. "Now you know the urgency of our mission. We must attack and stop this bomb. Or at least delay it until it no longer represents a threat to the Fatherland. We have no choice."

The Hitler Youth corporal who had spent so much time ogling Beverly apparently didn't like the idea. He blurted, "But there will be security forces. Surely they would not leave such a secret unprotected."

"Yes, there will be security forces," Kleber said. "But they will not be expecting us. If necessary, we will fight our way to prospective targets. Key scientists. Equipment. Stores of purified uranium. We will destroy them. We will do our duty. Then we will withdraw."

Rumbles rose from the ranks. It was beginning to sound too much like a suicide mission. Kleber placated them with outstretched palms and said smoothly, "There's good news as well. The Führer recognizes the importance of our mission and has done everything in his power to guarantee our survival. The U-boat that brought us weapons will be waiting off the coast of Mexico in ten days. After we complete our assault we will break into small teams and make our way south. Those who reach the rendezvous in Mexico will be taken aboard the U-boat for a victorious journey home. You will all return to the Fatherland as heroes."

"Enough," Waldau said. "Let us celebrate this moment with breakfast." He smiled, trying to look friendly and reassuring, but it didn't come off too well. The soldiers rose to their feet hesitantly, splitting into small groups. A natter of disgruntled low-level conversation buzzed in the background, like bees ordered to sting themselves to death.

Dryden had also heard enough. More than enough. He gestured to Beverly and Creighton and led them into the kitchen to load the coffee pot. Beverly came slowly, watching the milling groups over her shoulder. "What was that all about?" she asked.

"A lot of craziness," Dryden said. "We're in the hands of a bunch of nut cases. These guys are chasing some kind of will-o'-the-wisp superweapon. A pipe dream."

"But what did they say?"

"They think there's some kind of big bomb in the works. Up on the mesa where I used to go to school."

"Could they be right?"

"Not a chance," Dryden said. "I know the mesa. I sure as hell never heard of any such bomb. And no one could keep something like that secret."

Los Alamos Ranch School wasn't even a dot on Kleber's map. No wonder. As Dryden knew, there was nothing at the school except a few sprawling, hand-hewn log buildings that served as classrooms, unheated dorms, the headmaster's house, and housing for the other faculty. There was nothing to do except study and play soccer. There was nothing to see except pines, clouds, and the clean, clear immensity that was northern New Mexico.

Dryden had been an anomaly at the small boys' academy. It mostly attracted sickly sons of eastern seaboard industrialists, who shipped pale boys out to the high, isolated mesa and received back tough, suntanned young men. "Do you some good to make back-East contacts," Big Sam had pronounced unsympathetically when Dryden's mother decided the academy would give him better schooling than a country high school. Probably it had. While the school was small in size, the teachers took a wide view of the world. But Los Alamos Ranch School churning full-tilt as the site of a secret bomb factory? It would take a bunch of real nuts to believe it.

Dryden figured he had it made. True, he had to get Beverly, Creighton, and himself away from the Germans, but a cross-country trek on familiar ground would offer plenty of possibilities. Then he needed only to get to the nearest community with a Forest Service telephone line and holler for help in rounding up a bunch of maniacs. Dryden had tried to explain it all to Beverly and Creighton in quick whispers. Creighton's disbelief in the idea that an important new bomb was being produced anywhere in New Mexico was as strong as Dryden's, but Dryden warned himself not to get careless. The fact that the Germans were insane didn't make them less murderous.

So he gritted his back teeth and was silent when the Germans motioned him to the stables. A small team of men went to the area used by the blacksmith when he made house calls to shoe the horses. They began banging and hammering, but most of the Germans gathered to watch the choice of mounts from the best of the Dryden breeding stock. Kleber and Waldau deferred to Strikfeldt, who was clearly the most expert horseman, but Dryden saw quickly that Strikfeldt's real expertise was apparently limited to hunters. He didn't know beans about trail horses. Best of all, the guy was a sucker for a spirited, good-looking horse. Not the horses with the long, free strides. Not the natural trail horses that floated at the trot instead of pounding the ground. Strikfeldt did go straight to Southern Starr, who was almost everything a horse could aspire to be, but he left

Starrs and Bars, who had it all, quietly munching red oats in his box.

With something approaching anguish Strikfeldt presented Southern Starr to the Oberst, obviously wishing he could keep the horse for himself. "The best in the stables," Strikfeldt assured Kleber. "Look at the short back. The well-defined withers. He could carry you all the way to Germany."

"Does he behave well?" Kleber asked. "I am not a wild-West rider." The Oberst's voice was gruff, no doubt concealing uncertainty. Strikfeldt turned to Dryden.

Dryden tried. "He's a racehorse. He can outrun a Thoroughbred on a short track, and that's what he'll try to do on the trail. He won't let another horse get ahead of him. You can count on it. The mare in the next stall is·a much better distance horse."

Waldau said idly, "Yes, mares are always gentler."

Kleber stiffened. "I shall be in the lead anyway," he said. "I shall take this horse. Perhaps you would like a mare, Colonel Waldau?"

Not Waldau. He and Kleber were obviously still on the outs. Waldau had to have a stallion, the bigger the better. He turned down Rebel Raider and Jesse James and smiled only when Strikfeldt had Creighton bring out Wild Bill, who had not been given his name for nothing. Dryden concealed a smile of his own. Wild Bill wasn't one to buck, but he was a forger, with a ground-jarring trot. Dryden couldn't have chosen better for the SS colonel himself.

One by one he and Creighton saddled the horses as Strikfeldt chose every last snorty, overeager, knotheaded horse in the stable before starting on the reliable citizens. Creighton could hardly keep the happiness from his chronically bloodshot eyes, especially when Starrs and Bars came out of his box limping and was ordered back with a negligent wave of Strikfeldt's hand. When the young lieutenant finished, though, there wasn't much left in the stables. Creighton went to the mule barn for pack animals and Young Jeb, his favorite riding mule. Dryden saddled the last horse, a nice gaited mare he had reserved for Beverly, then took a canvas bag and headed for the office next to the tack room.

As Dryden touched the door handle Waldau said, "Wait. What do you want in there?"

"Medical supplies," Dryden told him.

Waldau shook his head. "The nurse gathered medical supplies at the POW camp. Naturally, we took the liberty of going through the cabinets in the house to supplement the kit she brought with her."

"These are medical supplies for the horses," Dryden said.

"Why should horses need medicines?"

"Well, for starters, how about muscle soreness, lameness, sprains, laminitis, azoturia, fractures, stringhalt, epizootic cellulitis, strangles, tetanus, septicemia, urticaria, colic—"

"Enough!" Waldau said.

Dryden was glad to stop. Creighton, not he, was the expert on horse ailments, and Dryden was none too sure of the string he had rattled off, partly in German, partly in English when his German failed him.

Waldau called Pavel to translate, and Pavel called Frischauer, who, as a farmer, presumably knew about horses. He knew more than the city men, that was sure. Dryden had seen Frischauer watching carefully as each horse destined for the enlisted men moved out of the stables and covered a little ground before latching onto a pair of long-swinging trotters for Pavel and himself.

Frischauer was assigned to accompany Dryden to collect the horse first-aid kit. He watched dutifully as Dryden dredged up a hoof pick, a handful of horseshoe nails, scissors, and a thermometer, then lost interest when he spotted two pairs of leather work gloves on top of a dusty filing cabinet. With an apologetic look at Dryden he pocketed them. A slicker and a pile of horse blankets next caught Frischauer's eye. Dryden got on with his own collecting.

Yes, he'd thought so. Arsenic, down in the bottom drawer of his father's desk. It could rev up an indifferent appetite and put a bloom on a horse's coat. Creighton and Big Sam had gotten stung that way by a Mesa Cherisco horse trader, and when the occasion arose they had stung the trader back. Dryden didn't know what he would do with the arsenic, but he had plans for the bottle of chloroform he picked up next. He threw in a canvas chloroform muzzle and a sponge to make it look right. Leg wraps, gauze, compresses, ah, three vials of morphine, syringes, a half-dozen hypodermic needles, a flashlight.

Dryden soon had such a pile that he discarded his canvas

174

bag and packed it all into a heavy-duty saddle bag. Frischauer gratefully retrieved the canvas bag and packed his own findings into it. Thank God everything was out of sight when Kleber entered the stable office followed by Creighton, Waldau, and the spy from Mexico.

Kleber had his maps out again. He had road maps for the entire route, from Texas to New Mexico and down to the Mexican border, but he seemed to know he couldn't rely on mere highway markings and town dots in New Mexico ranch country. He wanted information from Dryden and Creighton in planning a cross-country route to Los Alamos.

Damn Linares. It was good that Kleber recognized Creighton's value as a guide. If the foreman's life depended on his usefulness, Dryden urgently wanted the Germans to realize he was indispensable. But whereas Kleber and Waldau clearly thought the entire country was wilderness, filled with nothing but mountain lions and bears, Linares kept asking questions about the many tiny, unmapped Spanish communities that dotted the mesas and the Sangre de Cristo foothills. He had probably encountered their counterparts in Mexico. At least the spy seriously underestimated the natural watchfulness of the Pueblo Indians Kleber and Waldau so confidently planned to avoid when they had to cross the Rio Grande. A point, Dryden figured, for the home team.

"We must avoid this road, this Highway 85," Waldau said, studying the line that ran northeast of the Dryden ranch on over to Santa Fe. "We will also avoid this city of Santa Fe, and all should go smoothly."

Linares questioned Creighton about it, and Creighton said, "You gotta cross eighty-five somewhere if you want to work up north. You got you a railroad underpass here east of Bernal. That might do."

Waldau waited for the translation, then said, "What if we are seen? Surely car and truck traffic can be expected on a highway."

"We are not talking about the famous autobahn." Linares told him. "This is a small New Mexico road. And traffic has greatly decreased since the Americans started rationing gasoline. Also, I have confirmed with Herr Creighton that numerous hunting parties go out at this season to shoot deer. If we put the men through the underpass only five or six at a

175

time, we would resemble to the casual eye only another hunting party."

"Do you rely on the word of a mere *Schwarze?*" Waldau asked.

*Schwarze*. It literally meant black, but Dryden felt his cheekbones turn red with indignation at the way it was said. He drew away from the Germans, leaving them to confer, and said quietly to Creighton, "I found that arsenic you and Dad used that time on those bay mules. There are a couple of these Germans I might hate to use it on, but if I volunteer to make a stew for dinner tonight, you be sure not to eat any. Make sure Beverly knows, too."

"Arsenic? I got rid of that years ago. Buried it. It was too dangerous to have around."

"Are you sure? Powder, in a little blue can in Dad's bottom desk drawer?"

"Heck, that's nothing but styptic powder."

Dryden nodded, not altogether unhappy. There were kinder ways to kill. "Maybe it's just as well," he said. He glanced at the Germans to make sure they were still distracted, then said, "What magic did you use on Starrs and Bars to make him limp at just the right moment?"

Creighton grinned. "That was no magic, that was a blister. Starrs, he turned up lame this fall in a flexor tendon, and I finally tried one of those blistering paints on him. Didn't do much good. Rest and lots of liniment did it. But my, he hates that blister paint. I dabbed a little on him when I went in to bridle him, and he was trying to shake it off."

"Good work."

"Yeah. At least we'll have us one good horse to come back to."

"We're going to bring them all back. Tonight."

"You got a plan?" Creighton said. "Good. The sooner the better. It's gonna snow. Maybe not today, but it's coming."

Snow? When the Germans were packed, mounted, and ready to leave, Dryden eyed the northern rim of Mesa Apache, where low, dark clouds drifted. The morning was cold. But there was nothing on the wind. He swung onto the horse he had saved for himself, a dappled gray. The gray might not look like much, but he had a sweet fox trot that would go a long way toward keeping a bashed hip and out-of-shape muscles from crippling Dryden by nightfall, when

176

it was time to move. Dryden eased Sky to the front of the line with Kleber. Southern Starr predictably danced ahead, unwilling to have Sky draw up beside him. Locked safely in the stables, fed, exercised, but already lonesome, Pots and the other two ranch dogs began to howl as the horses moved out.

Near the end of the day, near the back of the string of horses, Beverly opened her black bag and slipped a syringe with a naked hypodermic needle into her jacket pocket. She contemplated sticking it into Erich Huber's eye. The needle was three-quarters of an inch long, made of the sharpest steel. It would slide into the eye easily. Of course, it would only be a puncture wound. Would that be good enough? If left untreated, if it became thoroughly infected, the wound might cause the strutting youth the loss of an eye, but there were always those ifs, and he might recover. She really wanted to maim him for life.

Maim him or kill him? For that matter, did wanting to murder a baby-faced young man simply because he was a tit-grabber and an ass-pincher trivialize both oneself and the act of murder? Beverly thought perhaps it did. She also thought it might be worthwhile to do something permanent about the way her young guard smiled when he put his hands on her. Machine-gunning all the Germans was only a fantasy inspired by that smile. Yet Beverly was so seriously angry with Huber that when she learned at the noon rest period that Dryden's arsenic was really only aluminum chloride, her first reaction was deep disappointment. Poisoning the bunch of them to make sure the smiling Hitler Youth died seemed only moderately extreme.

Oh, like Dryden, she'd spare a few Germans if the opportunity arose. Their two kitchen helpers, little Willi and shy Herr Boberach, had gravitated to the tail of the train to help Creighton with the pack mules. And the big man named Frischauer, who had joined the amateur mule skinners, also seemed inoffensive. She wouldn't kill them. But the others lacked cause for mercy. Especially Waldau and his ape, Voight, who had killed her two patients in the schoolhouse. She wouldn't even spare the handsome young lieutenant, Strikfeldt. During the day Strikfeldt had frowned at Huber

177

several times when he'd seen him feeling her up. But a frown wasn't enough.

Jolting along beside her on a dapple-gray horse, struggling to stay in the jouncing saddle without actually sitting on it, wincing with pain, Huber had no opportunity at the moment to slide a hot hand along her hip. His hands were too busy with the reins, and her hips were securely seated in a surprisingly comfortable western saddle on a mare named Little Lil. Maybe just maim him. Beverly reached a gloved hand into her jacket pocket and felt the hypodermic needle again.

She would have to wait. Mr. Creighton had passed the word to her. Make no trouble. Lull the Germans. They would sneak away that very night, chloroforming Huber or the other guards, if need be. Not a bad idea, that. Put Huber under deeply so he couldn't cry out. It would only take a few seconds with the needle to carve her initials on his face, say a quarter-inch deep.

Comfortable with her thoughts, Beverly looked to the head of the string of riders, at Dryden, riding smoothly behind Kleber on another dapple-gray gelding. Its name was Sky. Beverly didn't know the name of Huber's horse. She didn't care. It looked enough like Sky to be a brother, but she refused to be interested in Huber's horse because Huber was riding him. Huber didn't like his horse. He cursed a lot in German. Beverly was glad. Maybe she'd ask Mr. Creighton the horse's name after all.

Creighton was right behind her with the mules, loaded with food, barbed-wire cutters, hatchets, shovels, rope, horse feed, and cooking utensils, all clanking and banging. They didn't move quietly. It didn't matter. There was no one in all this empty vastness to hear. They had ridden up from piñons to pines, gaining altitude, getting colder all the time, resting rarely, and then only for the sake of the horses. Cold biscuits and cold meat were handed out at noon by Willi and Boberach to men groaning with pain. Saddle-sore. Like Erich Huber.

Darling Ned, there at the head of the train. Take two aspirin every four hours, he'd told her. If things got really bad, he had something stronger for her. So sweet. So naïve. Still, the aspirin was good advice for someone not accus-

178

tomed to horses and saddles. Stay ahead of the inevitable inflammation and pain, or at least stay even with it.

She hadn't been allowed to exchange a direct word with Ned all day. Mr. Creighton was the messenger. Dutifully, she took her aspirin. She also administered them to Willi, Boberach, and Frischauer. Mr. Creighton only grinned. What did it mean to him to be saddle-sore? Nothing, apparently. And nothing is what she offered to Huber. Let the bastard ache and groan. He had barely managed to fondle her more than twice at the noon break. What possible fun could there be in it for him? She was bundled up in so many layers of sweaters and jacket that he surely couldn't feel anything, just imagine the flesh beneath. And smile.

They stopped before sundown two miles on from a creek where they watered the horses. It would be a gray sunset. The whole day was gray. Once the order to stop was given, the men all but fell off their horses. They were tired as well as sore. Kleber gave them ten minutes to groan before setting up a proper military camp. Guards were directed to the perimeters of the camp. Food and blankets unloaded for the night. Dryden left on foot to guide a scouting party that presumably would investigate the surrounding area. Mr. Creighton waited for no instructions. He strung long ropes between pine trees, tethered the horses to the ropes, and began unsaddling them. Beverly went to help rub the horses down, hoping Dryden would eventually come.

"Where are we?" she asked Creighton as she worked on a tired Little Lil.

"Maybe five or six miles from Rowe," Creighton said. "Not that Rowe's much. It's just a couple of stores. Fishermen use it as a jumping-off place when they're going up higher. We're in the Santa Fe National Forest. Pretty good fishing."

"I could fancy about a dozen rainbow trout right now," Beverly said.

"Let's just hope the biscuit and beef hold out," Creighton said. He nodded through the pines toward Kleber, who had stopped a man with an armload of wood. The man reluctantly put the wood down. "Looks like it's gonna be another cold camp," Creighton explained.

"No fire?" Beverly said. She stopped, appalled. Had she

179

whined? She added matter-of-factly, "Oh, well, it doesn't matter."

"They probably don't want to take the chance on smoke," Creighton said. "I don't think we're more than three miles or so north of the highway. Probably afraid smoke would be spotted."

He moved to the next horse. Willi and Frischauer roused themselves and came to help, but little Boberach remained on a log on which he had collapsed. Beverly thought he looked dangerously tired. The prisoners who had been on American rations longer had much more stamina.

They were also more enterprising. A young corporal named Lampe who hung out occasionally with Huber came seeking his saddle and blanket roll, and it wasn't just to look for blankets. A bottle clinked. Lampe stuffed something under his jacket and edged off through the trees. Huber and two other men followed him. The Dryden liquor supply, Beverly inferred, had been raided again.

Huber and the others went back and forth from the trees several times before Beverly finished rubbing down the five horses she'd allotted herself. Dryden returned from his patrol accompanied by Strikfeldt, and both headed over to help with the horses. Dryden slipped the bits out of their mouths so they could graze on the dried grass that grew between the pines. Strikfeldt said something cheerful-sounding in German and gestured at the mules, then moved on to help Creighton take them to a farther clearing. Dryden lingered for a moment with Beverly.

"I love you," he murmured. "You smell of horse sweat. Once we get out of here tonight and get the horses home, I think I'll make love to you in the barn."

"Is horse sweat erotic?" Beverly asked.

"Maddeningly," Dryden said.

"Then I won't bathe first."

"I won't give you a chance."

"I might be too saddle-sore to open my legs."

"There are ways," Dryden said wisely. "There are ways."

Strikfeldt called, and Dryden walked on. Ned was limping, poor darling. The hip. Beverly, too, was summoned, by Pavel, acting as translator for the Oberst. "You must stay with your guard," Pavel said. "Oberst Kleber asks that you please do not wander about the camp or converse with Captain Dryden."

"My guard has been drinking," Beverly said. "Assign me someone who is decent. And sober."

"Drinking?" Pavel said. He conversed rapidly with Kleber. "Impossible," he translated. "You are mistaken."

"Because your dear little Hitler-bastard Huber is a proper German soldier? The mistake is yours. He *has* been drinking, and at the best of times he is cat vomit."

Pavel looked less certain than Kleber sounded on the next translation. "You are not to indulge in personal likes or dislikes," Pavel relayed. "You are here to minister to the men. All are extremely sore from unaccustomed riding. What medication have you that would be appropriate?"

"Only aspirin," Beverly lied.

"Then kindly give them aspirin."

Kleber turned away, and several of the Germans who had edged within listening distance fell back. One drifted toward Huber. The youth watched Kleber's back recede, then swaggered straight to Beverly, eyes glazed, staggering slightly. He reeked of whisky.

Huber didn't bother speaking. Failing common language, he had only one means of communicating his displeasure, and apparently only one interest anyway. He didn't try to fondle her surreptitiously this time. Bottle courage made him direct. He reached out, jerked Beverly's jacket open and put both hands on her breasts, squeezing hard. And smiled that red-lipped, superior smile.

Over by the horses someone shouted. It was Dryden, of course. Across Huber's shoulder Beverly saw Dryden start to run toward her. Strikfeldt and Creighton both ran after him. There was no time. This was Beverly's war, and Ned had to be kept out of it. Huber squeezed harder, hurting, obviously expecting her to try to break away. Instead, Beverly stepped closer to his grinning face, her right hand dipping into her jacket pocket.

She stabbed. Not directly. Not in his groin, her first thought. Not in his eye, her second. With a swinging, roundhouse motion, she brought the needle horizontally across Huber's smiling mouth, then stepped back, shouting, "Hah!"

Huber tried to scream, but the full, curling upper lip was

neatly pleated together with three-fourths of an inch of sharp stainless steel.

"E-e-e-e-e-e-e-e," Huber squealed. He danced away from Beverly. "E-e-e-e-e-e-e-e."

His hands fluttered around the bobbing syringe attached to the needle. Too much of a momma's baby to touch it, Beverly thought contemptuously. Too scared to pull it out himself.

Huber fell on his back, still screaming that high-pitched animal scream. Beverly whirled, ready to grapple with Dryden, ready to try to keep him off Huber, but Creighton had already done the job. Dryden was down after a pell-mell tackle. Only Strikfeldt came on. Beverly braced herself, but Strikfeldt carefully circled around her and went to Huber. He put one foot on the squirming youth's chest, not at all gently, and reached down. With one quick jerk he pulled out the needle. Then, to Beverly's joy, Strikfeldt spat in Huber's face.

"Schweinerei," Strikfeldt said to Huber. Beverly couldn't understand what else he said, and Pavel, who came running back with Kleber, was too busy to translate. Beverly stood her ground while questions were fired. Strikfeldt hissed accusingly at Huber, who mumbled back, all but blubbering. One of his drinking buddies shamefacedly produced the nearly empty whisky bottle. Many of the Germans had seen what had happened. They all talked at once until Kleber turned to Beverly, speaking apologetically. That was all she had waited for—assignment of the blame. She turned her back on him and walked with dignity to Dryden and Creighton.

But once she slipped her hand into Dryden's she began to tremble. "I'm sorry, darling," she whispered. "I know we weren't supposed to do anything until tonight, but some bad situations have to be dealt with directly."

"You're goddamn right they do," he growled. "I'm the one who's sorry, baby. You've been right all the time, and I've been wrong."

Wrong. Wrong not to have butchered the SS captain, Grebling, in the kitchen last night when he had a knife in his hand to cut up beef. Wrong not to have strangled Frischauer this morning when they were alone in the stable office.

Wrong not to have seized any one of a dozen opportunities during the day to knock Kleber from his horse and stage a bucking-bronco act with Sky, trampling Kleber to jelly.

Dryden had no trouble staying awake that night, waiting to be sure his German bunkmate, the man with the crippled arm, Franz Eggers, had gone soundly to sleep. The previous night at the ranch he wouldn't have killed Eggers. Tonight he would. Bad situations had to be dealt with directly.

The same problem persisted, of course. Kill one German and face twenty-one more. Impossible to protect Beverly and Mr. Creighton when you're that severely outnumbered. But he'd been protecting the damned Germans, too. Why? When had he started regarding them as his personal charges? Back in the POW camp, when they were fairly docile prisoners? Aliens in an alien land. Soldiers like himself. Good guys who just happened to be fighting on the side of the bad guys. Bullshit. Which one of them was truly more deserving to live than Waldau and Voight? Or the young cur Beverly had mangled? Round them up. Get them back in some squirrel-cage prisoner-of-war camp. That's all he'd been thinking. Wrong. Wrong.

Dryden knew he still looked an impasse straight in the face. Anything he did would affect Beverly and Creighton. That's why he waited so long that night, listening to Eggers snore, before easing out of the blankets they shared. It was Kleber's idea, to bed down his prisoners with their guards: One person couldn't move without disturbing the other. Beverly's bunkie and new guard was Frischauer, who, Kleber explained carefully, was a decent, quiet family man who respected women. But Kleber had underestimated the fatigue of his men. Eggers never stopped snoring while Dryden slipped from the blankets with his pack of medical supplies.

There were armed guards patrolling out in the darkness somewhere. Dryden took no chances. He moved soundlessly into the trees above the camp and readied his bottle of chloroform and sponge before circling back down to get Beverly. The plan was for him to go to Creighton first. That was before they saw Beverly being led toward the center of camp with Frischauer carrying her blankets. Beverly was as smart as she was beautiful. She had balked, as if priggishly, and insisted on withdrawing near the tree line, away from the bulk of the men.

It went easily. Beverly was awake. Dryden could see her face turn slightly to watch him. She lay motionless until the chloroform-soaked sponge went over Frischauer's mouth and nose, then rose to her elbow and poised a shapely hand holding a pair of sharp scissors from her first-aid kit over Frischauer's jugular. Ready, once again, to deal directly with a bad situation if Frischauer tried to struggle.

Frischauer only gasped, a reflex. His chest heaved briefly before he sank into a different sleep. Dryden dripped more chloroform on the sponge, then more, until Beverly silently rose and leaned close to Dryden's ear.

"He'll do," Beverly said. "Ned, a guard has been walking back and forth just below the horses. There's another over to the west. He keeps stepping on sticks when he walks. Mr. Creighton is between us and the horses."

"I saw," Dryden whispered back. "Come."

They almost missed Creighton in the darkness. He was lying next to Linares, perhaps the only German who didn't object to Creighton's black skin, and the spy had pulled his blanket up over his head. Creighton's dark face was lost in the greater blackness of the night, until Dryden saw his eyes move whitely. Like Beverly, he was awake and ready. Creighton gently pulled the blanket from Linares's head and lifted a huge black hand above Linares's throat, ready, again like Beverly, to clamp down and deal directly with the possibility that the spy would struggle.

Linares never stirred. Creighton's eyes rose to Dryden, then his hand rose warningly, and he eased the blanket back over Linares and slid away from the sleeping man.

A horse snorted. They had been prepared for that, but Dryden jerked away. Creighton didn't speak until they were well above the sleeping Germans, into the trees, then he said, "It's gonna have to be the mules, Mr. Dryden. That guard's sticking due south of the horses. No guards by the mules. Get Young Jeb for Miss Beverly. Bring any old mule for you and me. Once you get her up on Jeb, start yelling out in German, 'Bears! Bears!' That'll be my signal. I'll have the horses loose before you can say Jack Robinson, and I'll be driving them straight north. You and Miss Beverly head straight east. I'll find you later on."

"The devil you say. You're coming with us."

"Sort of like the devil. Black. I got the advantage, Mr.

Dryden. That white face of yours, I saw you coming in the starlight. No guard's gonna see me sneaking around in the middle of the horses. Now, once you get near the mules they're gonna start whistling and stamping around. That's why you better go ahead and call out. They'll be making racket enough to wake the camp anyway. All right, let's get going.''

Dryden might have protested, but the black man melted into the night. Dryden took a deep breath and started to move back into the trees with Beverly. Was the plan workable? Even a good riding mule would be hard for Beverly to stay on. And the special knots with which Creighton had tied the horses might not slip free fast enough for Creighton to get away safely. Should they have worked it all out more carefully?

A polite German voice came from Creighton's direction, a short distance away. It said, "Oh, you startled me. I beg your pardon. I was just—'' The voice stopped abruptly. Then, an octave higher, it shouted, "Help! Halt! Guard! Guard!'' Through the darkness a small figure came running toward them.

"Jesus, it's little Willi,'' Beverly breathed.

Dryden grabbed for Willi Roh and almost collided with Creighton. They both wrapped arms around the wriggling little man. Dryden had him by the collar when another sound stopped him.

A metallic click as a machine pistol was ratcheted and primed. Then another click, this time from a handgun, and a beam of unsteady light hit them.

"Halt!'' a voice cried in German. "Halt or I shoot the woman!''

Within seconds, grappled by a half-dozen alarmed men, pinned by the dancing flashlight beam, Dryden lost sight of Beverly and Creighton. He panicked and drove an elbow into the nearest throat, trying to locate her, but then he heard her icy voice in back of him: "Touch me and I'll give you what I gave that bastard Huber.''

Dryden got cuffed several times in the struggle. He went down on one knee, and someone almost simultaneously snaked out both hands and grabbed his ankles. He jerked and kicked, and someone went over backward. By the time he was hauled to his feet Kleber was in front of him.

185

"Get that flashlight out of my eyes!" Kleber ordered. "Keep it on them. Do you have all three of them? Are they all here?"

"Yes, Herr Oberst," someone said.

"The horses?"

"Lieutenant Strikfeldt is checking them now. He thinks they are all secure."

"What happened here?"

Voices hummed. Then Willi Roh's voice spoke out: "Herr Oberst, I apologize. I had to empty my bladder. I walked to the trees, to avoid fouling the vicinity of the camp, and on my way back I—well, I almost collided with Herr Creighton. They were trying to escape, Herr Oberst."

"Yes, of course they were," Kleber said. He sounded disgusted. If so, it was with himself, for he went on, "In an attempt to ease your difficulties as a prisoner, Captain Dryden, I have been too lenient with you. From now on you will be tied when we stop for the night—you, Nurse Bennington, and Herr Creighton. You will be kept tied hand and foot nightly from now on. You may thank yourself for this, for you have brought it on yourselves. Do you understand?"

Dryden didn't try to plead for Beverly. He knew she wouldn't want it. "Oh, yes," he said quietly. "I believe I understand everything now."

*Thursday*
*December 28, 1944*

# TEN

Despite himself, Pavel felt happy almost up to the minute of the accident on the third day. He blamed himself later. He would have paid closer attention to the new look in Dryden's eyes if he hadn't been so busy gawking admiringly at the high mesa country into which Dryden led them after they left the dark forests of pine. Nor would he have brushed off his vague suspicion that the American officer was guiding them over unnecessarily rough terrain. He told himself that Oberst Kleber and SS Standartenführer Waldau, not Dryden, had set the route. He told himself that Dryden obviously loved his horses, not to mention the beautiful nurse, and surely wouldn't expose either the animals or the woman to treacherous switchback trails if easier paths could be found. But mostly he was preoccupied by the glory of the strange land they labored to cross.

He had served in the deserts of North Africa. He had found nothing there to love. To Pavel, the desert land in which he had fought was like a waterless sea, with the sea's same crushing indifference to the welfare of any creature that chanced upon it, but without the sea's grandeur. This high desert was different. It spoke. There was a message in the mountains far behind them, where ragged gray clouds caught and tore on the peaks. There was faint music in the rocky slopes, even in the gnarled piñon pines and junipers, and most of all in the immense empty dome that was the sky. Pavel didn't know the language of this great and lonely land, but he could understand the song.

The broken country unnerved some of the men. "It's like the moon," Boberach complained fearfully in midafternoon. The Oberst had changed the order of march. Herr Boberach no longer trailed behind with the mules and the dark-skinned foreman, but rather rode near the front of the train beside Pavel.

"You are just hungry," Pavel said. Why wouldn't the poor man be? Nothing but cold scraps for breakfast. Only apples for lunch. Boberach was not a soldier. He was unaccustomed to the spartan ways of the military man. "Here, eat this," Pavel told the little scientist. He took a treasure from his shirt pocket. "I saved half a biscuit from this morning's rations."

Boberach accepted the biscuit but said, "I am not just hungry, Pavel. I am hungry, and I am cold, and I have been on this horse so long that my legs feel like they are going to break off at the hips. I wish they would. Then maybe I would not hurt so much."

Pavel laughed. "You should have finished the German atomic device sooner, Herr Boberach. Then you wouldn't be riding a horse across an American desert."

Boberach responded so softly that Pavel could barely hear him over the thud of his horse's hooves and jingle of its reins: "I will tell you a secret, Pavel. None of us wanted to finish the bomb. It is too terrible a weapon to put into the hands of a fanatic like Hitler."

Pavel was startled. "Then why are we here?" he asked. "If you felt that way, why did you even tell us about the American bomb? Why not let them finish it and end this damned war?"

"No one wants to see Germany destroyed, either," Boberach said. "Oh, we talked about it. Let the Americans win. But the price of their victory would be too high to pay. It would be almost as bad as giving the bomb to our lunatic Führer."

Pavel rolled walleyes at the horsemen behind them, Waldau and Grebling. "Shhh," he said.

Boberach looked chastened. "Do you want your biscuit back?"

"No, man, eat it. With your mouth shut."

Ahead, Kleber raised his hand to signal a halt, and Pavel felt a moment's panic. Could the Oberst have possibly overheard? But, no, Kleber only wanted to confer with Dryden about a huge buff-colored rock outcropping above which Dryden had started his horse. Pavel spurred forward to listen.

Kleber said, "Surely it is easier to pass below the rock, Captain Dryden. While it is clear that you are guiding us in the correct direction, your choice of routes always seems to be the slowest."

"Sometimes slow is safest," Dryden said. The cold, speculative look in his eyes roamed over Kleber. He gestured. "There's a pretty good drop-off below. The rock is loose. The horses are tired. I don't advise it."

Not only the horses were tired. Pavel thought Oberst Kleber looked haggard. The horse he rode fought him continuously, still trying to supplant Dryden's horse in the lead position. The brute was stubborn, that's what, but no one had dared suggest trading with the commandant.

"Save your advice for the question of our night's stopping place," Kleber said. "Tonight the men must have shelter. We must be able to build a fire. An abandoned barn would do. Or some out-of-the-way building. Are there no such structures on our route?"

"I know a cave," Dryden said. "It's not very deep, but it's sheltered under a rock ledge. It's a small Indian ruin I used to climb around in when I was a boy. There are several cave dwellings up where we're headed."

"A dwelling?" Kleber said. "Rooms? Walls?"

"Yes."

"That should serve us well. We will spend the night there."

"Not unless you pick up the pace," Dryden said. He smiled, a smile as cold as his eyes. "The cave is in a canyon near Los Alamos. Somehow I don't think you'll get there by nightfall."

"You are deliberately trying to provoke me," Kleber said.

"That's fair enough," Dryden said. "I've been provoked from time to time on our little jaunt."

Kleber made an impatient motion with his hand. Instantly his horse shied. Dryden reached for the horse's bridle. "Easy, boy," he said to the horse.

Waldau, perhaps curious, decided to join them. He dug booted heels into his horse's sides. That was also a mistake. The horse leapt forward, shouldering Pavel's horse out of the way. Dryden slid off his own mount to intercept Waldau. He quieted Waldau's horse easily. Waldau asked Kleber, "Are you calling a rest stop? Such surroundings are uninviting, but I think the men need rest time now."

"No, I was conferring with the captain about shelter for the night," Kleber said. To Dryden he said, "So if we will not reach your cave by nightfall, why not a mine? Those abandoned mine shafts we saw this morning—are any of them safe? Are there more in the vicinity?"

"Dozens," Dryden said. "Detour down to Madrid and there are old coal mines all over the area. Of course, it'll add fifteen or twenty miles to the trip."

Waldau almost groaned. He looked scarcely less haggard than Kleber, as his horse was almost equally unmanageable. He said to Kleber, "Surely you would not consider such a detour. The men could not tolerate additional time on these damnable animals."

"I agree, it's out of the question," Kleber said. "We shall risk an open fire tonight. The men must have warmth and cooked food. We must move on now. The lower path, Captain Dryden. Since you are fearful, I shall take the lead."

Kleber didn't wait for Dryden to remount. He gave his horse its head, and the animal started along the faint downward trail at a trot, followed by Waldau, perhaps willy-nilly. Pavel clucked to his horse and squeezed with his legs, coaxing it to fall in behind. Poor horse. It was moving well, but not eagerly, as it had yesterday, and keeping up with the other horses no longer appeared to interest it.

Had Pavel not lagged behind, could he have prevented the accident? He didn't think so, but he at least could have tried. As it was, he could only see it coming. Waldau kicked his horse, trying to catch up with Kleber. The horse lunged forward just as Kleber started below the big rock. The trail was wide enough, at least ten feet, but it sloped toward the outer edge. Loose rock littered it, and more rock plunged down a steep incline. Waldau's horse bumped Kleber's. Kleber's horse slipped on the loose rock.

It happened slowly. Later, Pavel could see it happen again and again in his mind's eye. Kleber's horse tried to regain its balance but teetered, then it toppled toward the edge. Kleber fell with the horse. It landed heavily on top of him, on its side, sliding, sliding.

The horse wrenched its whole body strongly, kicking, trying to get purchase with its rear legs. By then Dryden was rushing on foot past Pavel, followed by, of all people, Herr Boberach.

"Grab his head!" Dryden shouted. He shouted it in English, but Boberach appeared to understand what was needed. Dryden gripped the horse's tail, dodging flying hooves to do it, and pulled hard, sliding the frightened horse off Kleber and away from the edge. Pavel forgot his aches and leapt to help them.

Scrabbling, kicking, eyes rolling wildly, the horse plunged to its feet on the trail instead of plunging over the edge. It stood uncertainly, trembling, well clear of the Oberst. That was when Kleber screamed.

Pavel was four steps away. Dryden backed the snorting horse up the trail, away from the fallen man. Pavel threw himself to his knees beside his commanding officer. "Sir!" he cried. He ran his eyes frantically along Kleber's body. "Where are you hurt? Are you bleeding?"

Kleber was quickly stolid about the pain. "I believe I'm a little shaken," he said in an almost normal voice. "I can't seem to get up."

"Don't move," a woman said in English. Pavel fumbled the translation, but Kleber didn't move anyway. It was the nurse, hurried from the back of the train by Bernd Strikfeldt.

Kleber looked at Strikfeldt rather than the nurse. He said, "Perhaps you should return to the pack animals, Herr Leutnant. The Americans must not be allowed to seize this chance to get away." Then Kleber took a deep breath and began to shudder all over.

Kleber was more than shaken. Summoned from Kleber's side a half hour later with the nurse to a general council of war, Pavel mumbled worried translations to the men, all of whom gathered close.

"The general's right arm and shoulder are dislocated," the nurse reported. "He may have some spinal damage as well. My best guess is that at least two spinal disks are cracked and impacted. Damage to internal organs is another possibility, but I can't tell. His heartbeat was very rapid immediately following the fall, but it's normalizing now. I think it's just a response to shock. Otherwise he has a nasty gash on one knee and his leg. That's about the only thing I can treat."

SS Captain Grebling seemed to be in charge of the meeting. He said, "The arm and the spine—could they be broken?"

"Without X rays I have no way of telling," the nurse said.

"There are no bones protruding?"

"Don't you think I would have noticed? I've taped the shoulder. We can keep him warm. I've given him morphine for the pain. I hesitate to suggest a hospital, having seen how you treat your hospital cases. But unless you can get him to one soon, there's little more anyone can do. He could keep a whole hospital staff busy all by himself."

Grebling said, "So Oberst Kleber should not travel on?"

"Certainly not," the nurse said.

Pavel hesitated before translating her crisp reply. The words had a dread familiarity. And finality.

But Grebling had recognized the negative tone. He said, "And the assault team cannot wait. Colonel Waldau, my recommendation is that we leave the Oberst on the trail, with food and water, of course, and press on."

Strikfeldt said, "That's the same as killing him!"

Grebling nodded slowly. "That might also be a good idea."

"No," Pavel said.

Waldau showed quickly where the real power lay. He snapped, "What did you say, Sergeant?"

"There will be no knife in the throat for Oberst Kleber," Pavel said. He looked hard at Albert Voight, who stood behind Waldau.

Grebling said, "The Oberst is incapacitated. Colonel Waldau is therefore in command. You will obey *his* orders. All of them."

"No," Pavel said again. He had heard Dryden use the short, effective monosyllable and had seen it work. He was astonished at how easily the word came out. After a lifetime of soldiering the habit of obedience was strong—but not unbreakable.

Pavel wasn't carrying his machine pistol. He had left it by Oberst Kleber's side. He didn't care. Still, obedience was only a part of a soldier's life; the art of politics had to be practiced, too. So Pavel stared into Grebling's eyes, not Waldau's, and addressed the young officer, rather than deliver his challenge directly to Waldau.

"The Oberst will not be killed," Pavel said. "The Oberst will not be left behind. The Oberst is a veteran Afrika Korps officer, and that is not the Afrika Korps way. If the Oberst must be tied to his saddle in order to travel, he will be tied to his saddle. But he will travel with us."

There was silence. It lasted long enough for the greater silence of the desert to sweep in. Then Jürgen Frischauer, his own Schmeisser held casually, stepped up wordlessly to stand beside Pavel. Franz Eggers followed right behind him. Lieutenant Strikfeldt quietly took a place on Pavel's other side. A few Schmeissers rattled, and men drifted to join them. Willi Roh, Basil, the tanker, Lampe, Maschmann. The nurse started to say something, then she, too, fell silent.

It was the other outsider, the hulking spy Linares, who finally broke the silence. He said. "We can get another ten miles before dark. Then there's only one more day between us and Los Alamos. If there is enough morphine, Kleber would probably prefer trying it."

Grebling objected, "If he slows us down . . ."

"Why should he?" Linares said. "He'll be feeling no pain."

Waldau raised an eyebrow. His tack was oblique. "This morphine," he said. "Many of the men are also in pain, perhaps not as acute but certainly continuous. I had not heard there was more morphine, or I would have suggested its use long prior."

Pavel discussed the morphine situation quickly with the nurse, then translated. "The morphine is a veterinary-grade opiate," he said. "Brought from the ranch. She says she has used it on the Oberst as a measure of desperation and will continue to do so if we require it."

193

"Veterinary grade! Pah!" Waldau said. "Better to be saddle-sore. Very well. It would appear that any search teams that have been delegated to find us are still in disarray. I have seen no aerial surveillance, no sign of troops. If the situation changes, I may be required to change my position. In the meantime, my orders are that we shall ride on as soon as the Oberst can be tied to his horse. I must say I do not envy him the journey."

Colonel Christopher felt irked. The man he sat facing was fully fifteen years his junior, yet he was already a full colonel and therefore superior to a mere lieutenant colonel such as himself. That trim mustache. An obvious attempt to look older. Christopher almost uttered a small, disgusted snort, then thought it better to keep his opinion to himself.

Christopher and Sergeant Kieran had been called on the carpet. At present the sergeant was literally standing on the dun-colored carpet that graced—or disgraced—Christopher's office floor, since Christopher had already been handed his own reprimand. The carpet crunched a little as Kieran shifted nervously. Everything one touched in McLean was always covered by a thin layer of dust and sand, blown by the eternal, infernal wind. Now, for Christopher, it would be Washington, D.C. Hot and humid in the summer, cold in the winter. At least there would be less dust.

They had told Christopher before they called Kieran in, this Colonel Scott and the FBI man, an older civilian who never quite finished a sentence. Christopher was on his way to the new Pentagon. At last! But it was also, again, at the least. Procurement. Toilet paper, Christopher was willing to bet. He was being bucked upstairs to a harmless office. Bucked upstairs—a promotion? Full colonel? His first act, once he'd solidified his contacts and mended some fences, would be to phone this young jerk and tell him where to get off.

"No sir," Sergeant Kieran said stubbornly. "You asked me, and I'm telling you, those Germans are still somewhere in the area. Captain Dryden probably has them hid in a farmhouse or something until things quiet down."

The FBI man said, "Since you are unable to provide any proof whatever, Sergeant, that Captain Dryden . . ."

Colonel Scott waited politely for the FBI agent's words to

trail off into the dusty air. Then he said crisply, "Nothing in Captain Dryden's dossier indicates any common feeling or uncommon sympathy for the German prisoners of war, Sergeant. Your suspicions, if you had any, should have been reported long before now. Am I correct, Colonel Christopher?"

Christopher nodded eagerly. If he cooperated, maybe they'd give him pens and pencils to procure instead of toilet paper. Maybe they'd give him an office with a window. "Quite right, Colonel Scott," he said. "I regret to say it, but while Sergeant Kieran complained verbally more than once about Captain Dryden, it always boiled down to complaints that the captain insisted on the proper discharge of the noncommissioned officers' duties."

For once the FBI man uttered a complete sentence. "And what did you do about it, Colonel?" he wondered aloud.

"I . . . uh . . . I always gave Captain Dryden my full support," Christopher said.

"After-the-fact excuses are unconvincing, Sergeant," Colonel Scott said. "In the future, if you have any complaints about a superior officer, put them in writing and file a correct report. In short, cover your ass. Speaking of which, you're hauling ass out of here, Kieran. You're being shipped to Alaska. Point Barrow. Cold storage for the duration."

"My God!" Kieran gasped. "Alaska? What about Colonel Christopher? It's all his fault. My God!"

"Colonel Christopher is not your concern," Scott's eyes wandered to Christopher, then back to Kieran. "You've left us with a nice mess here, both of you. There's no sign of the Germans. Twenty-four goddamned men! Vanished! We have extended roadblocks and checkpoints on a hundred-mile radius. Nothing. Police have been alerted from here south to the Mexican border, and the Border Patrol put on alert. Still nothing. We've got planes sweeping the highways and countryside to the east, just in case they're trying to get to a seaport. And still, by God, nothing. Just what the hell do you suppose happened to them?"

Kieran all but stuck out his lower lip and pouted, turning accusing eyes to Christopher. "All right," he said bitterly. "I can see who's going to get all the blame here. If they aren't hiding somewhere close like I said, then what about

195

that report about a dead sheriff on the highway west of Amarillo? Or those two unidentified bodies they found in that New Mexico schoolhouse? That sure sounds like Germans to me. Maybe they went west. Maybe they got out through the wire, and Dryden got them away fast before we could set up roadblocks, and—''

Scott waved him quiet. ''You're grasping at straws, Sergeant. Mr. Green, will you tell Colonel Christopher and the sergant your views on the death of the sheriff?''

The FBI man said, ''Well, it's hard to find a connection of any kind with . . . After all, it happened so soon after the break, less than five hours, and how could the Germans get that far that fast? . . . There's just no logical reason for the escaped Germans to go running off to the middle of nowhere if they're trying to get out of the country, and . . .''

Colonel Christopher stopped listening. His eyes turned to the drawer in which he had hastily tucked his bourbon bottle. If only everyone would go away. One of his Texas toddies would go nice about now. A celebration. The Pentagon. A promotion. No more POWs. No more Texas. It would all be so promising, if only he could be sure there was some way to sneak his toddies into his new office once he reached Washington.

The FBI agent droned on in fragmented sentences, explaining the facts as he knew them. Unfortunately, he knew absolutely nothing about the project at Los Alamos. It was too sensitive. So sensitive that even the FBI had not been informed. General Leslie Groves, head of the huge Manhattan Project, had insisted on the strictest possible security. Only the president and a few top-level government people were aware of it. Not even Vice President Harry Truman had been told. Paranoid secrecy had shut the door to the west and to Los Alamos. The hunt for the escaped Germans turned eastward.

With Waldau in charge, risks were taken. Two mule deer were spooked in an arroyo as Dryden led the train off the mesa country toward a small spring, and Waldau allowed them to be shot, issuing orders that any humans attracted by the sound of gunfire also be shot. The men ate venison that night, cooked over a fire incautiously large, and Waldau similarly allowed a fire to be built before dawn the next morning so the men could have hot food and coffee before riding on.

"Waldau is relying on force of arms," Dryden told Beverly. "Kleber preferred stealth." They had just left the injured commander, accompanied by their two guards. Almost speechless with pain, Kleber had nevertheless grunted his thanks to Beverly as she administered the morning's first morphine shot.

"I'm really worried about him," Beverly said. "He's bearing up remarkably well, but I'm pretty sure he ruptured a kidney in the fall."

"Poor bastard," Dryden said. "How can you tell?"

"The urine sample—bright, dark red, with a lot of sediment."

"Can you do anything?"

"Nothing. But he'll feel easier soon. The guards had to jostle him quite a bit to roll him over for the injection."

"It's nothing like the jostling he'll get when Pavel lifts him back on a horse."

"God, so true. Ned, do you want a shot? Your hip . . ."

"No, save the morphine for Kleber. I'm doing okay."

"You're sure?"

"Hell, yes. I was so tired last night I went to sleep before they could even tie me up again. Hey! And no more bad dreams. Maybe I was too sound asleep to dream. How's that for a plus? Besides, Kleber's going to need all the morphine you've got. We lost about five miles yesterday, because of the accident and the great deer hunt, and Waldau plans to make it up. Bev, watch out for your little buddy Huber. I saw him take a few shots at the deer, and it seems to have helped his morale. He's beginning to strut again."

"But he isn't smiling," she said. She giggled. "His lip's still too swollen."

"Just be careful."

"You, too."

Dryden left her with Frischauer, her new guard, and went with his own guard to help saddle the horses. No chance to talk to Creighton. Linares stuck too close to him. The first opportunity came as they neared a two-lane asphalt highway that ran south from Santa Fe toward Albuquerque. Waldau and Linares huddled to discuss how to cross the road without being seen, and both Dryden and Creighton were called in again as consultants.

Creighton smiled when he heard the problem. "Good luck," he said. "You got no cover around these parts."

It was an understatement. They had ridden through hills each more barren than the last to a wide plain. No piñon pine grew here. Even juniper was scarce. Low greasewood bushes and cactus were the only spots of green from horizon to horizon. Dryden had kept them low, following arroyos, to get this far without attracting undue attention.

"Are there no railroad underpasses?" Waldau insisted. For Creighton's sake and to keep the discussion moving, Linares translated everything to English.

"None I ever saw," Creighton said. "What about you, Mr. Dryden?"

Dryden shook his head. "About the best we can do is cut a couple of miles to the north. There's a pretty good rise up there. The road cuts between two cliffs, and it winds a little. You could probably post a man at the top of the cliffs to watch for traffic. He can wave you across, a few men at a time, when the road is clear."

As usual, Waldau objected to any thought of a detour, but Dryden pointed out that they had to start moving north soon anyway. He managed to get in a few words with Creighton as Linares and Waldau worked out the details.

"You see those two Indian boys on that little hill about four miles back?"

"Sure did," Creighton whispered. "I don't think anybody else saw them, though. They ducked pretty quick."

"Any chance they'll pass the word they saw a big party of armed men?"

"Only to another Indian," Creighton said. "You know how Indians like to stay to themselves."

"Listen, if we get spotted on the trail and any shooting starts, you're the one who's closest to Beverly."

"Don't ever think I'd forget it for a minute. I'm gonna scoop her right off that horse and lie down on top of her until the shooting stops, and you can bet I'll take it from there."

Dryden sighed. "Thanks."

"Don't thank me unless I get a chance to do it, Mr. Dryden. And I'd kind of rather I didn't. Stray bullets don't much care who they hit. Is that why you're heading the Germans north of that empty store building with the cistern? The horses are plenty thirsty, and I brought a bucket."

"Yeah, but there's a little gas station a quarter mile down the road that the Mexican family used to run."

Creighton nodded. "They still do. The woman's a widow now, but she's still running it, her and the kids. I guess there's no reason to get them shot. River's close now. The horses can wait and water there."

That was what Dryden had decided. A bit hesitantly, he made another decision and interrupted Waldau and Linares to warn them that once they'd managed to cross the highway and headed toward the Rio Grande they would start encountering a steady string of Indian pueblos, all with outlying farmlands surrounding them; in such inhospitable country, civilization, both new and old, clustered around water.

"We'll have to stop riding so bunched up." Dryden said. "Send out one or two scouts to see if the way ahead is clear. Otherwise you're going to have to shoot your way to Los Alamos, and even if that doesn't bring troops down on you, you'll be out of ammunition once you get there."

"I decline to feel concern about a few Indians," Waldau said. "We will avoid them if we can, of course, but speed is essential."

"Not just a few Indians," Dryden said. "More like a few hundred. The population of some of the pueblos easily runs that high. Like the Santo Domingos. Theirs will be the first pueblo we have to get around. Shoot a half dozen of them, and you're going to see how real American Indians act when they're on the warpath."

Dryden didn't mention that the Pueblo Indians tended to be peaceable people. It wasn't necessary. Were Waldau to shoot down any of their number, peace would be a thing of the past anyway. He was glad to see that Waldau, however sullenly, took his advice and sent out an advance guard as they moved on. Dryden knew they would be seen, no matter what they did. He could even hope that the Germans' trespass in such numbers would be offensive enough to cause someone to complain to the law. He couldn't be sure what might happen after that.

When they finally reached the Rio Grande Dryden gave no advice at all. That was because Waldau looked at the river, smiled at its size, and sent Albert Voight across first to scout the far bank. Dryden lounged as comfortably as his aching hip would allow on Sky's broad back and enjoyed the show.

Except in the spring melt, when it could roar down its sandy channel in a two-hundred-foot-wide torrent, the Rio Grande looked narrow and docile. Doves whistled out of the cottonwoods that lined the bank, and tiny sandpipers rose in panic from a midstream sandbar as the German party approached. But a deep, narrow current boomeranged unpredictably from side to side in the river, carrying the year-long flow south, and Dryden knew what would happen when Voight started across the far side of the sandbar.

So did Voight's horse. Voight was on Gypsy Belle, a big mare of mature age and placid outlook, but Gypsy didn't lack for horse sense. She splashed willingly through the icy water on the shallow side of the river, although she wanted to stop and drink, but she balked when Voight tried to move her on across the sandbar. He prodded. She stamped. He kicked. She gave him a look that meant she was thinking about rolling over on her side and getting rid of him, an old trick of Gypsy's when she was cross. Voight doubled his fist and leaned forward to slug her on the top of her head, but Gypsy must have sensed that the blow was coming. She started forward abruptly and instantly plunged into six-foot-deep water.

Gypsy kept her head above water. That was more than Voight did. The mare rose riderless and started swimming steadily, letting herself drift slightly to hit the far shore at an easy place to climb out. Voight appeared in her wake, splashing and wallowing, then sank again.

"His weapon!" Waldau cried. "Did he lose his weapon?"

No one seemed concerned about Voight. Dryden concurred. Let the bastard drown. But even weighed down with heavy wet clothes, Voight came up again and needed to swim only a few strokes to grab the trailing branches of a thicket of willows. He heaved himself ashore, then stood, staring across with open mouth, his heavy body already shivering.

Waldau turned angrily on Dryden. "Why didn't you warn us about deep water?"

"The river changes all the time," Dryden said. "Besides,

even a fool could see from the current that the bottom drops out over there. What does that make Voight?"

"An imbecile who has lost a valuable weapon," Waldau said. "Very well. What do we do now?"

"Let the horses water first," Dryden said. "That will quiet them. Then ride out to the sandbar and dismount, and swim the horses the rest of the way. Without men on their backs they'll go more willingly."

"What of our clothing?"

"If you're smart, you'll strip before you set out," Dryden said. "Otherwise you'll be wearing wet clothes the rest of the day, and you'll be as cold as Voight is. Knock a few tree branches together and make a small raft. Put your gear and guns on it and let a couple of men bob it across. You'll find the water a little cold for nude swimming, but at least you'll keep your clothes and weapons dry."

"You will be wet and cold, too, Captain," Waldau said.

"I'm counting on it," Dryden said. "I could use a bath."

He was worried, though. About Beverly. For the men to strip was one thing. For a woman to have to skin down to panties and bra in front of the men was something else. But when he nudged Sky over beside Little Lil, Beverly had only one objection.

"Ride around with cold, dripping undies in this kind of weather? You're surely joking," she said.

"Then leave them off when you put your clothes back on," Dryden said.

"Think again, darling. I'm not exactly flat-chested, as you know very well. I'd be bobbling and jiggling every time Little Lil started trotting. I'll send my clothes over on the raft, like everyone else. Undies included."

Creighton and the pack animals crossed to join Voight while a couple of the men gathered branches and formed a raft. The rest of the Germans shuffled, obviously expecting Beverly to retire to the shelter of the big cottonwoods that grew along the river so they could shuck their clothes. But she did no such thing. She studied them with bland interest as they stalled and waited and finally began to strip. Then she trained her eyes on Erich Huber. A rosy flush climbed to his forehead, and he turned his back on her to take off his shirt. He hopped from one foot to the other to get his shoes. He looked back over his shoulder to find her eyes still on him, and only an impatient order from Grebling forced him out of his pants and shorts.

"My, my," Beverly mocked loudly. "My, my, my. The little dear won't turn around. Angle over in front of him, Ned, and see if he really has a penis."

Huber bolted for the river, leading his horse. He hesitated when his bare foot first touched the water.

Beverly laughed. The back of Huber's neck turned red, and he threw an angry look at her. Briskly, calmly, Beverly then began to take off her clothes.

She might have been alone in her bedroom. First her jacket came off. Then the top sweater. Then the second sweater, revealing the form-fitting top of a set of long johns. She folded each garment neatly and stacked them on the jacket. Shoes and woolen socks next, then her woolen slacks, then the long johns. Without a pause she removed her bra, then her panties, folded them into the jacket, tied it into a sausage, and handed it to Dryden for the raft. White-fleshed as a goddess, full-breasted, firm-hipped, she turned a serene smile on Dryden, then looked back at Huber and thumbed her nose at him. She let her hand fall and stood still for a moment.

Look, every line of her white body said silently, Look at what I've given the man beside me. Look at what you'll never have.

Huber looked. Then he turned away hastily and stumbled awkwardly into the river. Ignoring all other glances, Beverly led her horse across the shallow water, then waded in unhesitatingly for the brief swim.

Dryden had to scramble to strip off the rest of his own clothes in time to lay them on the raft and follow. Right ahead of the raft, Pavel and Jürgen Frischauer were trying to ease their injured commander, still on horseback, across the channel. They had removed his shoes and trousers for him. The gash on Kleber's leg still looked nasty, Dryden saw. Nastier, in fact, with redness and inflammation spreading out from the wound. A healthy body would be healing without so much difficulty, but Kleber's poor body was hardly in a healthy state. At least he was on a quieter horse, good, reliable Starrgazer, whom Pavel had traded for Southern Starr.

Starrgazer was perfectly willing to go for a little swim, but his preference was to get it over with fast. The men, Pavel on one side and Frischauer on the other, were leading him too slowly. When the sandy river bottom began to slope steeply, Starrgazer jerked and tried to plunge ahead. Frischauer cried out.

"Keep him steady!" Pavel said.

"I'm sorry," Frischauer panted. "He stepped on my bad foot."

"Don't drag behind," Pavel said. "Come, horse. Come. Good horse. Now, swim!"

Somehow they all made it. The tail of Kleber's long flannel shirt was wet when he got to the other side, but Pavel, after waiting discreetly until Beverly was dressed, borrowed her scissors from her first-aid kit and cut off the shirttail, then hastily got Kleber into the rest of his clothes. Everyone was chilled. Voight, in his soggy clothes, looked frozen. Not one man offered Voight a dry shirt or the loan of a blanket. They had not forgotten their dead comrades.

Waldau finally relented and told Grebling to give Voight a saddle blanket, and the weather cooperated for a while as they pushed north, soon climbing again. Pale, wintry sunshine broke through the high cloud cover that had dogged them. It lasted two hours, then north wind blew the clouds back. Waldau allowed no rest periods the rest of the afternoon. He pushed the men hard, anxious to get to the final campsite before nightfall sent the temperature plunging back below freezing. Night came early at the winter solstice, and the wall of the twisting canyon they followed at the end of the day cast its own gray shadow even earlier than the night.

Waldau finally stopped. "How much farther to this cave of which you spoke to Oberst Kleber?" he demanded of Dryden.

"Maybe two miles," Dryden said. "Caves, actually. Don't expect too much. Most of them are little more than shallow pockets in the side of the canyon."

"I will need reconnaissance. This road that shows on the map. The one that leads to Los Alamos. How far is it from the caves?"

"Maybe another two miles," Dryden said. "But they're tough miles, up and over a difficult mountain. You'd be better off sending them now. They can backtrack and climb out of this canyon through the pass behind us. There's another canyon on the far side."

"You will give detailed instructions to Herr Linares," Waldau said. "Captain Grebling, you and Herr Linares will form a small scouting party to check for patrols. Take two men with you. Report back to the caves when you are finished."

"But sir, it will soon be dark," Grebling objected in a high-pitched whine.

"So?"

"But . . . how do we rejoin you? We have not seen the caves. We might not be able to find them in the dark."

"Captain Dryden will instruct Herr Linares. Once you are close, your horses will smell and hear the other horses. Then you will know you are back."

"We haven't eaten since—"

"You forget yourself, Grebling. I know when you last ate. Now do your duty. Do it efficiently and you will soon return. There will be food waiting."

The carrot and the stick. Waldau was good with both of them. For Dryden, the carrot alone seemed sufficiently tempting. In a few minutes they would reach the caves. Food and a chance for Beverly and Creighton to rest and get warm, a chance to look after the horses and to rest and get warm himself. Dryden didn't demur about giving directions to the spy. An interesting choice to lead a scouting party. Dryden had a mental image of the giant German skulking around the dry mountains of New Mexico, busily spying on whatever he found occurring there. Linares was matter-of-fact about the assignment. He questioned Dryden closely and briefly, then rode off to the rear with Grebling and his men as rapidly as the horses were willing to move.

The horses were ready to call it quits for the day. Even Sky walked with his head down and his ears drooping. In the last of the light Dryden pulled Sky gently to a stop and studied a crook of the canyon that faced south. Relief welled up. Some forty feet above the canyon floor, well above flood level, a deeper shadow loomed. The caves, at last.

Waldau was eager to explore, but for Dryden the horses had to come first. Just this side of the caves, still facing south, the canyon wall folded back among thick trees, creating a wide-mouthed enclosure. It wasn't quite a small box canyon, but close enough. Creighton rode in promptly on Young Jeb to check the canyon walls. Within a few minutes he rode back to the pack mules and chose one to unsaddle. Waldau stiffened as Creighton unpacked a large ax.

"Got only one ax, but we got the hatchet, too," Creighton said. "Mr. Dryden, you and the Germans start chopping tree limbs. We pile up enough slash, we can close the stock right in. That what you had in mind?"

"It's what I hoped," Dryden said. He translated quickly to Waldau, who chose Albert Voight, sullen, still soggy, to wield the ax. Perhaps it warmed him. As a temporary measure, Dryden stretched rope among the trees and waved the horses in. Cold hands stripped off wet saddles. Dryden had them stacked in a line on loose boulders at the foot of the wall, where they would at least have a chance to dry. Someone went to relieve Voight with the ax. They had to dig flashlights out of the supply packs to check the wall of brush when it was finally done. Then, laden with their kit bags, blanket rolls, and weapons, the Germans contemplated the forty vertical feet between them and the caves.

"Give me a flashlight," Dryden said. "There are steps and handholds. We just have to find them."

"Hurry," little Otto Boberach said. "I shall freeze soon if I don't get out of this wind."

"So move around and keep your blood circulating," Dryden said. He ran the beam along the smooth face of the rock. "Look for dead wood. There won't be any firewood in the caves."

"We have to carry it up there?"

"All the way," Dryden said. "Ah, here we are. The steps start here."

No regular stair steps and risers these. Here and there among the rocks shallow footholds had been chopped from the living rock with stone axes. Dryden climbed slowly, calling directions in both English and German. "Move to your right now. . . . Feel overhead, about head-height. . . ."

The rock was cold. The hands that had clung to it when the little ruin was last occupied were seven centuries dead. They gained a wide, flat ledge that overlooked the canyon floor and gazed into darkness at the back of the cave, from

205

which an even colder current of air seemed to ooze forth to halt them.

"*Mein Gott,*" Waldau said to Dryden. "Didn't you tell the Oberst there were rooms? Houses?"

"There are. What's left of them. Nobody's been around to do any maintenance." Dryden shone the flashlight beam inside the shallow sandstone cave. Clinging to its coldness was the crumbling cliff dwelling, mostly roofless, but with many stone walls intact. Some of the apartmentlike rooms were two stories high, but most were one story, honey-combed together, nestling against the back of the biggest cave. Around the ledge another cave yawned blackly. All the dwellings here were smaller. The suburbs.

The ruin had obviously been a modest, workaday sort of place, housing a small population that farmed the flat land above the canyon rim and hunted on the canyon floor.

"Home," Dryden said cheerfully. "Come on in."

"What of snakes?" Waldau asked.

"They'll all be asleep this time of year. But keep your eyes open. And stay out of the top stories. The floors weren't any too stable the last time I was in here."

"Bring lanterns," Waldau ordered. "Who has brought firewood? Quickly now. We shall build a fire."

Everyone bustled. Beverly, left guardless, came instantly to Dryden. Together they peered through small, square doorways and windows into small, empty rooms. They saw nothing but sandstone blocks that had slipped to the floor so long before that everything was covered with the same fine layer of windblown sand. The standing walls still showed traces of the reddish adobe mud used to plaster them. Rat turds littered the dirt floors, but even they looked ancient.

"Cozy," Beverly said. "Nice thick walls. It ought to be well soundproofed. I can't say much for the decor, though."

"You'll love it," Dryden said. "It's got cold and colder running water. At least, there used to be a spring. Come."

It was difficult to get from room to room. No doubt the original builders, whose very names had been lost with the civilization they had created, had found it good protection to slow down potential invaders. Dryden and Beverly had to edge nine feet along a narrow passage that led deeper into the ruins. Willi Roh and Franz Eggers squeezed after them, no doubt at Waldau's orders. There were two rooms at the

206

end of the passage. Dryden gave Beverly the flashlight and knelt to lift a heavy stone from the floor. The beam of light joined with water, clear and unmoving, seeping from the sandstone floor of the cave.

"Is it drinkable?" Beverly asked dubiously.

"Sure. It's probably why the Anasazis chose this particular run of caves for occupation," Dryden said. "Hauling it along the passage won't be fun, but it's better than going thirsty."

"Who are the Anasazis?"

"It just means 'the Ancient Ones.'"

Their flashlight was commandeered when they returned. Eggers gave Waldau a report on the spring, and Waldau looked pleased.

"Excellent," he said. "The ruins are somewhat uncanny, but in all they will make an excellent staging point. You have done well, Captain Dryden."

"What's my reward? I suggest it be that Lieutenant Bennington doesn't have to be tied up tonight."

"And I suggest it be that I allow you to live one more day," Waldau said. His customary crispness returned. "Lieutenant Bennington, you will now take your medical kit and attend to Oberst Kleber. Oh, and take a look at Private Frischauer. He apparently reinjured his foot earlier when crossing that river. Nothing to bother a man on horseback, but he's limping now. Perhaps I shall have the black cowboy make him a crutch. I want him rested and able to walk on his own two feet tomorrow. Captain Dryden, you will be my guide as I assign sleeping spaces to the officers and men."

There were far too few intact dwellings to go around, but the men seemed happy to bunk in together. With another man sleeping against your back, you have more warmth on such a cold night. A small fire was built in the very back of the cave, and the big coffeepot was soon bubbling. Creighton and Dryden, both guarded, were back with the horses, rationing out oats, when the scouting party returned.

"I want to hear this," Dryden whispered. He left Creighton with the last of the oats and climbed up after the scouts. He climbed more quickly this time, his hands and feet remembering old patterns, but Grebling was already at the fire, holding numb fingers to it, by the time Dryden gained the caves.

"The wind has dropped, but it seems colder now," Grebling complained.

"I do not wish a weather report," Waldau told him. "What of the road?"

Linares said, "Patrolled by troops, as you anticipated. It is only a dirt road, and the patrol is sporadic, but we saw at least one truck or jeep pass every twenty to twenty-five minutes."

"There are guard posts along the road?"

"None that we saw, but I suspect we would have found some if we had looked further. Captain Grebling was, um, convinced we should return promptly with our report."

Waldau looked worriedly at the fire. "And the outlying territory? This canyon? Also patrolled?"

"No, Colonel. Only the road to Los Alamos."

Waldau looked relieved. Dryden wasn't. He withdrew from the circle of men who had edged close to listen and walked to the lip of the ledge to look out. There were no lights. Anywhere. He could see only dark masses that were trees and the opposite wall of the canyon. Was Linares lying? Had they actually ridden as far as the road? If so, were there really trucks and jeeps filled with soldiers on the road, the dirt road to Los Alamos?

But hell, it was dark. How could Linares know for sure that the vehicles were military or the men inside soldiers? Maybe there was a celebration at the school for the inevitable students who couldn't make it home for the Christmas holidays. Maybe it was just the cook and his helpers coming home with supplies.

Disquieted, Dryden glanced back at the German soldiers around the fire. And even the smell of venison beginning to roast brought him no comfort.

# ELEVEN

The angry horse reared, hooves flashing, pounding at his shoulders. Pavel pushed the big blonde to safety, threw aside his half-eaten chicken wing, and reached for his machine pistol. He rolled over, tangled in his blanket, and raised the weapon. It was only Willi Roh, trying to shake him awake.

"God preserve us," Pavel muttered. He returned the Schmeisser to its place against the scabby rock wall and fought his way out of the blanket. His mouth felt like a ball of fur. He smacked his lips, trying to rid himself of the aftertaste of sleep. "Damn you, Willi. You wrecked a beautiful dream. I was on a picnic with a big milk cow of a wench, drinking cold beer and eating roast chicken. I thought you were one those *verdammt* horses."

"Come quick," Willi said.

Pavel heard murmurs outside the crumbled wall of the cubicle in which he had slept. The voices came from the mouth of the cave. His senses became more alert. "What is it?" he asked. "What's wrong?"

Willi's mousy features were ashen. He said, "You have to see for yourself, Pavel."

Quickly, Pavel pulled on his boots and retrieved his weapon. "I'm ready. What is it?"

Outside the ruin Pavel could see comrades at the broad cave entrance, clustered against the light, staring outside. Franz Eggers, Erwin Maschmann, Lampe, Detthard. He swung his eyes across the other dwellings, seeking Dryden and the girl. Had they tried once more to escape? No, they were both by a cook fire, huddled with the black cowboy in the back of the cave. Jürgen Frischauer sat near them on a rock, watching them. What then? Troops? A patrol?

Pavel hurried to the natural stone balcony that overlooked the canyon. Untied boots flopping, he nudged enlisted men out of the way and stared out at a world of silent brilliance. Snow everywhere. A mantle of white marched across distant mesas. It layered the canyon floor with a thick, shadowed carpet. Pine boughs sagged under its dazzling white weight. Even the horses, standing in their sheltered enclosure with their tails to the wind, wore a film of white across their flanks.

Willi Roh said, "It came in the night, Pavel. I felt the first flakes when I was on duty, but I didn't think it would get this bad."

"Have the officers seen it?" Pavel asked.

"Lieutenant Strikfeldt was here a moment ago," Willi said. "The others are still asleep."

"You'd better get them," Pavel said. As the little rifleman started toward the officers' dwelling Pavel called after him, "And tell Oberst Kleber what is happening."

Franz Eggers massaged his crooked elbow, as if the cold was getting to him. He said, "What now, Pavel? We can't mount a hit-and-run raid with snow on the ground. Not if we want to get away. We'd leave a trail a blind man could follow."

Erwin Maschmann said, "We have food enough. If we go on short rations, maybe we can wait for the snow to melt."

"We can't wait," Pavel said. "The U-boat is lying off the coast of Mexico. We've only six days to finish here and get to it."

Eggers shivered. "A U-boat will do us little good if the Americans track us down and kill us."

Maschmann said, "Maybe we shouldn't attack at all, not with so much snow. Why can't we just head for Mexico?"

"That kind of talk could get you a bullet in the head," Lampe said. "Colonel Waldau has a short temper."

"Sure, put yourself in Waldau's hands," Eggers sneered. "That bastard doesn't care if he gets us all killed."

Maschmann said morosely, "Pavel, do you think it's true? What the officers said about that atomical bomb? Could one plane blow up a whole city?"

"I don't know," Pavel said. "Oberst Kleber believes it. And he's a smart man. Perhaps there's something to it."

"A whole city?" Maschmann siad. "With everyone in it? What kind of monsters would explode a bomb like that?"

"We would, if we had it," Lampe said. "You heard the Oberst and Herr Boberach. We're trying just as hard to make the same kind of bomb. If it could end the war, don't you think we would use it?"

"The whole thing is a fairy tale," Eggers said. "It's an excuse to get us to throw our lives away. Nobody can make a bomb out of little atoms. Wait and see. We'll get up there and discover it's for nothing."

Pavel heard the rapid clop of boots coming toward the cave entrance. "Careful what you say," he murmured. "Waldau is on his way."

Ulrich Waldau marched up to them, decked out in his best SS field uniform, complete with decorations, death's-head cap, and high-topped boots. The tunic had been mended at the shoulder seams and across one torn pocket, and it was wrinkled from its journey in Waldau's knapsack, but it still looked good. Waldau's Standartenführer collar tabs had a bracing effect on the enlisted men. Pavel noticed they all stood a little straighter.

Waldau stared out at the snow and said, "Well, Sergeant Pavel. An invigorating sight, isn't it?"

"Yes, sir," Pavel said without conviction.

Waldau eyed Pavel's dirty, rumpled civilian clothing. "You should get rid of those rags, Sergeant. Get back in military harness. Go put on your uniform. It will make a new man of you."

"Yes, sir," Pavel said. "My uniform, sir?"

"A precautionary move," Waldau said. "We are close to the Los Alamos military reservation. I intend to take a small party to look it over. If we were to be captured, our intentions would be obvious. In civilian clothing we could be

211

arrested and executed as spies. As soldiers in uniform we merit the protection of the Geneva accords. Assuming we are caught, of course.''

"Yes, sir," Pavel said. "Some of the men were worrying about that, sir. They were wondering how we can mount an attack in deep snow without leaving a trail."

"There's an element of uncertainty in any battle," Waldau said. "That's what makes a soldier's life worthwhile. Spice for the stew." He waved a hand, dismissing the danger. "After coming this far I consider the prospect of capture highly unlikely. The important thing is to make certain the attack succeeds. We will manage. Oberst Kleber assures me you are the best soldiers he's ever led into battle."

"It would be nice if we had some chance for survival," Pavel said.

Waldau's cheerful expression wavered. He said, "I'm in good humor this morning, Sergeant Pavel. Don't spoil it." He swung his chin, regarding each face in the ring of soldiers. "Perhaps Oberst Kleber was overly optimistic about you," he said. "Like Pavel, you seem to have forgotten how to think and behave as soldiers. Perhaps you've been locked away in a prison camp too long. Too much time away from the plow can ruin the best of oxen. We shall rectify that, beginning now. I want everyone back in uniform immediately. All of you. From now on we shall function as a proper German fighting unit, with full regard for the proper chain of command. Understood?"

Pavel's cheeks burned from the rebuke. "Yes, sir."

More figures approached the cave entrance. Waldau looked around to see Dieter Grebling, also in SS uniform, coming from the Indian ruins, prodding Dryden before him. "Now we shall see," Waldau murmured quietly. "Sergeant Pavel, I want you breakfasted and ready to ride in a half hour. We'll need six horses. Lieutenant Strikfeldt and Herr Boberach will go with us. Also the American officer, Captain Dryden. Corporal Voight will ride along to watch over him."

"Yes, Herr Standartenführer."

Waldau waited until Dryden reached the stone balcony, then swept his hand, indicating the snow-white vista outside. He said, "Well, Captain? What do you think? Beautiful, is it not?"

"I like it," Dryden said. "It doesn't look so good for you, though."

"Perhaps," Waldau said. "Has the snow ended?"

"Not a chance. There's more coming. Maybe a lot."

"When?" Waldau asked.

Dryden looked at the leaden sky and turned his face to the wind. "Flurries later today. Noon, maybe. Mr. Creighton says by midafternoon for sure. There could be a hell of a storm tonight. Enough to trap you here for days."

"A bitter storm? With cold winds?"

"Arctic," Dryden said. "Plenty of ice as well as snow."

Waldau's eyes glittered. "Does that satisfy you, Sergeant Pavel?"

Pavel cocked an eyebrow, then sighed. "Yes, sir. I understand."

Waldau nodded smugly. "Come, Captain Dryden. We'll see to breakfast. Then you will accompany me on a ride."

As soon as they were out of earshot, Maschmann whispered, "What did he mean, Pavel? Why should more snow satisfy any of us?"

Pavel sighed. "He plans to use the storm," Pavel said. "We'll attack tonight, under cover of darkness. The snow and wind will cover us. I hate to admit it, but that SS bastard may know what he's doing."

"He knows enough to get us all killed," Eggers muttered. "Let's get some coffee before the officers drink it all. At least the condemned men should have a hearty meal."

Dryden gave Sky a nudge in the flank and turned into the trees. The Pajarito Plateau was a windblown washboard of soaring tabletop mesas and deep canyons, dotted with pine forests. Icy streams trickled through the canyons, nurturing stands of aspen, fir, and spruce. Heading west through the trees along the rim of one of the many rugged canyons, Dryden caught glimpses of the dark Jemez mountains just ahead. To the rear, looming beyond Santa Fe, rose the massive purple toe of the Rocky Mountains, the Sangre de Cristo range.

Dryden led the small band of uniformed Germans along snowy deer trails, working them in careful stages up the side of an incline. They were headed up the back of a rolling, jagged mountain covered with Ponderosa pine, looking for a secluded vantage point at the top. On the far side of the mountain, still hidden from their view by a rocky ridge, wound a wider canyon that Dryden knew well from his youth. Down the center of the canyon snaked a shallow, sandy stream hidden by groves of cottonwood trees. The wide canyon and the mesa beyond took their Spanish name from the thick cottonwoods: Los Alamos.

It was another gray day. They'd been in the saddle for almost three hours, plowing through drifts of snow when they had to, keeping to the trees as much as possible. Strikfeldt handled his mount well even in snowy terrain. Waldau had finally wised up and changed Wild Bill for a less stubborn mount, and he, Voight, and Pavel were holding their own. Only Boberach seemed to be having difficulty. The little man was still awkward with horses, and Dryden had to slow down time and again to help him up a rocky rise or through a cleft of boulders. Twice, when the trail torqued close to the hillside and fell off precariously to deep drifts, Dryden made them all dismount and walk the horses across. He told them it was for their own safety, but he was more worried about his stock. As Kleber had proved, even a surefooted animal can lose its balance when a trail has poor footing and the hand at the reins is inexperienced.

He paused to survey the heights above them. The trees thinned out about a hundred yards from the top. A hidden vantage point, Waldau had insisted. A ledge with boulders or trees from which they could see the mesa where the old ranch school rested. Dryden knew just the place, but he had made the trip as long and as hard as possible.

He could see the rocky approach to the ledge now. The horses would be left when they reached the end of the trees. To get to the ledge above they would have to traverse the top of a steep cliff just below the peak, a slab that dropped off at least sixty feet into a deep V-shaped crevasse between two sheer rock faces, plugged at the bottom with a deep mound of snow. Maybe the Germans would take one look at the icy footing along the cliff and lose their resolve.

"How much further?" Waldau asked. Steam rose from the horses' flanks as they rested.

"Up there," Dryden said. "Just above the trees."

They spurred the horses on. Now that they were this close, Dryden was eager. It had been years, at least eight or

214

nine, since he last saw the old Ranch School. But it was alive in his memory. The stables where they kept the horses, including some of his dad's. The faculty cottages where he and a kid from Maine had once sneaked in to steal a box of cigars from the biology teacher, Mr. Welch. The huge old Fuller Lodge, a stately log building with a wide veranda where school authorities held graduation ceremonies. And Ashley Pond, south of the lodge, which froze solid every winter. Dryden had spent many an afternoon on the frozen pond with the other students, cutting blocks of ice for the Ranch School ice house.

Would the school be the same? As hard as he tried, Dryden still couldn't imagine the rustic boys' academy as a hidden factory for secret weapons. The road on which Linares claimed to have seen patrols was a rutted dirt trail that wound thirty-five miles down to Santa Fe, clinging to the mountainside. His dad wouldn't drive to Los Alamos in the family car. Not even to pick Dryden up for summer vacation. Dryden had to catch a ride to Santa Fe with the good-natured school cook while his dad waited at La Fonda Inn, drinking bourbon and water and playing poker with Santa Fe cronies. If big Sam Dryden refused to drive the road even at the beginning of summer, how could Army trucks and factory workers make the trip on a daily basis when winter weather turned the road into a slippery, icy monster?

They reached the edge of the pines, and Dryden reined Sky to a stop. He dismounted and looped the gray's reins around the trunk of a pine. "You may as well stretch your legs," he told them. "We'll have to walk the rest of the way."

Strikfeldt and Waldau dismounted easily, followed by Voight. Pavel slipped from his saddle and helped Boberach down. Boberach arched his back and groaned. While Pavel and Voight tethered the officers' horses, Waldau took two sets of binocular cases from his saddlebag. He handed one case to Pavel and looped the other over his head. Strikfeldt folded several sheets of paper and slipped them into his tunic. Dryden watched silently, wondering what the paper was for.

Waldau gazed at the rocky path. The sixty-foot drop from the cliff near the top must have given him pause. He cocked an eyebrow at Dryden and said, "The path is iced. Is this the only way?"

"It should be okay," Dryden said. "The cliff ledge is wider than it looks. Just stick close to the mountain and pick your footing." He offered Waldau a look of challenge. "Unless you'd rather turn back."

"If you are prepared to walk it, then so will we," Waldau said. "Lead us to the top."

The wind picked up as they moved into the open, rattling their collars and whipping their trousers around their ankles. The snow was shallow on the windblown scree, and brittle. It crunched underfoot as they wound up the side of the mountain toward the narrow cliff.

Boberach began to breathe heavily after only a few strides. "It must be the altitude," he panted. "I find it difficult to catch my breath."

"You'll get used to it," Dryden said. "We're only at about eight thousand feet."

They worked their way to the cliff, fighting the chill wind. Pavel followed on Dryden's heels. They were only halfway across the ledge when Pavel suddenly muttered to himself and gripped Dryden's shoulder, pushing him to his knees. Dryden felt his body slip and begin to slide on the ice toward the V-necked drop. He clawed at Pavel's boots and held on. "Down," Pavel called to the others. "Everyone, quick. Down."

The Germans hit the icy surface of the cliff top. Dryden clung to Pavel's leg and inched back to firmer ground. "Are you crazy?" he hissed at Pavel. "You could have knocked me over the edge."

"What is it?" Waldau demanded. "What's wrong?"

"Riders," Pavel said. He pointed. "Two men. There. On the horizon. Below that far ridge."

Waldau brought his binoculars to his eyes. Dryden craned his neck and scanned the area, then finally saw them. At least a mile or two to the east. Two armed men in park ranger hats leading a pack mule along the top of a hogback. They were clearly patrolling the area. They rode slowly and purposefully, staying on high ground so they could see the broad sweeps of countryside below. Dryden frowned. Why would park rangers be out patrolling such wild, empty land in weather like this? Unless . . . Oh, God, he'd been praying the Germans were wrong about the Ranch School at Los Alamos. Could there really be some truth to Boberach's secret superbomb story?

The two riders continued along the hogback, tiny figures in the distance, moving in and out of piñon scrub. The clouds had been thick all morning, but as Dryden and the Germans lay watching, a hole broke through above them and a shaft of noon sunlight came beaming down, pinning them to the snow and ice. Pavel cursed softly. "You lied," he said to Dryden. "Now the sun is shining. Where is this storm you predicted?"

"Keep your lederhosen on," Dryden said. "The sun won't last. The storm is coming. I can smell it."

The riders moved slowly in the distance, paying no attention to the shaft of sunlight or the men caught beneath it. Waldau tracked their progress through the binoculars. Dryden wished for a way to signal the two riders, but they were too distant and the Germans too close, hugging the ground behind him. He stretched his neck to look over the side of the cliff, down the steep funnel-shaped drop that had almost claimed him. It was at least sixty feet to the bottom, but snow had spilled into the crevice from the top, forming a cushion some ten or twelve feet deep at the bottom. Perhaps even enough to have broken his fall. Could he have survived? Come out of it with no more than a busted rib or two? Perhaps. He was glad he hadn't been forced to find out the hard way.

"They're moving toward the valley," Waldau said. He tracked them with the binoculars. "They haven't seen us, but they appear to be coming in this direction." He glanced at Dryden. "How long before they reach the canyon below us?"

Dryden looked across the valley, judging the distance. "At least an hour," he said. "They'll have to cross three ridges. They'll be out of sight most of the time." As he spoke the two riders and the pack animal dipped below a far ridge. "There," Dryden said. "They're gone now."

"Let us get on with our business," Waldau said. He put his field glasses back in the leather case and gestured Dryden to his feet.

They inched across the rocky slab of the ledge and followed a worn path toward the top of the hill. The deer trail changed direction and started downward, and Dryden led them the rest of the way up by memory, climbing across a table of stone. Pavel grunted hard and tried to keep up with him, but the others began to fall behind. Dryden neared the sun-washed crest and hoisted himself up the last incline. He dropped into a cluster of rocks below the rim. Moments later Pavel dropped in beside him.

"What is this place?" Pavel asked.

"Another boy and I used to come here when we were sick of school," Dryden told him. "It took us almost half a day to hike across the canyon and climb the mountain, but it was worth it. We could sit in the rocks and watch the other kids move around on the mesa without being seen. It made us feel godlike, looking down majestically on all the antlike humans. I'll bet that's how Waldau feels when he orders you around."

"Your mouth never stops, does it?" Pavel said. "Well, I understand now what you did to Oberst Kleber. You stung him and stung him, like a fly, until he became impatient, and his impatience drove him to have that terrible accident. That won't work with me, Captain."

Waldau's head appeared near the crest. He climbed up too quickly, lost his balance, and sat down hard on the rocks. Boberach came next, blowing air through loose cheeks and pausing every few seconds to push his glasses back up on his nose. Strikfeldt and Voight clambered after him.

"Where is the Los Alamos mesa?" Waldau asked.

Dryden hooked a thumb over his shoulder. "Across the canyon," he said. "All you have to do is stand up."

Waldau eased himself up. He gazed in silence for a moment, then his face smoothed into a smile. "Wonderful," he murmured. "Remarkable." He rested his elbows on the surface of the rock and screwed his eyes to his field glasses again. "Yes, yes, a perfect view," he said. "Strikfeldt. Come. Look."

The junior officer slid up to join Waldau in the sunlight. Boberach and Pavel rose as well. Even Voight, who was supposed to be watching Dryden, swung his eyes to the vista below. Only Dryden resisted. He rested his back against stone and steeled himself, trying to work up his nerve. He was scared to death to look, dreading what he might find. He had hoped Waldau would take one quick glance at the mesa across the canyon and curse in disappointment, with nothing to see but the familiar log buildings of the old school. But it was too late. The moment was past. Waldau's face, pressed to his binoculars, radiated only satisfaction.

"It's larger than we were led to expect," Boberach breathed. "So many buildings. How many people would you say?"

"Two thousand," Waldau said. "Perhaps three."

Dryden blinked. Two thousand people? On his mesa? There couldn't be room for that many people. The necessity to know had to be faced. He pushed to his feet to see what had to be seen.

What he saw was like a blow to the stomach. On the far north side of the wide canyon loomed the cloudy, gray Los Alamos mesa, rising from the canyon floor like an aircraft carrier. The old Ranch School buildings were still there, but you had to look hard for them. The nearest rim of the mesa held a sprawling assortment of large wooden structures surrounded by barbed wire. Buildings he'd never seen before. The rest of the mesa was covered by a jumble of house trailers, quonset huts, and barracks buildings. A curtain of smoke hung over the flimsy buildings as hundreds of coal furnaces and wood burning stoves struggled to heat them.

"Barbed wire around the bigger wooden buildings," Waldau murmured. "That must be the technical area."

Strikfeldt pointed. "And a second ring of wire around the entire area, including the sleeping quarters. We'll have to cut through both."

Pavel made a sad sound. "It looks like a POW camp."

Dryden leaned in rigid silence against the rock, stunned by what he saw. His rustic old school, once charming in its isolation, had become an ugly teeming town. Barbed wire. A wooden water tower among the larger laboratory buildings. Rutted dirt streets, covered with snow. No sidewalks. Frail clapboard apartment houses with drab gray and green siding squeezed together in crowded clusters. Rows of quonsets sat flank to flank. Los Alamos mesa topped off at 7,200 feet, some 800 feet lower than their vantage point, and they could see the congestion clearly.

"So many people," Boberach said. "They can't all be

atomic scientists. There aren't that many good physicists in the world."

"It would seem the American army has constructed a small town for them." Waldau said. "As with any military encampment, it would require a sophisticated population. Technicians. Wives and children. Doctors. Teachers. Support people to run their stores. Military guards."

"I must make notes," Strikfeldt said. "We'll need a detailed map." He extracted the folded sheets of paper from his tunic and smoothed them on a rock. "Pavel, be prepared to assist me."

Pavel popped his binocular case and pulled out the second set of field glasses. While he waited he caught the silent look of shock on Dryden's face. He hesitated, then placed the binoculars wordlessly in Dryden's hands. Dryden pressed the field glasses gratefully to his eyes and focused on Fuller Lodge, seeking comfort in the familiar. It was still there by Ashley Pond, great polished log columns fronting the veranda, but it was crowded mercilessly from all sides. Gone were the wide sweeps of grass and clean-smelling pines, crowded out by the temporary living quarters and boxy working structures. He could see a few figures slogging through the snow, heads bent against the cold wind. South of the pond, toward the technical area and the road to Sante Fe, a huge curved building had been constructed as some kind of main office. Checkpoints spanned the road. Signs bearing the insignia of the Army Corps of Engineers prohibited entrance without a pass.

Waldau chuckled appreciatively behind his own glasses. "The fools. They've set their primary security to guard against trespass from the road. Very little has been done to protect the perimeter. Pavel, how many armed men would you estimate?"

Pavel retrieved his field glasses from Dryden and picked out the military barracks buildings. He studied them, then counted sentry boxes and guard posts scattered along the road and stretched around the barbed-wire technical enclosure. "At least sixty guards standing duty at this moment," he said. "Add a few mounted guards and figure three revolving shifts. I'd say a total military complement of some two hundred men."

"Two hundred men?" Boberach said nervously. "Two hundred against our twenty? How can we succeed?"

"Surprise is our greatest weapon," Waldau said. "Secret movement to the objective. Silent penetration. Brief and bloody combat. Rapid disengagement. Swift withdrawal."

"But what if they see us coming?"

Waldau chuckled, pleased with what he saw. "They won't see us. We'll cross the canyon under cover of darkness. We can leave the horses in the trees below and scale the mesa from the south. Most will be asleep in their bunks."

"And the scientists?" Boberach asked.

"Easily managed," Waldau said. "Once we have infiltrated the target area we will assemble in a temporary command post. The main action group, led by Lieutenant Strikfeldt and Sergeant Pavel, will disperse to seek the designated targets and prepare them for destruction. A special task force under my command will remain at the command post to collect the renegade scientists. We'll be in and out before they realize what has hit them."

Dryden stared at Waldau, quietly appalled. Was the man serious? Did he really plan to attack an armed stronghold like Los Alamos mesa with only twenty men?

"There is a guard tower on the rim of the canyon," Pavel pointed out. "And I see a patrol path just inside the wire fence. We'll have to be careful if we approach the slope from below."

"Show it to Lieutenant Strikfeldt," Waldau told Pavel. "We'll want every sentry post marked on the map."

Pavel passed the binoculars back to Dryden and bent over Strikfeldt to indicate the tower and sentry boxes. Strikfeldt marked each, then continued sketching and making notes on his folded sheets of paper, forming a preliminary map of the mesa top.

"We should select our command post in advance and put it on the map as well," Waldau said. "Perhaps one of the houses. We need a quiet location where we can assemble the scientists while the assault team sets explosive charges."

The sun drifted behind thick cloud for a moment, plunging them into gray half-light. Dryden grimaced.

"There are several primary scientists on my lists," Boberach said. "But I had not expected so large an installation. How will we find them?"

"That may not be so difficult as you think," Waldau suggested. "If I understand your list correctly, we are concerned only with the leading intellects, a handful of men who will be accorded special treatment. For example, whom among them would you consider the most important?"

"They are all respected," Boberach said. "Fermi. Bethe. Frisch. Ulam. All of them. But perhaps . . . yes, Niels Bohr, the Dane. He would be the most honored. Most of us have studied under him at one time or another."

"Let us consider this Niels Bohr, then," Waldau said. "I assure you he will not be living in common housing with the store clerks and army personnel. We are seeking scientists with giant egos who consider themselves irreplaceable. Look for the better houses. Your Danish scientist and others like him will almost certainly be found in the finest quarters." He swept the mesa with his binoculars. "There, those houses among the trees. Beyond the green apartment complexes." He handed his glasses to Boberach and pointed him in the right direction. "Do you see the houses I mean? We'll pick the largest and use it as our command base. Perhaps the one with the American jeep in front of it. The size indicates an inhabitant of importance, possibly even this Bohr person. The identity of the inhabitant doesn't concern me. No matter who lives there, he can be forced to help us."

Dryden swung his borrowed field glasses to see which houses the SS colonel was talking about. He found them quickly, the commodious old log cabins that once housed the faculty at the ranch school. More specifically, a big log cabin with a jeep in front of it, the cabin that the head schoolmaster had once inhabited. A sprawling place with its own bathtub. Waldau could be right. Someone of importance must surely be living in it. An armed khaki figure stood by the jeep, shivering in the wind. None of the other cabins were guarded.

"The houses are deep in the complex," Pavel objected. "Reaching them will be dangerous."

"Not if we are covered by the storm," Waldau said. "Remember, the key is silence. Rapid movement. Cover and concealment. Keep low at all times. Avoid open areas. Once we seize the house, you and Lieutenant Strikfeldt can lead the assault force to the technical area to set the charges. No alarms. No shooting. We must not be discovered before

222

the explosions begin. You will so instruct the assault team. Stealth and silent death only. The knife and garrote."

"How many explosive charges will we need?" Strikfeldt asked. "Can we determine which buildings are to be destroyed?"

Waldau swung his glasses to the technical area. "The buildings we seek will almost surely be within the smaller fenced area," he said. "Perhaps we can determine the purpose of each from its shape and size. Herr Boberach, is that possible?"

Boberach stood on tiptoe and looked over the edge of the rock, concentrating on the technical area. "Probably the larger buildings," he said. "There will be a chemistry laboratory and a physics building among them. And some of the machinery—the Cockcroft-Walton generator and the big Van de Graff machines, for example—would need space, as would the Harvard cyclotron. They may even have a cryogenics laboratory. If we hope to cripple the project permanently, it might be safer to explode all of the buildings in the technical area. Especially the larger buildings."

"I count seven large buildings within the wire," Strikfeldt said. He made additional notes on his chart. "It would be easier with timers, but we can try mixing slow fuses with fast fuses and time them to go off together. I'll estimate distances and splice them before we leave the caves. Is that acceptable?"

"You may need an eighth charge," Boberach said. "If the Americans have any appreciable amount of the purified uranium isotope, it will still be quite small. Perhaps no more than ten pounds. They could easily store it in one of the smaller buildings. We cannot allow it to survive. Someone will have to seek it with the Geiger counter."

"If it's so small, why bother?" Pavel asked. "Can't the Americans replace it?"

Boberach shook his head. "Not for months, and only at great expense. Purified uranium is the heart of the bomb. My colleague, Werner Heisenberg, estimates the first ten pounds of usable purified uranium will cost the Americans at least twenty million of their dollars. Perhaps twice that amount."

"If the purified uranium exists, we will find it," Waldau said. "We'll need someone small enough to slip through any window. Pavel, who would you suggest? Private Roh? Yes, he's small. He will carry the Geiger apparatus. Herr Boberach can instruct him in its use when we return to the caves."

Dryden could see heavy storm clouds thickening on the horizon. He still couldn't know whether Waldau and Boberach were correct about a crazy big bomb being constructed on his mesa, but something major was obviously happening there. Waldau's strategy was daring, dangerous, even foolhardy. But what if it worked? Who could stop them? If the storm came before nightfall, the Germans could slip across the canyon and up the side of the mesa with no problem. Once there, they could do a lot of damage.

"And if we are discovered?" Pavel asked.

The sun slipped into the open again, washing the canyon and the hilltop with a temporary layer of bright gold. It wouldn't last long. The storm clouds were rolling in rapidly from the north.

"Yes, I suppose that possibility exists," Waldau said. "We will hold the scientists hostage in the main house until the explosions begin. If the Americans stumble across members of the assault team and open fire, we will execute the scientists. Otherwise we will wait until we hear the first of the explosions."

Boberach looked pained. "We won't have to kill anyone if we aren't discovered, will we?"

Waldau gave him a queer look. "Why should it matter to you? They're all Jews and renegades. Men who fled the Fatherland to avoid service to the Führer."

"Some of them were my friends," Boberach murmured.

Pavel seemed unsatisfied. "Let us get back to the possibility of discovery," he said. "How do we escape?"

"Don't be an old woman," Waldau said. "Our major concern should be the success of the mission. If we do our duty and carry out our tasks, escape will take care of itself."

"A bit of planning would help," Pavel said. "The men will fight more readily if they are convinced they have a chance to survive."

Waldau chose to ignore him. "We'll need a reasonable approach from the floor of the canyon," Waldau said. He leveled his field glasses again, scanning the mesa. "Look for a path, or steps, or a deer trail up the side of the slope."

Pavel's face was grim, but he joined in with the others, looking for the best route to the top.

Dryden knew he had to do something. He had to alert the guards on the mesa somehow. Perhaps the men manning the guard tower, overlooking the canyon. He glanced at the field glasses in his hand, then at the position of the sun. Flashes from the lenses? If he could judge the angle correctly, he might catch someone's eye.

"There's a small building on the canyon floor below the technical area," Boberach said. "See the concrete blast walls? They probably use it to test the initiator explosives. Perhaps there is a pathway from the top."

Waldau swung his binoculars. "Yes, I see the blast walls," he said. "No, even with a path the bluff appears too steep. And perhaps too well guarded. I prefer a gentler slope, something away from the technical center. There, near the road. See how the ground stretches out? We could come up that way, cut through the fence, and make our way to the houses."

Dryden judged the sun again, then lowered the glasses and tilted them, exposing the lenses. He waggled them experimentally, looking for a telltale spot of reflected light across the mesa. On his fourth try he thought he saw a flicker dancing among the technical buildings. He waggled again.

"Yes, that will be our path of access," Waldau said. "Manageable, even through snow. A circuitous route to the big log houses. And from there to the target buildings." He panned the glasses to the technical area. "The assault team can breach the inner fence just below—" He stopped and focused his glasses, then whirled on Dryden, his face a mask of fury. "Stop him!" he said.

Dryden dropped the field glasses to his chest, but too late. Voight and Pavel clamped his arms, yanking him away from the rock. Waldau stepped in and snatched the glasses from his neck. "You were trying to make sun signals!" he said.

"Blow it out your asshole," Dryden said.

He offered it in English, but Waldau may have understood the general drift. He smacked Dryden across the face with an open palm, then fumbled his Walther P-38 from its holster. With a quick motion he drew back the slide and raised the cocked pistol to Dryden's head.

Pavel stepped in quickly. "No, Colonel, don't!" he

blurted. "You cannot! A shot would be heard. It would give away our position!"

Waldau held the pistol level for a moment, then let his hand fall. He lowered the hammer and jammed the pistol back in his holster. "Get him out of my sight," he told Pavel. "Take him down from the crest and wait below for us."

Pavel unlimbered his Schmeisser and nudged Dryden in the back. Dryden went willingly. As they clambered away from the rocks and worked their way down the rugged slope toward the narrow cliff edge the sun disappeared again. This time for good. The clouds rolled in, thick and angry.

"You're a fool," Pavel muttered, following Dryden down the slippery path. "What possessed you?"

"I'm a soldier, like you," Dryden said. "What would you have done?"

"I wouldn't throw my life away," Pavel said. "Do you know how close he came to shooting you?"

"No risk, no gain," Dryden said. But his legs trembled as he lowered himself the last few feet to the cliff ledge, and it wasn't all from muscle strain.

The cliff slab was level and windy. Pavel said, "We'll wait here for them." He gestured with the Schmeisser, indicating Dryden was to stand at the edge of the cliff, away from him. As they waited the first light flakes began to fall.

Dryden said, "You see? I told you the snow would come."

"Don't be so lighthearted!" Pavel snapped. "What's the matter with you, man? Can't you see the trouble you are in? You're a fool. Waldau is not Kleber. He will not forgive you."

Dryden shivered. The wind rose, swirling flakes past his head and shoulders. "What will he do?"

An icy pebble rolled down the side of the mountain. Pavel looked up. "They're coming," he said. He shook his head. "You must face your fate alone. I can't help you."

Waldau came first, leading the way down the rock trail, with Voight behind him and Strikfeldt assisting Boberach in the rear. Waldau, when they reached the cliff ledge, was cold and calm. He gazed at Dryden and said, "You have outlived your usefulness sooner than I anticipated, Captain. Now you will die."

Pavel and Strikfeldt exchanged looks. Strikfeldt took a

half step forward and said, "Sir, that would be a mistake. We still need him."

"No longer," Waldau said. "His stubbornness has created difficulties for us from the beginning. He has attempted to suborn the loyalties of our men. He has tried consistently to foil our progress through escape attempts. Now he has attempted to expose our position to the enemy. His continued disobedience outweighs his utility. I say he must die. Without delay."

"Sir, please," Strikfeldt pleaded. "I must respectfully remind you, we are bound by the Geneva accords. Captain Dryden is a military prisoner. Wait at least until we return to the caves. To kill him without trial or due process is wrong."

"We have no time for such niceties," Waldau said. He dipped his chin at Voight. "Corporal Voight, execute the prisoner. Your knife, please. Do it silently."

Strikfeldt, still troubled, drew himself up. "I wish to go on record with my objection, Herr Standartenführer. I have no wish to be labeled a war criminal."

Belatedly, Pavel stepped forward and said, "I also object, sir."

With an obvious lack of concern, Waldau said, "You may rest your consciences, gentlemen. Your objections are noted. And disregarded." For a moment he studied the two men, on the verge of commanding them to hold Dryden for Voight's knife, then he gave up the idea. "Corporal Voight, carry out my orders."

Voight unsheathed his knife. Dryden's mouth went dry. He hadn't expected it to go this far. He took a step back, but his heel hit a loose stone at the edge of the cliff. He heard it click and fall. Voight advanced slowly, readying the blade. Dryden flicked a look over his shoulder, seeking room to retreat. Less than a foot to the edge. His eyes were drawn to the knife, coming closer, closer. Good God, he didn't want to die. He couldn't die. Not now. His gaze touched the deep V-shaped cleft, falling starkly into the gray gloom. An unthinkable thought, born of desperation, clawed for his notice. He remembered the deep snow mounded at the bottom. Sixty feet down.

Voight slashed at Dryden's midsection, testing his reactions. Dryden sucked in his gut and backed to the edge, but his foot slipped and he had to fight for balance. Voight grunted. The big corporal tried to keep a blank face, but it was obvious from the glitter in his eyes that he had seen Dryden's momentary slip on the icy surface. He circled to Dryden's left. Dryden edged toward the deep cleft, feeling with his heel for the rim of the cliff. It was a terrible idea, but he had no alternative. Could he find the nerve? He must, if he wanted to survive. The big German waited until Dryden stopped moving, then feinted with the knife. Dryden allowed himself to be intimidated and ducked away too quickly. His feet begin to skitter on the slippery ledge. It was all Voight needed. He swung the knife, slashing at Dryden's stomach. Dryden yanked away at the last moment, felt the knife slice through the outer edge of his jacket, felt the ground drop away beneath his feet, felt the rush of air as he toppled backwards, flailing. It was a long fall. Far longer than he had expected. The stone sides of the V-shaped funnel swept past, narrowing. He remembered wondering vaguely if the cushion of snow could really be as deep as he'd hoped.

Then he remembered nothing.

Pavel gasped. It had happened so quickly. One moment Voight was swinging the knife, and then it was over. The icy footing. A single wrong step. A sharp cry. The vision wouldn't go away. Dryden slipping, falling, his arms wind-milling frantically. A soldier deserved a better death.

"Is he dead?" Waldau called.

Voight stood at the edge of the cliff, staring down. "Yes, Herr Standartenführer, I think so. It's a long way to the bottom."

Strikfeldt moved cautiously to Voight's shoulder to check. Pavel followed, carrying his Schmeisser. He poked his head over the edge and looked down. The drop was dizzying. Far below, half buried in snow, Pavel saw Dryden's head, arms, and one leg.

"Yes, he's dead," Strikfeldt said. He gazed at the far ridges. "Someone should climb down and hide the body. If the riders come this way, they might see him from below."

Waldau nodded, satisfied. "Then do so. Send someone. We can't risk discovery now."

"It's too deep," Pavel said. "We'll never make it."

Strikfeldt sighed. "I'll try." He paced around the mouth

of the cleft, looking for the best way down, then lowered himself over the edge. He began a careful descent, picking his footholds. The snow continued to fall.

"What will we do now?" Boberach asked Waldau timidly. "He was our guide. When the assault is done and the American pursuit begins, who will lead us out of the mountains to safety? How will we get to Mexico?"

"The black cowboy will guide us," Waldau said. "The woman will tend our wounded and the cowboy will lead us to safety. Once we reach the Mexican border, their usefulness will be at an end as well."

Strikfeldt was forced to stop before he was ten feet down. The snow was coming harder, and he was having difficulty finding handholds. He tried another route without success. Finally he called, "I can't get down from here. I'm coming up."

It was Voight who saw the riders. He murmured to Waldau and pointed. They were closer now. Their horses had crossed another ridge and were slogging along in the blowing snow. The men's faces were masked by scarves. Pavel called to Strikfeldt to hurry.

The artillery lieutenant climbed faster. Pavel reached down to help him to the top. Strikfeldt took several deep breaths, then said, "Perhaps we can reach the body from below."

"Enough," Waldau said. "Leave him. Get to the horses."

Strikfeldt looked down at Dryden. "But what if he's visible from the ground? What if they see him?"

Waldau turned his face to the wind. "Let him be. The snow will cover all traces. Come. It's time to return to the Indian caves."

# TWELVE

Soldiers were waiting for them at the cave entrance. Several of the troopers crowded around with questions, but Waldau shooed them away. Pavel accepted a tin cup of hot coffee from the sentry and listened while Waldau told Strikfeldt and Grebling to assemble the troops. Pavel drained his coffee quickly. He wanted to see Oberst Kleber before the meeting, to tell him what had happened on the mountaintop across from Los Alamos mesa.

Pavel felt oddly disoriented as he crossed the stone balcony toward the ruins. His eyes, subjected to the blinding white-on-white brilliance of an afternoon snowstorm, hadn't yet adjusted. The primitive buildings at the back of the cave seemed dark. They were also incredibly inviting. Pavel was tired after the long ride, and hungry. He thought of his pallet in the cubicle next to Kleber's. To roll quietly under his blankets. To close his eyes. God, it sounded good. Waldau was determined to leave with the assault team as soon as it was dark. Two hours from now. Surely there would be a chance to rest before they mounted up.

Franz Eggers came through a crumbling stone wall and saw Pavel. He nudged Willi Roh, and the two of them hurried to intercept him. "Did you find the assault site?" Willi asked.

Pavel nodded.

"What was it like?"

"Awesome," Pavel said without breaking stride. "A small town atop a mountain. Surrounded by barbed wire."

They followed him a few steps. "Can we do what Waldau wants and get out with our skins?" Franz Eggers asked.

Pavel shrugged. "Perhaps," he said. "Go and hear for yourselves. Waldau has called a meeting." The two men exchanged looks and peeled off to the cave entrance. Pavel called after them, "Willi, check with Herr Boberach. There is a special assignment for you." He kept walking.

Escape. Survival. That's all any of them would be thinking. Waldau was a fool not to recognize it. To hell with them all. Pavel wasn't their keeper. He would be taking the same chances. It was part of the business of being a soldier.

The black cowboy and the nurse were under guard beside a small fire in front of Kleber's cell. The guards, Erwin Maschmann and Jürgen Frischauer, seemed even more grateful than the two Americans for the warmth, but as Pavel approached, Frischauer reached for a pine pole crutch and hobbled to his feet. Maschmann lifted his chin nervously and said, "Is it on?"

"It's on," Pavel said. "We leave at nightfall."

Maschmann poked the fire. "Damn."

The nurse gazed past Pavel, searching through the figures at the cave entrance. "Where's Ned?" she asked. "Captain Dryden? Why isn't he with you?"

Pavel switched to English. "He's dead," he said.

The color drained from her face. After a moment, she said, "How?"

Pavel, repenting his abruptness, said, "It was an accident. A patch of ice. He fell off the mountain. I do not think he suffered."

The black cowboy glared. "You're lying. Eddie knows how to handle himself on snow, ice, you name it. He wouldn't fall off a mountain unless he was pushed."

"I can only tell you what I saw," Pavel said stiffly. "He slipped on the ice and fell. It was very quick." He broke eye contact with the black and slipped back into German, speaking to Frischauer and Maschmann. "Prepare yourselves. We

231

leave in two hours. Only Herr Linares will remain behind, to guard the prisoners. Is Oberst Kleber awake?"

Frischauer said, "I think so. I took him an extra blanket a few minutes ago."

Pavel bent over to slip through the breach in the wall. Kleber was lying on a pallet in the corner. A candle from the ranch flickered near his head. His face was pale and covered with sweat, in spite of the chill, but he dredged up a smile when Pavel came through the opening.

"Friend Pavel," he said hoarsely. "How went the expedition?"

Pavel squatted beside him. "Not as well as I would have liked," Pavel said. "The American is dead. Waldau ordered it."

Kleber's face registered dismay. "Why? What happened?"

"We caught him trying to signal the mesa," Pavel said. "Lieutenant Strikfeldt wanted to bring him here for punishment. Waldau insisted it be done immediately."

"I see," Kleber said. "He was an honorable enemy. Was his death fitting?"

Pavel sighed. "He died with some dignity, if that's what you mean," he said. "I'm sorry, Herr Oberst, but I've seen too many needless deaths lately. I'm beginning to think no one dies well when he is alone or far from home."

"Don't despair, Pavel. You'll come through this."

"I was thinking of my comrades," Pavel said. "Waldau is a bloodthirsty prick. His only concern is the success of the assault. He doesn't care two pfennigs whether the rest of us live or not."

"He's a good officer," Kleber said. "You may not agree with his values, but you must trust his judgment. He'll bring you through this ordeal."

Pavel shook his head. "I've seen the mesa. And I've listened to Waldau. We may succeed in our mission, but I doubt many of us will survive it. The country is too wild. They'll hunt us down and cut us to pieces before daybreak."

Kleber was silent, then reached out to touch Pavel's sleeve. "Yes, Pavel, I know. Escape is unlikely. I've known from the beginning. It seems a great deal to ask, the sacrifice of so many young lives. But the alternative is far worse.

Hundreds of thousands of innocent civilians may die if you fail.''

"I don't need a sermon," Pavel said roughly. He rose, staring down at Kleber's extended form. "I'll do my duty. We all will. If we die, we die. But the blame falls squarely on you. Damn it, you had no right to get hurt. We needed you. Many of us followed you through Africa, and we would have followed you to hell in America. With you in command we could have accomplished anything. Perhaps even survival. Now you are useless to us. By default, Waldau is our leader. If none of us makes it back, our blood will be on your head.''

Kleber's seamed face caved in. "I'm sorry you feel that way, Pavel.''

Pavel gazed at him a moment, then relented. "No, that's not how I feel. I'm tired, Herr Oberst. Nothing more. It's been a long day.''

Kleber turned his face to the wall. Pavel stood above him, trying to think of something else to say, something that might diminish the damage he had done. Nothing came. Wordlessly, he hooked the machine pistol over his shoulder and left the crumbling cubicle.

Frischauer hobbled over, leaning on his pole. He nodded toward the cave entrance where the uniformed soldiers had gathered, carrying their weapons. "Look at them," he said. "Feel the electricity. It will be a brisk night, full of danger. May I ride beside you, Pavel?''

Pavel regarded his friend for a moment, then said, "You aren't going. New orders from Oberst Kleber. He doesn't think you can climb the mesa. You will stay behind with Herr Linares to guard the two prisoners. If the assault goes against us and we do not return, it will be your duty to see that Oberst Kleber reaches safety. Can you do that?''

Frischauer blinked. Realization came slowly. His face stayed blank, but his eyes betrayed his relief. He said, "Take the Oberst to safety? Yes. Yes, of course. We can manage that.''

"Good," Pavel said. He stepped toward the stone balcony to join the others. Yes, it would be a brisk, dangerous night. Perhaps Dryden was the lucky one, after all.

\* \* \*

Dryden opened his eyes to swirling snow. Cold. So cold. He was in a deep snowdrift at the foot of the funnel. The wind had shifted with the increased intensity of the storm, and now the snow was whipping out over the mountainside above him. He tried to move and sagged back. His whole body ached. The distance from clifftop to snowdrift must have been greater than he thought. Or the cushioning drift not as deep.

He lay half-buried in the snow, sorting through sensory perceptions. A pulsating ache here. Soreness there. Pain in the hips. Stiffness. Cold all over. Was anything broken? Only one way to find out. The fingers first. Good, they moved. Try the arms. Yes. Now lift the shoulders. Jesus, sore as hell. But they seemed to work. Okay, pull the legs from the snow. He tugged his right leg free, then his left, wincing with the effort. He rested briefly, then raised a hand slowly to his face to wipe snow away. What about the feet? Yes, he could feel his toes. Could he move his ankles? A little pain, but they responded. Legs? Hips? He tested each slowly.

He hurt like an old dog forgotten and left outside in a storm, but he was still in one piece. Were the Germans gone? He lifted his eyes to the top of the funnel. No one. How long had he been here? He spread his elbows and grunted to a sitting position. Snow fell from his chest in cakes. He swung his gaze to the open side of the funnel, seeking clouds and horizon, wondering what time it was. There was no horizon. Only thick, fat flakes whipping silently past the cleft, obscuring his vision. It was a heavy snow. Almost a blizzard. At least it still seemed to be daylight. With his cold but protective blanket of snow removed, his teeth began to chatter. He tugged his collar closer to his throat and shivered.

He knew he had to get down from the funnel soon and find shelter or risk freezing to death. He rolled over and tried to stand. His legs plunged deep into the snow again. He pulled them free gingerly and crawled to the stone slab, spreading his weight. Which way? Up? He raised his eyes to the cliff. No, too steep. He'd never make it. Down to the base then? He inched his way to the outer edge of the snowbank, clinging to the vertical slab. Wind whistled past his cheeks as he looked down. Yes, perhaps. He couldn't see the bottom; the snow was falling too thickly. But he knew where it was. If he could ease himself past some fifteen feet of ragged outcropping, he might reach the trail.

It wouldn't be easy. He pulled numb hands from the icy slab one at a time and blew on them, trying to warm them. His fingers tingled. He flexed them and gripped a broad sliver of stone leading to the exposed face, then pulled himself carefully to his feet. Hand over hand he edged out to the lip of the cleft and found a foothold. Snow broke loose beneath him and toppled into the void. He hugged tight, listening for the soft shush as it plunged to the bottom. He heard nothing but wind. Slowly he began to move again, picking each foothold, each handgrip with meticulous care. His body rebelled at first, offering stabbing aches and twinges with each movement, but the harder he strained and worked, the less it bothered him.

The wind racketed and sleet mixed with snow stung his cheeks. He found a good grip and paused, then felt carefully for the next hold, testing. His fingers encountered a slight glaze. The sleet was beginning to stick. Much more and he would be in deeper trouble. He tried to hurry his pace, picking each handhold just as carefully, but holding it for a briefer time. Urgency propelled him. He worked his way across the stone face as swiftly as he dared, teetering between compulsory speed and caution. Sleet pelted him, rattling against the stone. And then, unexpectedly, his foot touched solid ground. He stopped and felt with his toe, seeking the limits of the footfall. Was it the path, or only false hope?

He craned his neck to peer over his shoulder. What he saw sent a surge of gladness through his body. He laughed softly to himself. It was the path. Snowy. Narrow. Steeply inclined. But relatively safe. He strained for a new handhold and dragged himself inches closer, then lurched to rocky security. His lungs swelled with relief.

He sagged to a tumble of snow-covered rocks and rested for a moment. The wind blustered, and he groaned back to his feet. He had to keep moving. Would the horses still be down in the trees? No. The Germans were long gone by now. He'd have to make his way through the storm on foot. And suddenly, with a rush, he realized the potential advantage of his situation. As far as the Germans were concerned, he was dead. Nothing he did now, no decision he made, could harm Beverly or Creighton. He could only help them. He was free.

But where would he go? Los Alamos or the caves? Los Alamos was on the other side of the mountain and across the canyon. It was a long trek through the snow and wind, but he could warn someone about the Germans. Assuming he had the time it would take him to get there. The Indian caves were closer. He could reach the caves easily if he stayed on the canyon floors and avoided the circuitous rolling route he had shown to Waldau and the others. But the Germans were still there. And he had no weapon. How could he help Beverly and Creighton?

Which was it to be? Off to warn strangers of an impending attack, or back to the ruins to save his love and his old friend? Up the mountainside, toward Los Alamos? Or down through the trees, toward the caves? In the end the decision was easy. Terrain and freezing cold helped him make it. Without a horse Los Alamos was just too far away. He gritted his teeth and began to pick his way along the snowy trail. Downward. Toward the Indian ruins.

Pavel finished oiling his machine pistol and threw the rag in a corner. He stashed spare clips in his knapsack, then unwrapped the Geiger counter from the blanket with which Herr Boberach had covered it, fretting about the effect on it of the ubiquitous dust in the ruins. Scientists were silly men. Boberach should have worried about himself and kept the blanket for extra protection against the storm.

Pavel threw the blanket over his shoulder to give to Boberach later and took another blanket for himself. He had listened carefully when Boberach instructed Willi on the operation of the Geiger counter. If Willi were to take a bullet, someone would have to fill in, so it was only prudent. And it was a good use of his time. Pavel hadn't bothered to write any last notes to leave with Frischauer, as some of the men were doing. If he didn't make it back, he had no one at home in Germany to care.

Willi was waiting outside Pavel's ruin. His face was pinched, and his eyes moved constantly, like those of an animal backed in a corner, seeking escape.

Pavel handed him the Geiger counter. "Are you confident you can use this?" he asked.

"Yes, of course," Willi said. His eyes darted. "You'll tell Colonel Waldau how carefully I studied it, won't you, Pavel?"

"Why?" Pavel said.

"It might help me later. Pavel, can we win this battle?"

"If the raid goes as smoothly as Waldau outlined it, we will," Pavel said.

The eyes moved again. "Yes, but the question is what happens afterward," Willi said.

Pavel tried to hearten him. "Don't worry so much," he said. "Waldau is right about the storm covering our retreat. The falling snow will hide our trail."

"For how long?" Willi said. "And what happens when it clears? When word of this attack gets out, the Americans will go mad. Franz says they will have planes out looking for us. Police. Armies. We're three hundred miles from Mexico."

"But we have horses," Pavel said.

"Yes, we talked of that. And there's the *schwarze* cowboy. He can lead us through hidden ways, keep us out of sight. Can't he?"

Pavel sighed. "That depends on the cowboy."

"No, it depends on us," Willi said. "We'll make him cooperate. We'll threaten the woman, just as the officers did with Captain Dryden. If the cowboy refuses to help us, we'll kill her."

Pavel looked at Willi more closely. Before a battle all soldiers were tense, but Willi was close to the edge. The little mouse threatened to turn into a frantic rat, lashing a naked tail, snapping its fangs, ready to bite and slash at anything that came near. That could happen. Pavel had seen it before. He had, he thought wearily, seen just about everything before.

Pavel decided to shame the little man. "Listen to yourself," he said. "A soldier using a woman's skirts as armor. You're beginning to sound like Waldau. Shall we kill everyone who gets in our way?"

The eyes quested, avoiding Pavel. "Oberst Kleber started it. That first night at the POW camp, when we escaped. From the very beginning he used the woman to make Dryden behave."

"That doesn't make it right," Pavel said. Shame hadn't

237

worked. He switched to an authoritative tone. "If you are so eager to start killing, I'll give you enemies who can fight back. The soldiers at Los Alamos. Go outside and see if Maschmann's detail has finished feeding and saddling the horses. We leave in five minutes."

Willi ducked his head and rose, unwilling to meet Pavel's gaze. He picked up his machine pistol and the Geiger counter and sloped toward the cave mouth.

Pavel hooked the knapsack over his shoulders and walked along the crumbling walls. Soldiers were gathering their weapons and streaming down to the cave entrance. Frischauer and the huge spy were lurking near the split in Kleber's wall. Linares, alert and scowling, was wearing his war face. Frischauer was also sober, but obviously delighted that he wasn't going along on the raid.

Pavel nodded a curt greeting. "Have you a weapon, Herr Linares?"

The man from Mexico pulled a Walther P-38 from his belt. "Yes, this one," he said. "Colonel Waldau gave it to me. It belonged to the Oberst."

"Belongs," Pavel corrected. "The Oberst will want it back when he recovers." He motioned for Frischauer to join him. Frischauer hobbled over. "Be careful with the woman and the cowboy," Pavel said quietly. "Take them into Oberst Kleber's room where you can watch them all."

"Yes, Pavel."

"There's rope among the stores," Pavel told him. "Send Linares to fetch it. Tie the black one's hands tightly. I don't trust him. The woman, too, if necessary. But keep them safe. Let no one else near them, especially if we have to separate and come back a few at a time during the retreat. Only the officers or I are to give orders concerning them."

Waldau, standing with the other officers at the cave entrance, wrapped a blanket around his shoulders and called the soldiers together. It was time.

"I must go," Pavel said. "Take care of yourself."

"And you," Frischauer said.

Dryden heard the horses in the darkness. Snorts of resentment. A disparaging fart. A querulous whinny in reply. He threw himself behind two great trees, but he needn't have bothered. They weren't that close. It was a trick of the storm, sound carried on wind.

He stepped out of the trees, looking for the cave. It must be near. He could smell woodsmoke. Snow danced in dizzying eddies, falling silently in the deepening night. Some fifty yards away, faintly visible through the swirling flakes, a column of horses and riders headed up the canyon. How many? Hard to tell at a distance. At least twenty men, heads down, wrapped in blankets. He thought he recognized Waldau in the lead, but it could have been Strikfeldt. Even Pavel.

Dryden waited until the horses were swallowed by the night, then made his way through snow-capped boulders. The smell of smoke was stronger now. And food. Someone had cooked the last of the venison. His mouth watered, and he reproached himself silently for thinking of hunger when Beverly might be lying inside the cave, dead or dying. No, don't even think it. She was alive. She had to be alive.

A soft nicker sounded in the black night ahead of him, and he stopped. Something moved. He crept forward a few feet, enough to see forms in the gloom. Horses, moving restlessly behind their brush barricade. One was Sky, eyes wide, nostrils flared, stretching his neck over the brush so he could see the man about whom his sense of smell had already told him. Dryden moved silently to the gray's head and rested a calming hand on his muzzle, murmuring assurances.

"Good boy," Dryden whispered. He patted Sky's neck and stepped carefully through the trees. Now his sense of direction was back. If the horses were here, the Indian ruin had to be a few feet above him and to his right. Yes, there. Through the snow flurries. The wide mouth of the cave, yawning in the night. He moved closer, then stopped again.

Someone there, standing in the cave entrance. A pinpoint of red floated in the black maw, just beyond the falling snow. Dryden slipped behind a tree and watched. The pinpoint rose slowly to mouth level and glowed. A man smoking. A very tall man, judging from the altitude of the mouth. Dryden looked back and counted horses. Too many. His own gray, Sky, brought down the mountain after they'd left him for dead. Beverly's horse. Kleber's. Creighton's mule. The pack mules. And two other horses. The Germans had left two men behind. Of course. Kleber was injured. Someone had to watch over him. And stand guard over Beverly and Creighton.

The cigarette rose again, a deep drag this time. In the glow Dryden saw the high, angular features of Herr Linares, the German spy from Mexico. The cigarette lingered for a final puff, then arced across the night as Linares flipped it out into the snow.

He waited until Linares turned away, then shuffled across the last few feet of snowy ground to the bulge of rock below the cave. He hesitated, feeling for the handholds cut in the sandstone, then hauled himself up and slipped onto the natural balcony. The cave was darker than the night, except for embers of a dying fire in the back of the ruins. Dryden's eyes quickly adjusted, and he saw Linares pacing along the flat balcony, a good forty feet ahead of him. A pale flicker of light danced inside one of the ruins. Another fire, probably. This one fresher, still burning. That would be Kleber's dwelling.

Dryden moved away from the balcony and circled along the cave wall toward the ruins, trying to keep pace with the tall spy. Linares paused and peeled off toward Dryden's side of the cave. Dryden ducked back. He pressed against the cave wall and froze. Linares didn't seem to be looking for anything or anyone in particular. He walked with head down, in a determined manner, straight for the end of the balcony, and his path carried him to a point ten yards from Dryden. Dryden waited, tensing, half expecting the German to whirl on him. But Linares was only pacing, like a mechanical soldier in a clock tower. He came to a stop by a pile of firewood at the end of the stone ledge, then braced one hand against the rock and leaned forward, looking down.

Dryden darted toward the German's back. He ran on the balls of his feet, trying to cover ground quietly and quickly. It should have worked, but it didn't. Linares must have heard something—perhaps a scrape of shoe leather or a whisper of cloth—for the tall German jerked around, clawing at a gun in his belt.

Dryden dived for the gun and knocked it spinning, but the towering agent dipped a shoulder and threw a short, powerful punch that caught him in the ribs. Dryden ended up on the balcony floor, blinking in surprise. He tried to scramble to his knees, but Linares kicked him in the kidney. It hurt like hell. He rolled over, grunting, trying to get away from both the German and the edge of the balcony, and Linares bored in, stamping at his face. Dryden wrenched away, but not fast enough. A boot grazed his cheek and caught his ear, ripping the skin. The German was astonishingly quick for his size. And he obviously knew something about street fighting. His early moves were dirty and deadly. He was all feet, fists, and elbows, and he seemed to be trying to hit Dryden with every one of them.

Dryden warded off blows as best he could. And then suddenly the blows stopped. He blinked and rose to his elbows and saw Linares snatch up a huge chunk of firewood. The German raised the heavy stick with both hands and leaned in close, aiming it at Dryden's head. Dryden teetered back and kicked viciously at the German's face. Both heels caught the man on the forehead, and the skin tore. The blow must have ruptured a small vein, because copious amounts of blood spurted. Linares staggered back a step, with blood streaming into both eyes. The piece of firewood slithered loose and tumbled to the balcony floor.

Linares was half-unconscious already, but Dryden grabbed the fallen chunk of firewood and scrambled to his feet. He yanked Linares around and positioned him deliberately, setting him up, measuring him for the kill. When the big German was properly set, swaying on his feet, Dryden cocked the stick like a baseball bat, reared back, and swung for the fences. This time everything was right—weight, shift, timing. He banged Linares on the side of the neck, just below the skull. The German's head snapped to the side, and he fell slowly, stretched out full length, arms dangling. His chin smacked the stone floor a split second before the rest of him. It was like watching the Empire State Building topple.

The entire violent encounter had taken only seconds, but it had seemed incredibly prolonged and incredibly loud. Dryden groped for the gun and dropped beside the German, waiting to see if anyone in the ruins had heard the struggle. He lay in silence, watching. Surprisingly, Linares was still alive. He could hear the big man breathing and see the deep rise and fall of his chest. Dryden eased a hand to the German's shirt and felt the heartbeat, strong and steady. He was a tough son of a bitch.

Firelight flickered through the fragile wall of Kleber's dwelling, and a faint murmur of voices drifted to the balcony. Nothing else moved. Dryden wondered how anyone could have missed it. All that noisy shuffling and the blows and grunts. An abnormal sound characteristic of the cave, most likely. The high stone ceiling was like an echo chamber, filled with acoustical anomalies. He remembered strange occurrences from his student days. In some of the hot acoustical areas you could whisper and be heard clearly thirty yards away. In other parts of the cave, where the sound was deadened, you could drop an armload of canteens and scarcely be noticed. He thought hard, trying to recall the hottest sound areas. It would be hell to come through a noisy rough-and-tumble, then get caught creeping through the ruins on tiptoe.

A voice drifted again from the ruins. Normal level. No excitement. He fumbled with the German's gun, groping for the safety. The P-38 was an automatic pistol, half a pound lighter than the .45 Dryden was used to and with a higher muzzle velocity, but relatively simple. He made sure it was ready to fire, then gathered himself and ran at a crouch.

Kleber's cubicle was just below two of the taller structures. There was a roofless ruin beside it, and the remains of walls that might once have supported higher ceilings. Beyond Kleber's ruin was another very narrow passage to the spring. Rough ladders, now rungless, led up to the next tier. None of the Germans had bothered to explore the higher units. The few floors and walls that remained looked too unstable.

Dryden reached the edge of the ruins and crept toward Kleber's rubbled outer wall. The smell of venison grew stronger. So did the murmuring voice—a man speaking in German, encouraging Kleber to eat. Dryden peered inside. Kleber was propped up in his blankets near the fire. A man leaned over him with a bowl of broth and meat, trying to tempt him with a spoonful. An MP-40 machine pistol rested against the wall a few inches away.

Movement in the far corner caught Dryden's eye. Deep in the shadows, too far from the fire to be comfortable, Clarence Creighton worked his wrists energetically, trying to loosen his ropes. Beside Creighton, leaning forward to obscure what he was doing from the two Germans, was Beverly. Dryden felt a wave of relief so strong that it made him nauseated. Or maybe it was hunger. The stewed venison smelled like heaven.

He eased through the opening, pistol in hand. Beverly saw him first. Her head jerked. She opened her mouth to speak, then caught herself and clamped it shut. She nudged Creighton. The black face turned upward and saw Dryden. Eyes and teeth gleamed in the shadows. The man with the soup bowl murmured again, urging Kleber, trying to cajole him into another bite. It was the big farmer, Frischauer.

Dryden stepped carefully over fallen rock and moved toward the two Germans. His foot clicked against a pebble. Frischauer ignored it. Kleber raised his eyes, expecting to see Linares. When he saw Dryden instead, his body twitched. He rasped to Frischauer, "The American. The gun. Quickly."

Frischauer wasted a precious moment understanding, then dropped the bowl and grabbed for the machine pistol, but he was too late. Dryden had kicked the Schmeisser out of reach and pressed the P-38 against his jaw, just below the cheek. He said, "Easy, friend. If you want to see home and family again, be very still."

Frischauer turned into a block of granite. "There's another one," Beverly said quickly. "The man from Mexico."

Dryden nodded. "I know. He's out cold by the cave wall."

Creighton tugged at his wrists. "They told us you were dead," he said.

"I almost was," Dryden said. He nudged Frischauer with his foot. A hard nudge. "Get up. Untie my friends."

The big farmer rose cautiously, head down. He worked on Beverly first. Her rope fell away. She sprang to her feet and rushed to Dryden. She threw her arms around him, hugging him so tightly that he almost groaned. "Darling," she said. "Ah, darling. You don't know how glad we are to see you."

He hooked a hand around her waist, keeping the pistol free. "I think I do," he said. "It runs both ways, you know."

Frischauer, who had bent over Creighton, seemed surprised to find the black's bonds already loose, almost off. He finished untying them. Creighton pushed himself up and rubbed his wrists, grinning at Dryden. "We never doubted

243

for a minute you were alive, Eddie. Takes more than a handful of Germans to put a good man down."

Beverly said, "Liar. We cried like babies."

Creighton came shyly to join them. "Well, maybe a little. When we thought no one was looking."

Dryden offered him the pistol. "Keep an eye on things, will you, Mr. Creighton? I've got to haul Linares in where we can watch him."

Creighton waved the pistol away. "You just sit," he said. "I can handle Mr. Linares."

Dryden nodded gratefully and sagged to his haunches, keeping the pistol on Frischauer. Creighton came back a few minutes later, dragging Linares by the shoulders. The big spy's face was a bloody mask. His head lolled on his chest, but he managed to sit up clumsily when Creighton lowered him to a position against the wall.

"You really messed him up," Creighton said admiringly.

"Tie the bastard," Dryden said. "Let Frischauer do it, then tie him up as well. Tie them good and tight. Especially Linares. That son of a bitch is strong. He damn near caved my ribs in."

Creighton picked up a rope and handed it to Frischauer. He used gestures to communicate. Frischauer knotted the rope carefully around the big spy's wrists. When Linares was secure, Creighton picked up the other rope and tied Frischauer's hands behind his back, none too gently. He tested the knots, then nodded, satisfied. "Okay, that takes care of the bad guys. What now, Mr. Dryden?"

Dryden shook his head. "Back to 'Mr. Dryden,' are we?" He took a deep, weary breath, then braced a hand on the floor and creaked to his feet. "So much for rest and relaxation. Time to get cracking. I've got to do what I can to stop the German raid on Los Alamos."

"I'm ready," Creighton said. He picked up Frischauer's Schmeisser and raised questioning eyebrows. "How do you shoot this thing?"

"Use the cocking handle on the bolt," Dryden said. "It's touchy. Move the handle inward to lock it once the bolt is open, or a jar could discharge it."

"Yeah, I see. Let's go."

"You aren't going with me," Dryden said. "You're going to get Beverly to safety. Double back to one of the pueblos

244

and ask the Indians for help, or get to a road if you can and flag down a car or a truck—''

Beverly interupted vehemently. "Don't be ridiculous. Mr. Creighton and I aren't about to let you go out there and chase twenty Germans all by yourself. I'll stay here and wait for you. It'll be my turn to guard some prisoners."

"I haven't got time to argue," Dryden said. "I want you both out of the caves, safe."

Creighton braced the Schmeisser on his hip. "Can't do it," he said. "Your lady is right. Seems to me as how two men would have a better chance to stop the Germans than just one man alone."

Dryden sighed wearily. "Please, Mr. Creighton, listen to me. It's not safe for Beverly to stay here, and it's sure as hell not safe for her to wander off alone looking for help. Believe me, that's a blizzard out there. She could get lost and freeze to death. You, you old buzzard, no snowstorm could stop you."

Beverly said, "That's right, and that's why you need him with you to warn the authorities at Los Alamos. As soon as you talk to them, they can send a small army here for me. Both of you bundle up good and warm." She picked up the cast-iron Dutch oven and hefted it like a club. It made a formidable weapon, shaped like a skillet, with an iron handle, but twice as deep and twice as heavy. "I'll be fine. I'll wait here, all nice and warm, and stand watch over these three. If anyone moves, I'll bean him."

Dryden dithered, trying to decide. He didn't want to leave Beverly in the cave with three Germans, even if Kleber was badly hurt and the other two were tightly tied. And yet he welcomed the thought of Clarence Creighton at his side.

Creighton helped the decision along by saying, "Whatever we do, we better do it quick. The Germans got a good head start on us. They'll be a couple of miles from here by now."

The temptation was strong. Dryden said uncertainly, "We could probably cut them off on horseback. The trail I showed them takes the long way around. Or we could go over the ruins on foot and head straight for Los Alamos. Get there almost as quick as they do."

"Given a choice, I say since we got to go to Los Alamos mesa anyway, let's catch up on horseback and follow along behind," Creighton said. "The last man in a line, he's easy pickings. In a storm like this we could water them down pretty good."

Dryden nodded, testing the thought. "We might, at that," he said. He handed Kleber's pistol to Beverly. "Keep this. If anyone wiggles, shoot him."

"You'll need it," she objected.

"There'll be plenty of guns where we're going," Dryden said. "I'll pick one up along the way." He put a hand on Creighton's shoulder. "Let's go. We'll need blankets and heavy jackets. Whatever we can find. And a couple of horses. I'll help you saddle up."

"Sounds good to me," Creighton said. "It'll be just like old times."

Dryden grinned at the black foreman. He gave Beverly a quick hug and hurried off to find saddles and blankets. He was suddenly feeling much better. And he thought he knew why. He had been frustrated, outmanned, and outmaneuvered since the Germans first pounced on him that night back at the POW camp. But the odds had changed. The Germans still outnumbered him, but now they were in Dryden's country. Riding on ground he knew, whipped by winter, unsuspecting. Fighting their way through an unpredictable New Mexico blizzard. And Dryden and Creighton were loose behind them, free to range at will.

Even the aches subsided. It was almost inviting. His outdoor life as a rancher's son, his knowledge of these very hills would serve him well. And he knew it. With Creighton at his side he could cut the Germans out of the column one by one and decimate them. Maybe kill every damned one of them.

Or die trying.

# THIRTEEN

Creighton rose in his stirrups and pointed. "Below us, in the canyon." Dryden followed Creighton's point. Two hundred yards east a string of horses slogged through stifle-deep drifts of snow. The German assault team, at last. They were moving down the lower ridges. The ground leveled off below them. Across the forested canyon lay Los Alamos plateau, less than an hour's ride away. The lead horses were nose to tail, but gaps grew wider as the line lengthened. German stragglers had lagged behind, strung out in disarray along the rocky trail. Dryden recognized the horse at the extreme rear. It was Starr Fire, a bay gelding.

"They'll reach the trees in a couple of minutes," Dryden said. "If we ride ahead from here, we can cut through the scrub and catch them before the line closes."

"How do we take them?" Creighton asked.

"One at a time," Dryden said. "We'll split up and go for the stragglers. I'll take the last one. You angle ahead and lie in wait for the next. We'll meet up the trail when we finish."

"Do we do it quiet or noisy?"

"Quiet," Dryden said. "Once they spot us it's over. See you in a few minutes."

Creighton leaned forward in his saddle. It was the only signal his horse needed to follow the trail. Dryden turned Sky down the slope. He caught glimpses of the Germans through light snow flurries, but not for long. The storm clouds opened up and dumped fresh misery on the plateau. Wind and snow thickened quickly.

The bulk of the German line, at least twelve of the horses, were already past by the time Dryden tethered Sky and crawled to a good position among the tumbled rocks. He hugged his blanket around him, waiting. Long gaps began to appear between riders at the rear of the column. Stragglers, plodding along in isolation, followed the tracks of the other horses. One horse passed so close to Dryden's rocks that he could have reached out and touched it on the flank. He crouched, waiting for Starr Fire to appear. When the horse sidestepped skittishly into view, a German, swathed in a blanket, was slouched on his back, clinging to the pommel, head lowered against the wind. The man must have assumed he was alone at the rear of the column, but the horse knew better. Starr Fire's ears were up, and he was chewing at the bit. He was clearly aware of another human's presence in the darkness.

It was easier than Dryden had expected. The horse was already alert and nervous. Dryden sprang into the open, practically under the gelding's front feet, and unfurled his blanket like great bat wings. Starr Fire whinnied in fright and reared. The German, off balance, toppled down Starr Fire's croup and flopped to his face in the snow. Dryden was on him in an instant. He planted a knee on the German's back and grabbed the blanket in both hands, seeking the neck. A Schmeisser, looped over the shoulder, rattled. Dryden pushed the German's bundled head into the snow and held tight, squeezing, choking. The man kicked frantically and clawed, fighting for air. Dryden held on. The thrashing continued for almost a minute, but each movement grew progressively weaker. Even after the man stopped struggling Dryden held his face in the snow. He didn't relax his grip until he was sure the man was dead. Then he tugged the Schmeisser from the German's shoulder and dragged him off the trail to leave him behind the rocks.

Starr Fire was long gone, frightened away by the gasping grunts in the snow. There was no time to look for him now.

There were other stragglers to isolate. More damage to inflict.

Dryden was on his way back up the slope to get Sky before he realized what he had done. A cold shudder rocked through him. He had dragged the German's body behind the rock and left it without looking at the face. The thought had never occurred to him. He had killed his first German POW and he hadn't even bothered to see who it was.

Erwin Maschmann twisted in his saddle, trying to catch sight of his missing companion. Lampe had been behind him a few minutes ago, bringing up the rear. Pavel had told them to keep up, but it was damned hard to do when you were in the middle of a raging blizzard, freezing your ass off. Not even the Russian front could be colder.

Maschmann glanced over his shoulder again. Come on, Lampe. Hurry up. Maybe he should turn back for a look. No, to hell with it. Fall too far behind and he'd never catch up. He kicked his horse in the flanks, urging it on, but the horse snorted uneasily and pranced in place, staring at the trees and shadows ahead as if unwilling to go on. Maschmann peered into the darkness. What now? Wolves? He slipped a hand under his blanket to touch the cold metal of his machine pistol. Stupid horse. There was nothing there. Just a big cottonwood tree, leaning over the trail, limbs hanging low. He muttered and banged his heels into the horse's belly, demanding movement.

Reluctantly the horse edged forward. Maschmann smiled to himself. He couldn't blame the animal. Some of these dark shapes in the snow looked almost human. This one, for example. A tree with thick snowy limbs stretching down to scrape a careless rider. Almost like arms. Good thing he was alert. If he'd been looking back over his shoulder for Lampe, it could have knocked him right out of the saddle.

He raised an arm to brush the snowy limb out of the way. And froze in terror. The limb reached back for him. At the end of a long, sinewy arm a hand as black as night clawed at his throat. Another hand joined the first. Maschmann recoiled, trying to lean back in the saddle, but the momentum of the horse carried him right into the dangling arms. The black hands clamped down on his windpipe and dragged him upward. Maschmann's heart thudded with the adrenaline

249

released by his fright and he felt his bowels loosen. He was in the grip of some horrible demon of the forest. Just before he died he saw a flash of white teeth in the middle of a spectral black face, grinning down at him from the thick tangle of cottonwood boughs.

Pavel checked the compass once more, then reined in to wait for the officers. Waldau and Bernd Strikfeldt rode up. "If we keep on this bearing, we should shortly reach the mesa," Pavel said. "Then we need only find our ascension point and leave the horses."

"Acceptable," Waldau said. He wore a muffler around his ears. "That will put us within the community by midnight. We'll have a good six hours of darkness to accomplish our tasks."

Pavel started to speak, then held his tongue. He wanted to suggest that survival depended on completing all tasks in considerably less time. The men would need at least two hours of deep darkness to retire to the horses and make good their escape. But Waldau had steadfastly refused to discuss the possibility of withdrawal until the goals of the mission were fully realized.

Strikfeldt came to Pavel's aid. "I see no difficulties. Barring unforeseen circumstances, we should be able to set the charges with reasonable dispatch. We can disengage and make our way back across the canyon well before sunrise."

Pavel welcomed Strikfeldt's assessment, but the young lieutenant had barely finished speaking when the first unforeseen circumstance occurred. A man cried out near the end of the column, a shrill shriek of panic that rolled through the snowy night.

"What the devil was that?" Waldau demanded.

Pavel wrenched his reins, turning his horse to the rear. "I'll find out," he said. He spurred back along the column past huddled figures, all still now, twisted in their saddles to stare in the direction from which the sound had come. The startled cry had lasted for only a moment, but the man who had uttered it was still badly frightened. As Pavel closed in on the rear of the column he heard whimpering. He reined in.

"Who shouted?" Pavel asked. "Was it you?"

Blinking eyes met Pavel's. It was an Afrika Korps tanker,

the grizzled turret master called Basil. He pointed a quaking finger at the trees. "I saw something," he babbled. "A wraith among the branches. A horrible face, with rime on the eyes and nose."

Pavel twisted for a look. "There's nothing there."

"I saw it, I tell you. Grinning at me. An evil thing."

Pavel gazed rearward, along the trail. "Where the devil are Lampe and Maschmann? They were behind you, were they not?"

The man snuffled. "I think so. I haven't seen them for some time now."

A horse whinnied and came trotting through the snow, catching up from the rear. Pavel felt a surge of relief. "Here they come." But as the horse drew near, taking shape in the falling flakes, Pavel realized it was riderless, reins dragging at its feet. He snatched the reins and pulled the horse to a stop. His nose wrinkled. The saddle reeked with the smell of voided bowels. "Maschmann's horse," he said. "Something must have happened to him."

The tanker swallowed. "Maybe . . . *it* . . . got him."

"Don't be a fool," Pavel snapped. "There is no *it*. Perhaps his horse threw him."

"I know what I saw," the man said.

Pavel scowled at the empty trail. Still no sight or sound of Lampe. "You may be right," he said. "Not with your talk of wraiths, but there may be someone tracking us." He furrowed his brow. Dryden? Not possible. He'd seen Dryden fall from the cliff. Who else could it be, then? The black cowboy, escaped somehow from Linares and Frischauer? Indians? An American patrol?

He turned back to the column and gestured with a sweep of the arm to the next man up the line. "You," he called. "Come here."

Basil's eyes widened. "What are you doing?" he asked. "We must move on, catch up with the others."

"Not with someone behind us," Pavel said. A rider plodded back to join them. Pavel glanced at the newcomer and said, "I'm leaving the two of you as rear guard. Find Lampe and Maschmann. If someone is tracking us, kill him."

Basil swallowed again. "We shouldn't split up," he said. "You need us, Pavel. With Lampe and Maschmann missing

251

we're down to fifteen men and three officers. What if it gets us, too?"

"Don't be a damned fool," Pavel said. "If anyone is out there, he's human. Find him and dispose of him. No shooting. Kill him quietly. Then catch up with us at the canyon wall."

When the sound first came Dryden and Creighton were on foot, leading their horses below a steep slope. Blowing snow had partially filled the Germans' tracks, replacing sharply delineated hoofprints with shallow, rounded depressions. Another half hour and the prints would be gone. Dryden put a hand on Creighton's sleeve and stopped. Soft voices murmured in the darkness ahead, carried by the whipping wind. "Two men," Dryden said. "On foot. Coming this way."

Creighton nodded to show he'd heard them, then gestured with his chin toward the hill. "Not too good, where we're at," he whispered. "Slope's too steep. Ripe for avalanche. We'd best backpedal."

"Avalanche? Are you sure?"

Creighton shrugged. "Best indicator is the angle. At least sixty degrees, maybe seventy. Anything over thirty degrees gets to be right dangerous. No trees to speak of, either. Looks like it may have dumped before, in other storms. Leeward side, out of the wind. Snow pretty deep along the top. Wouldn't take much to bring it down."

Dryden cocked his ear. "I don't hear the rest of the column."

"They probably went on ahead," Creighton said. "Left these two to take care of us. That's what I'd have done."

"We can detour around them," Dryden said.

Creighton shook his head. "I'd feel better with no Germans at my back," he said. "But this sure isn't the place to take them on. Any little old noise could bring a load of snow down on us."

"Or on them," Dryden said. "If I lure the Germans under the slope, could you break the snow loose?"

Creighton surveyed the incline. "Maybe," he said slowly. "Maybe I can work my way up the side and get set up near that steep shelf. If you can lead them under me, I'll give the snow a good whomp, and we'll see. Might bring her pouring down."

"Let's try," Dryden said.

Creighton gave him a serious look. "You better know what you're doing, boy. You make any noise, or slip and fall, and the impact might be enough to set the whole thing off. You could be ass over teakettle, trapped under a ton of snow."

"I'll be careful," Dryden said.

Creighton nodded. "Tie the horses out in the trees," he whispered. "Snow's gonna spread out pretty wide." He handed his reins to Dryden, then picked his spot and began climbing, working his way gingerly up the slope.

Dryden led the two mounts to safety and hurried back. Creighton was already high above the snowpack and out of sight. The slope blocked most of the wind, but an occasional gust broke through, carrying snatches of anxious conversation. The voices were nearer. Someone fretting about ghosts.

Dryden cut cautiously beneath the slope. He tried to think only of voices ahead of him and the trail he intended to lay for their benefit, not the menacing mound of snow. Don't think about it. Don't think about it? Easy to say. He remembered a standard challenge from the upperclassmen on Los Alamos mesa. "Hey, Dryden. Don't think of the word *elephant* for the next fifteen seconds." He started scuffing the snow, leaving a line of footprints for the Germans, while his mind screamed, "Elephant! *Elephant!* ELEPHANT!"

He was halfway back when the two Germans rounded the far end of the slope and came into view. Dryden ducked. They were walking with heads down, huddled against the cold. Behind them, trailing on reins, were two of Dryden's horses. He peered through the snow, agonizing. He still had time to move on, out of range. He'd left enough footprints to keep them coming. But his mind painted a picture of the horses, wheeling in terror, fighting to escape as the side of a mountain roared down on them.

He took a deep breath. He had to get the Germans to drop the reins. Give them a peek, maybe. Let them spot him and run like hell. Maybe they would abandon the horses and come after him. He raised questing eyes to the top of the slope, seeking Creighton. If only he could warn him somehow, tell him what he was about to do. Running Germans would be harder to time than walking Germans. Would Creighton be ready?

One of the Germans stopped and pointed. The other unlimbered his Schmeisser. Too late now. They'd seen the footprints. They came on faster, tugging the horses, following the trail. If he was going to do it, it had better be quick. He inhaled deeply and lurched into the open.

They saw him almost immediately. The man with the Schmeisser racked back the cocking lever, and Dryden dived for cover. He hit the snow and rolled. He heard a soft rumble overhead, and snow sifted down the embankment. It was a dangerous moment, and Dryden knew it. Even if his acrobatics didn't jar the face loose, a rattle of gunshots would surely do the job. But nothing happened. The other German cursed and yammered something about no shooting. They were apparently under orders not to alert the mesa. Dryden jumped to his feet and raced away.

The invitation was too inviting to resist. Both men dropped their reins and plowed down the trail after him. The mountain creaked, disturbed by the thudding feet. Dryden ran hard, gulping cold air. He risked a look over his shoulder and saw them gaining ground, running well. Too well. His battered hip twinged as he forced it into high gear, but they still seemed to be closing the distance. As he passed under the steep shelf he heard a loud *whomp* overhead. He flicked a look upward and saw Creighton hurl a huge rock into the midst of the snow. It landed with another loud *whomp*. The top of the hill teetered. Creighton hurled a third rock, then a massive pine bough. Still the snow held. Dryden ran on, side and hip aching. Had his friend miscalculated? Would the damned thing never go?

And then, as the two Germans pounded down on him, it went. Softly at first, a few spills of snow pouring down the sides, then a low rumble and a creak as larger fragments broke loose. Like dominoes, each falling fragment gouged more chunks from the side of the hill. The rumble grew noticeably louder. It was turning into a full-blown avalanche. Dryden, aware of the danger, ran even faster. The Germans didn't. Startled by the sound, they pattered to a stop and looked up. The last thing they saw was a wall of snow roaring down on them at breakneck speed. It hit bottom like a train, enveloping the two men, sweeping them off the trail, burying them under tons of rock and snow.

Nor did it stop. When it hit level ground it broke up like

water from a waterfall, spreading in all directions, a surge of snow ten feet deep flinging thick gobbets of snow ahead like shrapnel. Dryden ran until he could feel its cold breath closing on him, then dived behind a boulder. The snow surged past, rumbling beyond his boulder, spilling in toward his feet, covering his legs. He clung to the ground for interminable seconds until the sound died, then lifted his head, surprised to find himself alive.

He shook himself loose and rose, peering over the boulder toward the top of the hill, worrying about Creighton. And saw him. Standing at the crest, shaking his head in awe. Creighton's voice drifted down to him. "You weren't supposed to cut it so close, boy. Maybe I still got a thing or two to teach you."

Pavel, helping Otto Boberach climb the snowy mesa toward the road, heard the soft, distant rumble and stopped. The little scientist was startled, too. He gripped a bush to keep from slipping and said, "What was that?"

"I'm not sure," Pavel said. "It sounded like a rock slide." He looked down past the climbing Germans. Guns and kits rattled faintly as each man pulled himself hand over hand through snow-whitened brush. The low rumble had sounded close, but it was probably a trick of the storm. The trees at the foot of the mesa were untouched. That meant the horses were safe. Thank God for that.

Grebling, the SS captain, climbed to Pavel's perch and hissed, "Why are you standing? Keep moving."

"Did you hear the sound?" Pavel asked him.

The SS captain gestured impatiently. "Falling rocks. What difference does it make? Keep moving. We're almost to the top."

"Herr Boberach needs a rest," Pavel said.

"No time," Grebling said. "If he can't keep up, carry him."

Pavel grimaced and took Boberach's elbow, boosting him to the next level. The ground was rough, though gently angled. It would have been an easy climb under normal conditions, but the snow made footing treacherous. The little scientist had slipped to his knees twice and might well have gone tumbling down the mountain, knocking soldiers along like tenpins, had Pavel not been holding onto him.

255

"Is it much farther?" Boberach asked.

Pavel craned his neck. "No, just a little more. I see some of the men on top already. Come. Step here."

Whispers reached them as they scaled the last few feet. Strikfeldt looked down from the lip and gestured for them to hurry. Pavel hefted Boberach to the top and climbed up after him. Strikfeldt pointed. A hundred yards up the road, visible through falling snow, stood a checkpoint and sentry box. German soldiers were fanning into a field, away from the checkpoint. Ahead Pavel saw a wall of wire. Waldau was already there with a team of wire cutters, opening the way. By the time Pavel and Boberach reached the fence men were pouring through. Dim structures loomed beyond. Light gleamed faintly through frosted windows. Tendrils of smoke curled from a few chimneys. They'd made it. The edge of the encampment at Los Alamos.

Pavel and Boberach slipped through the gap in the fence and huddled with the others. It was a strange settlement, filled with flimsy buildings and narrow dirt streets. No street names that Pavel could see, only numbers. The living quarters all looked alike. Wooden boxes and rounded quonset huts. Some of the windows were lit, but most were dark. No one visible on the streets. The storm had apparently driven everyone inward. "Stay close to me," Pavel whispered to Boberach. "And no talking. Do as I tell you without hesitation."

Strikfeldt studied his map briefly and took the lead. As the first Germans moved away at a crouch into clustered buildings, the snow whirled. Pavel touched Boberach's arm and gestured him into the flow. Walls rose about them. Wind gusted. The wire fence vanished, swallowed in the thickening snow. They hugged the buildings, moving in jerks and starts through snow-capped structures, strung out along both sides of a silent, narrow street.

Strikfeldt's hand-drawn map quickly became their one link to reality. Following his hatchwork of hastily sketched streets, they swept deeper into the compound, darting from building to building, skirting sentry posts, streaming across empty, windswept intersections, padding silently through ankle-deep snow. No one spoke. No weapons jingled. They moved in classic combat fashion, rapidly, staying low, com-

256

municating only with hand signals, avoiding open areas. Constantly alert, expecting the unexpected.

The first unexpected moment was a late Saturday-night party, a premature New Year's Eve celebration in one of the two-story apartment buildings. Footprints in the snow suggested a gathering of as many as twenty or thirty people. Music drifted down from the upper level. Tinkle of glasses. Male guffaws. Laughing women. The Germans hesitated, but the party proved no danger. No one ventured outside as the Germans streamed past. It was too cold, and the party-goers seemed determined to ride out the storm.

The second discovery came as a pleasant surprise. Strikfeldt's map worked. His accuracy at laying out streets wasn't entirely unexpected, but it had seemed almost too much to hope for. By counting streets and following the map meticulously Strikfeldt managed to bypass military checkpoints and bring them through the squeaky-new tin houses and flat-roofed apartment buildings and into an older area with trees and rambling pre-war log cabins. And wonder of wonders, there before them was the big two-story log house Waldau had selected, just as the map said it would be.

Strikfeldt stopped the Germans with a hand signal and conferred briefly with Waldau, then gestured Pavel forward. "Stay here," Pavel whispered to Boberach. "Don't come until the house is secure."

The house was surrounded by shrubbery and a low hedge. Dark logs with white chinking. Light gleamed from the living room and an upper window. An armed sentry was on the road, sitting in a closed jeep. The sentry looked uncomfortable, bundled under the steering wheel, chin tucked close to his chest. Snow whipped past the jeep's isinglass flaps.

Pavel picked faces from the darkness and signaled them into position. Two men to the rear of the jeep. Others to the far side and back of the house. Willi Roh and Franz Eggers to accompany him to the near side. The house teams broke apart, moving swiftly, darting first to the hedge, then to the shadows of the building. Pavel hugged the logs near a lighted window and nodded to two men at the rear of the house. One unfurled a grappling hook on a scaling rope and tossed it up to snag a stone chimney. The rope was knotted at one-foot intervals. The first man held it taut while his partner climbed hand over hand. Pavel peered around the corner of the house to make sure the road team was in place, crouched behind the jeep, then gestured to Willi Roh.

The rest came instinctively. They moved with clockwork precision, like a superbly choreographed dance team. Pavel used the butt of his Schmeisser to smash the window. The sound of shattering glass triggered the man atop the wall, and a second window crashed in. Pavel handed the barrel of his Schmeisser to Franz Eggers to form a platform, and together they boosted Willi over the sill and through the broken panes. Willi, the smallest man in the unit, went flying into the room. The American sentry, startled by the muffled sounds of breaking glass, spilled out of the closed jeep and started for the porch. He managed only a few steps before two shadows rose and engulfed him.

Eggers dropped to his hands and knees below the window. Pavel planted a foot on his back and climbed through after Willi. Wood splintered as someone broke through the back door. A man stood in the center of the room, confused by the melee of sounds. He was a thin man, almost tubercular. He couldn't have weighed more than 130 pounds. Pavel reached through the window to drag Eggers over the sill. The curtains billowed and snow swirled in after him.

Willi Roh pushed the man against the wall. "Who are you?" the man stammered. He coughed, the sound of a heavy smoker. "What do you want?"

Pavel tugged his blanket off, exposing his uniform, and tossed it to Eggers. He told Eggers to pin it over the window, then said in English, "Who else is in this house?"

The man stared at Pavel's uniform wth slack-jawed fascination. "No one," he said. "I'm alone." The answer came too quickly.

Feet tramped up on the front porch, and the door burst inward. More soldiers came flying in, Schmeissers questing. Waldau and Grebling hurried through after them with weapons drawn. Waldau gazed about the room. "Is this the house of Niels Bohr?" he asked.

Pavel grasped the man by the collar and said, "We are seeking the famous scientist Niels Bohr. Where is he?"

The man blinked blue-gray eyes. "I . . . I don't know. In Washington, I think. Why are you looking for him here?"

"Does he not live here?"

"No. I do."

Pavel translated for Waldau. The SS colonel said, "Nonsense. This is the finest house of all. It must belong to Bohr. Only the leader of the project, a world-famous physicist like Bohr, would be allotted such quarters."

The man stiffened and said in haughty German, "I *am* the leader of the project."

"You speak German?" Pavel said.

"Most physicists do," the man said. "German is the language of science."

Soldiers came in with the cases of explosives and fuse cord, and the road team hurried in after them, dragging the unconscious sentry. Strikfeldt and Boberach were the last to enter. The door swung shut. Boberach shook snow from his hair and reached for his spectacles. "Have you found Doktor Bohr?" he asked.

Pavel gestured with his gun toward the thin man. "This one says he is not here."

Boberach squinted at the man, then smiled and stepped toward him. "You are the American scientist Robert Oppenheimer, are you not? We met once. It was a seminar at Göttingen. You presented a paper to be published in *Zeitschrift für Physik*."

The man said cautiously, "Yes, I'm Robert Oppenheimer."

"I thought your paper was brilliant," Boberach said. " 'On the quantum theory of continuous spectra,' as I recall. I am Dr. Otto Boberach. I was a fellow *Privatdozent* in Göttingen at the time, but we had little chance to talk." He frowned. "Why are you here, Dr. Oppenheimer? Are you also working on the American project?"

Pavel interjected, "He says he's the leader of the project."

"Yes, of course," Boberach said. "They would have to put an American in charge, wouldn't they?"

A man, the German who had scaled the wall, clattered onto a second-floor landing above them and called down, "There's a woman up here, and two children. One is a baby."

The scientist, Oppenheimer, shrugged and said, "My wife, Kitty, and my children. They're not important to you."

"Neither are you," Waldau said coldly. "Lieutenant Strikfeldt, prepare your explosives and fuses. As soon as

259

this man sends for the people we seek and they begin to arrive, the assault team will leave for the technical area. Herr Doberach, produce your list."

Boberach pulled a folded sheet of paper from his pocket and said apologetically, "I'm sorry, Dr. Oppenheimer. There are people we wish brought here."

Waldau snatched the sheet from Boberach's fingers and unfolded it. "There are twelve names on this list," he said. "You will produce them. The German Jew Hans Bethe, who once taught at Tübingen. The German renegade Rudolf Peierls, who studied under Bethe. The Austrian defectors Victor Weisskopf and Otto Frisch. The Italians, Enrico Fermi and Emilio Segrè. The three Hungarian Jews, Eugene Wigner, John von Neumann, and Edward Teller. A Pole named Stanislaw Ulam. George Kistiakowsky, the Russian. And Niels Bohr, the infamous Dane who inspired them all. These men must be summoned immediately to your quarters."

Oppenheimer's thin, ascetic face registered concern. "But why? What do you want with them?"

"That is not your business," Waldau said. "Do as you are told and send for them quickly, and you may live to find out."

"You've named some of our busiest people," Oppenheimer said. "They often take work home. It's late. There's a storm. They may not want to come."

"Then you must be persuasive," Waldau said. "Your wife and children depend on it."

There was movement at the top of the stairs. The soldier came out on the landing, leading a pretty, dark-haired woman with a baby in her arms. A small boy followed at her side. Oppenheimer's gaze lifted. He said quickly, "Kitty, are you all right?"

"Robert, these are Germans," the woman said accusingly, as if her husband himself had produced them.

Waldau let his P-38 drift to her. "Decide, Herr Doktor." He smiled faintly. "You may tell the men on the list that you have received important intelligence about German progress on an atomic bomb similar to yours. Tell them you must meet with them immediately."

The slim scientist stared at his wife. He undoubtedly had a quick mind, but he was in shock, and his thought processes seemed to function slowly. He remained silent for several heartbeats, then let his shoulders slump. "Very well," he told Waldau. "But I can't deliver them all. Eugene Wigner is away from Los Alamos for the weekend. Dr. Bohr hasn't visited the site for weeks."

"Then summon the remainder," Waldau demanded. "Ten men. Make certain they come. Be assured, I will question them as they arrive. If you have lied about Wigner and Bohr, or if you lie and make excuses for any of the others, your family will answer for it."

Creighton led the way at the end. His sense of smell was so keen that he swore he could smell horses on the wind. He hustled through the cottonwoods on foot, following a trampled path in the snow, and spotted them hidden under the trees at the foot of the mesa. He called softly to Dryden, "Over here. I found them."

The horses were tethered in bunches, all seventeen of them, rumps turned to the cold wind, snorting nervously. "Any sign of the Germans?" Dryden asked when he caught up.

"Nope," Creighton said. "Looks like they're long gone."

Dryden nodded. "I found boot tracks leading to the mesa. They could be on top by now."

Creighton said, "I got an idea. Those two back at the slope, they acted like they were afraid to shoot at you."

"They couldn't," Dryden said. "A shot might have alerted the mesa."

"Then why don't we take a shot or two of our own? Just pop a couple off in the air. That's what we want, isn't it? To warn folks up on the mesa?"

"I wish we could," Dryden said. "But we don't know for sure where the Germans are. They might already be holding the scientists hostage. If we raise the alarm from down here, Waldau might kill them. No, we'll have to climb up and alert the guards. Then we can round up some people and maybe take the Germans by surprise."

Creighton checked his Schmeisser. "Let's get going, then."

"Not yet," Dryden said. He sighed, a mournful gust of breath. "First we turn the horses loose."

Creighton stared at him in disbelief. "What are you talking

261

about, boy? You want to send them out in this storm? Some of them could die."

"We have to take the chance," Dryden said. "We can't leave them here. If any of the Germans get away, they'll grab horses and head straight back to the caves. And Beverly."

Creighton gazed at the horses, appalled. "We can't, Eddie. Whatever don't get lost or killed, the Indians will steal. Couldn't we just take them off somewhere and hide them?"

"In this snow?" Dryden said. "Hell, we followed their tracks clear across the canyon. What makes you think the Germans couldn't do the same?" He thumped Creighton on the arm and said, "Come on, old-timer. I know it hurts, but we have to do it."

Creighton followed him reluctantly to the horses. As Dryden started untying them Creighton moaned. He moved to another bunch, slipping reins, but he finally stopped and said, "All of them?"

"All of them," Dryden said. "Including our own two horses. Don't leave anything."

The horses pulled loose one by one. A few bolted, dashing away into the trees. Others recognized friendly scent. They stamped and snorted and made circles in the snow, but they seemed content to stand their ground, waiting for human instructions.

"Make them go," Dryden said. "Scatter them good." He whipped off his blanket and flapped it at the nearest horses. They spun against each other, eyes wide. Creighton whirled his own blanket at them from the other side. They reared in amazement, betrayed by men they trusted. Dryden and Creighton rushed in, flapping their blankets and making deep hostile sounds in their throats. Panic spread and the horses plunged away, beating paths through the woods.

Creighton stopped with his blanket dangling from his hand, dragging in the snow, and watched the horses pound through the trees. "God damn, that hurts," he muttered. "Those Germans better watch their asses. I'm getting good and mad."

* * *

Pavel stood by the front curtains, peering at the road. "Someone approaching," he said. "Two men in overcoats coming up the walk."

"Good," Waldau said. "Is Lieutenant Strikfeldt ready?"

"Yes, sir, He's in the back with the assault team, going over the assignments."

"Let us wait no longer," Waldau said. "As soon as the first hostages are in our hands, call the assault team together. Gather your explosives and leave by the back door. Herr Boberach and I will hold the hostages until you return. Captain Grebling and Corporal Voight will stay here at the command post to help us."

A knock sounded. Pavel and Waldau slipped to the wall on either side of the door. Waldau pulled the P-38 from his holster and gestured a chastened Oppenheimer off the couch. "Greet them," he hissed. "Get them inside." Oppenheimer shifted to his feet. Boberach, who had been sitting on the couch with the frail American scientist, jumped up and padded to the door after him.

Oppenheimer swung the door open. Two men, one tall with tangled hair sticking up like a fright wig and the other shorter, balding, stamped snow from their galoshes and stepped in out of the wind. "You picked a terrible night for a meeting, Oppy," said the tall one. His English was accented. "Fermi had to drag me out or I wouldn't have come."

"Hans," Boberach said with delight. "Hans Bethe. Hello, old friend."

The man unbuttoned his overcoat, peering at Boberach. Recognition dawned, and he said, "Otto? Is that you? How did you get here? I thought you were in Germany."

Boberach's smile faded. "I was," he said. He bobbed his chin beyond the two men at Waldau and Pavel, standing behind them. The tall one turned and saw the German uniforms and the guns. His body jerked.

Waldau closed the door and smiled. He said, "Sergeant Pavel, you may leave now."

*Sunday*
*December 31, 1944*

# FOURTEEN

Studying the trampled snow, Creighton said, "They crawled through the fence here and went up through those buildings. Do we go after them?"

Dryden slipped through the cut in the wire and followed the German footprints a few yards. "No, there are still too many of them. Now we go for help."

"Where?" Creighton asked. He surveyed the dark huts and buildings. "Looks to me like everyone is buttoned down for the night, safe and warm."

"There are guard posts along the main road," Dryden said. "And barracks for the military. I saw them earlier today from the mountain across the canyon. Someone's bound to be on duty."

Creighton examined the German tracks, seeing how they scattered through the buildings before they were swallowed by the night. "Looks like we left fifteen or sixteen men. What do they want up that way?"

"The old schoolmaster's house," Dryden said. "That's where they'll hold their hostages. Then the main assault team will head for the technical area, down on the rim of the mesa."

"I guess we still don't do any shooting, huh?"

"Not yet," Dryden said. "If I've got Waldau figured right, he'll cut loose on the scientists the minute the alarm sounds."

"Hostages aren't much good if they're dead," Creighton said. "Maybe he'll keep them alive as bargaining chips."

"I wouldn't bet on it."

They loped through the buildings. Dryden was totally unfamiliar with the streets and the welter of small buildings, and the snow was falling so thickly that they could scarcely see twenty yards in any direction, but he knew the mesa like his own backyard. He'd played on it, explored it, suffered homesickness on it. Bulldozers and new buildings might alter the cosmetics, but they couldn't change the terrain. This was still his ground.

Buildings forced detours, but even without stars or landmarks to guide them Dryden led them with scarcely an error to the old Fuller Lodge. They stopped in its shadows, and Dryden wasted a moment staring up at the big log columns. Even Big Sam had made the trip when his own son graduated, driving up the ragged road in the family Packard. Dryden could see him clearly, sitting on a folding chair by Ashley Pond with the other parents, grinning ear to ear as his boy received his diploma.

If only Big Sam were here now. He'd know how to handle Waldau. Dryden pointed. "The pond is out there," he said to Creighton. "The technical area is just to the south. Keep low. The Germans could have gotten there first."

Proof came in moments. As they skirted the pond they encountered a trail of fresh footprints coming from the faculty houses, barely dusted with new snow. Creighton bent to study the ground. He gauged the depth of the prints and felt the texture of the snow. "I figure twelve men here," he said. "Maybe thirteen. Not more than ten or fifteen minutes ahead of us."

The trail led to the lower corner of the mesa, crisscrossing from trees to structures, the footprints falling farther apart and obviously running across open ground. The technical buildings loomed ahead, rising darkly across the main road. Another barbed-wire fence, fifteen strands high, blocked the way. At the top more barbed wire projected outward to discourage climbers. Several strands of wire hung limply where they'd been cut.

A dim halo of light caught Dryden's eye from down the road near the main gate. One of the sentry posts. "Keep your eye on the fence," he told Creighton. "I'll see if I can rouse the guards."

He left Creighton in the shadows watching the broken wire and hurried along the silent road toward the light. The halo expanded as he drew nearer, then took form in the night—a brightly lighted window in a small wooden building. Around the building, cars and trucks sat unattended in a small parking area, mounded with snow. The American military presence, like the scientists and technicians who lived above Fuller Lodge, had shut down for the night, waiting out the storm.

Dryden could see a solitary guard through the window, huddled near a potbellied stove for warmth, head tucked in the folds of a khaki parka and hands wrapped carelessly around an M1 carbine. A coffeepot perked away on a hot-plate, but the guard didn't seem to be interested. His chin was nodding, and he looked half-asleep.

Dryden pushed the door open and stepped inside. He said, "Soldier, call your duty officer. We've got a problem."

Startled, the guard reared back from the stove and clambered to his feet. He fumbled the carbine to his shoulder and said, "Hold it. Who the hell are you?" He looked at the big, oily machine pistol in Dryden's gloved hands. "Put that gun down, mister. Do it quick or I'll turn you into Swiss cheese."

"Easy," Dryden said. He laid the Schmeisser delicately on the table by the coffeepot. "No fuss or noise, soldier. I'm Captain Edward Dryden of the U.S. Army. Just let me talk to someone. We need troops. And we need them quietly. We don't want to raise an alarm."

The guard stared. Dryden wore his uniform under his flapping blanket, but it was rumpled and dirty after five days on horseback, and his face was ragged with beard. "I never saw you before. If you're an army officer, where's your pass? How the hell did you get in here?"

"I came through the fence," Dryden said. "Following a German attack force. They're here to sabotage the bomb."

"Yeah, sure, Germans. That does it. Just leave the gun on the table and step back."

"Listen to me," Dryden said. "There are Germans in the technical area at this very moment, setting explosive charges. Get your duty officer in here. We've got to round up help and stop them."

"Germans with explosives? Christ almighty, mister. Even if I was crazy enough to believe you—which I sure as hell don't—I couldn't call anyone. You should have done your homework. We've got no phones in the guard posts. Only the top scientists and officers have telephones up here on the mesa. We're out in the middle of nowhere, and the security officers want to keep it that way. Germans, huh? And I suppose the Japs have invaded San Francisco? You must think I'm some kind of horseshit hick to feed me a story like that."

Dryden said urgently, "If you have no telephone, then go get someone. We may not have much time."

"I'm not going anywhere," the guard said. "Neither are you. You're under arrest. Put your hands where I can see them and sit down. The duty officer will show up in an hour or two, making his rounds. We'll wait nice and quiet until he comes. Then he can take you to whatever loony bin you escaped from or shoot you as a spy. Either way is okay by me."

Creighton poked his nose in the door and said, "Eddie, come quick. They're laying fuses. I just saw—"

The guard gaped. Another apparition in flapping blankets. He tried to swing his gun at Creighton, but Dryden snatched the coffeepot from the hot plate and hurled it at him. The hot pot bounced off the guard's head, and he crashed to the floor. Steaming coffee flew across the room, just missing Creighton's legs. Some drops must have hit. The black man jerked back and sucked in his breath.

"Sorry," Dryden said. "I didn't have time to plan it. You were about to tell me something?"

Creighton nodded. "I just spotted two Germans ducking between buildings. They were playing something out from a spool. Detonating wire, maybe. Or fuse cord. If we're going to keep them from blowing up the mesa, we'd better get busy." He looked down at the unconscious guard. "No help from the army, huh?"

"I'm afraid not," Dryden said. "We'll have to handle it."

\* \* \*

Boberach bobbed his chin. "Yes, we were aware of the new element, but we've had no time to study it. You say it fissions like U233, but it can be chemically separated from uranium? Remarkable."

Otto Frisch, nephew of the magnificent Lise Meitner, said, "Segrè and Seaborg isolated it. Since uranium and neptunium were named for the planets Uranus and Neptune, we decided to stick with the scheme. We call it plutonium, after the planet Pluto."

Boberach said, musingly, "Pluto. Greek god of the underworld. God of the dead." He shuddered. They were in Oppenheimer's bedroom, several of the Los Alamos scientists under the guard of Albert Voight, who stood at the door, watching. Unable to resist shop talk, Boberach had joined them.

"It has made all the difference," Frisch said. "We calculate the slow-neutron fission at 1.7 times that of U235. We believe we can produce enough for nine bombs a year, but they are harder to explode than the uranium gadget. We need an implosion device—high-explosive lenses, fitted precisely—to make them work. Kistiakowsky and von Neumann are working on the problem."

Boberach gasped. "Nine bombs a year?"

"You shouldn't be discussing our plutonium experiments," Enrico Fermi told Frisch. "The security people would go crazy."

"What difference does it make?" Frisch said. "It's too late for Germany. What can they do?"

"That isn't the point," said Rudolf Peierls. "This man works for Nazi Germany. He's an enemy. We shouldn't even be talking to him."

"Otto Boberach?" Frisch said. "He's a pure scientist. And a friend. Tell them, Hans. He was your friend, too."

Hans Bethe snorted. "Friends change," he said bitterly. "War changes them. I once counted Hans Geiger a friend. Until the Nazis came to power. Then he turned on me."

Boberach looked embarrassed. "I knew there was bad blood between you and Geiger, but he never told me why."

Bethe shrugged. "A small matter, perhaps. But important to me. He was on vacation when the Nazis ordered the university in Tübingen to dismiss me, so I wrote him, asking him what I should do. He wrote back a completely cold letter, telling me that the changed situation made it necessary to dispense with my services. That was all. No concern, no expression of sympathy. We had been friends for years, and yet he treated me like a total stranger."

"Many of us were too frightened to say anything in those early days," Boberach said.

"Not everyone," said Emilio Segrè. "Walter Bothe argued with the authorities for weeks, trying to keep us in Europe. And after some of us came to America, Werner Heisenberg wrote an emotional letter telling me how much he regretted the way the Nazis were treating us."

"Surely, a letter," Peierls said. He was a round-faced German Jew with thick glasses and rabbit teeth. His wife, also a scientist, was Russian. "Anyone can write a letter. But what did Heisenberg do? Even for people he knew. Take Edward Teller, or Fermi, for example. Did he put his neck on the line for them? No, he stayed behind in Nazi Germany to work on a bomb for Hitler."

"Yes, we stayed behind," Boberach said. "But our work hasn't gone well." He glanced at Voight and lowered his voice. "Hitler is a fool. He puts his faith in rockets and jet aeroplanes. We hold the key to the universe, and he prefers silver trinkets."

Oppenheimer, smoking quietly, seemed to wake up. "Your work in Germany hasn't gone well? How far have you progressed?"

The question was asked in a casual manner, but Oppenheimer's soft eyes glittered too brightly. Boberach knew he was being pumped for information, but he didn't care. It no longer mattered. He said, "We're in the same quarters at the Kaiser Wilhelm Institute. We have 664 cubes of metallic uranium in our pile and one and a half tons of heavy water to moderate it."

"But that is nothing," Peierls said. "No threat at all."

Boberach shrugged. "Not only have we made no substantial progress, but we're continually harassed by Allied bombing raids. They're thinking of moving everything to a little resort town in the Black Forest. Haigerloch. They're going to put us in a cave. That should tell you how far behind we are. In a cave. Can you imagine putting everything you've developed over the last five years in a cave?"

Oppenheimer sighed. "We were worried about you," he said. "We were afraid you were ahead of us."

"You worried for nothing," Boberach said. "Hitler has stymied us at every turn."

"So you've come to destroy our work," Peierls said. "And us."

A few of the scientists exchanged looks. Hans Bethe put it into words. "What will happen to us, Otto?"

Boberach firmed his jaw and stood up. "Nothing," he said. "Trust me. I will see to it."

Voight let him out of the bedroom, and he hurried to the front of the house, seeking Waldau. He found the SS colonel in the living room with Grebling, pacing by the window. Oppenheimer's wife, who had been instructed to sit in clear view on the couch, was trying to keep her children quiet, but her eyes, dark and fine, flashed every time she looked at the Germans. Boberach said, "Colonel, we've been talking, the scientists and I. The Americans have made remarkable theoretical progress, but even with their giant reactors in Tennessee working full-time they haven't been able to separate any substantial amounts of enriched uranium."

Waldau parted the curtains and peered out the window. "So?"

"Don't you see? Their bomb can't work without a radioactive core. The American atomic device won't be ready for months. Perhaps as long as a year. The war in Germany will be over by then. None of this is necessary."

"What makes you think they would tell you the truth?"

"We're scientists," Boberach said, affronted. "We aren't bound by political squabbles and petty security matters." Waldau looked at him skeptically, and Boberach tried for words the man might understand. "A scientist's life is based on sharing information, spreading the horizons of knowledge. Don't you see? All that really matters to a scientist is the intrinsic and ethereal beauty of science itself."

"All I see is a fool," Waldau said. "Go back to your scientists."

"But this raid isn't necessary," Boberach protested. "I swear to you, the American device is months from completion. We can leave now. No one need be killed."

"It's too late," Waldau said. "We're committed."

\* \* \*

Pavel stood guard in the dark west wing of the main chemistry and physics laboratory watching Franz Eggers and Bernd Strikfeldt place charges under the Cockcroft-Walton generator. Others were laying waterproof fuses outside, running them from four different buildings to a central igniting area. As soon as Strikfeldt finished setting charges here they would move on to the cyclotron building. With so much heavy, wet snow on the ground Strikfeldt seemed happier with the clumsy navy fuses.

Pavel checked the windows for the fourth time, feeling impatient. Strikfeldt was superb with explosives, but too meticulous. Pavel wished he would hurry. Boberach had marked six buildings for demolition, and they still had two to go. How long could their luck hold out? The fuses were carefully measured and timed to give them plenty of time to get clear. But until all buildings were charged and fuses laid they couldn't even consider retreat.

A click sounded in the hall. Then another. Coming closer. Pavel swung his machine-pistol to the door. It was only Willi Roh, carrying Boberach's peculiar Geiger counting device. He came in, breathless, and glanced at Strikfeldt and Eggers, then said, "Pavel, I've looked everywhere. I've pointed this thing at every corner and door I can find. I keep getting clicks, but nothing large enough to be important. Maybe they don't have much of that radioactive uranium stuff."

"Perhaps not," Pavel said. "Herr Boberach told us it was difficult to purify."

Willi looked relieved. "I'm through with the Geiger counter, then? Thank God. A soldier likes to have a gun in his hands, not a tick-tock machine."

"No, we have to be certain," Pavel said. "Keep looking." Willi grimaced. Pavel could see he didn't like going into the quiet buildings by himself. He added kindly, "Get Erich Huber to accompany you. But hurry. Two more charges and it will be time to fire the fuses. Once they're lit, we have to get out of here."

"It can't come too soon for me," Willi said.

Two bodies now lay in the shadows behind Dryden and Creighton. The third German hadn't seen them yet. He came toward them, walking backward through thick snow flurries,

271

playing out a length of thick fuse cord from the cryogenics laboratory. The passageway between buildings was narrow, and Dryden was sure the man would pass near one of them.

Creighton gestured. Dryden poked his head around the corner of the building for a quick look. He saw the man closing in on the propane tank behind which Creighton was hiding, but the man stopped short. He backed into a snow-hatted tub of sand, one of many Dryden had seen in the technical area, presumably as a precaution against flash laboratory fires. The German glared at the tub and cursed softly, then veered toward Dryden.

Dryden waited until he was only a few feet from the corner, then reached out with his machine pistol and looped the shoulder strap over the man's head. The man dropped the roll of fuse and clawed at his neck, but Dryden twisted the Schmeisser, tightening the strap, and yanked the man off his feet. Creighton was on him in an instant, smashing his face with the butt of his own Schmeisser.

"Three down," Creighton whispered.

Dryden hooked the German's armpits and dragged him back in the shadows with the other bodies. "Don't get cocky," he cautioned. "There are still nine more in here somewhere."

"Yeah, but they'll never get those fuses to burn," Creighton said. "I've worked with dynamite. You know what they say. You got to keep your fuses dry."

Dryden nudged the roll of fuse. "I don't know. This doesn't look like any fuse I ever saw. Heavier. Stiff. Taking the Germans out one by one won't do us any good if they manage to blow the buildings."

"You could be right," Creighton said. "Stuff does look different. So let's figure out where he was going with it. Those Germans I saw earlier were laying fuse to the southwest. If we put this one and the others together, I reckon they'd join up somewhere in those buildings over there. Maybe that's where they plan to set them off."

"We'll take a look," Dryden said.

They skipped out of the shadows, angling from cover to cover. They passed a small supply building and headed for the larger structures. They stayed close together, but the snow fell so thickly that Dryden lost sight of Creighton. He doubled back, groping, and found his friend sprawled in the snow.

Dryden grabbed his arm. "Are you okay?"

Creighton raised his face, grinning. "Look what I found," he said. He lifted a length of fuse, half buried in the snow. "We must be on the right track. Damn thing tripped me."

They followed the fuse the rest of the way, hunched close to the ground, fingers lifting the cord inches from the snow, just enough to see where it led. It took them quickly between buildings and close enough to hear whispering voices. Dryden tugged Creighton behind a snowy wooden stoop and pressed a finger to his lips.

The wind whipped toward them, carrying murmurs. Voices seemed to be arguing. Dryden heard Willi Roh's words tumbling. "Pavel said you had to. Someone has to cover my back." The other voice—was it the Hitler Youth, Erich Huber?—grumbled something, then said, "Yes, all right. But make it fast."

The wind softened. Dryden peered over the stoop and cursed quietly. He could see three figures down the alley between buildings. One hunched over the fuse terminal, tying fuses, but the other two were coming toward him. Willi Roh was carrying Boberach's Geiger counter. Their heads were down, and it seemed unlikely that they would see Dryden or Creighton hugging the snow, but neither could Dryden or Creighton make it across open ground to intercept them without being seen. The stoop was too exposed.

Dryden pushed Creighton below the stoop and rolled across him. He held very still until the two Germans passed along the far side of the alley and rounded the corner. Creighton lifted a snowy face. "Close," he whispered.

Dryden stared after the two Germans. "Willi Roh is looking for the uranium," he said. "Do you think you can handle the fuses alone?"

Creighton checked the remaining German, poised on his hands and knees over the fuse terminal. "Easy as pie," he said.

"Get rid of him any way you can," Dryden said. "Then drag him out of sight and cut the fuses. Make your cuts far enough away from the box so no one will notice. I'll meet you out at the small supply building when I finish."

Willi and Huber were headed toward an office building

behind the big laboratories. Dryden could see them vaguely from the corner, a good fifty feet ahead. He didn't follow them across the open. There was another stoop ahead of him, with a shrub-lined walkway from labs to the office building. He stayed close to the lab wall, waiting for the shorter distance from portal to portal.

Sticking close to the big lab structure seemed a good idea at the time. But it almost cost him. His eyes were on Willi and Huber. When they reached the wooden office building and stopped to force the door, Dryden dropped beside the laboratory stoop, concerned that one of them might look back and see him. He concentrated on them so intently as they slipped inside that he didn't see the German come out of the lab building right above him, carrying a half-empty box of explosives.

Dryden rose to dart across the walkway and ran smack into the man. The German oofed and staggered back. His eyes went to Dryden's face and he goggled, unable to believe what he was seeing. He dropped the box and reached for the strap of his machine pistol, but Dryden lowered a shoulder and hit him again, driving him to the wall. The man bounced, wincing, and opened his mouth to shout. Dryden swung his machine pistol in a short arc, clubbing the man in the face. The German fell in a heap, weapon clattering against the stoop.

Too loud. Too damned loud. Anyone in the lab building could have heard it. Dryden took off for the offices on the run, expecting a cry of alarm from his rear. Even the chatter of a Schmeisser. The office building loomed ahead. Would Willi and Huber be alerted, waiting for him? Too late for caution. He jerked the door open and threw himself inside.

The hallway was empty. He held still, listening. A flight of stairs led upward at the end of the corridor. Somewhere above clicks sounded. Faint clicks. The Geiger counter. Moving from room to room. Willi was already on the second floor, scanning for uranium. Dryden cracked the door to peer across the way. Sure enough, another figure appeared on the lab stoop, barely visible through the blowing snow. A German, brought by the unexpected noise. The man stared at his fallen comrade, then stepped quickly back into the lab building.

Dryden tried to rationalize. Maybe he thought his friend

274

had fallen on the ice. Hell, it was slippery outside. A man could slip and hit his head. But Dryden knew better. The second German had stepped back into the lab building too quickly. If he really thought his friend's fall was an accident, he would have gone to his aid, not ducked back inside. And there were footprints trampled in the snow. Dryden cursed his luck. Anyone could see signs of a struggle and tracks leading from the stoop to this building.

Okay, he was blown. Germans upstairs and Germans across the way. He was caught between them. He had to handle Willi Roh and Erich Huber fast and lower the odds. He let his breath out and hustled to the stairwell.

"Where?" Pavel said.

"By the back door," Eggers chattered excitedly. "He was lying at the bottom of the steps. Someone caved his face in."

"Damn," Pavel swore. "Who? A guard, do you think?"

"I didn't wait to find out," Eggers muttered. "I saw tracks and Detthard bleeding in the snow, and I took off. Christ, Pavel, if they know we're in here, they could be surrounding the building."

"It can't be more than one or two guards," Pavel said. "Any more and they'd be storming the building by now." He made a fist and banged the wall. "Damn, I knew something was wrong. Too many men disappearing. They're picking us off one by one."

"They'll kill us all," Eggers moaned. "I tried to tell you, Pavel. This whole project was doomed from the start."

"It's time to cut our losses," Pavel said. "To hell with the other two buildings. Go get Strikfeldt. I'll check Detthard. We'll fire the fuses and get out of here."

The Geiger counter stuttered in the darkness ahead of him. Dryden slipped to the top of the stairs, treading lightly, and paused to orient himself. Doors lined the dark hallway. Staccato clicks, like bursts of radio static, came from one of the rooms at the end.

He stayed by the wall, following the clicks. A few doors were ajar. He could see dark desks piled with papers and blackboards covered with unintelligible figures. He moved cautiously. The corridor floor was uncarpeted, and he worried about creaking boards. Willi would be busy, concentrating on the Geiger counter, but Huber was a careful bastard.

The Geiger counter clattered, and Dryden zeroed in on the sound. The clicks seemed to come from an open doorway just a few feet ahead. He stepped lightly. He was almost to the open door when Willi called, "Erich?" Dryden pressed against the wall. Had he given himself away? Willi's voice bubbled on. "Erich, hurry. Come. I may have found something."

Dryden felt quick relief. Willi didn't know he was outside the door. But just as quickly another realization tumbled in. Huber wasn't in the room. That's why Willi had called to him. He could be anywhere. And Dryden was pinned to the wall in plain sight. He spun around. And saw Huber. Coming casually through one of the offices near the stairway, carrying a carton of cigarettes and a turnip watch, pockets bulging with booty.

Almost simultaneously Huber saw Dryden. He dropped the cigarettes. They stared at each other along the dark hallway, then Huber whirled and vaulted the bannister, disappearing down the stairwell. Dryden heard him land on the steps with a clatter, then heard his boots pounding toward the front door. Moments later he was outside. Not a word of warning to Willi. Nor to anyone else. No shouts. Just the muffled sound of running feet, rapidly fading away.

Willi called again. "Erich? What's keeping you? I need help."

Dryden gripped his Schmeisser and slipped through the open door. Snowflakes twirled past a tall window on the far side of the room. Willi squatted in front of a thick floor safe, concentrating on the Geiger counter. He played it back and forth along the bottom of the safe's heavy door slab. Clicks rattled in jerky pulses.

Willi heard Dryden step across the floor, but he must have thought it was Huber. He said, "The reading isn't as high as Herr Boberach told us it would be, but there's something in here. Maybe it's that uranium stuff. If we can get this safe door open, we can—" He glanced up and saw the Schmeisser inches from his nose. His eyes rose from the barrel to Dryden's face. Recognition came, and Willi's mouth opened. He gasped, a soft, audible sigh.

Dryden suffered a moment of indecision. He'd intended

to coldcock the little rifleman, a crack to the head with the butt of the Schmeisser, but Willi's eyes, pale white flashes in the darkness, looked so frightened, so defeated, that Dryden almost lost the will to do it. In that brief tick of uncertainty Willi's eyes turned fierce.

The little rifleman shot to his feet and came at Dryden in a frenzy, swinging the Geiger counter. Dryden dropped back, using the Schmeisser to ward off the blow. Willi kept coming, arms swinging, shouting in German. The Geiger counter slammed against the machine pistol again, knocking it from Dryden's grip. Weaponless, Dryden swept his arms out and looped them around Willi's shoulders, trying to pin the Geiger counter. Willi struggled, then butted at Dryden with his head, catching him under the jaw. Dryden held tight. He could smell a cold sweat of fear coming from the little German, and fear made Willi strong. They wrestled across the room, banging into a desk, spilling a welter of papers and books.

Willi tore free. The little German stepped back toward the window, a look of triumph on his face, and cocked the Geiger counter for a coup de grâce. The look of triumph changed to one of disbelief as his foot slipped in the litter of papers and he toppled backward against the windowpanes. His shoulders smashed through glass and wooden moldings. Jagged splinters flew into the night. Willi teetered on the sill for a moment, then plummeted after them.

Dryden groped for his Schmeisser, then hurried to the window. Willi was lying below in a spray of glass, some half-sunk in the snow. Snow had cushioned Willi's fall, and he seemed unhurt. Dryden watched as he opened his eyes and struggled to his feet. The little rifleman staggered drunkenly, then raised stunned eyes to the window. Dryden didn't understand what was wrong until Willi clawed over his shoulder, trying to reach something behind him. As he turned slowly, grasping, Dryden saw a jagged hunk of glass imbedded in his back and a steady flow of blood washing down to his hips. Willi circled twice, and the color drained from his cheeks. His eyes rolled under lids, and he toppled to his side. He twitched and grew still. The Geiger counter lay in the snow beside him, still clicking.

*　　*　　*

277

Hunched over Detthard's body, Pavel saw Erich Huber pound through the snow, heading away from the buildings. What was he running from? Who put the feather up his ass? And where was Willi? He put a finger hurriedly to Detthard's throat, knowing there would be no pulse. The man's nose was battered into his face. A hell of a blow. Probably drove a bone fragment back into the cerebrum. He would have died in moments.

As Pavel rose, thinking about Huber, wondering what had sent him toward the fences in such panic, he heard a crash of glass and jerked around in time to see Willi come flying through a second-floor window of the building across the way. He saw Willi smash down in a spray of glass shards. He would have run to Willi's aid, but he saw Willi stagger to his feet and clutch at the glass in his back. He saw Willi fall for the final time, and he saw Dryden's pale face looking down from above.

Pavel ducked back inside the lab building. God damn the sorry luck! So that was what had been happening to his men. Dryden. Still alive. And here. In the technical area compound. The bastard had surely alerted the American guards by now. Troops would soon be swarming all over the place. He had to warn his comrades, tell them to flee. He heard Strikfeldt and Eggers hurrying toward him from the lab, and he called, "Not this way. They know we're here. Use the other doors. Give me the igniter. I'll light the fuses. You round up everyone you can. Get them through the fence."

Strikfeldt fumbled for the electric igniter and tossed it to Pavel, then he and Eggers spun around and darted the other way. Pavel ducked around a corner and ran toward the side door. Who was left? Lieutenant Strikfeldt and Franz Eggers, yes. And he'd sent Weber to work on the fuses. Erich Huber running in fear through the night. Who else? There were at least two men dead that he knew. Willi and Detthard. Another three men that he hadn't seen for almost an hour. Four men missing back on the canyon trail. Good God. So many men unaccounted for. What had happened to them? Dryden? Alone? How the devil could Dryden make such deadly headway against so many experienced soldiers?

He threw the side door open and dropped into the snow. He expected to see Weber lurking near the fuses, but the man was gone. Damn fool. He was supposed to stay close, in case the fuses needed to be fired early. Pavel hurried to the fuse terminal, determined to set them off.

Pavel squeezed the button of the electric igniter, and the filament glowed. He leaned over the fuses, then stopped. He could see marks in the snow, ridges that cast shadows in the red glow of the igniter filament. Someone had been here, sneaking up behind Weber. Two sets of footprints. Signs of a brief struggle. Other footprints tracked along the fuse lines, three fuses to the north and three to the south, but they could have been left by the men who laid them. He studied the ground more closely. Drag marks. A furrow. Something heavy, like a man. And in the middle of the furrow a pair of ruts. Heel marks. Someone being pulled away, out of sight. Dead or unconscious.

Pavel released the button, and the glow died. He knew Weber was lost. Someone had surprised him at the fuses and either killed him or rendered him unconscious, then tugged him away to hide him. The fuses looked intact. But they were plainly visible, obvious to anyone. Why would someone expose himself to danger, slipping up on Weber, then go away without cutting the fuses? Unless . . .

He gripped his Schmeisser and followed the furrow, his eyes swiveling from the heel marks to the half-buried line of fuses running beside the building. He was out of the alley before the furrow stopped, and footprints led to the fuses. Pavel detoured to the wall, following the tracks. The fuses were buried, but he tugged them out of the snow and found the cuts. Right through the center. A foot-long gap missing from each. Pavel clamped his teeth. Smart bastard. Thought he could cut the fuses away from the terminal and no one would notice. Not this time.

He paused to calculate, then leaned close with the igniter. The slower fuse lengths were behind him. The rest would burn terribly fast. He could light all three fuses and run and still have time to reach cover behind one of the buildings. But he would never make it to the fence. Not before the first explosion. Once the explosions started the whole settlement would come awake. Would escape still be possible? Perhaps, in the confusion. Perhaps not. He had no choice. The charges had to be touched off.

He heard a sound coming in his direction, footsteps crunching through the snow, moving rapidly. Strikfeldt?

Eggers? One of the American guards? Pavel bent quickly over the fuses and pressed the button. The red glow heated instantly. He touched the filament to the first fuse. It sputtered and caught. He moved the igniter to another. Across the way, near a small equipment shed, a dark figure rose from the shadows. The *schwarze Neger*, attracted by the glowing wire and the spewing fuses. The black cupped his hands and yelled, "Eddie! He's lighting the fuses. Stop him!"

Pavel heard the footsteps again, increasing in speed. He touched off the final fuse and started to run, but Dryden bowled around the corner and tackled him, sending him sprawling in the snow. In better times Pavel might have enjoyed the encounter. He owed Dryden much. But the three fuses were burning, and he knew he didn't have the time. He coiled his legs and kicked, knocking Dryden loose. Dryden came flying back at him. He kicked again and scrambled to his feet, taking off on the run. The black's voice rose. "The fuses, Eddie! Get the fuses."

Pavel pounded to the far end of the alley and threw himself into the snow. He rolled behind a concrete foundation and poked his head out. He saw Dryden stamp out one fuse. The black loped into the alley with a knife in his hand and hacked at a second like a snake, slashing frantically. Dryden chased the third fuse, trying to stamp it, smother it, yank it loose, but the fuse burned on. The black turned back to help, but the fuse was moving too rapidly. As they closed in it curled up the side of a building and ran through an open window. The two men looked at each other, then dived for cover.

Pavel jumped and dodged toward the fence, running as hard as he could. There was a moment of deep silence behind him as the fuse burned its way to the explosive charge, then the building erupted. A shattering boom rolled across the mesa, followed by flame and showering glass. The shock wave almost knocked Pavel from his feet. He clutched his Schmeisser and ran on. His mouth tightened. Too bad, Dryden. You shouldn't have pressed your luck.

Dryden and Creighton drove their faces into the snow and covered their heads with their arms. The wall blew out above them. The sound was deafening. The blast lifted them from the ground, and a pressure wave hurled them back. Flame belched in boiling waves and curled to the sky. Glass and metal fragments rattled against nearby structures. Smoke rolled over them like quick fog, then followed the rising fireball, sucked up by heat. Boards and siding, blown high by the force of the explosion, rained down in huge chunks. Something hit Dryden's leg with a clatter, and smaller scraps pelted around him.

His senses shrieked. Blinding light. Buffeting shock wave. Sharp heat. Pain. Choking smoke. The incredible, battering noise. His ears rang with it. Even after the rain of fragments ended the noise seemed to roll on. He kept his head down, waiting for it to end.

And then he realized it had ended. The persistent ringing in his ears was only residue. He lifted his head cautiously from the crook of his arm and looked up at the building. Half the wall and a portion of the roof were gone, and flames crackled deep in its belly. The blazing alley was as bright as day. He tried to rise, but something lay heavily on his leg. He twisted to an elbow and looked back. A jumble of timbers rested at an angle against a large piece of sheet metal that hadn't been there before. Dryden wriggled his body, tugging at his leg until it slipped loose.

He found his Schmeisser and staggered to his feet. Where was Creighton? His ears sang on, buzzing loudly in the silence. An enormous white blur, imprinted on his retinas by the flash, blotted his vision. He lurched through the clutter of planks and wreckage seeking his foreman. And found him, under the debris. Only a foot at first, sticking out beneath a shattered layer of singed roofing. Dryden shoveled wood and panels of siding with both hands, then dropped to his knees and dug for Creighton. He reached the man's armpits and pulled him, as gently as possible, out into the snow.

Creighton opened an eye and looked up at him. "Whoo-eee," he murmured. "Those Germans really know how to give a party."

"Can you walk?" Dryden asked.

"I'd rather not."

"Try it," Dryden said. "We've got to get to the fence."

Creighton winced. "You go on. Just leave me here for a spell."

"Not a chance," Dryden said. "This place will be buzzing

with guards in no time at all. They'll shoot at anything that breathes.''

"You're the boss," Creighton said. "You may have to give me a hand.''

Dryden helped him to his feet and looped an arm around his waist. Creighton tried to walk, but his left leg collapsed on the first step. He didn't cry out. He just sank. Dryden looked down at the leg. The knee was badly mangled. He said, "Sorry, Clarence. I'll have to carry you. It may not be comfortable, but it'll get us out of here faster." He boosted Creighton to his shoulder and started for the fence. The fire raged on behind them.

Lights were blinking on all over the mesa. The snow kept falling. Dryden made for the fence, jouncing Creighton. He heard shouts from the east, the direction of the guard huts. Poor slobs. What would they think, awakened by a blast on an isolated hilltop dedicated to the construction of the world's most tremendous superbomb? Would they think the big bomb had jumbled its atoms and exploded prematurely? That it was all over? Damned right they would. It must have happened nightly in their worst dreams.

Somewhere in the darkness a pair of M1 carbines barked. A Schmeisser chattered back. Dryden put his head down and ran for the wire, scarcely feeling Creighton's weight. More guns opened up. The guards were out in force now, and Dryden heard shouts and challenges above the sound of gunfire. They seemed to be centering their attention on an area some sixty yards or so to the east.

When he reached the breach in the fence he saw why. Fresh footprints, fewer than had come in, went through the wire and turned away from the technical area. But in their panic the German survivors had turned the wrong way and run headlong into the guards spilling from the military police huts. Dryden could see them now, hunkered behind snow-covered cars, exchanging fire at the end of the road.

Dryden ducked through the fence with Creighton. Was Pavel among them? He could see five or six Germans at most behind cover, and at least fifty Americans sprawling ahead of them, peppering them with gunfire. One big American, bare-chested and in stocking feet, completely unmindful of the snow, seemed to be rallying the others for a charge. Dryden saw a flash behind the cars as a grenade went off, and a German officer, Strikfeldt, staggered and fell. The bare-chested American whooped and ran toward the cars, firing from his hip. It was wasted bravery. One of the Germans opened up with his Schmeisser, and the big man went down, face and chest plowing into the snow. Some of the Germans broke away from the cars and ran toward the shadows.

A stray shot whistled overhead. Creighton shifted and groaned. "Do you think we could keep moving, Eddie? This don't seem the best place in the world to linger."

Dryden hefted Creighton to a more secure position and moved as rapidly as he could away from the shooting, heading toward the schoolmaster's house.

Pavel burst into the headmaster's house, startling the woman and the two children. Waldau and Grebling, standing by the window, whirled on him. Waldau was enraged. "You fool!" the SS colonel bellowed. "Why did you allow an explosion to sound prematurely?"

Pavel leaned against the wall, gulping for air. He said grimly, "Be satisfied, Colonel. It may be the only explosion you'll hear. Dryden is alive."

Waldau's anger subsided. "Yes, I know. I heard."

"Heard?" Pavel said. "How?"

Waldau waved a hand, dismissing the question. "You allowed him to best you. A cripple. By himself. I find that hard to believe."

"Tell that to the men he's killed," Pavel said. "Only a handful of us got out. I thought they were ahead of me until I heard the shooting. I'm going back for them. I'll need Voight and anyone else who's willing to come. What about you, Herr Standartenführer?"

Grebling said, "No, no. This is our command post. We must wait here. Those who escape will come looking for us."

Pavel knew the SS captain spoke from fear. Still, what he said perhaps made sense. The others would disengage if they could. He tuned his ear, listening. Had the firing abated already?

"Summon Voight and Huber," Waldau told Grebling. "Have them bring the scientists. Let us finish what we came for."

Pavel swung his head. "Huber is here?"

Grebling pounded on the bedroom door, Voight stuck his head out, and Grebling murmured to him. The door swung wide, and Voight ushered the scientists into the living room. Boberach and Erich Huber followed. Huber glanced nervously at Pavel. His scabby upper lip trembled.

Pavel grabbed him by the lapels. "You bastard!" he snarled. "You saw Dryden and you ran out on us. Not a word of warning to anyone."

"Let him go," Waldau said. "It was important that I be warned."

Pavel said incredulously, "Let him go? I ought to kill the little bastard. Some of my men might be alive right now, except for him. And your precious explosions might have gone off on schedule."

Waldau raised the flap of his holster. He said, "Sergeant, do as I say. Release him. We need every man we can find. It's time to execute the hostages and retire to the caves."

Boberach picked his way through the scientists. "But Colonel, we don't need to do that," he said. "I told you. It isn't necessary. The bomb is no problem. It can't possibly be ready in time."

"My orders are to execute the hostages," Waldau said. "And I intend to do so. Step aside."

Boberach seemed frightened by what he was about to say, but he said it anyway. He drew himself up and backed into the middle of the scientists. "If they are to die, Herr Standartenführer, then I am prepared to die with them."

It didn't bother Waldau a bit. "As you wish," he said. "Corporal Voight. Shoot them all."

Pavel sighed and primed his Schmeisser. "Hold it," he said. "No one is going to die. Not yet. Not until my men get here. I will not have them robbed of their chances for survival."

Voight hesitated. He glanced at Waldau for a sign. Waldau glared at Pavel. "Lower your gun!" he snapped. "That's an order, Sergeant."

"Stuff your orders up your ass," Pavel said. "My men come first."

He expected trouble from Waldau, and perhaps from Voight and Huber. He didn't expect interference from the frightened SS captain, Grebling. And that was his downfall.

Grebling, seeing his chance for escape evaporating, flung himself at Pavel's gun. He grabbed the barrel and pushed it to the ceiling. Pavel tried to fight the SS captain off, but Voight and Huber came flying in at him and dragged him to the floor.

Dryden couldn't believe his eyes. He lowered Creighton to the porch and peered through the parted curtains. Pavel was against the wall with hands above his head and a gun at his back. The cocky Hitler Youth, Erich Huber, stood behind him. Waldau and Grebling were nearby. Albert Voight was on the other side of the room, holding a gun on frightened strangers. The scientists, most likely. Still alive, thank God. But why Pavel? Why had they taken Pavel prisoner?

Waldau murmured something, and Voight cocked his weapon. Dryden tensed. It looked like the shooting was about to begin. He backed up a couple of steps, got a good grip on his Schmeisser, then threw himself through the window. He blasted into the room in a shower of glass. Someone shrieked. He thought at first it was the woman, but it sounded more like the SS man, Grebling.

Huber and Voight froze. The scientists, expecting death, threw themselves to the floor, bodies tumbling in every direction. Dryden rolled and came up with the Schmeisser. He loosed a burst and saw Huber's arm jerk, spotting red. The Hitler Youth cried out, clasping a hand to his shoulder. Pavel ducked for cover. Dryden swung to Voight and fired again. Voight dived into an alcove. Bullets stitched across wood molding above him, gouging chunks and splinters. Waldau jerked his pistol from his holster and started shooting, but he seemed to be spraying shots at random, without aiming. Dryden shifted the Schmeisser and pressed the trigger, aiming at Waldau's stomach. Nothing happened. The damned gun had jammed. He slapped the priming lever, trying to wrestle it open. All that activity in the technical area. Maybe he'd used it as a club once too often.

In the moment of frantic silence Waldau and Grebling whirled and raced for the rear of the house. Huber scrambled to his feet with one arm dangling and leapt through the broken window. Dryden threw the jammed gun to the floor, intent on chasing them down, but Voight chose that moment to come flying out of the alcove. One of the scientists shouted a warning, but it was too late. The big German plowed into Dryden and knocked him spinning.

Dryden thumped face-down on the floor. Something or someone landed on his back. He was conscious of immense weight. Voight planted a ham-fisted hand on his neck, trying to grind his face through a black-and-white Navajo rug. Scientists chattered shrilly in the background, sounding concerned, but no one did anything to help. Dryden tried to move, but his arms were pinned and he couldn't get leverage. He strained against the pressure, but the big hand stayed on the back of his neck. One hand. Only one hand. Where was the other? Absurdly, he found himself worrying about Voight's missing hand. Was it holding a Schmeisser? Was he about to start shooting? Or God, the knife! Was Voight fumbling for that knife he'd used to kill the soldiers in the Tucumcari schoolroom?

It was the knife. Dryden didn't see it, might never have lived to learn about it, except for Pavel. The knife came sliding out of Voight's tunic and was poised to strike when Pavel grabbed the big man and wrenched him off Dryden's back. With the weight suddenly lifted Dryden rolled to his elbow, wondering what the hell had happened. He saw Pavel with a choke hold locked around Voight's neck, and he saw Pavel reach down for the knife wrist and turn it, then pull it back sharply into the big man's stomach, just below the ribs. Pavel didn't say a word to Voight. Just planted his hand on the knife and drove it deeper. All the way to the wooden handle. Then he released Voight and stepped back.

One of the scientists murmured, "Oh, my God." Voight had a look of pure surprise on his face. He tried to rise. He actually made it to one knee. He touched the knife handle in wonder, then flicked a look of confusion at the scientists and folded to the floor. Dryden snatched Voight's Schmeisser from the Navajo rug.

"I'm indebted to you," he told Pavel.

"You owe me nothing," Pavel said. "It was a pleasure."

Dryden hurried to the back, looking for Waldau and Grebling, but they were gone. The kitchen door stood wide, with snow and cold air blowing in on the linoleum. He cursed and shut the door.

When he returned to the living room the scientists had taken stock and had discovered that two of them had been nicked by Waldau's wild shots. One man, a beanpole with an imposing dome of forehead, had a hole through the palm of his left hand. The woman, Kitty Oppenheimer, attempted to stanch the bleeding with a piece of window curtain. She fussed as she worked on him, and Dryden wondered if she was more worried about the wound or the blood spotting her furniture. But the man had an amused expression on his face and seemed to take no offense.

The other wounded scientist was Boberach. He sat on the floor, rocking back and forth with both hands clamped around one bare foot. His shoe lay beside him, with a neat hole punched through the leather toe. Only Pavel paid any attention to him. Dryden started to ask Boberach how he felt, then realized with a start that Pavel was holding a Schmeisser. He jerked Voight's weapon to his hip and racked the lever back. The noise caught everyone's attention—Kitty Oppenheimer, the milling scientists, Boberach, And Pavel, of course. It was a sound German soldiers knew well.

Pavel looked up in disgust. "They took it from me earlier," he said. He offered the gun to Dryden. "If it makes you nervous, put it away."

Dryden hesitated. Pavel had just saved his life. Still, the man was a German soldier. He said, "Yes, thank you, Pavel. I hate to sound ungrateful, but I think I'd feel better if it was unloaded."

Pavel removed the magazine and tossed it to him, then laid the machine pistol on the floor. "In your place, I'd do the same," he said.

"How is he?" Dryden asked, nodding at Boberach.

"A flea bite," Pavel said. "He'll need a new pair of shoes, but I've seen worse wounds on kindergarten playgrounds."

Boberach looked furious. "It hurts," he said.

Dryden stepped out on the porch, looking for Clarence Creighton. Creighton had managed to slide against the wall, and he had a snowy rock in his hand, cocked and ready. When he saw it was Dryden he lowered the rock and said, "You took your own sweet time coming back. Who was shooting at who?"

"Good guys and bad guys," Dryden said. "I'm afraid most of the bad guys got away."

"Oh, crap," Creighton said. "They'll head for the caves. They've got no place else to go."

"I know," Dryden said. The door opened and Pavel stepped out. Creighton did a double take and raised his rock, but Dryden said, "It's okay, Clarence. He's one of us now. I'll explain later."

Pavel stared down at Creighton. "What happened to you?"

Creighton said, "What the hell you think happened to me? That explosion you set off. Busted the hell out of my knee. How about getting me inside? It's cold out here."

Together they lifted Creighton. As they carted him toward the door Pavel paused. He cocked an ear, listening. "Soldiers," he said. "Headed this way."

"Your men?" Dryden asked.

Pavel shook his head. "Too many. The Americans. Probably coming here."

Dryden helped Creighton into the living room. "I can't hang around," he told the black. "They'll have questions. Beverly is alone at the caves. I've got miles to go and things to do." He turned to Kitty Oppenheimer. "I hate to turn your house into an aid station," he said. "But I've got another big emergency, and I'd like to think my friend is in good hands. Will you take care of him?"

She looked down at Creighton. "You're sure he's not one of them? I personally will help him bleed to death if he's one of these foul Germans." Her eyes shifted challengingly to Pavel's uniform.

Dryden said, "No way, ma'am. My friend is Mr. Apple Pie. As American as they come. He's been out fighting the Germans who were trying to hurt you. Now he's hurt."

She nodded decisively. "Then I'll take care of him."

Dryden said, "There are soldiers on the way. Make sure they know he's one of the good guys, will you?"

The fine eyes flashed. "I'll make sure the soldiers understand," she said.

Pavel put a hand on Dryden's arm. "I'm going with you."

"You can't," Dryden said. "You're a German soldier."

"And a good one," Pavel said. "You'll need me. Unless you think you can handle Waldau, Grebling, and Huber by yourself."

"I've done pretty well so far."

288

"Yes," Pavel said. "Because none of us knew you were behind us. Now Waldau knows. Perhaps you can manage him alone, but what if not? Who suffers? The nurse?"

"Why should you help me?"

"I am not thinking of you," Pavel said. "I am thinking of Oberst Kleber. That Nazi bastard Waldau will kill your woman without a qualm and head for Mexico. He will kill Kleber, too. He will leave no one to tell pursuers which way he has gone."

"Can I trust you?" Dryden asked.

Pavel shrugged. "As much as I could trust you in similar circumstances."

Dryden stared at him. It was a dangerous idea, but with Beverly's life hanging in the balance he wanted the help. Welcomed it. Needed it. He picked up the spare Schmeisser and handed it to Pavel.

"Okay, Sergeant. Let's go."

*Sunday*
*December 31, 1944*

# FIFTEEN

Lighted windows stretched before them. The settlement had come awake, thanks to the explosion. The technical building was still burning, and the sky was bright with flames on the southern rim of the mesa. Dryden and Pavel skirted boxy houses, trying to reach the hole in the fence without being spotted. The wind had weakened with the dying storm, and the snow had thinned. In a way it was both a help and a hindrance. Without the wind and stinging snow in their faces they could move faster. Visibility had increased, making it easier to see guards on the streets and alter their course. But there was a downside. What they could see, could also see them. If anyone spotted them now and challenged them, they were finished. Pavel's German uniform was fully visible. Dryden was wearing the proper uniform, but it wouldn't have done him any good. He was still an outsider, someone who had no official business being on the mesa, and a challenge for either would mean delay, questions, maybe even a bullet.

They swerved to avoid clusters of people standing outside some of the living structures, staring at the burning horizon, but most of the lit windows signaled empty quarters. The majority of the mesa's residents had bundled up in coats and gone streaming down to help fight the fire. Some of the guards had joined the fire brigade as well, but most of them were out looking for intruders. Dryden could hear them clearly, shouting signs and countersigns among the buildings. He also heard a few shots, but he had no way of knowing whether they were shooting at shadows. Either way, it was a bad night to be out in the open.

They were almost to the fence when they encountered their first civilian body. A man in a plaid mackinaw and blue jeans, lying in the doorway of a flat-roofed McKee house. A pair of horn-rimmed spectacles lay askew on his nose, and he had a bullet hole in his neck. Dryden and Pavel detoured for a quick look. Pavel put a finger to the man's throat. No pulse.

"Stray bullet?" Dryden asked.

Pavel shook his head. He indicated booted footprints, then slipped a finger into a thumb-sized depression in the snow and pulled out an empty shell case that had melted through the crust. "Waldau," he said. "At close range."

Dryden pulled the mackinaw off the body. "Poor bastard. He must have opened the door at the wrong moment."

"He wasn't the first to die tonight," Pavel said. "Nor the first to be taken by surprise." His eyes flicked to Dryden, and for a moment there was fire in them.

"I did what I had to," Dryden said.

"Yes, we must talk about that some day," Pavel said.

Dryden clamped his teeth. "We can talk now, if you want to."

Pavel got to his feet and stuck his jaw in Dryden's face. "That would give me pleasure," he said.

Frustration had put Dryden on edge, and he leaned forward, aching to fight. Then he thought about Beverly. He settled back on his heels and thrust the mackinaw at Pavel. "Shut up and put this on," he said. "We've got other priorities."

Pavel sobered. "Yes, I suppose Waldau must come first."

"Let's go," Dryden said. "We can settle our differences at the cave."

"I can wait," Pavel said.

*　　*　　*

291

At the fence Pavel paused again. "They are several minutes ahead of us," he said. "Here are their tracks. Two sets The boots of officers. Waldau and Grebling. The snow is only now beginning to fill the depressions."

"I can read the signs," Dryden said. He pointed at another set of tracks. "They've got company. Flecks of blood. Huber, probably. I caught him in the arm back at the schoolmaster's house."

"No, not with them," Pavel said. "Behind them. The footprints are clearer, more sharply defined. Perhaps he's trying to catch up."

A guard's voice sounded. Too near the fence for comfort. Dryden glanced over his shoulder. "Okay, so we can both read tracks," he said. "Let's postpone the competition and get out of here. Maybe we can work together for a change."

They ducked through the gap in the fence and followed the tracks. The fire in the technical area was burning less fiercely. The glow in the sky had paled, and the sounds of confusion had fallen to a murmur.

The tracks led to the rim of the mesa and spilled down at the nearest point without bothering to make for the gentler slope they'd used earlier. Dryden and Pavel tumbled after them. Pavel lost his footing halfway down and slid a good fifteen feet before he managed to snag a bush and pull himself to a stop. Dryden helped him up, and they descended the rest of the way more cautiously.

The tracks reached bottom and turned toward the trees where the Germans had left the horses. As Dryden and Pavel followed through deep snow Dryden told Pavel how he'd scattered the horses. The big German grunted in appreciation. Huber's tracks paralleled those of the two German officers, but only for about fifty yards. Then Huber had stopped. A small trampled area showed where the Hitler Youth had milled about indecisively before striking off in a new direction.

"He can't be far ahead," Pavel said. "Do you want to go after him?"

The blood flecks followed Huber's tracks, but less profusely. Perhaps he'd finally thought to apply pressure to the wound. A pity. Dryden liked Kitty Oppenheimer's idea. He had hoped Huber would bleed to death. He said, "No, let him go. Waldau is the one we want."

The tracks of the two officers led into the trees and circled, seeking the horses. When they reached the area where the horses had been, panic must have set in. The strides grew longer, leading first one way, then another. Dryden and Pavel moved from cover to cover warily. Without horses, Waldau and Grebling might still be in the trees somewhere, hiding.

As it happened, only Grebling was there. Dryden saw the signs first. Hoofprints in the snow. A trampled circle. One of the loose horses had apparently wandered back into the trees. Waldau and Grebling must have seen the horse and separated to slip up on it. Both sets of boot tracks came together in the trampled area, and both obviously got their hands on the reins. Hoof marks showed where the horse had tried to break away. The two officers had settled the horse down, but only one of them had climbed into the saddle and ridden away. Grebling lay on his back at the edge of the circle, a bullet in his throat and another between the eyes. With only one mount available, Waldau had discarded him.

"Now we know why Huber peeled off on his own," Dryden said.

"You believe he heard the shots?"

Dryden nodded. "And probably knew what they meant."

Pavel stared at the hoofprints leading from the circle, stretching out at a gallop. "We'll never catch him now."

"We have to," Dryden said. "We might still get there first, if we move hard enough and fast enough. We know the way. He's riding blind."

"He knows the trail," Pavel said. "You showed it to him."

Dryden shrugged. "He'll have a hard time following it in the dark. Besides, I never said it was the fastest trail."

Pavel's eyes narrowed. "You duped us?"

"Cooperating with the German Army was never my strong point," Dryden said. "Let's just say I held something in reserve."

They abandoned Waldau's trail and moved across the canyon at a steady clip, breaking a new path through the snow. The first mile was over relatively flat terrain, but the snow depth varied and the pace was tiring. They didn't talk much. When they reached the stream they stopped. Ice had formed at the edges, but the water ran fast and cold in

293

the center. Pavel spotted a pair of beaver-toppled aspen, and they dragged them to the near bank and laid them over the middle to create a temporary bridge. Once across, they resumed moving fast. The worst of the storm seemed to be over. Even the light, feathery flakes stopped falling. The wind softened. A patch of night sky broke through on the southern horizon. They moved on, breathing hard, toward the mountain facing Los Alamos mesa.

They rested briefly when they reached the foot of the mountain, then Dryden gestured up at a low saddle. "This is the tough part," he said. "We can work our way around, or we can go across the top. If we can get to the top, the other side should be easier."

"You intend to climb this mountain? At night? In the snow?"

"Just to the saddle," Dryden said. "It isn't as bad as it looks. In good weather it would be a Sunday stroll. But watch your step. One slip and you're out of action. I won't stop to help you."

"If you can climb it, I can climb it," Pavel said.

Dryden hooked his Schmeisser over his shoulder and started up the slope. Pavel fell in behind him. It was easy going on the lower hip of the mountain, but the snowy slope became progressively rockier. They picked their way with care. At the midway point the incline leveled off at the end of a ledge, and they were able to hike across a broad, sloping table for almost a quarter of a mile. The wind, unfettered, pummeled across the barren table, stabbing them with needles of blowing ice crystals, but the snow was shallower, and they moved all the faster. There was a hint of light in the eastern sky. A promise of dawn. Dryden tugged his collar close and led Pavel to the south side of a boulder, out of the wind. "We'd better take a break," he said.

"Can we afford the time?" Pavel asked.

"I think so," Dryden said. He pointed. "The caves are down there. We can make it in another half hour. But we'll need our wits about us. There are the same kind of toeholds going down to the caves as there are going up, but we'll probably hit ice."

"Then a rest sounds good," Pavel said. He swung his Schmeisser off his shoulder and sagged to his haunches against the boulder. He relaxed with eyes closed, then opened them. "I have been wondering," he said. "How can you justify the zealous intensity of your pursuits on Los Alamos mesa?"

Dryden dropped to the ground beside him. "I thought we were going to leave all that until we put Waldau out of action."

"I don't mean what you did to my men," Pavel said. "That was war. No, I mean working so hard to rescue the atomic device. You heard what Herr Boberach said. It isn't a military weapon. It's a terror bomb. Meant to kill women and children."

"I wasn't saving the bomb," Dryden said. "I was trying to save lives. The scientists. Waldau had every intention of killing them."

Pavel nodded. "I suppose," he said. "Still, the scientists are responsible for the construction of the bomb. And the bomb is meant to kill civilians."

Dryden gave him a sideways glance. "What if the bomb was a German weapon, and I had set out with troops to cripple it? Wouldn't you have tried to stop me?"

"I don't know," Pavel said. "Perhaps not. Some things should be left to God and nature."

"What about duty? What if you were ordered to stop me?"

Pavel shrugged. "I've always believed in the concept of duty," he said. "But in this case, I'm not sure. I'd still have to live with my conscience."

Dryden grinned. "There may be hope for you yet, Pavel."

Pavel turned a serious face to him. "And what of you, Captain? How will your conscience fare?"

"I can live with it."

"Perhaps," Pavel said. "Let us hope you have no cause to regret what you have done this night."

They were just starting to inch down the steep face of the canyon wall above the ruin when Pavel spotted movement below, a man and animal plugging along the canyon floor in a rush to reach the cave. "There," Pavel said, pointing. "Waldau approaches. He's moving hard."

Dryden leaned out for a better look. He recognized the chestnut mare, even at a distance. It was Christina Rosetti, a friendly, trusting creature, too fine-boned for a good quarter horse, but what she didn't have in stamina she made up for in heart. She didn't know how to say no. Demand speed and she would give it until she collapsed. Even from here he could see the SS colonel whipping her. Steam blew in gusty snorts from her nostrils. "Bastard," he muttered. "He'll ruin her, the way he's driving her."

"Will he reach the caves before us?"

"He might," Dryden said. "Oh, God, he might."

Beverly stamped on a long branch, cracking it, and fed the fire. Smoke curled into her eyes. She picked up the pistol and sat facing Linares and Frischauer. It would be daylight soon. Hours had passed since Ned and Mr. Creighton left the caves. Where were they now? Were they still alive? No one else had come. She'd heard a single muffled boom in the darkest hours of morning. Distant. Indistinct. A horrible sound. Like a bomb. Her imagination had worked overtime, summoning dreadful images. Newsreels of the London Blitz. Screams and smoke. Burning buildings. Frantic digging. Ned, lying below piles of debris, bleeding, trying to stay alive until rescuers reached him.

Staying busy helped. The German commandant, Kleber, had passed a bad night. He was feverish and in considerable pain. She had changed the dressings on his leg, but the infection had worsened. Odd that the most minor of his injuries should give him the most trouble now. But mostly he was awake and out of his head, rambling in German, shouting at shadows.

And it was cold. She'd tried to keep the fire going, but smoke was a problem. There were holes in the roof over Kleber's ruin, and the smoke should have dissipated easily, drifting out into the cave. For some diabolical reason it hung in the air. It wasn't as bad at floor level where Kleber lay, and where the other two Germans were tied and resting. As long as she stayed low with them she was all right.

Kleber moaned again. She sighed and laid the pistol on his blankets and reached for the pan of water she'd brought from the spring in the adjacent ruin. She dipped a compress in it and wrung it out, then laid it across his forehead. The other two Germans were moodily quiet. The spy, Linares, was openly hostile. He wasn't in very good shape after his fight with Ned. His massive face was crusted with dried blood, and both eyes were swollen, but he stared at her balefully, watching her in hateful silence. Frischauer, leaning against the tattered stone wall with his hands tied behind, looked terribly depressed. Probably upset because he was a captive again. Or perhaps he was just cold. He had slept for a long while, and he'd surely feel even chillier now that he was awake.

As she glanced at Frischauer he stirred. He suddenly sat straighter. He said, "Bitte, Fräulein. Please." He murmured something in German.

Linares lashed out with a boot, kicking Frischauer in the thigh. The spy snarled angrily in German. Frischauer ducked his head.

Beverly picked up the gun and pointed it awkwardly with both hands. "What is it?" she demanded. "What did he say?"

Linares scowled. "Nothing of importance," he muttered. "He whined like a baby that he was cold and asked for more wood on the fire. I told him to shut up. We do not require your ministrations."

"Oh," she said. She laid the gun back on Kleber's blankets. "I'm glad you feel that way, smart ass. It's getting too smoky in here anyway. Tough it out."


"I know some words of English," Frischauer whispered. "Enough to understand what you said. Why did you speak of wood on the fire? I told her nothing of the cold. I mentioned only that I heard a horse approaching."

"You have a big mouth," Linares grumbled. "If she didn't hear the horse, that's her lookout. You owe her nothing."

"But she's distracted, tending the Oberst. I wanted only to put her mind at ease, to tell her that her friend was perhaps returning."

"Fool. It might be our people."

"Not likely," Frischauer said sadly. "Pavel said it was a suicide mission."

Frischauer wished he could escape into sleep again, but instead he listened more carefully. He thought he heard snorted greetings, an exchange among the trees, but it could have been restlessness on the part of the animals left to fend for themselves through the storm. Another faint sound drifted to the ruin a few moments later. Click of pebble?

Scrape of boot leather? The crackling fire popped and shifted. He couldn't be sure whether he was hearing light footfalls or only imagining them.

The woman seemed to notice nothing. Frischauer watched the weary look on her face as she dipped the compress and wrung it. Kleber had begun to rave again, rambling about British tanks in the Sahara, calling for artillery support, demanding more gasoline. She had much on her mind. Concern for the Oberst. Watchfulness for her two prisoners. Fear for her friend, the American captain.

Linares nudged him. Frischauer looked around, saw the swollen eyes gesture toward the broken wall. He swung to the spill of masonry and was startled to see a haggard face rise in the darkness. The SS colonel. Waldau. Frischauer looked back at the woman. Still deeply involved with Oberst Kleber, trying to quiet him. The gun was at her knees, in the blankets. He wanted to call out to her, to warn her. But he did nothing. He couldn't. Waldau was too close.

Linares shifted, straining his arms to show his roped wrists. The SS colonel, standing silently outside the breached wall, stared down at the ropes. His face, seamed with exhaustion, looked murderous. Now muscles flickered in his jaws. His hand dipped to his holster, drawing his weapon. He stepped quietly inside.

The woman had a hand on Kleber's brow, murmuring. Waldau stepped across the room, arrogantly confident. He was within four feet of her before she looked up. Frischauer saw the look of shock spring to her face. Her free hand drifted toward the blanket. He shook his head violently. No, no, not the gun. He'll shoot.

Perhaps she saw Frischauer's warning shake of the head. Perhaps not. Either way, she seemed to have reached the same conclusion. Her hand moved to the edge of the blanket and turned it, covering the pistol. Then she rose to face Waldau. Good girl, Frischauer thought. Hide it and step away. Maybe your chance will come later.

Linares struggled to his feet, grinning. "I knew someone would come," he said.

Waldau stepped around the big spy to get at his bound hands. "How did this happen?" he asked.

"The American captain," Linares said. "He's alive."

298

Waldau's jaw muscles flickered again. "Yes, we saw him on the mesa. He came here? Where is the black cowboy?"

"They went away together," Linares said. "Don't let the woman get close to the blankets. My gun is there somewhere."

Waldau tugged the final knot loose and let the rope fall to the floor, then looked at the woman and gestured her to the wall with his gun. His face was dark with anger. "Damn all, the black was to lead us out of here."

Linares rubbed circulation back into his wrists. "We don't need him. There are horses. And pack animals. And Mexico is south."

"And an army at our heels," Waldau said.

Linares looked up. "You were successful on the mesa?"

"Only partially," Waldau said. "Can you get us to Mexico and the submarine?" The spy nodded. "Then come," Waldau said. "We must leave quickly. Gather what food you can."

"We'll have to rig a sled to one of the horses," Linares said. "The Oberst is in no condition to travel by saddle."

"The Oberst is my responsibility," Frischauer said. "Untie me. I can help."

Linares started toward Frischauer, but Waldau stopped him. "Leave him," Waldau said. "Neither he nor the Oberst will accompany us. We have no time for cripples."

Linares hesitated. "You may be right. Just the two of us, moving with all haste. Our chances would be better."

Frischauer looked at them, not believing his ears. "No, please," he said. He labored to his feet and presented his bonds to Waldau. "Please, Colonel. Untie me. I can be useful."

"Wagging tongues may be dangerous," Linares said. "We'll be on the trail for days. They could point the way to the submarine."

Waldau proposed the inevitable but simple solution. "Retrieve your gun," he said. "Shoot them all. The Oberst as well."

Linares stepped toward Kleber's pallet. The woman spoke no German, so she couldn't have followed the discussion. But she knew what Linares wanted from the blankets, and she broke from the wall, trying to reach the gun first. Linares flung her away, spinning her toward the cooking fire.

"Run!" Frischauer yelled.

She didn't. She fell to her knees. Without hesitation she snatched the big venison pot and scrambled up. She took a swipe at the spy, stunning him, then spun toward Waldau. She was at least six feet away, but she didn't let the distance deter her. She threw herself at him. Waldau, though mildly surprised, reacted calmly. He raised the pistol and aimed, preparing to fire.

Frischauer squeaked in outrage, then lowered his head and butted Waldau in the back. Waldau's arm lurched and the pistol went off.

"That's his horse," Dryden said. The young mare stood among the trees, steaming in the cold. Waldau couldn't have beaten them by more than a few minutes. "Come on," he told Pavel. "I left them in Kleber's ruin. We've got to get to her."

Pavel put a hand on his arm. "Let us go with caution," he counseled. "The colonel will have untied Jürgen and Herr Linares by now. Someone could be watching the entrance."

"I don't give a damn," Dryden said. "If those bastards have touched her . . ." He clambered down to the stone balcony in front of the ruin, his Schmeisser cocked and ready. Pavel followed.

The balcony was clear. They hurried toward the dwellings, moving swiftly and silently. Dryden could see firelight flickering in Kleber's cubicle. He heard voices, Waldau and Linares, talking quietly. Then Frischauer's voice, sounding plaintive. The voices grew silent, then something seemed to happen. Sounds of a struggle. Frischauer calling out, telling someone to run. A moment of silence, then a shot. Dryden broke into a full run, heart pounding with dread. Pavel raced at his heels.

They made a terrible clatter running across the wide ledge, but no one heard them. The sounds from the ruin were too intense. Waldau cursed and called for help. A woman's voice rose in shrill counterpoint. "Drop it, you bastard, drop it!"

Dryden leapt to the wall a step ahead of Pavel and poked his head in. He saw Waldau against the side wall, warding off blows. Beverly was all over him like a she-cat, kicking, swinging the Dutch oven, straining for his gun. Frischauer, hands still bound, helped as much as he could, driving at

Waldau like a battering ram, pummeling him with lowered head and shoulders. Across the room, near the fire, the big spy dug a gun out of Kleber's blankets and rose, looking for a clear shot.

"Hold it!" Dryden demanded.

The spy whirled and fired. Adobe chinks flew from the wall near Dryden's head. Dryden and Pavel cut loose simultaneously. The Schmeissers bucked, and Linares blew back across the blankets and into the fire, scattering embers and burning wood. Sparks spiraled upward.

The roar of the machine pistols, deafening in the small cubicle, and the acrid, burning smell of cordite brought the tableau at the wall to a halt. Three faces turned. Frischauer buckled gratefully and slid to the floor. Beverly's face, savage with determination, softened. Waldau's gaze fell on Pavel, and he, too, seemed momentarily relieved. Then he must have remembered the state in which he had left Pavel. He roused himself and swung an arm, backhanding Beverly toward the gap in the wall, and raised the pistol to fire.

With Beverly stumbling toward them neither Dryden nor Pavel had a clear shot. Waldau's first bullet whistled past her ear, gouging a chunk from the rock wall. Dryden bounded over the fallen rubble and grabbed her, wrestling her to the floor. Pavel tried to get a bead on Waldau as soon as she was down, but not in time. Waldau's second shot caught Pavel in the clavicle and spun him around. He fell, firing the Schmeisser, and slugs stitched across the rotting ceiling.

Waldau fired again, throwing a shot at Dryden, but he didn't wait to see the results. He turned and bolted through a gap in the rear of the ruin, skittering through the dark passages. Dryden lifted his head. He heard Waldau's boots scrape on stone as he ran through the spring room. A pebble clicked and fell into the water. Then hasty steps weaving through the maze of inner chambers.

"Are you okay?" Dryden whispered to Beverly.

She nodded.

He looked around at Pavel. The big sergeant was bleeding below the neck but still had his wits about him. He waved toward the gap in the back wall. "Go," he said.

"Stay out of the line of fire," Dryden told Beverly. "If Waldau comes back, duck and sing out."

\* \* \*

The cave dwellings, forged by ancient builders with little safety in their lives, were difficult of access. No more than two structures led directly into one another. Some rooms could be reached only by narrow passages, some only by low tunnels. They were like a jumble of mismatched children's building blocks, boxes stacked one on another at the back of the cave, protected only from the elements. Steep, tall ladders, easily pulled up if an enemy approached, had been the sole means of entrance to the upper stories, but the crumbling of many of the walls, in whole and in part, had created a stair-step effect in some areas. In others, ceiling beams had rotted. Roofs had collapsed. Like the dwellers who had inhabited them, the dwellings were slowly returning to the earth that had formed them.

Dryden checked his Schmeisser. Half a magazine left, and a spare tucked in his waist. Forty rounds, more or less. He wondered how many spare clips Waldau might have for the P-38. Not that it mattered. If he couldn't track the man down and finish him off with a magazine and a half, he had no business stalking him at all.

And then, from deep in the ruins, the voice came. "Captain Dryden. Give yourself up. The rest of my men will be here shortly. They will hunt you down without mercy. Surrender now, and I will let you and the woman live." Waldau, sounding desperate. Perhaps he was shorter on ammunition than Dryden thought.

Dryden crept silently through the inner chambers, smelling the decay. Dark, dusty rooms filled with debris from floors above. A rabbit warren. He passed a broken wall with the top portion missing. A huge hunk had fallen from the ceiling above. He had prowled these same chambers as a youth, but nothing seemed the same. He stopped and listened for Waldau. He heard low, moaning wind, a drip of water, sputter and crack of the dying fire in Kleber's ruin. And movement. A creak of boot and rustle of cloth. Adobe fragments rattling down a wall. Flutter and groan of roof beams. Waldau was climbing to the upper chambers.

Which way? The sound seemed to come from his left. Dryden ducked through a sagging portal and tried to cross a spill of rocks, but his foot clicked against a rock and dislodged it. Another opening beckoned. He approached it warily. It opened into a roofless area with a narrow half wall at the back, stone rising raggedly toward the upper chambers. He paused in the darkness, listening. No sound at all now. Waldau was somewhere above, watching the wall, waiting for him.

"Answer me," Waldau called. "I am willing to negotiate."

Sure, Dryden thought. Waiting with a P-38 in his hand, ready to negotiate a hole in Dryden's head the minute he stepped into the open. Dryden pressed against the doorway and raised the Schmeisser, but the gun came to his shoulder too hastily, and the magazine housing scraped against the edge of the stone lintel. The click of metal against stone seemed horribly loud in the silence. He froze, listening. Waldau must have heard it, too. There was a rustle of twill beyond the opening and soft footfalls as the German officer shifted position.

Dryden tracked the movement from below. He was coming this way. Dryden scanned the upper walls. Several feet from the rear of the cave, gravity and time had formed a crack in one of the surfaces, about six inches across, splitting down the middle. He shifted the Schmeisser and waited for Waldau's face to appear. A sudden sharp cry rolled up from Kleber's ruin, freezing his blood. Beverly's voice. "Ned! Trouble!"

Dryden hesitated, then wrenched back toward her voice. Oh, God. Something had startled her. Not Waldau. He knew it couldn't be Waldau. Waldau was above. And Beverly wasn't the type to shriek at shadows. What then? Another voice rumbled indistinctly from Kleber's ruin. Male. German. Weary.

Panic overcame good sense. Dryden ran faster, skittering and scraping through narrow passages. He should never have left her, not even to hunt Waldau. He bounded across a pile of rubble and skidded into Kleber's cell, intent on reaching her. His noisy, fumbling entry was dusty, ungraceful, and sudden. And apparently unexpected. He heard gasps. Heads swiveled. Beverly, crouching above Kleber, gaped. Pavel, propped on his elbows with a wad of bloody gauze pressed to his clavicle, stared with open jaw. Frischauer, motionless near a mound of rubble, stiffened. And a sudden intake of breath from the breach in Kleber's wall. Erich Huber. Holding a gun,

Dryden ground to a halt. Huber's gun wavered from Beverly to Pavel. Dryden held his own Schmeisser at arm's length. He didn't raise it. His thinking processes, addled by desperation, slipped slowly into gear. He stood very still, eyes riveted on Huber. Huber peered back. Frostbitten. Covered with snow and rime. Gasping. Chest heaving.

"You don't need the gun," Dryden told him.

Huber rubbed a shaking hand across his scabbed upper lip. "Dead," he said. "So many dead."

"Put the gun down," Dryden said. "Don't make me shoot you."

It was an empty threat for the moment, with Huber's gun covering Beverly and his own gun hanging at his side, but Huber either didn't notice or didn't care. He slouched against the wall, his gun steady. "What happened?" he asked vaguely. "I don't understand. How could so many die?" He glared at Dryden and his voice grew louder, grating. "Was it you? Did you kill them all?" The gun barrel rose.

Pavel seemed to recognize Dryden's predicament. He looked for his own machine pistol, lying too far away, then eased his hand to a loose stone. His fingers closed on it.

Footsteps approached warily from above. Waldau. He must have been close enough to make out Huber's words. The padding feet paused, and his voice called cautiously from an upper chamber, "Huber? Erich Huber? Is that you?"

Huber's backbone straightened. "Yes, Colonel. I am here." He turned his head, a dazed look in his eyes. "Where are you?"

"Shoot the American," Waldau shouted. "Shoot them all."

Huber's body sagged. His posture said he was a beaten man, too weary to cope, but he had been given orders, and he was ready to give it a try. He raised his machine pistol. Everyone in the cell seemed to move at once. Frischauer lowered his head and butted Huber from the blind side. The Hitler Youth lurched. Beverly snatched a burning stick from the fire and whistled a roundhouse swing at his shoulders. Sparks flew, and Huber staggered back. Pavel tossed the

304

stone awkwardly. Dryden swung his machine pistol into firing position, but Frischauer and Beverly were too close. Beverly swished the burning stick, trying to wallop Huber again. Dryden looked for a clear shot.

It was all too much for Huber. He collapsed in a sobbing heap, arms flung over his head, overwhelmed, too exhausted to fight back. Beverly crowded close with the burning stick, considering one more swing, then tossed the firebrand aside and snatched Huber's gun. She stood over him menacingly with the machine pistol in both hands, looking like a savage Amazon.

Waldau's voice rolled out of the darkness. "Damn it, man. Shoot!" Scrape of shoe leather. Closer. Dust sifted down. Dryden shifted the Schmeisser and followed the puffs of dust, trying to guess Waldau's path. Then, suddenly, Waldau's face appeared above the roofline. The P-38 pistol rose to blast away. Dryden ducked and opened up with the Schmeisser. He fired until the already depleted magazine was empty. Adobe crumbled. Spent cartridges rattled to the floor. In the silence that followed, Dryden heard Waldau pound away, running back through the ruins.

Dryden discarded the spent magazine and fumbled for a fresh one. He followed the overhead thumps into another chamber, a wide room with a small circular depression at the center, a fire pit. Waldau was moving fast. Too fast. He should have known better, but panic can do strange things to intellect. Dryden stopped by the fire pit and fired a quick burst at the ceiling to keep the panic boiling. The thumping feet quickened. Dryden heard a mushy crack of wood and masonry. The ceiling sagged. Feet scrabbled for balance. Flakes of adobe plaster popped. Waldau's leg appeared first, bursting through to the hip, then the surface crumbled and the roof caved in. Waldau's voice wailed like a dropping bomb, a startled sound that plunged from the upper level to the floor of the chamber. He landed in a shower of debris not twenty feet ahead.

Dryden worked his way through the wreckage. The SS officer was lying on his side, pinned by a pile of pine poles. His left arm was folded peculiarly under his body in a way that elbows weren't meant to function. His gun was within reach of his right hand, but the fall had stunned him. He looked up at Dryden with resignation.

"You're going to kill me," he said. It was a statement, not a question.

"Don't tempt me," Dryden said. "A bloodthirsty bastard like you? It would be no great loss to the world if I did."

"You are no better," Waldau groaned. He took several shallow breaths. "You pretend to be so civilized. You speak of a few inconsequential deaths. How can they matter? I had one goal, to destroy the American atomic facility. To save my country. All else was unimportant. And what of you? You butchered my men. You matched me, bloody deed for bloody deed, in an effort to save the atomic device. You will live to regret this night."

"You're the second person to say that to me," Dryden said. "From you, I don't much like it."

"Weakness," Waldau said. "The voice of a civilized man." His eyes touched the fallen gun, then flicked back to Dryden. "Because of you the device may go forward. Hundreds of thousands will perish. How much blood will be on your hands? Which of us is the real homicidal maniac?"

"Why don't we find out?" Dryden said. He looked down at Waldau's pistol. "Go ahead. Pick it up."

"You will kill me either way," Waldau said.

"Maybe not," Dryden said. "I'm a civilized man, remember? Maybe you'll get lucky."

Waldau extended his hand a few inches toward the Walther P-38, then hesitated, staring up at Dryden. "I am injured," he said. "You will allow me a fair chance to reach the gun and raise it?"

"As fair as you've ever been."

Waldau's eyes narrowed uncertainly, and he grabbed for the pistol. Dryden let the SS colonel's fingers close on the grip, then opened up with the machine pistol, cutting him in two.

"You're very quiet," Beverly whispered. The sun had risen outside the cave, and pale reflected light now reached the inner depths of Kleber's chamber. With its help Beverly was rigging a sling for Pavel.

"Got a lot on my mind," Dryden said.

"Like what we're going to do with them?" She nodded at Frischauer, squatting beside the Oberst, and Erich Huber, wrapped in a blanket and sound asleep. "Do you want me to stand watch while you go for help?"

"I don't think we'll have to do anything," Dryden said. "By now Clarence has probably told the authorities at Los Alamos where to find us. They'll be along eventually."

"What is it, then? What's bothering you?"

Dryden grinned. "Something Waldau said. I guess the shakes are wearing off, and I'm having a look at myself."

Pavel lifted his chin. "Second thoughts, Captain?"

"Something like that."

"Don't regret too quickly," Pavel said. "I want you strong when we face each other."

Dryden regarded Pavel's pale face. "Tell you what, Pavel. I'm going to do you a favor. I'm not going to beat your brains in until you feel better."

A low, quick laugh rumbled up from Pavel's belly, shaking his body. He winced. "Thank you, Captain. I appreciate that."

Horses whinnied outside the cave. Saddle leather squeaked as bodies lowered themselves to the snow. Dryden picked up his machine pistol and stepped to the opening in Kleber's wall, hoping it was scouts from Los Alamos. He saw three exhausted men climb to the ledge outside the cave. Franz Eggers and another man, breathing hard, scraped wearily toward the ruins, supporting a wounded Bernd Strikfeldt between them. They saw Dryden and stopped dead.

Dryden waved the Schmeisser. "Come up and join us," he said.

Eggers released a gust of air and came the rest of the way with his two companions. They entered the ruin quietly and dumped their guns in the middle of the floor, then sagged against the wall and slid to their haunches.

"Place is getting crowded," Dryden said.

"We could relieve the congestion," Beverly said tentatively. "We could let Pavel and his friend go. We owe them something. Pavel saved your life. And I don't know what I would have done without Frischauer's help."

Pavel glanced at Kleber, sleeping restlessly on his blankets. "Thank you, Fräulein. It is a kind thought. But I think I would do better to stay with the Oberst. The idea of travel does not lure me this morning."

"What about your friend?" she asked.

Pavel shifted his gaze to Frischauer and murmured. Frischauer nodded energetically. Pavel looked up at Dryden. "Yes, please," he said with sudden hope. "Jürgen is a gentle man, Captain. He wishes only to rejoin his family. I have no right to ask it, but I would appreciate your consideration in this matter."

Dryden said nothing.

Pavel searched Dryden's face and seemed to take his silence for assent. He reached up and squeezed the big farmer's wrist. "It's all right," he told him. "You can leave. Go easy. Pace yourself. Travel only as fast as your foot will allow. But get there before the submarine leaves. You have five days."

Frischauer took a cautious step toward the breached wall. He looked at Dryden warily, as if expecting to be called back. Franz Eggers looked up enviously from the floor, but he was too exhausted to do more than call, "Good luck, Jürgen!"

It was Beverly, not Dryden, who stopped the German POW. "Wait," she said. "You'll need food. And blankets. Give me a moment and I'll get them for you."

Strikfeldt raised a bloodless face. "I have the American money they gave us at the camp," he said. "Franz, will you help me get it? It's in the pocket of my jacket."

Eggers roused himself. "I have money, too. Take it, Jürgen." He dug in his own pockets.

Pavel slipped a hand into his trousers. "I still have the compass," he said. "You'll need it. I also have a warm jacket, but it's bloody."

"He can have my jacket," Eggers said. "And quickly, Jürgen, get out of that uniform. Put on a civilian shirt and trousers."

The exhausted men spent the last of their energy in a short, busy stir, outfitting their companion for the journey. Beverly quickly packed all the available rations in a knapsack and handed it and two blankets to Frischauer.

Dryden let Frischauer hobble out of the ruin, then gathered up the loose weapons and followed him. Frischauer looked back fearfully at Dryden, then picked up his pace, moving faster. He hobbled to the balcony, then stopped,

308

eyes shut tightly. His shoulders were squared, as though he expected to be shot.

Christina Rosetti looked up from the trees. Two new horses had joined her in the early morning sunshine, brought by Eggers and the others. Behind their brush barricade the pack animals stirred nervously. Dryden dumped the guns by the cave entrance. "Take Beverly's horse," he said. "She's better rested than the others. Her name is Little Lil. Treat her right and she'll get you there."

"You would allow me to take your horse?" Frischauer said.

"Go on, get out of here," Dryden said.

Frischauer nodded gratefully and half climbed, half slid down to the floor of the canyon. He hurried into the stock pen for Little Lil and saddled her, then led her past the barricade and carefully pulled it closed behind him. He mounted quickly and rode into the trees, heading up the canyon. Dryden was pleased to see that he didn't press her.

Beverly came out on the balcony and joined Dryden. She linked her arm in his and said, "That was good of you, Ned."

"It's nice to see at least one person come out of this with hope."

She rested her head against his shoulder. "Do you think the soldiers from Los Alamos will be here soon?"

"Any minute now. Hey, let me look at you. Are you crying?"

He turned her face up to his. She gulped and shook her head. "Just a little," she said. "I loved Little Lil."

Dryden felt the weight of weariness and loss as well. "I loved her, too," he said. "Maybe we'll get her back one day. All our saddles are stamped with the name and address of the ranch. Maybe someone will see it and sell her back to us."

Beverly laughed shakily. "Let's change the subject before I start bawling," she said. "It would be nice to have a bath. Do you suppose the soldiers from Los Alamos will let us clean up before they start asking questions?"

"If the scientists on the mesa tell them the truth about what happened, they'll probably treat us like heroes."

"Or throw us in prison for the duration," she said.

He laughed softly, but without mirth. A curl of horses wound toward them from far down the canyon.

Beverly saw them, too. She looked quickly to be sure Frischauer was out of sight, then plucked at Dryden's sleeve. "Ned, if they let us go back to McLean, will you still try for active duty?"

He shook his head. "Not after this." He shaded his eyes, staring at the distant horses. "I'm obsolete. If the scientists finish what they've started on the mesa, my kind of war is over."

"If the bomb is as terrible as they say, maybe the whole concept of war is obsolete," she said. "There might never be another. Perhaps you can all go home."

Dryden slipped an arm around her. "Maybe. But I doubt it. I feel a little like Pandora. Like I've helped to open a door that should have stayed shut. God knows what will come out."

"It's done," she said. "Try not to think about it."

"Yes, it's done," he said. "For now."

# SUSPENSE, INTRIGUE & INTERNATIONAL DANGER

These novels of espionage and excitement-filled tension will guarantee you the best in high-voltage reading pleasure.

__**FLIGHT OF THE INTRUDER** by Stephen Coonts 64012/$4.95
__**TREASURE** by Clive Cussler 70465/$5.95
__**DEEP SIX** by Clive Cussler 69382/$5.50
__**ICEBERG** by Clive Cussler 67041/$4.95
__**MEDITERRANEAN CAPER** by Clive Cussler 67042/$4.95
__**RAISE THE TITANIC** by Clive Cussler 69264/$5.50
__**DIRECTIVE SIXTEEN** by Charles Robertson 61153/$4.50
__**A SEASON IN HELL** by Jack Higgins 69271/$5.50
__**CARNIVAL OF SPIES** by Robert Moss 62372/$4.95
__**NIGHT OF THE FOX** by Jack Higgins 69378/$5.50
__**THE HUMAN FACTOR** by Graham Greene 64850/$4.50
__**THE CROSSKILLER** by Marcel Montecino 67894/$4.95
__**JIG** by Campbell Armstrong 66524/$4.95
__**SHAKEDOWN** by Gerald Petrievich 67964/$4.50
__**SWORD POINT** by Harold Coyle 66554/$4.95
__**SPY VS SPY** by Ronald Kessler 67967/$4.95

POCKET BOOKS

**Simon & Schuster, Mail Order Dept. SUS**
**200 Old Tappan Rd., Old Tappan, N.J. 07675**

Please send me the books I have checked above. I am enclosing $_____ (please add 75¢ to cover postage and handling for each order N.Y.S. and N.Y.C. residents please add appropriate sales tax). Send check or money order—no cash or C.O.D.'s please. Allow up to six weeks for delivery. For purchases over $10.00 you may use VISA. card number, expiration date and customer signature must be included.

Name _____

Address _____

City _____ State/Zip _____

VISA Card No. _____ Exp. Date _____

Signature _____ 318B-10